After leaving her convent school, **Miranda Lee** briefly studied the cello before moving to Sydney, where she embraced the emerging world of computers. Her career as a programmer ended after she married, had three daughters, and bought a small acreage in a semi-rural community. She yearned to find a creative career from which she could earn money. When her sister suggested writing romances, it seemed like a good idea. She could do it at home, and it might even be fun! She never looked back.

Cathy Williams is a great believer in the power of perseverance as she had never written anything before her writing career. From the starting point of zero, she has now fulfilled her ambition to pursue this most enjoyable of careers. She would encourage any would-be writer to have faith and go for it! She derives inspiration from the tropical island of Trinidad and from the peaceful countryside of middle England. Cathy lives in Warwickshire her family.

Melanie Milburne read her first Mills & Boon at age seventeen in between studying for her final exams. After completing a Master's in Education, she decided to write a novel and thus her career as a romance author was born. Melanie is an ambassador for the Australian Childhood Foundation, is a keen dog lover and trainer, and enjoys long walks in the Tasmanian bush. In 2015 Melanie won the HOLT Medallion, a prestigious award honouring outstanding literary talent.

Irresistible Italians

Irresistible Italians:

A Scandalous Proposition

MIRANDA LEE

CATHY WILLIAMS

MELANIE MILBURNE

MILLS & BOON

First Published in Great Britain 2023
by Mills & Boon, an imprint of HarperCollins*Publishers* Ltd,
1 London Bridge Street, London, SE1 9GF

www.harpercollins.co.uk

HarperCollins*Publishers*
Macken House, 39/40 Mayor Street Upper,
Dublin 1, D01 C9W8, Ireland

Irresistible Italians: A Scandalous Proposition © 2023 Harlequin Enterprises ULC.

The Billionaire's Ruthless Affair © 2016 Miranda Lee
Cipriani's Innocent Captive © 2017 Cathy Williams
Deserving of His Diamonds? © 2012 Melanie Milburne

ISBN: 978-0-263-31877-7

This book is produced from independently certified FSC™ paper
to ensure responsible forest management.

For more information visit: www.harpercollins.co.uk/green

Printed and Bound in the UK using 100% Renewable electricity at
CPI Group (UK) Ltd, Croydon, CR0 4YY

THE BILLIONAIRE'S RUTHLESS AFFAIR

MIRANDA LEE

CHAPTER ONE

I SHOULD BE HAPPIER, Alex thought as he picked up his mug of coffee and carried it out onto the terrace of his penthouse apartment, shivering slightly when the crisp air hit his face. Not that it would be cold for long, the sun already peeping over the horizon. Winter in Sydney was a picnic compared to winter in London. He *was* glad to be back home. But not all that happy, for some reason.

Alex surveyed the panoramic view of the city skyline, telling himself that a man would have to be a fool not to be happy when he'd finally achieved everything he'd ever vowed to achieve.

At thirty-four, Alex was no fool. He was, in fact, a very successful businessman.

A Rhodes scholar, Alex had first become an entrepreneur back in England over a decade earlier, going into partnership with his two best friends from Oxford in a dilapidated old wine bar, which probably should have been demolished, but which they'd turned into a going concern. As it turned out, one wine bar had eventually become two, then three, then ten, till finally they'd formed a franchise.

Sergio's idea, that.

Alex smiled for the first time that morning. Thinking of Sergio always brought a smile to his face. Jeremy, too.

Yet those two were as different as chalk and cheese. Sergio was inclined to take life way too seriously at times, whereas Jeremy... Lord, where did one start with Jeremy? Though some people might describe him as a playboy, Alex knew Jeremy was a decent man at heart, generous and loyal, though with way too much charm and money for his own good. And he'd have even more money now, the recent sale of their wine bar franchise having made them all billionaires.

Alex's smile faded somewhat as he realised that the sale of their franchise had now severed the main connection between the three men. Whilst he didn't doubt they would always remain friends, it would not be the same as when they'd gathered together in London on a regular basis. Sergio had now returned to Milan to take up the reins of his family's ailing manufacturing business, whilst he himself would have no reason to return to England.

Still, that was life, Alex supposed. Nothing stayed the same. Time and tide waited for no man, he knew, a quick glance at his watch showing that it was almost eight.

He was going to be late for work, which was a rarity.

Harry would be wondering where he was. Alex hoped she wasn't upset over the way he'd spoken to her yesterday. Not that she'd seemed offended. Though relatively young, she was without doubt the best, most sensible PA he'd ever had.

Gulping down the rest of his coffee, he hurried back inside, stashed his mug in the dishwasher, snatched up his phone and keys, then headed for the lift. Just as the lift doors opened, his phone rang. A wry smile lit up Alex's face when he saw that it was Jeremy.

Speak of the devil!

'Jeremy...mate... I was just thinking about you.' Alex

strode into the lift and pressed the button for the basement car park.

'That's a worry,' Jeremy replied in that deeply masculine voice which always surprised people. 'Haven't you got anything better to do with your life? You should be out there making more millions. Though, perhaps not. You'd only give the lot away.'

Alex grinned. 'You've been drinking, haven't you?' It would be late evening in London.

'You could say that. I'm at a party. An engagement party.'

Alex suppressed a groan at the thought that another one of Jeremy's brothers—perhaps even his mother or father—were on their way to the altar again. You didn't have to look far to understand Jeremy's negative attitude towards love and marriage. Clearly, he didn't trust either to last.

Alex wasn't into love and marriage himself, either, but not for reasons of scepticism and cynicism. He knew full well that true love existed and lasted, if you found the right person. Alex just wasn't interested in finding his soul mate. He had personal reasons for staying a bachelor, the main one being the promise he'd made to his mother on her deathbed.

'God made you extra smart for a purpose, son,' she'd told him with her last breath. 'Promise me you won't waste your talents. Use them for good. Make a difference.'

Alex had done just that. But being a dedicated philanthropist took a lot of time and energy. He simply didn't have enough left over for a wife and family. Though, if he was strictly honest, Alex liked being a bachelor. Liked living by himself. Liked being free of emotional entanglements.

The lift doors opened at the basement and Alex headed for his nearby SUV at a clip.

'So who's getting hitched this time?' he asked Jeremy. 'Not your mother, I hope.' Jeremy's mother had divorced her third husband last year after she'd discovered he was sleeping with his personal trainer.

'No, thank God. No, this is someone far more surprising.'

'Really?' The mind boggled. 'Look, hold it a sec. Have to get in my car. I'm on my way to work.' Alex jumped in behind the wheel and swiftly connected his phone to Bluetooth. 'Right. All systems go,' he said as he backed out of his spot.

'Do you ever do anything except work?' Jeremy said drily.

'Sure I do. I eat out, work out and have lots of great sex. A bit like you, dear friend.'

'Are you still dating that Lisa chick, the girl you told me about with the grating giggle? Or did you break up with her as you said you were going to as soon as you got back to Sydney?'

'Yeah, she's gone,' Alex said with a scowl on his face. Lisa was still a sore point with him. He'd been going to tell her tactfully this last weekend that it was over between them when she'd actually had the hide to break up with him first, informing him that she'd taken a job on a cruise ship that was setting sail for Asia that very week.

He should have been relieved. Instead, he'd felt decidedly disgruntled. 'I don't want to talk about Lisa,' Alex ground out. 'I want to know which surprising person is getting married.'

'Trust me when I say that you're going to be more than surprised. It's Sergio. *He's* the one getting married.'

Though slightly taken aback, Alex was not exactly

shocked. 'What's so surprising about that? He said he was going to find himself a wife when he got back to Italy. It is a bit quick, though.'

Jeremy laughed. 'You don't know the half of it. The wedding's set for just over two weeks' time.'

'Good grief! Why all the hurry? The bride-to-be can't possibly be pregnant. He's only been back in Italy a little over a fortnight.'

'As far as I know, Bella's not pregnant.'

Alex's foot slammed on the brake, bringing an angry hoot of the horn from the car behind him. He was on the car park exit ramp at the time. Gathering himself, he drove on, trying to stay calm and not cause an accident.

'You shouldn't tell me something like that when I'm driving,' he said a lot more calmly than he was feeling. For Bella was *the* Bella, the darling of Broadway and Sergio's one-time stepsister. Sergio had confessed to his friends a couple of years back that he'd always had the hots for her. Naturally, they'd both urged him to move on and forget her.

Clearly, he hadn't taken their advice.

'Trust me, I'm just as shocked as you are,' Jeremy said in droll tones. 'Even worse, I've had to witness Sergio's crazed obsession first-hand.'

'What do you mean?'

'I knew Sergio was staying at his villa on Lake Como, so I decided to fly over yesterday and surprise him for his birthday.'

'Oh, God, his birthday. I forgot, as usual.'

'You always forget birthdays. Anyway, back to my story. Naturally, I thought Sergio would be alone. He'd said he wanted a holiday before tackling the family business. Apparently, I'd got that wrong. Because when I arrived, he was in Milan, with Bella installed at the villa.

She claimed she was suffering from burnout and had tried to rent the villa from Sergio, but he'd invited her to stay as his guest instead.'

Alex's teeth clenched down hard in his jaw. 'So the upshot is she wangled her way back into Sergio's life and then seduced him.'

'That's not how Sergio tells it. He says *he* seduced *her*.'

'That doesn't sound like Sergio.'

'I agree, but apparently he did. And then the poor bastard fell in love with her.'

'Yes, but did she fall in love with him back, or is this a case of like mother like daughter?' Bella's mother was a cold-blooded, ambitious woman who'd married Sergio's widowed father to finance her daughter's singing and dancing career, then divorced him once Bella's career had taken off. 'Does Bella know he's a billionaire now?'

'Don't know. It's been a madhouse here.'

Alex rolled his eyes. 'You must have got some impression of Bella's sincerity. Or lack of it.'

'Well, as unlikely as this will sound coming from an old cynic like me, I think she might be genuinely in love with Sergio.'

'Don't forget she's an actress,' Alex pointed out sharply.

'Now who's being a cynic? Anyway, the wedding's set for the thirty-first of July. I have no doubt that Sergio will be in contact with you shortly. He wants us both to be his best men. I told him we'd be honoured. So when he asks you, try to act thrilled, because there's no way he's going to change his mind about this. The man's crazy about her. All we can do is be there for him to pick up the pieces if and when everything goes belly-up.'

Alex wasn't sure how much help he could be from

Australia. But of course he would go to the wedding. He would be proud to stand at Sergio's side as his best man.

'Just book a flight that will get you to Lake Como the day before the wedding. No, make that two days before. I want to take you into Milan and have you fitted with a decent dinner suit. This might prove to be a disastrous marriage, but that's no excuse not to look our very best. We must do Sergio proud on the day. We are, after all, his best men.'

A lump formed in Alex's throat, rendering him speechless for a moment. Fortunately, Jeremy wasn't similarly afflicted.

'Have to go now, Alex. Claudia has just come out onto the terrace looking for me. Now, don't forget to book your flight, and for pity's sake sound thrilled when Sergio calls you. *Ciao*,' he said with a wry laugh. 'When in Rome, you know.' And he hung up.

Alex groaned at the thought of having to sound thrilled when Sergio contacted him. But he would do it for Sergio's sake. Fate wasn't being kind to him, letting him fall for a woman like Bella. Their getting married was a disaster waiting to happen.

Such thinking reinforced Alex's own decision never to get tangled up in the whole 'love and marriage' thing. Loving and losing someone—either through death or divorce—was never going to be on his agenda. No way would he risk ending up like his father, or becoming the victim of some clever gold-digger. That was why he always dated girls who never had a hope of ensnaring his heart. Girls who just wanted to have fun.

Alex quickly realised there would be no time for fun during the next two weeks. His nose would be pressed to the grindstone every single day. At least it would be when he finally got to the damned office. Poor Harry. She was probably close to sending out a search party!

Harriet didn't mind at all that her boss was running late that morning. When she'd arrived at the office shortly before eight, she'd been dreading having to tell him her news, news which she should have told him when he'd first come back from London. But at the time her emotions had been too raw. She would have wept in front of him. She knew she would. And she didn't want to do that. Alex would have been embarrassed. And so would she.

So she'd let the days tick away without confessing that her engagement to Dwayne was no more, her anxiety increasing as each day passed. She'd rather hoped her boss might notice that she wasn't wearing her engagement ring, but he hadn't. Alex didn't notice personal details like that. He was a man with tunnel vision most of the time. When at work, he worked.

It did irk Harriet slightly that no one else at Ark Properties had noticed, either. But that was her fault. Whilst she was friendly with everyone who worked there, she didn't socialise with the rest of the staff. She never went with them for drinks on a Friday night. Harriet had her own group of girlfriends she had drinks with, Emily of course being the main one. Then of course, up till recently, she'd had Dwayne.

Naturally, things would be different from now on, with no Dwayne to complain if she didn't hurry home after work. It worried Harriet, however, that her suddenly single status would change the wonderful working relationship she'd always had with Alex. He was a great boss. She liked him a lot and felt sure that he liked her back. Yet when she'd walked into his office to be interviewed for the job last year, Harriet had gained the immediate impression that she was a non-starter. Alex had looked her up and down with sceptical eyes. With hindsight, maybe he'd been worried that she might make a play for him. He was, after all, one of Sydney's most eligible bachelors.

Whatever; as soon as he'd discovered she was engaged, his attitude had changed. Though he'd still put her through the mill during the interview. She must have pleased him with her answers, because he'd hired her on the spot.

Of course, her résumé *had* been second to none—provided you overlooked her poor pass in her Higher School Certificate. Which Alex had, once she'd explained that her dad—who was a miner—had lost his job during her high school years and that the family finances had been so tight that she'd taken not one but *three* part-time positions to help make ends meet, her studies suffering as a result. A little white lie, that. But not one she felt guilty about. The boss of Ark Properties didn't need to know the ins and outs of her past life. Alex had seemed suitably impressed by her work ethic, plus her career in real estate. He didn't care that she'd never actually been a PA before. He wanted someone who could take over the office whenever he was away, which up till recently had been quite often. He had business ties in England which she wasn't privy to; Alex could be secretive at times.

But those business ties had apparently been wound up and he was back in Sydney permanently. Harriet might have felt pleased if she hadn't been in a state of apprehension at the time. That apprehension had now reached such a level that it was interfering with her sleep. So Harriet had resolved last night to bite the bullet and tell Alex the truth this morning. Which would have happened already if he'd been here when she'd arrived, she thought with a flash of irritation. All of a sudden, his being late didn't seem quite so desirable, the delay in confessing twisting her stomach into more knots.

Sighing at the sight of Alex's empty office, she headed straight for the staff room, where she filled the kettle in readiness for the mug of black coffee Alex always wanted first thing on arriving. He'd probably send her out for a bagel, too. That man was a bagel addict! Maybe she'd leave off telling him her news till he'd downed his coffee and bagel. Alex wasn't at his best till he'd eaten. The kettle on, she opened the overhead cupboard and took down one of the small tins of quite expensive cat food she kept there. The snapping sound of the ring pull had a rather large moggy dashing into the room, purring his welcome as he wound his way around Harriet's ankles.

'Hungry, Romany?' Harriet said, quickly scraping the food out onto a saucer and putting it down on the floor. The cat pounced, gobbling up the food like he was starving.

'You spoil that cat.'

Harriet whirled at the sound of Alex's voice, surprised that she hadn't heard him come in. He looked impossibly handsome as usual, dressed in a dark blue business suit which deepened the blue of his eyes and contrasted nicely with the fair hair. His shirt was a dazzling white, his tie a stylish blue-and-silver stripe.

'You ought to talk,' Harriet said, thinking of all her boss had done for Romany. 'Might I remind you that *you* were the one who insisted on buying all the top-of-the-line cat accessories.'

'Had to do something to stop my PA from crying her eyes out.'

'I wasn't doing any such thing.'

'You were close to,' he reminded her.

I suppose I was, she thought as she picked up the

plate, washed it thoroughly and put it away, not wanting any of the staff to start complaining about the smell of fishy cat food. Not that they would. They all loved Romany. Unlike Dwayne. He hadn't loved Romany at all; had complained like mad when Harriet had brought the poor starving animal home a couple of months ago after she'd found him cowering and crying under her car one Saturday night. He'd insisted she take it to the RSPCA the very next day, which she had, hopeful that they would find him a good home.

Impossible, they'd said. No one would want a seriously old cat like Romany. Unable to bear leaving him there to be put down, in desperation she'd taken him to work on the Monday, where she'd asked if anyone would give him a home. When no one had put their hand up, Alex had said he could be the office cat. Always a man of action, he'd immediately had a cat flap installed in the store room, then had taken Harriet out to buy whatever was necessary to keep the cat happy and clean. The cleaners had been informed of Romany's presence so that precautions could be taken for him not to escape.

Harriet recalled feeling overwhelmed by Alex's generosity and kindness at the time whilst seething with resentment over Dwayne's meanness. As she bent and scooped the cat up in her arms, she realised that the incident with Romany had been the beginning of the end of their relationship. Being an animal lover was, after all, one of her checklist points. After that, she'd begun to look at Dwayne with different eyes. The rose-coloured glasses that came with falling in love had definitely come off. His constant refusal to give any money to charity was a sore point. So was his not doing his share of housework around the flat. When she'd complained to Emily about this, she'd just laughed, saying Harry expected way too much from men.

'They expect their women to look after *them*,' her best friend had told her. 'It's in their DNA. They're the protectors and providers, whilst their women are the homemakers and nurturers.'

Harriet hadn't agreed with Emily, hoping the world had moved on from expecting women to be happy with such narrow roles in life. No way was she going to settle for less than what she wanted in life, which was an interesting career, as well as a husband who ticked all of the boxes on her Mister Right checklist. Dwayne had certainly ticked the first three, but had begun seriously falling down on the rest. His suggestion a month ago that she buy her wedding dress second-hand on the Internet had been the last straw!

'So has the kettle boiled?' Alex asked, interrupting Harriet's none-too-happy thoughts.

'Should have,' she said.

Dropping the cat gently on the tiled floor, she set about getting two mugs down from the overhead cupboard. 'It's not like you to be late,' she added, doing her best to ignore the instant churning in her stomach. Maybe she wouldn't tell him today after all…

'I slept in,' he replied. 'Then traffic was bad. I'm going to need a bagel with my coffee.'

'Fine. Oh, and, Alex…' she said before he had the opportunity to walk away and before she could procrastinate further. 'When you have a minute, I…um…I need to talk to you about something.'

He sighed a rather weary-sounding sigh. 'Look, Harry, if you're going to complain about the way I spoke to you yesterday, then don't bother. I'm sorry. All right? I was in a bad mood and I took it out on you, which I realise was unforgiveable, but I'm only human. If you must know, I broke up with Lisa at the weekend.'

'Oh,' she said, not really surprised. Of the three girls Alex had dated during the time she'd worked for him, Lisa had been the most annoying with that silly laugh of hers, not to mention the way she would drop into the office unannounced. Alex hadn't liked that, and neither had Harriet. 'I'm sorry,' she added a little belatedly.

'I'm not. Not really.' Alex stared at her hard for a long moment. 'You're not going to quit, are you?'

Her shocked expression must have soothed him, for his eyes immediately softened. But it underlined to Harriet that Alex was not a man who responded well to being crossed or thwarted. She'd always known he was a tough businessman, but she'd never seen him seriously angry. It wasn't in his nature to be mean, but she suspected he had a temper, like most men.

'No, nothing like that,' she said quickly.

'Then out with it, Harriet. I don't like to wait for bad news.'

'It's not bad news,' she said, startled by his calling her Harriet like that. She'd always liked the way he called her Harry. There was a subtle intimacy about it which made her feel like his friend as well as his assistant. Obviously, she'd been deluding herself in that regard.

'Well, not bad news for you,' she went on sharply, doing her best to control a whole range of emotions which began bombarding her. The sudden lump in her throat alarmed her.

'The thing is, Alex, I...I've broken off my engagement to Dwayne.'

His expression carried a measure of shock, quickly followed by one of genuine sympathy.

When tears pricked at her eyelids, panic was only a heartbeat away.

'I'm very sorry to hear that, Harry,' he said gently. 'Very sorry indeed.'

His calling her Harry like that completed her undoing, bringing a wave of emotion which shattered her pretend composure and sent a torrent of tears into her eyes.

CHAPTER TWO

ALEX'S SHOCK AT Harriet's news was eclipsed by her bursting into tears. For not once during the months she'd worked for him had she ever cried. Or come close to it, except perhaps over the cat. She was the epitome of common sense and composure, pragmatic and practical under pressure at all times. Even when he snapped at her—as he had yesterday—she just ignored him and went on with her job. Which he admired.

He didn't care for women who cried at the drop of a hat or used tears as a weapon. He'd been brought up by a woman who'd been very stalwart by nature, a legacy perhaps of being born poor in war-torn Hungary, she and Alex's father having migrated to Australia when they'd been just newlyweds. They'd hoped to make a better life down under. Unfortunately, that hadn't happened. But his mother had never complained, or cried.

'Crying doesn't get you anywhere,' his mother had told her three children often enough.

She had cried, however, when she'd found out she was dying of cervical cancer, a condition which could have been cured if she'd been diagnosed early enough.

Don't think about that, Alex. Attend to the here and now. Which is your usually calm PA sobbing her broken heart out.

After standing in the doorway for far too long, wondering how he'd forgotten that Harry was a woman with a woman's more sensitive emotions, Alex launched himself across the room and gathered her into his arms.

'There, there,' he said soothingly as he stroked her soft brown hair.

If anything she sobbed even harder, her shoulders shaking as her hands curled into fists and pressed against his chest. Romany meowed plaintively at his feet, obviously sensing distress in the air.

'Stop crying now,' he advised gently. 'You're upsetting the cat.'

She didn't stop crying and Romany ran off, the insensitive deserter. Alex wished he could do likewise. He didn't feel entirely comfortable holding Harry like this. He was never comfortable with excess emotion. Neither was he a touchy-feely kind of guy. He touched a woman only when he was about to make love to her.

'Oh! S-sorry.'

Alex's head swivelled round at the sound of Audrey's startled apology. Audrey was forty, divorced and a cynic and the expression on his receptionist's face suggested she'd instantly jumped to the conclusion that something of an intimate nature was going on between her boss and his PA. Alex knew he had to nip that idea in the bud before nasty rumours started flying around the office.

'Harriet is upset,' he said rather brusquely. 'She's broken off her engagement to Dwayne.'

Audrey's finely plucked eyebrows formed an even greater arch. 'Really? What did he do?'

Alex rolled his eyes at the woman's lack of compassion. All she seemed interested in were the grisly details. Though, now that he thought about it, Alex was curious about the circumstances as well. He could not imagine

Dwayne being unfaithful. He wasn't that kind of guy. Not that he knew him well. He'd met him only twice.

Alex had actually been surprised by Harriet's choice of fiancé. She was a very attractive girl—and smart as a whip—whereas Dwayne was just, well, ordinary, both in looks and intelligence. Alex had found him quite boring to talk to. He would have expected more interesting conversation from a high school history teacher, but Dwayne had come over as being interested in only his pay cheque and his holidays.

'More time to play golf,' he'd said rather avidly.

Perhaps that was what had gone wrong. Maybe he'd been spending too much time on the golf course and not enough time making love to his fiancée. Alex knew that if he was engaged to Harriet, he would spend quite a lot of time making love to her. Having her in his arms reminded him what a good figure she had.

When such thinking sparked a prickling in his groin, Alex decided to bring a swift end to his hugging Harriet so closely. Stepping back from the embrace, he leaned over to snatch a handful of tissues from the box that was kept on the counter and held them out towards her still-clenched hands.

'Dry your eyes,' he ordered.

She did as she was told, blowing her nose quite noisily.

'Now, I'm taking Harriet out for coffee. And we won't be back for a while,' he relayed to Audrey. 'Let the others know the situation when they come in, will you?'

'Will do,' Audrey replied.

'I...I'd like to fix my face before I go out anywhere,' Harriet requested.

'Fair enough,' Alex said. 'I'll meet you at the lifts in five minutes.'

* * *

Grabbing her handbag, Harriet dashed out of the office and along the corridor to the ladies' room, which thankfully was empty. She groaned when the vanity mirror showed flushed cheeks and red-rimmed eyes. Sighing, she splashed them with cold water, glad that she didn't wear eye make-up during the day. Otherwise she might have ended up looking like a raccoon.

Grabbing some paper towels, she dabbed her face dry, after which she swiftly replenished her red lipstick before running a brush through her shoulder-length brown hair. When it fell into its usual sleek curtain without a strand out of place, she conceded that her monthly appointment with one of Sydney's top stylists was worth every cent. It saved her heaps of time every morning and in moments like this. Because, when Alex said he'd meet her in five minutes, he meant five minutes. Patience was not one of her boss's virtues. Kindness was, however. And compassion. He'd shown both with Romany and now with her.

She should have known he'd be nice to her.

Not that she'd expected him to hug her like that. That had been a surprise. So had her bursting into tears in the first place. It wasn't like her to be so emotional. But she supposed it wasn't every day that your dreams for the future were shattered. Maybe if she'd cried buckets during the days after the split with Dwayne, she wouldn't have broken down just now. She hadn't even told Emily, knowing perhaps her friend's critical reaction. She'd just bottled up her feelings, then stupidly started worrying that telling Alex her news would jeopardise her job. As if he would be so cruel as to sack her because she was suddenly single. The very idea was ludicrous!

With a final swift glance at her reflection in the mirror, Harriet hurried from the ladies' room and strode quickly along the grey carpeted corridor which would bring her to the lift well. Alex was already there, his expression shuttered as he looked her up and down, probably searching for signs that she had herself under control. No way would he want her weeping by his side in public. She gave him a small, reassuring smile, but he didn't smile back, his gaze still probing.

'Better now?' he said.

'Much. You don't have to do this, you know,' she added, despite actually wanting to go and have coffee with him. 'We could just go back into the office and have coffee there.'

'Absolutely not. Audrey and the others can hold the fort.'

The lift doors opened and several office workers piled out, Ark Properties not being the only business with rooms on that particular floor, though theirs were the pick, with Alex's office having a wonderful view of the Harbour Bridge and the Opera House. 'Nothing like a good view of Sydney's spectacular icons to help sell property in Australia,' he'd told her on the day he'd hired her.

Harriet agreed wholeheartedly.

'So when did all this happen?' Alex asked her as he waved her into the now empty lift.

'The weekend you flew home from London,' she told him.

He threw a sharp glance over his shoulder as he pressed the ground-floor button.

'Why didn't you tell me straight away?' he went on before she could think of a suitable answer. 'Did you want to give yourself the opportunity to change your mind? Or for Dwayne to change it for you?'

'No. No, once I made up my mind, I knew I wouldn't

change it. Dwayne hasn't tried to change my mind, either. After our last argument, he knew it was over between us.'

'That must have been some argument.'

'It was.' A rueful smile teased the corners of her mouth. What would Alex say, she wondered, if he knew he'd been the subject of most of that last argument?

His eyes narrowed on her 'Want to tell me about it?'

She looked up into his gorgeous blue eyes, then shook her head. 'I don't think that would be a good idea.'

'Well, I do,' he stated firmly just as the lift doors opened on the ground floor. Taking her arm, he steered her across the spacious lobby and through the revolving glass doors which led out onto the chilly city street.

'So which café do you prefer?' he asked, nodding towards each of the two casual eating establishments that flanked the entrance to their building. It occurred to Harriet that Alex had never actually taken her for coffee before. She'd lunched with him a few times—always with clients—but only at the kind of five-star restaurants which catered for businessmen of his status.

'That one has better bagels,' she said, pointing to the café on their left.

'That one it is, then.'

He found them an empty table at one of the windows which overlooked the street, seeing her settled before heading for the counter. Harriet found it odd watching him queue up to order food, thinking he wouldn't have done that too often. But then she recalled that he hadn't always been rich and successful.

When she'd secured a second and personal interview for this job, she'd looked him up on the Internet, unable to find out all that much information, the best being an article written about him for a men's magazine a couple of years back. Harriet had been surprised to discover that he'd come from a down-at-heel migrant family, living in government housing in the outer western suburbs of Sydney. His near-genius IQ had given him access to special schools for gifted children, followed by various financial grants to help him through university, culminating in his being awarded a Rhodes Scholarship.

The magazine article she'd read had outlined his rise to success in Sydney, first as a realtor based mainly in the western suburbs, then as a property developer with his head office in the heart of Sydney's CBD. The article made no mention of any business interests in England, or his personal life, except to say that he was one of Sydney's most eligible bachelors. There'd been no mention of his family or friends.

Harriet rolled her eyes at what happened when Alex reached the front of the queue. The very pretty young brunette behind the counter beamed at him as she took his order, her eyes and manner very flirtatious. Harriet found herself decidedly irritated, hating the thought that Alex might have already found a replacement for that silly Lisa. The sudden thought that she might be jealous seemed ludicrous. Jealous of whom? And of what? And, more to the point, *why*?

Harriet frowned, wondering and worrying that Alex's hugging her earlier might have unlocked feelings which she'd always had for him and which she'd successfully hidden, even from herself. Harriet couldn't deny that she'd liked the feel of his big, strong arms around her; she liked his bringing her here for coffee as well.

Whatever, when Alex turned away from the counter and started heading towards her, Harriet found herself looking at him with new eyes, the same new eyes which had examined Dwayne with brutal honesty and had found him sadly lacking.

The word 'lacking' would never apply to the boss of Ark Properties. He had everything that any woman would want. In a boyfriend, that was, but not in a prospective husband.

So lock this unwanted attraction of yours away again, Harriet, and look elsewhere for your life partner. Because it's never going to be Alex Kotana!

Perversely, however, as soon as he sat back down at their table, she opened her silly, jealous mouth and said waspishly, 'I suppose that happens to you all the time.'

'What?' he said, sounding perplexed.

Whilst kicking herself, Harriet quickly found a wry little smile and a more casual tone. 'The brunette behind the counter didn't half make it clear that you could have put her on your order, if you'd been so inclined.'

Alex smiled. 'She did, didn't she? Unfortunately, she's not my type.'

'You don't like brunettes?' Now that she thought about it, his last two girlfriends had been blondes. She'd never met the first one, who'd come and gone within a month of her becoming Alex's PA, so she didn't know if she was a blonde or not.

His eyes held hers for a rather long moment, making Harriet feel decidedly uncomfortable. She hoped her momentary jab of jealousy hadn't been obvious earlier. If it had, then she might not be lasting long in her job. It was a depressing thought. Her job meant the world to her. It was interesting and challenging and very well paid. Now that she didn't have Dwayne in her life, she needed her job more than ever.

'Sorry,' she said swiftly. 'I shouldn't be asking you personal questions like that. It's none of my business.'

Alex shrugged his powerful shoulders. 'No sweat. I'm about to ask you a personal question or two.'

'Oh?'

'Come now, Harry, you don't expect me not to be curious over why you broke up with Dwayne. That's why I brought you down here away from the prying eyes and ears in the office. To worm out all the grisly details. You must know that.'

Harriet sighed. 'There are no grisly details.' Just mundane ones.

'So you didn't discover he was a secret drunk, or a drug addict?'

'No!'

'You didn't come home and find him in bed with your best friend?'

'Lord no,' she said and laughed.

'Then what on earth did the man do?'

Harriet knew it was going to be difficult to explain without her seeming like some kind of nutcase. But she could see she would have to try. When Alex wanted to know something, he was like a dog with a bone.

'He just didn't measure up as husband material.'

'Ah,' Alex said, as though understanding perfectly what she was talking about. 'I rather suspected that his golf playing might have become a problem.'

Harriet just stared at him. 'I had no problem with Dwayne playing golf,' she replied, feeling somewhat confused. 'Though it didn't go down well when he bought a very expensive set of clubs the same day he suggested I buy my wedding dress on the Internet.'

Alex's brows lifted. 'He wanted you to buy a second-hand wedding dress?'

'Yes,' she admitted tartly.

'Ah,' he said in that knowing way again, Harriet gratified that her boss understood that Dwayne's penny-pinching suggestion might have been a deal breaker.

'My father was a mean man with money,' she found herself elaborating. 'I vowed when I was just a teenager that I would never marry a scrooge.'

'I fully agree with you. But didn't you know Dwayne was tight with money when you first started dating him?'

'He wasn't like that then. He used to spend money on me like water. Took me to the best restaurants, the best concerts, the best of everything.'

'Yes, well, a man like Dwayne would have had to pull out all stops to impress a girl like you. And he succeeded, didn't he? You fell for him and agreed to marry him. But once he had his ring on your finger, he dropped the ball. Am I right?'

'Very right,' Harriet agreed, then frowned. 'What do you mean by "a girl like me"?'

Alex smiled a crooked smile. 'It must have been very upsetting to find out that your Prince Charming was nothing but a frog. And a stingy frog at that. What I meant was that you were always a cut above Dwayne, not only in looks but in intelligence and personality. He must have known on first meeting you that he would have to lift his game in every department if he wanted to win the heart of the beautiful Harriet McKenna. But the fool couldn't keep it up, which is what happens when you play out of your league.'

Harriet flushed wildly at his compliments, not sure whether to believe him or not. Alex could be inclined to flattery on occasions. Not with her, but with clients. Though he had said she looked gorgeous the night they'd all attended that fundraising dinner back in March. She'd been wearing a new red cocktail dress which had looked well on her with her dark hair and eyes.

'So what was the final straw?' Alex went on. 'The wedding dress business? Or something else?'

'The wedding dress suggestion certainly brought things to a head. But I'd been unhappy for some time. And worried. It was obvious Dwayne wasn't the man I thought he was. He certainly wasn't acting like the man I fell in love with. He'd become lazy around the house. And with me.'

'You mean your sex life had suffered.'

Harriet laughed and blushed slightly. 'What sex life?'

'The man was a fool,' Alex said sharply. 'What did he honestly expect would happen if he started neglecting you in bed?'

'I have no idea,' Harriet said with a sigh, thinking to herself that she couldn't imagine Alex neglecting any of his girlfriends in bed. That man had testosterone oozing out of every pore of his gorgeous male body. 'He obviously didn't expect me to break off our engagement. He couldn't believe it at first. When I tried to explain the reasons why I'd fallen out of love with him, he went into a rage, accusing me of all sorts of crazy things.'

'Like what?'

Harriet could see Alex was determined to hear the truth behind the break-up.

'Like I no longer loved him because I'd fallen in love with you...

'As if I'd be stupid enough to do something like that,' she raced on before Alex had a chance to jump to any potentially dangerous conclusions.

CHAPTER THREE

THE ARRIVAL OF the brunette with his order of coffee and bagels could not have come at a better time, giving Alex the opportunity to hide his peeved reaction to Harriet's somewhat scoffing reply to Dwayne's accusation. A perverse reaction, in a way, considering he didn't want any woman falling in love with him. But it wasn't very flattering for Harry to tell him that her falling for him would be *stupid*!

His throwing the waitress one of his super-charming smiles was more the result of a bruised ego than his desire to capture the girl's interest. He'd been right when he'd said she wasn't his type. She'd been way too eager to please. As much as Alex liked to date pretty young things—and the brunette was just that—he preferred independent, spirited girls who didn't gush or grovel, and who didn't have a single gold-digging bone in their bodies. Alex had known immediately that the brunette was not of that ilk.

'Is there anything else you'd like, sir?' the brunette asked after carefully placing the coffee and bagel on the table, her attention all on him, not having cast a single glance in Harriet's direction.

'No, thanks,' he said and resisted the impulse to give her a tip. Harriet was already looking seriously irritated.

As the waitress departed, Harriet sent him a droll look.

'Yes, I know,' he said drily. 'It does happen to me all the time. But she's still not my type.'

'Then perhaps you shouldn't have flirted with her.'

Alex clenched his teeth hard in his jaw whilst he struggled to control his temper. 'And perhaps *you* should tell me why you find me so unlovable,' he retorted, still smarting over her earlier remark.

She blinked at his sharpness before dropping her eyes, taking a few seconds to pour the sugar into her coffee and looking up at him again. 'I never said you were unlovable, Alex. I said I would not be stupid enough to fall in love with you. That's an entirely different concept.'

Alex's bruised ego was not to be so easily mollified. 'Would you care to explain that last statement further? Why would it be so stupid for you to fall in love with me?'

'Aside from the fact that I'm your PA, you mean?' she threw at him.

He had to concede that that was an excellent reason. It was never a good idea to mix business and pleasure, something which he was in danger of forgetting.

'Point taken,' he said. 'Is that the only reason, then?'

She gave him a long, searching look that he found decidedly irritating. This was a Harriet he wasn't used to. Up till today she'd been the perfect PA, never complaining or criticising, calmly obeying his every wish and command. She'd never before looked at him in such an assessing and possibly judgmental fashion. He didn't like it. He didn't like it one bit.

Frankly, he preferred the Harriet who'd wept in his arms.

'You're not eating your bagel,' she said as she coolly stirred her flat white. 'And your coffee will get cold. You know how you hate lukewarm coffee.'

'I also hate not having my questions answered,' he ground out, sweeping up his mug of black coffee and glaring at her over the rim.

Harriet knew she had annoyed him; knew he'd taken her statement as a personal criticism. It had been seriously foolish of her to tell him about Dwayne's accusation. But it was too late now. Somehow she had to explain her remark without offending Alex further.

Make light of it, girl. Turn it round so that it's your failing and not his. And don't, for pity's sake, repeat the word 'stupid' in context with falling in love with him. No wonder he took umbrage!

'The thing is,' she said in a lighter, less emotional voice, 'I realised a few years back that if I wanted to get married and have children...which I did; which I still do, actually...that I had to stop dating a certain type of man. I—'

'And what type is that?' Alex interrupted before she could go on.

'Oh, you know. *Your* type.'

'*My* type?'

Oh, dear, she'd done it again. She'd opened her big mouth and put her foot in it. 'Well, not exactly your type, Alex,' she said with a 'butter wouldn't melt in her mouth' smile. 'You are rather unique. As you are aware, I've worked in real estate ever since I came to Sydney when I was twenty. Girls usually date men they meet at work. It was inevitable that I would end up dating real-estate salesmen. Invariably, they were tall and handsome, with the gift of the gab, but not exactly the most faithful kind of guy.'

'I see,' Alex said thoughtfully. 'Go on.'

Harriet was glad to see that Alex had lost his disgruntled expression, his blue eyes no longer cold and steely.

'By the time I turned twenty-seven, I decided I was wasting my time on men like that. So I sat down and made a checklist of what I wanted in a husband.'

'A checklist?' he repeated, looking both surprised and amused.

'Find it funny if you like. Emily certainly does.'

'Who's Emily? Your sister?'

'No. Emily's my best friend. She's an English teacher who flatted with me for a while. It was through her that I met Dwayne.'

'I did wonder how you two met. Frankly, I never thought you were all that well suited. Still, Dwayne must have met your checklist to begin with.'

Harriet sighed. 'I thought he did, till he moved in with me and eventually showed his true colours. I now appreciate that it's impossible to know a man's true character till you live with him. Dwayne certainly met the first three requirements. When I made up my checklist, I decided that I wouldn't even go out with a man till he ticked those three boxes. That way I hoped to avoid falling in love with any more Mr Wrongs.'

Alex's mind boggled over what those three requirements might be. Harriet was right about his finding the idea of a checklist funny. He did. Though he shouldn't have. Didn't he have a checklist of his own when it came to the girls he dated? They had to be in their early twenties, pretty and easy-going. He had a feeling, though, that Harriet's checklist would be a lot more fascinating. And, yes, very funny indeed.

'Do tell,' he said, trying to keep a straight face.

'Promise me you won't laugh.'

'I promise,' he said, but the corners of his mouth were already twitching.

'Okay, well, the first requirement is he can't be too tall or too short. Whilst I find tallness attractive, I've found that too-tall men are often arrogant, whilst too-short men can suffer from the "short man" syndrome.'

Alex realised that at six foot-four he probably came into the 'too tall' category.

'Do you think I'm arrogant?' he asked.

'A little. But not in a nasty way.'

'Thank God for that. And requirement number two is?'

'He can't be too handsome or too ugly.'

Well, Dwayne had certainly been on the money there. As for himself… Harriet would probably label him in the 'too handsome' category.

'And number three?'

'He can't be too rich or too poor.'

'Right.' Well, that certainly ruled *him* out as a prospective date for Harriet. Not that he would ever ask her out. He'd have to be mad to date Harriet.

But, as he looked into her big brown eyes, Alex was struck by the startling realisation that that was exactly what he wanted to do. Take her out, then take her back to bed.

Bad idea, that, he thought and busied himself stuffing his mouth full of bagel whilst trying to work out where such a potentially self-destructive desire had come from. After all, Harriet didn't fit his own checklist for dating candidates any better than he fitted hers!

Still, it didn't take Alex all that long privately to admit that he'd secretly wanted to take Harriet to bed since the day he'd interviewed her ten months ago. The attraction had been there from the moment she'd walked into his office, looking deliciously nervous but beautifully turned out in a sleek black suit which had followed the curves of her very feminine figure. Her dark brown hair had been up in a professional and somewhat prissy style, but her lushly glossed mouth had betrayed her true nature. He'd immediately made the decision not to hire her, despite her excellent résumé—till he found out she was safely engaged, at which point he'd fooled himself into thinking he could ignore his hormones.

And he had, up till now.

They would have remained in control, too, if she hadn't broken up with Dwayne; if she hadn't cried and he hadn't hugged her. That had been the catalyst which had started the chemical reaction which saw him now being tempted to do something seriously stupid.

Thank God it was still just a temptation. He didn't have to act on it. Didn't have to suffer the humiliation of Harriet rejecting him, not just because he was her boss, but because he was too tall, too handsome *and* too rich.

His sudden laughter brought a reproving look into her velvety brown eyes.

'You promised you wouldn't laugh,' she chided him.

'Sorry. Couldn't help it.'

'In that case, I won't tell you the rest of my checklist. You'd probably crack up entirely.'

'You could be right, there. So I'll save up the rest of your checklist till a later date. Now, I think we should finish up here and get back to work.'

CHAPTER FOUR

HARRIET SIGHED AS she sat back down at her desk and turned on her computer. She hadn't wanted to go back to work; back to reality. She'd been enjoying having coffee with Alex, despite her many *faux pas*. She hadn't really minded his laughing at her checklist, which she now appreciated *was* rather funny. Whilst it did have some merit, such strategies simply didn't work out in real life, just like those silly matchmaking forms they made you filled in on online dating sites.

Most women ended up marrying men they met through work, Harriet accepted, thinking of her other married girlfriends. Actually, *all* her girlfriends were married, a thought which was rather depressing. Harriet was well aware that marriage and motherhood wasn't the only pathway to happiness and fulfilment in life, but it was her chosen pathway. That and a career. Yes, she wanted to have it all, which was possibly where she was going wrong. Having it all suddenly seemed beyond her grasp. This time next year, she'd be hitting thirty. After thirty, finding a husband became more difficult; all the good ones were already snapped up.

Even ordinary men like Dwayne weren't exactly thick on the ground. Maybe she shouldn't have been so quick to dump him. Maybe she should have ignored his failings and accepted him for the imperfect specimen he was...

Harriet was pondering this conundrum when Alex strode out of his office and perched his far too perfect body on the corner of her thankfully large desk.

'A couple of things I forgot to tell you this morning,' he said as he hitched his right knee up into a more comfortable position, indicating he was staying put for a while. 'First, I want you to book me a flight to Milan, arriving on the twenty-ninth of July.'

'Milan?' she echoed, forgetting that it wasn't a PA's job to question her boss, just to obey.

'Yes. Milan, Italy. One of my best friends from Oxford is getting married on the thirty-first. I've been ordered to be there two days before the actual wedding so that I can be attired suitably for my job as best man. The other best man obviously fears I might show up in jeans and a T-shirt.'

Harriet blinked her astonishment at such a ludicrous idea. The night they'd attended that fundraising dinner back in March, Alex had walked into the hotel ballroom wearing a magnificent black tux. He'd quite literally taken her breath away.

'How ridiculous,' she scoffed. 'You are one of the best-dressed men I've ever met.'

'You haven't seen me when I'm slumming it. Jeremy has.'

'Jeremy?'

'The other best man and possibly the best-dressed rake in all of London.'

Harriet's eyes widened. 'Your best friend is a rake?'

'Birds of a feather flock together, you know.'

'You're not a rake,' she defended. 'You just pick the wrong girls to date. The reason they never last is that you get bored with them.'

Alex stared at Harriet and thought how right she was. He did get bored with the women he dated. But that was exactly what made them safe. They never touched him with any depth of feeling, never moved his soul. Leaving them behind was so damned easy.

The truth hit that he wasn't unhappy with his life so much, but he was bored. Bored with dating silly young girls. Bored with never having a decent conversation with a woman.

He hadn't been bored having coffee with Harriet this morning. He'd been alternately annoyed, then angry, then amused and, yes, aroused. A whole gamut of emotions. He hadn't been able to settle back down to work afterwards; he'd been looking for any reason to come out and talk to her again. Having Harriet book that flight for him had just been an excuse. He could quite easily have done it himself.

I'm not going to be able to resist this attraction, Alex finally conceded, *no matter what the danger*. He suspected she would not reject him; the sexual chemistry which had sprung up today was not all on his side. Alex had noticed her pique when the brunette in the café had flirted with him.

He still hesitated to ask her out on a regular date, sensing that it was too soon for such a move. Clearly, she was still hurting over the break-up with Dwayne. On top of that, she was his PA, one of the many reasons she'd given to explain why she would never fall in love with him. Not that he wanted her love, just her body. If truth be told, he didn't want Harry to be his next girlfriend. He just wanted to have an affair with her. A strictly sexual affair.

He should have been disgusted with himself. But Alex soothed his conscience by reassuring himself that he would never hurt Harry. He could give her pleasure and fun, something which he suspected had been in short supply in her life for some time.

The only problem was finding a way to achieve his aims without offending her.

An idea struck, one which would sound perfectly reasonable but which would give him the opportunity to act upon his feelings away from the office. Of course, there was always the risk that Harry would still reject his advances. And, yes, she might even be offended by them. Alex suspected she was a stickler for propriety in the workplace. But it was a risk he was prepared to take. It had been a long time since he'd lived on the edge, so to speak, and it excited him. *She* excited him.

His eyes met with hers, his gaze intense as he searched her face for a sign that he'd been right about her body language when they'd been having coffee together. Alex was gratified when a faint flush bloomed in her cheeks.

'My having to go to Italy for days on end couldn't have come at a worse time,' he said, schooling his own face into a concerned mask. 'I need to be continually hands-on with that golfing estate if it's going to be up and running by Christmas. Someone has to be up there every week to crack the whip. While I'm away, that person will have to be you, Harry.'

'*Me?*' she squawked.

'Yes, *you*,' he insisted. 'I've heard you over the phone to our contractors when they've been giving us grief. You are one tough cookie when you want to be.'

'But doesn't that job already have a foreman in charge?'

'Yes, but even the best foreman can get slack when he's working that far from the boss. If I hadn't been driving up there on a regular basis, we'd be even further behind than we are. I don't want any more delays.'

'Right,' she said, still looking a bit hesitant.

'I thought we could drive up there this Friday, stay overnight, then drive back on the Saturday. We'll stay overnight. And not in some dreary motel, either. Book us a two-bedroomed apartment at a five-star resort in Coffs Harbour. That's only a half-hour drive from the golf course. Somewhere near the ocean, with a balcony and a sea view. And make sure they have a decent restaurant. In fact, we might stay another night, then drive back on the Sunday. You deserve a break after what you've been through.'

CHAPTER FIVE

HARRIET DIDN'T KNOW what to say. She had travelled with Alex only once before. To the Gold Coast, to meet with some Japanese billionaires who'd been staying there at the Hotel Versace and who were potential clients for his new golf resort. But they'd travelled by plane and she'd taken a taxi to the airport by herself. She'd also stayed in a totally separate hotel room. The thought of staying with her way-too-sexy boss in an apartment—for possibly two nights—made her feel...what, exactly?

'Panic' came close to describing her reaction.

Before today, Harriet would have been supremely confident that Alex would never make a move on her. But things were different now. Lisa was past history and so was Dwayne. A new intimacy had sprung up between them, first when Alex had hugged her, and then when they'd had coffee together, an inevitable result once you started opening up about your private life to another person, even when that person was your boss. Harriet knew that men found her attractive. Why should Alex be any different?

And then there was her own silly self. She'd always been blindly attracted to men who were tall, handsome and, yes, super-successful, a failing which she'd worked hard to conquer. But she was in a highly vulnerable state at the moment and, when she faced it, when it came to tall, handsome and super-successful men, Alex was at the top of the heap. To stay with him in an apartment for two nights was asking for trouble.

She didn't need any more trouble in her life. She did, however, need her job; the mortgage on her Bondi apartment barely manageable now that she didn't have anyone to help with the payments. Having an affair with the boss was a sure way to lose her job. Harriet had been around long enough to know how such relationships ended.

'Thank you for your kind offer,' she said in her best businesslike voice. 'But I can't stay away for two nights. Emily is getting back from Bali on Saturday and we're having a catch-up lunch on Sunday.' This was a bald-faced lie. Emily was away for a further two months. Harriet knew, however, that she needed a decent excuse to get out of this. Alex didn't like being told no.

'Pity,' he muttered, then shrugged his shoulders, his indifference indicating he hadn't had any dastardly secret agenda when he'd suggested a two-night stay. He was just trying to be nice to her again. Truly, she was letting herself get carried away here, thinking he had seduction on his mind, a prospect which she had found perversely appealing and painfully flattering. Oh, dear... She seriously wished he'd get off the corner of her desk. Or alternatively stop swinging his foot like that. He was making her way too aware of his body, his very hunky, handsome male body.

Harriet picked up a biro so that she could pretend to take notes and not look at him.

'I'll get onto those bookings right away,' she said. 'I presume you'll be flying first class to Milan?' This with a quick glance his way.

'Of course,' he replied and smiled at her.

When Harriet's heart gave a lurch, she told herself quite fiercely just to stop it. But she might as well have tried to stop the tide from coming in. Why, oh why, did women find men like Alex so damned attractive? She supposed it was a primal thing, the female of the species blindly surrendering to the alpha male because that was the way of nature. But that didn't make it any easier to endure. The last thing she wanted was to start suffering from some silly crush.

'What about a date for the return flight?' she asked crisply.

'Mmm. Can't say I'm sure when that will be. I might spend a day or two with Jeremy in London after the wedding. It's summer over there at the moment. Look, just make it the one-way to Milan. I'll organise the return flight myself when I'm over there.'

'Fine. I'll scout around and see what's the best first-class deal. Might take me a while. First, I'll look up the various five-star resorts at Coffs Harbour,' she went on, putting the biro down and clicking on the computer to bring up resorts at Coffs Harbour. 'Get your tick of approval whilst you're here. Hmm... An ocean view, you said. With a balcony. It *is* winter, you know. I doubt we'll be spending too much time on an ocean-facing balcony.'

'Possibly not,' he agreed. 'But I like apartments with balconies. They're usually larger and have better light.'

'A balcony it is, then. Here's one which should suit— the Pacific View resort just south of Coffs Harbour. They have a two-bedroom spa suite available for Friday night which has a huge balcony with an ocean view.'

'And the other facilities?'

'Everything you could possibly want. There's a heated indoor pool as well as a gym and not one but two restaurants—one a bistro, the other *à la carte.*'

'Great.'

'Shall I book it, then?'

'Absolutely. Oh, and, Harry,' Alex added as he slid off the corner of her desk. *Finally.* 'Perhaps it might be best not to mention where we'll be staying to the rest of the staff, especially Audrey. She might jump to the wrong conclusion, the way she did this morning when she walked in on my hugging you. We don't want to start up any rumours, do we?'

'Absolutely not. Right you are, boss. Mum's the word.'

'Good girl,' he said, before heading back into his office.

Harriet almost laughed. Because all of a sudden she didn't want to be a good girl. She wanted to be a very bad girl. With Alex.

She was in the process of making the bookings when a courier walked in, holding a huge bouquet of assorted flowers.

'Someone's a lucky girl,' he said, smiling a goofy smile. 'The lady on reception said they were for you.'

Harriet's first hideous thought was that they were from Dwayne, in some vain attempt to get her back. But when she opened the card which accompanied the flowers, the words written there brought tears to her eyes for the second time that day.

Hope you're feeling better soon.
Love from Audrey.
PS The bum wasn't good enough for you, anyway.

The PS made her laugh, which came as a relief to the courier, who was looking worried.

'Everything's fine,' she said to him, waiting till he

left before going out to reception and thanking Audrey profusely.

'Flowers always make me feel better,' Audrey said. 'So does a glass of wine or two. Want to come have a drink with me after work?'

'Love to,' Harriet said. She'd missed her girls' nights out with Emily since she'd gone away.

'Great,' Audrey said. 'You should join the rest of us on Friday nights as well.'

'I will in future,' Harriet said. 'But I can't this Friday night. Have to go north with the boss to inspect his new golf resort. He has to go away overseas again soon and he wants me to keep a personal eye on things up there,' she added by way of explanation. 'So I need to see the lie of the land and meet the foreman.'

'That's a long drive. You'll have to stay somewhere overnight.'

'Probably. Still, there are plenty of motels up that way.'

'True.'

'I'd better get back to work or the slave driver might come looking for me.'

'He can be like that, can't he?'

'He's a workaholic, that's for sure.'

'I wouldn't like to do your job.'

'I don't mind. I like it.' An understatement. She *loved* her job.

'Don't you get fed up with being at his beck and call all the time? I mean, the things he asks you to do some-times.' Audrey rolled her eyes.

Harriet just laughed. Alex had been very up-front at her interview over the menial tasks he might ask her to do. She honestly didn't mind getting his bagels, buying presents for members of his family or even organising his dry-cleaning. Better than sitting at her desk all the time.

It wasn't till Harriet was sitting back down at that same desk that she realised she would enjoy the drive up to the golf estate this weekend very much if she wasn't starting to have these awkward feelings for Alex. Still, at least these days she was capable of resisting such self-destructive desires, having become wise to her own weaknesses where the opposite sex   and sex—was concerned. In time, these feelings would pass and she would meet someone else, someone who could satisfy her in bed and tick at least some of the boxes in her checklist, someone more in her league than the boss of Ark Properties.

The man himself suddenly materialised by her desk.

'So what's with the flowers?' he demanded, his face decidedly grim. 'I hope they're not from your idiot of an ex, trying to get back into your good books.'

'Hardly. They're from Audrey. Wasn't that sweet of her?'

'Very sweet. Look, I have to go out. Family emergency. Hold the fort till I get back.'

Harriet frowned at his swiftly departing back as well as his brusque manner. She wondered what kind of family emergency. He never talked about his family. Yet she knew he had a father still living, and a married older sister who had two children, a boy aged ten and a girl aged eight. She knew because she'd bought Christmas and birthday presents for them.

Maybe she would ask him about his family during the long drive north on Friday. And maybe not.

Friday now loomed in Harriet's mind as a day fraught with unspoken tension. Life, she decided, wasn't being very kind to her at the moment.

But then she looked at Audrey's flowers and smiled.

CHAPTER SIX

IT TOOK ALMOST an hour for Alex to drive from the inner city out to Sarah's home in North Rocks. Sydney's traffic situation was getting worse with each passing year. No matter how many motorways they built, nothing seemed to ease the congestion, or the delays. But the level of his frustration when he finally pulled up outside the house he'd bought his sister some years back was not due to road rage but rage of a different kind.

Gritting his teeth, he jumped out from behind the wheel and stormed through the front gate, bypassing the front door and making his way hurriedly round to the back of the house to the entrance to the granny flat. The one-bedroomed very comfortable flat accommo-dated his father, his useless, drunken father, whom Sarah had kindly taken in but with whom Alex had totally run out of patience. He'd only come because Sarah had asked him to.

She was waiting for him in the doorway, startling Alex with how much she looked like his mother at around the same age. Both were petite and dark, though with blue eyes. Sarah was like her mother in nature, too, being strong and sensible. Alex loved her a lot and would do anything for her. He wasn't as fond of her husband, Vernon, who seemed to resent the things Alex bought for his family.

Though he'd taken the house, mortgage-free, hadn't he?

Still, Vernon did put up with his less than ideal father-in-law living with them, so he couldn't be all bad. Of course, he continued to benefit financially from the arrangement, Alex paying their rates and electricity.

'Where is he?' Alex asked, his tone sharp.

'On the floor in the bedroom,' Sarah answered, stepping back to let him enter.

The sight of his father sprawled on his back on the rug beside the bed was infinitely depressing. Not just because he was dead drunk but because of the deterioration of this once fine-looking man. Alex had inherited his looks from his father, who'd been a big blond hunk in his younger days. It was no wonder his mother had fallen for him. But there was nothing attractive about him now. Nothing at all.

'Good God,' he said, shaking his head as he stared down at the ruin at his feet. 'Whatever are we going to do with him?'

'It's not his fault, Alex,' Sarah said with her usual compassion. 'He started drinking to forget and now he can't stop. He's an alcoholic. It's a disease. A sickness.'

'Then he should agree to go into rehab.' Alex had lost count of the number of times he'd suggested rehab to his father, but it always fell on deaf ears. 'It's a pity we can't forcibly admit him.'

'I know. But you can't. He has to volunteer to go. Come on, help me lift him up onto the bed. I would have done it myself, but he's just too heavy and I can't afford to hurt my back again.'

Alex frowned. 'You've lifted him up off the floor before?'

'Only once. You were away and I didn't want to ask Vernon.'

'Don't try to lift him again, Sarah. Call an ambulance if you have to.'

Alex scooped his father up off the floor with ease and laid him down on top of the bed. He stirred slightly, making a disgusting snorting sound, before falling back into his drunken stupor, his mouth dropping wide open. His breath was foul. So was his whole body. He needed a bath, sooner rather than later. Then he needed a good talking-to. This situation simply couldn't go on. It wasn't fair to Sarah.

'I have to go to work soon, Alex,' Sarah said, anxiety in her strained face.

Sarah was an oncology nurse, an occupation which she'd decided on after their mother had died at home without too much in the way of nursing. It occurred to Alex that their mother's early and totally unnecessary death had resulted in two of her children choosing careers which they'd hoped would make a difference. Not so his pathetic father, who'd promptly fallen apart. His only decision about the future was to try to drink himself to death.

'You go,' Alex said. 'I'll stay with him.'

'That would be great. Thanks. Look, he honestly can't help it. He does try, you know. Sometimes he doesn't have a drink for weeks. I told him I wouldn't let him around the kids if he was drunk all the time. He even went to AA meetings. But last week was the anniversary of Mum's death. I found him at her graveside crying his eyes out. After that, he went on one of his benders.'

Alex sighed, finally finding some genuine compassion for the man who'd once been a decent enough father, if always a little weak. His mother had been the strength in the family and his father had adored her. He'd called her his soul mate, his rock. She'd always picked him up when he was down. Which was often, his work history not being the best. He'd constantly been made redundant, making money tight in the family. It had been inevitable that when she died he would fall apart.

Watching his father disintegrate over the years had reaffirmed Alex's own decision to steer clear of marriage, as well as avoiding any deeply emotional attachments. Loving a woman obsessively the way his father had loved his mother was not something Alex wanted in his life.

'I'll make sure he has a bath and eats some food,' Alex told his sister. 'And I'll wash those filthy clothes he's wearing. Then I'll do my best to talk to him, see if he'll try rehab. I have some contacts at the Salvation Army. They have some very good rehab places for alcoholics and addicts.'

'Oh, that would be wonderful!' Sarah exclaimed. 'Thank you, darling brother,' she added, coming forward to give him a hug, reminding him of that other hug he'd been involved in earlier that morning.

Sarah hurried off, leaving Alex alone with his father and his thoughts.

But he was no longer thinking about his father. He was thinking about Harriet and the danger of having an affair with a woman who was vastly different from his usual type of bed partner. Not only was she older and more intelligent, she was emotionally vulnerable at the moment. Frankly, Harriet was way more emotional that he would ever have imagined.

The risk he would be taking by sleeping with her was also far greater than he'd originally envisaged. What if she fell in love with him? Even worse, what if he fell in love with her? Hell! What in God's name had he been thinking? Clearly, he hadn't been thinking, not with his brain, anyway. He'd let his hormones take charge, let them cloud his usual good judgment when it came to matters concerning the opposite sex.

There was only one thing to do. He had to forget living on the edge and put Harriet firmly back into the strictly professional PA box which she'd occupied in his head for the past ten months. He actually would have called her and cancelled the trip up north if it wouldn't make him seem like a blithering idiot. He was thankful now that they would be staying in that apartment together for only one night. But, to be on the safe side, he'd put a dampener on his hormones by working out at length in the gym during the next two days. He'd also get out of the office as much as he could. There were several building projects he had underway around Sydney which he could visit. Out of sight was out of mind. By Friday morning, he'd have himself firmly under control again.

His father stirred again, this time opening his eyes, blinking blearily at Alex for several seconds before groaning.

'You're not going to lecture me again, son, are you?' he said wearily.

'No,' Alex replied in a firm, no-nonsense voice. 'This time, I'm going to tell you what you're going to do, and you're going to do it, whether you like it not.'

'Am I just?'

'Look, if you want to kill yourself, then do the decent thing and do it quickly. Just don't do it slowly in front of your daughter and your grandkids. They deserve better than that.'

'You don't understand,' he blubbered.

'Yeah, I do. Better than you think. You might not realise this, but Mum's death affected the whole family, not just you. You think Sarah and I didn't grieve? We did.

But eventually we all moved on, the way Mum would have wanted us to move on.'

His father looked away in shame.

'It's not too late, Dad,' Alex went on, his voice gentler. 'You can beat this thing if you want to. Sarah's going to need you when the kids get older. You could be here when she can't be. Keep an eye on them. Sarah's been good to you. Time for you to be good back to her. Time for you to step up to the plate and be a man.'

Tears sprung into his father's tired blue eyes. 'It's too late.'

'It's never too late,' Alex insisted. 'People can change, no matter how old they are. It won't be easy, but it will work, if you give it a chance. I'll help you, too, if you let me.'

'You're a good son.'

Alex experienced some guilt at this remark. He hadn't been such a good son. Sarah had been the one who'd shouldered most of the burden of looking after their father. He'd just opened his cheque book. But he vowed to do better in future.

'All right,' his father said with a resigned sigh. 'I'll give it a go.'

CHAPTER SEVEN

HARRIET SET HER alarm for five on Friday morning, having made arrangements with Alex to be at his place at six-thirty.

'Take a taxi on expenses,' he'd told her during the very brief appearance he'd made in the office last Wednesday morning, telling her at the same time that he wouldn't be in at all on the Thursday and that she was to use the extra time she would have to give their website a face-lift, something she'd been urging him to do for ages. He didn't explain any of his absences, as was often the case with Alex. She suspected it had something to do with his family emergency.

As the taxi sped towards Alex's Darling Harbour address, Harriet pondered again the nature of said emergency. She hoped none of his family was ill.

When the taxi pulled up to the kerb outside Alex's swish-looking apartment block, Harriet paid the fare, then climbed out, taking a few deep breaths as she waited for the driver to get her bag out of the boot. She no longer felt as nervous about this trip as she had the other day, but was not altogether calm. She'd spent an inordinate amount of time last night putting her wardrobe together for the two days, opting for smart casual, though at the last second she'd thrown in a dressy dress, in case Alex wanted to dine at the resort's *à la carte* restaurant.

Of course that had meant adding the right accessories to the growing pile of clothes.

'Going on holidays, love?' the taxi driver asked as he dropped the rather substantial bag by her feet.

'Something like that,' she replied.

'Hope it's somewhere a bit warmer than this,' he said jauntily as he climbed back in behind the wheel and sped off.

It was a bitterly cold morning, Sydney having been blasted by some air off the Antarctic overnight. Still, it would be warmer where they were going. Harriet had chosen to wear stretch black jeans for the drive, teaming them with black ankle boots and a cream cowl-necked jumper made of the softest mohair. She'd thrown on a fawn trench coat to keep out the early morning chill but which she would remove once they were underway. Alex's car was sure to be heated.

Pulling out her phone, she sent him a text to say she'd arrived.

Wait there, he texted back. I'll be right out.

Harriet was shivering by the time Alex pulled up next to her in his black Range Rover. She regretted not wearing a scarf; wearing her hair up was giving her no warmth around her neck.

'Get in,' he said as he jumped out. 'You look cold. I'll see to your bag.'

Harriet tried not to stare at him. But she'd never seen him in casual clothes before. He always wore a suit in the office. He looked great in a suit. In stone-washed grey jeans and a black leather jacket, however, he looked too hot for words. His fair hair was still wet from the shower, the top spiked up a bit, the sides and back clipped short.

She liked it that way. It was dead sexy, supplying an added edge to his already macho looks.

Harriet forcibly had to drag her eyes away, her heart alternatively flipping over, then sinking as she wrenched open the passenger door and climbed in.

And there I was, she thought irritably, *imagining I had this attraction under control.*

Hell on earth, thought Alex as he scooped up the bag and threw it in the back.

He'd taken one look at Harriet standing there, staring at him with those big brown eyes of hers, and he'd known for sure that this thing he felt for her wasn't a one-sided attraction. Alex was well versed in recognising the way women looked at him when they fancied him. And Harry fancied him. But possibly not as much as he fancied her. He was a man, after all, and she was seriously fanciable, especially in those sexy jeans and boots.

By the time Alex took his seat behind the wheel, his resolve not to act on the desire Harriet kept sparking in him was very definitely wavering, especially with her betraying her own feelings just now. Of course, his being her boss still created an ethical dilemma. Such relationships were definitely frowned upon, despite being quite common. Not always ideal, however. Inevitably, there came a time when the woman wanted more. Harriet would always want more. He wouldn't be doing her any favours by taking advantage of her, especially at this time in her life when she was on the rebound and emotionally vulnerable.

Hell, hadn't he been through this thought process before?

He'd already made up his mind to steer clear of her and that was what he should do. End of story. *So just be your normal, bossy self and for pity's sake keep your hands off! Then when you get back to Sydney tomorrow night, go out and find yourself a new girlfriend. With a bit of luck, by the time you go to work on Monday your head will be out of your trousers and back on business!*

Harriet forgot about taking off her coat, buckling up the seat belt over it and propping her large black handbag in her lap whilst doing her best to adopt a relaxed facade. But inside, that tension which she'd been fearing was gathering with force, making her jump slightly when Alex gunned the engine.

'You seem to have packed a lot for one night,' he said as he drove off.

Harriet managed a casual shrug of her shoulders. 'I'm never sure what clothes to take, so I always take more than I need.'

'It's a common female trait,' Alex said. 'When I took Hailey to Vanuatu for a long weekend, she had so much luggage I had to pay for extra baggage.'

Harriet had quite liked Hailey. Much better than Lisa. She didn't like any of Alex's girlfriends now, jealousy having raised its ugly head. Lord knew what she would do when the next one came along. And she would. There was nothing surer.

'I'll remember that when you take me to Vanuatu,' Harriet quipped.

Alex laughed. 'You mean you'd settle for Vanuatu? I would have thought Venice was more your style.'

Harriet winced as a memory hit her. 'You know, I wanted to go to Italy for my honeymoon. I'd always wanted to see Rome and Florence and, yes, Venice most of all. Imagine a city built on water! But Dwayne said

Italy was overrated and that Bali was just as good. And way cheaper.'

'He sounds like a gem,' Alex said drily.

Harriet snorted. 'Yes, a zircon. Everything about him was false.'

'You're well rid of him. But I have to confess I'm still curious over the other check-points on your list, the boxes Dwayne seemed to tick. At first, that is.'

'Oh, God,' Harriet groaned. 'Can't we just forget that stupid list?'

'Since *you* made that list, Harry, then I doubt it was stupid. Come on, tell your dear old boss all about it.'

She had to smile. The only thing right about that description of himself was the word 'boss'. 'Only if you give me your solemn word this time that you won't laugh.'

'If I do, I give you permission to hit me. Though not whilst I'm driving.'

They'd long passed through the harbour tunnel by then and were making their way towards Chatswood, the traffic growing with each passing minute. Like other big cities, Sydney never really slept.

'Well?' Alex prompted when she didn't say anything.

'Gosh, but you can be dogged at times,' she said, but smiling. It occurred to Harriet with a degree of surprise that their chatting away like this was making her relax. 'Okay, well, after Dwayne passed the first three boxes, the next one was that my husband-to-be was not to be boring or lazy.'

'Huh! I don't know about lazy, but I found him boring when I met him.'

'Yes, well, the rot was setting in by then. In the beginning, he showed me a good time. As for lazy... He went from sharing the housework and washing my car as well as his to being a couch potato.'

'I can understand how that would annoy someone as fastidious as you.'

Fastidious? Harriet wasn't sure if that was a compliment or a criticism.

'How am I fastidious?' she asked him enquiringly.

'Come now, Harry, you're a perfectionist! You always look great for starters, even at six-thirty in the morning. There's not a hair out of place, your make-up is on and your outfit is perfect for travelling. I'll also bet if I went into your place right now it would be spotless, with your bed made and the washing-up all done. Am I right?'

'Not at all. Yes, the bed is made and the washing-up done, but there's clothes all over my bed and the bulb in my bathroom isn't working. A perfectionist would have had it fixed by now instead of just moving a lamp in there so that I can see.'

'Really? I'm shocked.'

She had to smile. 'You're laughing at me again.'

'Never! Now, back to that fascinating checklist of yours. What comes after lazy and boring?'

'Look, I'm not going to go through every individual point with regard to Dwayne, except to say that he failed them all. I'll just recite the rest of the checklist the way it's written down.'

Alex smiled to himself; she clearly knew the list off by heart. 'My husband-to-be is to be easy-going and generous. He has to treat women as equals. He has to be a lover of animals and children. He has to have friends and interests other than work. He has to have empathy for others, especially those less fortunate than themselves. He has to be able to cook and doesn't think cleaning is beneath him. He has to respect me and trust me and love me and never, ever forget my birthday. And that's about it,' she finished, leaving off the last point which was about sex.

'Wow. That's some list. But what about sex? Don't you care what kind of lover he is?'

Harriet pursed her lips, a slight blush touching her cheeks. Trust Alex to notice that she'd bypassed that topic. She could never get anything past him at work, either.

'Well, naturally he has to satisfy me in bed,' she said, trying not to look as embarrassed as she felt.

'In that case, Dwayne must have satisfied you. At first, anyway?'

'I suppose so,' she said with a sigh. 'He could be quite good in bed when he wanted to be.'

'But not great.'

'No,' she admitted. 'Not great. Look, I don't feel comfortable talking about this,' she went on quite truthfully. The last thing she needed was to start thinking about sex when the object of her desire was sitting right next to her. 'Could we talk about something else? Work, perhaps, or the weather? And could you turn the heating down in this thing? It's very hot in here.'

Alex rarely felt shame, but he did at that moment. Asking Harriet personal questions like that was very definitely crossing the line, especially since he'd resolved not to act on the sexual feelings he'd been having about her. He couldn't help suspecting, however, that her flushed face was not entirely due to his putting the heater up too high.

Talking about sex could sometimes be very arousing, the brain being the most erotic area in the human body. The thought that she was sitting there in a turned-on state was not conducive to resisting temptation.

Gritting his teeth, Alex adjusted the temperature.

'I've turned the heating down,' he said. 'But perhaps you should take that coat off. I've only got a T-shirt on under my jacket, so I feel fine. You look like you've got a very warm jumper on.' And a very sexy-looking one, he'd noted earlier. All soft and furry, the kind you wanted to reach out and touch.

'I meant to take it off earlier,' she said. She was quick, the coat dispensed with in no time and her seat belt snapped back on.

'Throw it over onto the back seat,' he said when she went to lay the coat across her lap.

Alex glanced over at her as she twisted in her seat to do as he said, the movement bringing his attention to the swell of her breasts beneath her jumper. Her very nice breasts. It sent a message to his groin which made him wince.

Damn and blast! It wasn't Harriet who was sitting here in a turned-on state. It was his own stupid self. He should never have asked her about her sex life with Dwayne. He never should have organised this whole fiasco of a trip in the first place!

'I'll put the radio on,' he said brusquely. That way he wouldn't be tempted to ask her any more inappropriate questions. 'Do you want a news and chat channel? Or just music?'

CHAPTER EIGHT

'WHAT?' HARRIET COULDN'T think for a moment, her mind still on that look Alex had given her a moment ago. Had she imagined it or had he stared at her breasts?

Of course you were imagining it, you idiot, came the stern rebuke. *Why would he be ogling your very ordinary C-cups? They can't compare with Lisa's double Ds. Stop focusing on sex and just answer the man.*

'Just music, thanks,' she said, pressing her thighs together tightly in a vain attempt to bring her body under control, her silly, traitorous body which had become all hot and bothered. Talk about pathetic!

'Music,' Alex said to the computerised dashboard and a woman's voice came back with a request for more information. Whilst Harriet was technically savvy, her four-year-old car didn't have such advanced technology. She recalled Alex saying something about updating his SUV when he'd come back from London recently. So this had to be it.

'What kind of music do you like?' Alex asked her.

Harriet didn't really have a favourite style of music. But she supposed she had to say something. 'Country and Western.'

'Country and Western,' he commanded the computer and almost immediately a song came on that she liked.

'Amazing,' she said. 'You don't even have to insert a flash disc or a CD.'

'It's almost as brilliant as my PA.'

Harriet flushed with pleasure. This was another part of her job she liked—the way Alex would compliment her. Her previous bosses had never done that. Clearly, their fragile male egos had been threatened by her. Not so with Alex. Of course, there was nothing fragile about *his* ego. Or about him. He was a big man in every way.

'You did a brilliant job on our website, by the way,' he went on. 'I had a look at it last night and I was very impressed. It's better laid out and more user-friendly. And I like the way you included photos of the staff. Nothing like the personal touch.'

'That was Audrey's idea,' she admitted, not being one to take credit for something that someone else had suggested. 'We went out for drinks after work on Tuesday, and when I said I was going to revamp the website, she had quite a few excellent suggestions. She's an online shopping addict, so she knows what works and what doesn't.'

'She's a smart lady, Audrey. But inclined to gossip. Did you remember not to tell her we wouldn't be staying up here overnight?'

'Like you just said, Alex, she's smart. Audrey had already concluded we'd be staying somewhere overnight. But I let her think we'd be bunking down in separate rooms in an ordinary motel, not in an apartment at a five-star resort.'

'Good thinking. Did you organise someone to feed the cat while you're away?'

'Yes, Audrey's doing it.'

'That's good. Can't have the poor old thing passing

away from starvation while we're away. You'd blame me, and I don't think I could live with the guilt.'

'Don't be silly. You have nothing to feel guilty about where Romany is concerned. Did I ever thank you for letting him be the office cat?'

'Only about a hundred times.'

'Oh. Yes, well, it was still very good of you. Poor Romany,' she said with a sigh. 'I dare say he'll die soon. Still, at least we made the last part of his life a little happier.'

'You do spoil him rotten, Harry. Sometimes I almost feel jealous of that cat. Now, I don't want to stop again till we get to Port Macquarie, probably around eleven. I want to make the golf estate by two o'clock at the latest. Is that all right with you?'

'That's fine,' she agreed.

'If you need a break before then, just say so.'

'I'll be all right.'

'Good. Now, just settle back and relax and listen to the music. Eventually, though, I'll have to make some business calls. But not yet. It's still early.'

Harriet doubted that she would relax, but amazingly she did, the heated seats and the music melting away her earlier tension. She even drifted off to sleep, jolting awake when Alex started talking more loudly than the music. She listened, amazed at how much he could achieve on the phone in just a couple of hours, contacting all the foremen on his current building projects, demanding updates on their progress, giving them a hurry-up when needed.

Eleven saw them eating a disgustingly fattening lunch in the service centre near the turn-off to Port Macquarie, Alex scoffing at her comment that she'd end up with a backside the size of a bus if she ate that for lunch every day.

'No worries there, Harry. You would starve rather than eat this kind of food every day.'

'True,' she agreed.

'It doesn't hurt to bend your rules every once in a while, you know.'

She stared at him across the wooden bench, wondering what rules he was referring to. Probably that silly checklist of hers. Not that all of it was silly. In fact, a lot of those rules made perfect sense. The trouble was that men weren't perfect, so finding someone to fit all her far-too-many requirements was doomed to failure. All she could hope for was that the main ones might be fulfilled. The ones about love and respect and money and, yes, sex.

'You could be right, there,' she mused.

'I *am* right,' he pronounced. 'Now, drink up that cappuccino. Time to get going.'

He was back on the phone again as soon as they hit the road, chatting away with the sales team in the office, finding out how things were going and how many sales they'd had off their various plans. They had several blocks of units in a developmental stage, all of them in the far western suburbs and very reasonably priced. Most were likely to be sold before a single brick was laid. They also had a housing estate near where the new Sydney airport was to be built, which was proving popular with first-time buyers and builders. Harriet listened as Alex told each of the boys personally about his having to go away the week after next. When he finally finished talking, Harriet turned to glance his way.

'By the way, will *we* be handling the sales of the housing blocks on the golf estate, or are you going to give that job to local real-estate agents?'

'Both. And we'll advertise extensively online. That will be *your* job, Harry. Perhaps you can think about that while I'm away, since you won't be running around all the time getting your boss bagels and doing myriad other jobs which the lazy so-and-so could possibly do himself.'

Harriet laughed. 'I don't mind, really.'

'I know you don't. You are indispensable to me, Harry.'

'No one is indispensable, Alex.'

'You are to me. As selfish as it sounds, I'm almost glad that you've broken off your engagement. The thought of you getting married and leaving me to become a mother was filling me with dread.'

Harriet rolled her eyes. What a hopeless exaggerator he was! But, yes, it *was* selfish of him to say that. And rather insensitive.

'Sorry,' she said. 'But I still intend to get married and have at least one baby, so you'll just have to cope when that day comes. But don't worry. I have no intention of giving up my day job just because I'm pregnant. I'll waddle into the office right up to the last second. You might even have to drive me to the maternity ward if my husband is unavailable,' she added with a straight face.

CHAPTER NINE

ALEX WAS HORRIFIED at the thought, plus the image of Harry waddling into the office at some future date with a huge baby bump. He could see it now. Her desk would be littered with magazines that told you everything you needed to know about pregnancy and motherhood—plus everything you didn't need to know. She and Audrey would talk babies *ad infinitum*, spending every lunch hour buying baby clothes, not to mention oodles of those hideous stuffed toys. And, yes, there would be a bag packed and sitting in the corner, ready for the emergency of her suddenly going into labour.

'That won't be happening,' he ground out. 'Audrey can take you in a taxi.'

Harriet laughed. 'You should see your face. What's the problem, Alex? You're not afraid of babies, are you?'

'Immensely. They're noisy and messy and have no concept of doing what they're told.' He'd visited Sarah once or twice when she'd had newborns and had hardly slept a wink, what with the crying all night. It certainly wasn't something he craved for himself.

'No wonder you've stayed a bachelor if that's what you think.'

'It's what I think. Now, tell me what you think.'

'About what? Babies or bachelors?'

'No. About your surrounds. We're here.' And he pulled over to the side of the road and turned off the engine.

They were on the crest of a hill. Harriet's head swivelled round as she took in the land which would one day be an eighteen-hole golf course surrounded by privately owned homes and some holiday apartments. There would be a well-appointed club house, of course, as well as a small chapel with a lovely garden where weddings could be held. Big money in weddings, Alex had told her during the planning stage.

The land, she knew, had once been a banana plantation that had gone bust when the trees had developed some kind of fungus. A would-be entrepreneur had snapped it up for a bargain price, clearing the land before he himself had gone broke when his financing had fallen through and the stock market had crashed. Alex had stepped in, and here they were today.

She climbed out so that she could have a better look, standing on the grass verge with her hands on her hips whilst assembling her thoughts. The golf course itself looked nearly finished, but the buildings were still at the foundation stage, the rain obviously having held up that part of the project.

'Well?' Alex said as he came to stand beside her.

'It's going to be great. I love the artificial lakes. And the trees. But it's never going to be finished by Christmas,' she added.

Alex frowned. 'You're probably right. God, but I hate it when the weather works against me.'

'You can't control the weather, Alex.'

'I don't seem to be able to control anything much these days,' he muttered.

And then it happened. He turned towards her and she

saw it in his eyes—the very thing that she thought she'd imagined this morning. But she wasn't imagining this. The desire—no, the *hunger*—glittering in his sky-blue eyes was very real. Her hands slipped from her hips as she stared back at him, her heartbeat quickening.

Part of her didn't want him to want her like this. It would make Alex like all the other too-tall, too-handsome, too-successful men she'd slept with in the past. But there was no denying what he wanted, his hot gaze coveting her the way the big, bad wolf had coveted those three plump little pigs.

Unfortunately, Harriet knew she wouldn't prove to be the sensible pig who'd built his house out of bricks. She was the silly pig who'd built his house out of straw. One puff and it had fallen down.

Or one kiss, as it turned out.

He didn't say a word as he strode over and pulled her into his arms, all her defences dissolving well before his lips met hers. Her eyes closed as she lifted her mouth and her arms, sliding them up around his neck, pulling him close, her breasts flattening against his chest. Harriet could not recall a kiss affecting her as much as this kiss from Alex. Her head swirled as passion erupted within her like a volcano, her mouth gasping open. His arms tightened around her and his tongue delved deep.

Harriet had been kissed many times before—and by men who were good kissers. But Alex kissing her was something else entirely. His tongue moved back and forth in her mouth, then up, rubbing over the sensitive surface of her palate. She moaned with pleasure and excitement. She didn't want him ever to stop. She loved the way his hands started roaming over her back, sliding up and down her spine. One hand finally settled like a collar around the nape of her neck whilst the other splayed over her bottom, pressing her firmly against his erection. It blew her mind, just how hard he was.

The loud tooting of a horn plus some raucous catcalls had Alex wrenching away from her, his breathing ragged as he glowered at the passing car full of teenagers. Her eyes had flown open with the shock of his abandoning her so abruptly, leaving her still panting and flushed with heat.

'Damn,' he muttered, running his hands agitatedly through his short fair hair whilst scooping in several deep breaths. Shaking his head, he spun away from her, striding over to stand on the edge of the hill, his legs spread wide, his fists balled by his sides.

Harriet stayed where she was, staring over at him, dazed and more than a little shaken. It wasn't every day that she ached to have sex with a man within moments of their first kiss. Not that this was just any man, of course. This was Alex, her boss.

After staring down at the valley for several seconds, he whirled back to face her once more, though still keeping his distance.

'That shouldn't have happened,' he ground out. 'I never meant for that to happen.'

'No,' she said. Harriet didn't imagine for one moment that he had. 'Why did you do it, then?'

His laugh was very dry. 'Come now, Harry, don't play the ingénue with me. You've been around. You know how this works. If truth be told, I've been wanting to do that since the first day you walked into my office.'

Harriet blinked. 'What? You mean at my interview?'

'Yes, at your interview. Even then, I had some misgivings. But I fooled myself into thinking I could keep my hands off. I've never been partial to pursuing women who were in love with someone else, no matter how attractive I found them.' He dragged in a deep breath, then let it out slowly, his expression self-mocking. 'But fate conspired against me this week. I broke up with Lisa and you broke up with Dwayne. If I hadn't hugged you, then taken you out for coffee, none of this would ever have happened. I certainly wouldn't have organised for us to be alone like this.'

The meaning behind his last words took a few seconds to sink into Harriet's somewhat scattered brain, any flattery she'd been experiencing over his confessed attraction soon obliterated by shock.

'Are you saying that this so-called business trip was a deliberate ploy on your part to seduce me?' She'd imagined it might be for a brief moment earlier in the week, before dismissing the idea as ludicrous. 'You never really needed me to oversee this estate while you're away, did you?'

Alex shrugged his broad shoulders. 'No, I didn't need you to oversee this estate for me while I was away—and, yes, it was just an excuse to get you alone. Though I'm not keen on the word "seduce".'

'What else would you call it?' she threw at him angrily. 'You know full well I would never *want* to have an affair with you. You're my boss!'

'You didn't mind my kissing you just now,' he reminded her with brutal honesty. 'But all that is beside the point. I saw the folly of my ways in time and changed my mind about trying to *seduce* you, since you seem to like that word. Perhaps because it stops you from taking any responsibility over what just happened.'

'*You* kissed *me*, Alex. I didn't do a thing!'

'Nothing except look so deliciously sexy this morning that I haven't been able to think of anything else but making love to you all day.'

An already flustered Harriet homed in on his patently false words.

'You don't want to make love to me at all,' she snapped. 'You want to have sex with me. That's a totally different scenario.'

'True,' he said before walking slowly back towards her. 'But nothing changes the fact that we can't go back to the way it was between us, Harry. You want me as much as I want you. Don't deny it,' he said, close enough now to reach out and place his large hands on her suddenly trembling shoulders.

Harriet somehow found her tongue, despite it lying thick and dry in her parched mouth. 'That doesn't mean I have to do anything about it.'

'True again. But why deny yourself something which can give you pleasure? And I can give you pleasure, Harry,' he murmured, his right hand lifting off her shoulder to trace circles around her gasping lips. 'Lots of pleasure.'

'I didn't realise that you could be this wicked,' she choked out.

'There's nothing wicked about sexual pleasure, Harry,' he said, his bedroom-blue eyes going all smoky with desire. 'And there's nothing wrong with our having a sexual relationship, provided we keep it out of the office.'

He could say that, but she knew that if she did this—and her body was screaming at her to surrender—it might eventually cost her her job. Harriet knew of other women who'd had affairs with their bosses and they never came out on top. Never!

But her days of being weak where men were concerned was over. Harnessing every bit of backbone that she possessed, she stepped back, far enough to force his hand to drop away from her mouth and her still-burning lips. Her action surprised him, which made her smile a wry smile.

You don't know what you're dealing with where I'm concerned, Alex. But you'll learn.

'You're right,' she said crisply. 'About everything. But if we're going to have an affair, then I must set some rules.'

'Rules?' he echoed, his brows lifting skywards.

'Yes, rules.'

His rueful smile annoyed her, but she didn't let it show. She kept her cool and her resolve. Amazing, really, considering what she was about to do. Dwayne had been a big mistake, but Dwayne didn't have the power to hurt her as much as Alex could. Harriet had a history of falling madly in love with men like Alex. No matter how careful she was, it would probably still happen. But no way would he ever know that. The moment she felt even a smidgeon of love for him, her resignation would be on his desk.

'Shoot,' he said.

Harriet scooped in a calming breath before letting it out slowly. 'As you yourself said,' she began, her voice wonderfully cool and steady, 'there will be no sex in the office. That's a definite no-go. But also not during office hours. No sneaking out at lunchtime to some nearby hotel room.'

Alex scowled. 'Sounds like you've been down this road before.'

She hadn't, never having indulged in a secret affair before. All her relationships had been out in the open. But she wasn't about to tell Alex that. 'Like you said earlier, Alex, I've been here before.'

'Any other rules?' he asked, still sounding irritated.

'Only the obvious ones. You will use a condom at all

times.' She'd stopped taking the pill after breaking up with Dwayne. 'Also, whilst I'm sleeping with you, you don't sleep with anyone else. The day you take up with a new girlfriend, our relationship—such as it is—will be over.'

'Fair enough. Am I allowed any rules of my own?'

Harriet was taken aback. She hadn't anticipated this. 'But of course,' she said coolly.

'We will not have sex at all during the working week,' he surprised her by saying. 'When I work, I work hard. I can't afford to be wrecked the next day after being up half the night. But I expect you to spend every weekend with me. At my apartment,' he added. 'Starting from Friday night straight after work.'

A highly erotic thrill rippled through Harriet at the thought that he would want her that much. The prospect of spending every weekend at Alex's sexual beck and call was intoxicatingly exciting. She had no doubt he would be good in bed. No, he would be better than just good. He'd be fantastic. All of a sudden Harriet found it hard to concentrate on what she should be saying. But she had to. Her pride demanded it.

'Sorry,' she said crisply. 'No can do. I'll be going out for drinks on a Friday night with friends. I can't get to your apartment till much later in the evening.'

'No problem. I can wait. Waiting sometimes makes it better.'

Harriet suppressed a groan. She really was out of her league here. Yes, she'd had lovers before, but none quite like Alex. She could see that he was very experienced at playing erotic games. But there was no turning back. She wanted him too much.

'I also might have to go out with Emily on the odd

Saturday night,' she added, determined to make at least some show of independence.

'Can't you have your girls' night out during the week?'

'Sometimes, but not always. But back to the weekends. What do you mean by "at your apartment"? Aren't you ever going to take me out somewhere? For a drive, perhaps? Or to dinner, or to a show?'

'No. You're my PA, Harriet,' he added, showing her he meant business when he called her Harriet like that. 'You're also a marrying kind of girl. I don't want you to ever think that our affair has anything to do with love. It's about sex and sexual pleasure. It won't last. Maybe only a few weeks. But, let's face it, after what you've been through with Dwayne, you can afford a few weeks to indulge yourself in a purely selfish and strictly sexual relationship.'

Shock rippled through Harriet at the mention of Dwayne. Because she hadn't given him a second thought. The penny dropped that she hadn't been in love with Dwayne for a long time.

No, be honest, Harriet. You were never *in love with him. Yes, it was upsetting breaking up with him. But your heart wasn't broken, just your dreams.*

'When you're ready to move on,' Alex was saying, 'then just say so and we'll call it quits. Okay?'

Harriet just stared at him, stunned by the ruthlessness of his proposal and by her reaction to it. Sheer, unadulterated excitement. It was a struggle to stop the heat inside her body from reaching her face. Somehow, she managed.

'Okay?' he repeated, his eyes narrowing on hers.

'Okay,' she agreed, already afraid that calling it quits might prove impossible. Or it would whilst she was working for him. No matter what happened between them, it was perfectly clear that her days at Ark Properties were now numbered.

'Good,' he said, just a tad smugly. 'I'd kiss you to seal the deal, but I don't dare. After that last kiss, we'd probably end up having sex on the grass and, as much I occasionally fancy a quickie in the great outdoors, I prefer the comfort of a bed. Or a sofa. Or even a nice, warm spa bath.'

Harriet tried to banish the thought of having sex with Alex tonight in the spa bath, but it refused to go, evoking images which both aroused and tormented her. Dear God, but she could hardly wait!

'Now, we'd better get down there and pretend to do some work. I don't want Wally to think I made up some feeble excuse just so I could go away for a dirty weekend.'

But that's exactly what you did, Harriet thought dazedly as they both climbed back into the Range Rover. She didn't believe Alex's claim that he'd changed his mind about seducing her. He'd meant to have her all along. And now, he had her. Game, set and match!

CHAPTER TEN

ALEX STRUGGLED TO keep his focus on the job at hand in the two hours they spent with Wally, though he doubted the foreman noticed. He was too busy chatting away with Harriet and showing her everything. Wally seemed inordinately pleased that she would be visiting him in a couple of weeks' time, and not Alex. It seemed foolish to feel jealousy, but he did.

Alex might have worried about this uncharacteristic reaction more if his head hadn't been projecting forward to the evening ahead. He was impatient to have Harry in his arms again. Impatient to show her that he was the boss, even in the bedroom; that her ridiculous penchant for rules didn't apply to him. Yes, he would always use a condom. He wasn't a fool. But other than that he would not be dictated to, especially when she wanted him as much as he wanted her. He almost felt sorry for Dwayne. How could any man live up to that ridiculous checklist of hers? He'd have to be a saint.

Alex wasn't a saint. Not even remotely. But neither was he cruel or heartless. He was well aware that Harriet had just been through a tough time in her life. But he had no intention of hurting her. Hell, he would never hurt any woman, especially not Harry, whom he respected and admired enormously. Alex felt confident that having an affair with him would actually be good for her. It might encourage her to lighten up a bit. To live for the moment. To just have fun for a while.

By the time they left for the relatively short drive to the nearby resort, Alex had convinced himself that a strictly sexual affair with him was just what the doctor ordered for someone suffering over the break-up of a relationship.

Harriet didn't feel like chatting on the way to the resort, tension over the night ahead gathering in the pit of her stomach. Alex did his best to engage her in conversation, not very successfully. When he finally gave up asking her what she now saw as futile questions about the golf estate, she turned her head to gaze through the passenger window at her surrounds, noting idly that the countryside was very beautiful, with rolling hills and lush paddocks, the grass very green despite it being winter. Not many frosts this far north, she thought. Not to mention near the coast.

A sign came up saying that Coffs Harbour was only a few kilometres away.

By the time they turned into the resort, her nerves were jangling and her belly was as tight as a drum. Harriet still found it hard to believe that she was about to spend the night with Alex. *All* night, in his bed. Maybe even in his bath as well. It stunned her how quickly she had gone from engaged woman to suddenly single to her boss's secret mistress. Not that they'd actually done the deed yet. But it was a foregone conclusion. With the wild desires that were flooding her body at that moment, she couldn't have changed her mind even if she'd wanted to.

The resort was everything its website promised— several storeys high, the main building sat on a bluff overlooking the ocean. It faced north-east, with the back nestled into the rocky hillside. When they pulled into reception shortly after six, the sun had just set and dusk had arrived. Solar-powered lights were on everywhere, lining the circular driveway and winking in the tropical-style gardens. A parking valet descended on them as soon as Alex pulled up, taking care of their luggage while they went inside to book in.

Harriet was slightly taken aback when Alex told her to sit down whilst he handled everything. She was used to doing everything for him, but of course they were no longer just boss and employee; they were about to become lovers. She was glad to sit, her knees going to jelly at the thought.

The foyer was spacious and luxurious, with various seating arrangements dotted around. Over in a far corner was a bar and beyond that a large doorway with a sign over it, indicating the bistro-style restaurant she'd read about. She knew the *à la carte* restaurant was on the top floor, where the view of the ocean would be perfect during the daytime, as well as in the evening in summer, when daylight-saving time had it staying light till eight-thirty. She started thinking this would be the perfect place for future clients of their golf course to stay. She might contact the manager at a later date and see about their advertising on the Ark Properties website.

No sooner had Harriet thought that when she remembered she would probably not be working for Ark Properties for much longer. She sighed, then glanced over at where Alex was still at the desk, booking them in. Would it all be worth it? she wondered. Would the pleasure he'd promised live up to her expectations?

Harriet only had to recall the intoxicating expertise of his kiss to know the answer to that. Sex with Alex was going to be fantastic. Fantastic and unforgettable. It was the unforgettable part, however, which was the real worry. She couldn't imagine herself getting over him as quickly as she'd got over Dwayne. But when Alex turned from the desk and smiled over at her, all her concerns for the future fled. Her heart lurched as she watched him walk towards her. God, but he was gorgeous. Gorgeous and all hers. For now, anyway. Adrenaline shot through her veins, accompanied by the heat of a desire so strong that she wasn't sure she would be able to stand up.

'All done,' he said, still smiling. 'Our luggage has been sent up and they booked us a table for dinner at seven-thirty. Are you coming?' he said and held his hand out.

She put her much smaller hand in his large one, sucking in sharply when his fingers closed hot and strong around hers. He drew her up onto her feet, his mouth no longer smiling, his eyes darkening as they met hers.

'I'm not going to be able to wait till after dinner,' he said in a low, gravelly voice only she would hear. 'This is getting beyond bearing.'

'Yes,' she agreed, her face flushing wildly as everything she'd ever believed about herself was tipped on its head. She'd thought she knew how this kind of thing felt. She'd experienced sexual desire before. But this was different from *anything* she'd ever experienced.

'Don't say another word,' he growled and steered her hurriedly towards the bank of lifts against the back wall. 'When we get into the apartment, I want you to go to your bathroom and shower,' he told her on the way. 'I'll do the same in mine. Don't dress. Just put on one of their bathrobes. We'll meet in the living room. You have ten minutes. Not a second longer.'

There was another couple waiting to use the lifts and a fiercely aroused Harriet avoided their eyes. But she noticed when the woman started staring at Alex. It used to amuse Harriet when women ogled her boss, but this time she hated it with a passion, especially since this woman was young and attractive. Harriet knew she would have to get a grip on her jealousy if she was to survive her affair with Alex. He wasn't the type of man who'd appreciate a possessive lover.

She kept her eyes averted as they rode the lift upwards, the other couple alighting well before their own stop. Thank God. When the lift doors opened on their floor, Alex took her elbow and ushered her along the hallway.

The apartment was exactly as it had appeared on the website. Harriet already knew the floor plan by heart. The decor was no surprise, either, the website having detailed photos of all the rooms. The furniture was typical five-star-hotel furniture, comfy and classy. The colour palette was in blue, grey and white, the walls white, the carpet grey, the kitchen and bathrooms white.

Harriet didn't stop to look around, though she did notice that Alex actually had more luggage then she had, all their bags having been brought up and deposited in the entrance hall. She swept up her bag and walked swiftly through the living room and down the short hallway into the second bedroom, which she already knew had an *en suite* bathroom. Dropping her bag at the foot of the bed, Harriet raced into the bathroom, stripped off, then plunged into a hot, though far from relaxing, shower.

Harriet was way beyond relaxation. Alex had used the words 'beyond bearing' downstairs. She had already reached that point herself, her mind constantly filling with arousing images, her body balancing on a knife-edge of desire so sharp that the beating of the hot water against her erect nipples was actually painful. When she went to wash between her thighs, she had to stop for fear that she might come.

She was close. So very close. She had to stop thinking about Alex. Had to stop thinking about doing it with him. Had to stop *thinking*. Oh, God…

Harriet snapped off the shower and almost fell out of the cubicle, drying herself inadequately before drawing on the thick white bathrobe that was hanging on the back of the door. A quick glance in the bathroom mirror showed pink cheeks and messed-up hair. Sighing, she took her hair down, combing it with her fingers till it fell around her face in its usual tidy curtain. There seemed little point in bothering with make-up, though a quick spray of deodorant might be a good idea. So would cleaning her teeth. Dashing back into the bedroom, she pulled out her toilet bag and returned to the bathroom to attend to both matters.

More than ten minutes had definitely passed by the time she forced her jelly-like legs to carry her towards the bedroom door, her uncharacteristic tardiness not helped by a new and rather undermining train of thought. As much as she wanted Alex, she was suddenly terrified of somehow disappointing him. Maybe he would find her body too…well…ordinary. She didn't have spectacular breasts, an overly curvy bottom or legs that went up to her armpits. Her figure was very nice—she looked quite good naked—but it was nothing out of the box.

And then there was the worry about her own performance in bed. She'd never had any complaints before, but she suspected that Alex's standards were very high, and very demanding. He'd already demonstrated dominant tendencies, his rules for their affair clearly trying to turn her into some kind of submissive. And, whilst Harriet found such a scenario exciting, she wasn't sure how long she could sustain such a role. It went against her basic nature. Harriet was very independent in spirit, an organiser and a planner. Over the years she'd developed firm ideas over what she wanted in men and in life. Dwayne had gone as far as to call her bossy and controlling during their last argument, but Harriet didn't see herself that way.

Well, maybe a little…

It crossed her mind that her rather scandalous behaviour today could be her subconscious trying to break out of her usual sensible mould by doing something wild and rebellious.

Becoming the boss's secret mistress would certainly qualify as that!

CHAPTER ELEVEN

ALEX GLANCED UP when she entered the living room, his hands stilling on the bottle of champagne he was opening. It had been sitting in an ice bucket on the kitchen counter, along with two champagne glasses and a basket of fruit. Compliments of the management.

It had been over ten minutes since she'd fled his presence like the hounds of hell were after her. Her big brown eyes, he noted, looked just as they had that day he'd interviewed her. Deliciously nervous yet fiercely determined at the same time. He wondered how they would look when she was about to come. Would they grow wider, or scrunch up as she struggled not to let go?

He liked to prolong a woman's pleasure. Liked to prolong his own as well. Alex suspected, however, that there wouldn't be much prolonging this first time.

'Do you like champagne?' he asked.

She blinked, then stared at the bottle, as though she hadn't even seen it.

'Not really,' she replied. 'It gives me a headache.'

Alex laughed, then dumped the bottle back in the ice bucket. 'Well, we can't have that, can we? Should I make you some coffee, then? You must be thirsty.'

'I don't want anything,' she said before sucking in a deep breath. 'Just you.'

* * *

Harriet's bold admission shocked her. And him as well, judging by the startled look on his face.

But she simply hadn't been able to bear the thought of any more delay.

His surprised expression soon changed to one of hunger, his blue eyes clouding as they narrowed, then focused on her mouth.

She just wanted his hands on her naked body, and him inside her.

When he came out from where he'd been standing behind the breakfast bar, Harriet froze, needing all of her physical and mental strength to hold herself upright as he walked towards her. When he was close enough, he reached out and slowly undid the sash of the robe, Harriet's chest tightening as he parted it. When he slipped his hands inside and started playing with her tightly aching nipples, she gasped, then groaned. As much as she craved such attention, she craved him more.

'Please don't torture me, Alex,' she said shakily, her desperate eyes pleading with him.

'Don't torture *you*!' he exclaimed, then laughed. 'Sweetheart, you've been torturing me all day.' After shoving the ice bucket down to one end of the counter, he took a rough hold of her waist and hoisted her up onto the stone breakfast bar, pushing her back till her upper body was flat, parting her robe further, then parting her legs.

She could feel the cold of the stone counter through the robe, but she wasn't cold. Not at all. Harriet watched, eyes wide, as he moved to stand between her outspread legs, her head lifting a little when he unwound the sash on his own robe. She wanted to see him. Wanted to watch him.

Her mouth dried at the sight of his erection. He was

even bigger and harder than she'd imagined. And already sheathed with a condom.

'No, don't!' she cried out when he rubbed the tip against her clitoris, her nerve-endings already on the edge of release. 'Just do it.'

He swore, Harriet's head clunking back onto the bench top with relief when he pushed himself into her. Her relief was short-lived, however, as the dizzying pleasure of his possession was rapidly eclipsed by the speed and strength of the most intense orgasm she'd ever experienced. Spasm followed spasm, the sensations electrifying. Her mouth fell open as she dragged in a much-needed breath, her eyes closing when the room began to spin. They flew open again when Alex suddenly grabbed her hips, holding her captive with an iron grip as he came, his sex pulsating violently in tandem with her own contractions. Their mutual climax went on for ages, sating Harriet with the most overwhelming waves of pleasure.

Finally, their bodies grew still and calm, leaving Harriet lying there staring dazedly up at the ceiling whilst she struggled to gather her thoughts. For this was what she'd feared—a pleasure, a satisfaction, so out there that it would have her coming back for more, long after it wasn't wise. Hopefully, she wouldn't fall in love with Alex. Hopefully, she could keep it at just lust, or infatuation, or whatever this kind of sexual obsession was called. Already she was looking forward to those weekends where he wanted her to be at his sexual beck and call. There was nothing she wouldn't do for him. Nothing!

His lifting her up from the counter to hold her tenderly against him brought a moan of dismay to her lips. She didn't want tenderness from him. She just wanted sex. Alex might be able to indulge in tender post-coital embraces without letting his emotions get involved, but

Harriet wasn't of that ilk. She would have to put a stop to such hypocritical nonsense before disaster struck. After all, *he* was the one who said he just wanted a strictly sexual relationship. An affair, not a *love* affair. Which was exactly all *she* wanted from him. Clearly, he needed reminding of that fact.

Alex was taken aback when Harriet pulled back out of his arms.

'Wow,' she said as she lifted her hands to finger-comb her hair. 'I obviously needed that.'

Her remark sent Alex's teeth clenching down hard in his jaw. He hated to think that her urgent responses to him were the result of nothing but an intense sexual frustration. He preferred to believe she found him as attractive and desirable as he found her. He didn't like her implying that she was just scratching an itch with him. Surely she was just trying to find excuses for coming so quickly? Not that he cared. He'd come pretty quickly himself. And it had felt fantastic. Frankly, he hadn't had an orgasm that intense in living memory. Their coming together had helped, of course. God, the way she'd gripped his erection had been amazing. He could not wait to feel that again.

But he would have to wait, he supposed. They really should be getting dressed for dinner. But he was still inside her, damn it. And he wanted seconds.

Without asking, he slid his hands under her bottom and scooped her up off the counter. Thank God she was just a light little thing, but it still wasn't the most comfortable position with her legs dangling by her sides.

'What do you think you're doing?' she gasped, grabbing the lapels of his robe before thankfully wrapping her legs around him.

'That was a very nice entree, Harry,' he told her as he turned and carried her towards the main bedroom. 'But not nearly enough for me. My sexual appetite runs to five-course meals.'

He loved the wild glittering in her dilated eyes. She wanted seconds as much as he did.

'Don't worry,' he went on. 'We'll stop after the second course and save the rest till after we've eaten some real food. Nothing like a break to whet the appetite again.'

CHAPTER TWELVE

IT WAS AFTER seven-thirty by the time an elegantly dressed Alex steered a somewhat shell-shocked Harriet into the restaurant for dinner. Thankfully, she didn't look as shattered as she felt. The designer dress she was wearing, which had cost her a week's wages, fitted her figure like a glove, the emerald colour complementing her dark hair. Her make-up was perfect and her black patent leather bag matched her shoes, their four-inch heels giving her some much-needed height, especially when she was with Alex, who easily ticked her 'too tall' box.

Harriet did her best to exude an air of cool sophistication as their waiter showed them to their table. But it was a struggle to put aside the memories of what had just transpired. Less than twenty minutes earlier she had been stark naked in Alex's shower, her hands outstretched on the wet tiles, every muscle in her body tight as a drum as he teased her endlessly with a soapy sponge, then took her from behind, her moans muffled by the hot jets of water streaming over her back. She'd come quickly again, but Alex hadn't. He'd lasted and lasted and, astonishingly, when he'd finally come, so had she. Which was a first for her. She'd never come twice like that. Not in such a short space of time. Yet perversely, as soon as he'd withdrawn, she'd found herself wanting more. Before she'd been able to stop herself, she'd spun round and grabbed him, kissing him passionately.

It was Alex who'd put a stop to proceedings. Harriet flushed at the memory of his smacking her on the bottom and telling her not to be so greedy; that it was time to dress for dinner and she would just have to wait.

Harriet sucked in a deep breath as she sat down, the position reminding her that she was still on the sensitive side down there. Not sore, exactly. Just…sensitised. Feeling perversely embarrassed—really, what was there to be embarrassed about?—Harriet reached for the white linen serviette, flicking it open and placing it across her lap before the waiter did it for her.

'What would you like to drink?' Alex asked, forcing her to glance across the table at him.

Hopefully, her gaze was cooler than her cheeks. 'Something white and dry. But not too dry. I'll probably order seafood.'

'My thoughts exactly,' he replied, then handed the drinks menu to the hovering waiter, telling him to bring their best bottle of Verdelho.

'You trust him to pick for you?' she asked after the waiter hurried off.

'Why not? It's his job. I've never been a serious wine buff. I also don't drink much any more. I used to during my Oxford days—but I didn't have to pay for the wine at the time,' he added with a rather odd little smile.

'Why's that?'

'It's a long story. I might tell it to you one day, but not tonight. Tonight I want to find out a little more about you.'

'Me?'

'Yes, you, Harriet McKenna. So, tell me…what's your story? Before Dwayne, that is. I think I've heard enough about dear old Dwayne.'

Harriet pressed her lips tightly together. She really didn't want to open up any further to Alex. She'd already told him more than he needed to know.

'It's all in my résumé,' she said.

'Ah,' Alex said with a drily amused smile. 'You've decided to play the mysterious *femme fatale*, have you?'

Harriet shook her head at him. 'I'm not playing at anything, Alex. I'm simply keeping to the rules we set down when we started this strictly sexual affair. We don't need to know each other's life stories to have sex. In fact, telling each other all our past histories could be counter-productive. Exchanging confidences and secrets brings on emotional involvement. I don't want that. And neither do you.'

Absolutely not, Alex accepted. But, damn it all, he was curious about her. He suspected for the first time that there was a lot more to Harriet than he'd read in her résumé.

'We can't confine our conversations to sex, Harry. That could get a bit boring.'

'The sooner we get bored with each other, the better,' she replied. 'Then I can go back to just being your PA and you can find yourself another dolly-bird to sleep with.'

'I'm sick of sleeping with dolly-birds. I much prefer a woman I can talk to afterwards. Someone who's on the same wavelength as me. Someone like you, Harry.'

She rolled her eyes at him. 'In that case, we can talk about work as well as sex.'

Alex's exasperation was interrupted by the waiter arriving with the wine. Alex waved aside the tasting procedure and just asking him to pour, which he did, before placing the bottle in an ice bucket by the table.

'Would you like to order now, sir?' the waiter enquired.

'Come back in a few minutes,' Alex told him.

Harriet picked up her glass and took a sip. Alex did likewise, his mood turning dark as he glared over at her and thought how he much preferred her when she was naked and moaning with desire. No sooner had she put her clothes back on than the difficult woman was back, the one who liked rules and checklists, the one who was as intriguing as she was irritating.

Harriet picked up the menu and pretended to study the courses on offer, but her mind was still on things decidedly sexual. Various erotic images kept popping into her mind, all of them imaginative and wickedly exciting. In the end, she gave up, putting her menu down and picking up her wine glass.

'You order for me, will you?' she asked after a deep swallow of the wine. 'I'm not fussy, especially where seafood is concerned.'

'Right. How about we skip the entree and share a seafood platter? I'm not in the mood for waiting ages between courses.'

Harriet shivered as their eyes met across the table. When he looked at her like that, she wouldn't have minded skipping the whole meal.

'Fine,' she said and took another gulp of wine.

He frowned at her. 'I'd go easy on the alcohol till the food arrives, if I were you. Drinking too much on an empty stomach is never a good idea.'

Harriet's sigh carried exasperation. In truth, the alcohol *was* going straight to her head, but so what? It stopped her worrying about what she was doing and what she was suddenly craving. She was glad when the waiter came back and took their order; glad even when Alex's phone rang, leaving her to sit there and sip her wine in silence while he answered it, her ears pricking up when she heard Alex use the word 'dad'. She'd never heard him talking to family before. Not at work, anyway.

'That's good, Dad,' he was saying. 'No, it's not going to be easy, but it's the only way.'

A short silence, then he added, 'I'm proud of you. Look, I'll talk to you some more tomorrow. I'm out at dinner at the moment. With a very pretty lady.' This with a smile over at her. 'Yes, Dad, I will. Hang in there. Bye for now.'

He hung up, his smile disappearing as he put the phone away.

'My father,' he said unnecessarily, then added, 'He was the family emergency the other day.'

'Oh?' Harriet questioned, not wanting to pry, but naturally curious.

There was instant regret in Alex's eyes. Clearly, he wished he could snatch back those words. But then he shrugged and said bluntly, 'My father's a drunk. He's been living with my sister, Sarah, and giving her grief. Without going into unnecessary detail, I was finally able to get him to go into rehab this week. Hopefully, it will work, but I won't be holding my breath. Still, it gives poor Sarah a decent break.'

Harriet could see that talking about the situation was difficult for him. At the same time, she felt that perhaps he needed to talk about it. Men were their own worst enemy sometimes. They were poor communicators when it came to emotional issues. She wondered if Alex was secretly worried that he might become a drunk, too; that he might have inherited his father's weakness. It would explain why he was careful with alcohol.

'That's sad, Alex. Has your dad always been a heavy drinker?' she asked gently, forcing him to talk about it.

'No. Not at all. It didn't start till after my mother died. She was the love of his life. And the rock in the family. When he lost her from cancer way too early, he couldn't cope. None of us coped all that well. We all adored her, you see. Sarah was devastated. I can't begin to describe how I felt. I found it hard to come to terms with the fact that if she'd been diagnosed earlier, she would probably still be alive.

'Still, none of us kids handled our grief by turning to the bottle. My brother, Roy, eventually took off to the minefields in Western Australia, where he worked seven days a week and made a small fortune for himself. I gather he's married with children now, but we hardly ever hear from him. Sarah became an oncology nurse before getting married and having a family of her own.'

He stopped talking then and lifted his wine glass to his lips, leaving Harriet up in the air as to how *he* had coped with his mother's death. Whilst Harriet could see the danger in continuing with this conversation—her heart had already turned over in sympathy for Alex— she simply could not bear the suspense of not knowing.

'And you, Alex?' she prodded quietly. 'How did *you* cope?'

He shrugged, feeling uncomfortable. He put his glass down and smiled, though the smile didn't reach his eyes. 'I went to Oxford, found two great mates and joined the Bachelor's Club.'

Harriet's eyebrows arched in genuine surprise. 'What on earth is the Bachelor's Club?'

'I thought you didn't want to exchange personal details,' he reminded her.

'That was before.'

'Before what?'

'Before you whetted my curiosity.'

He laughed and the sparkle was back in his eyes. 'Women!' he exclaimed, but on a teasing note.

'Yes, yes, I know. Can't live with them, can't live without them.'

'True. I, for one, could not survive without a woman in my life. And in my bed,' he added, bringing Harriet back to cold, hard realty with a jolt. 'But I have found that the pleasure of a woman's company does come at a price. They invariably want to know way too much about your life, both past and present.'

Harriet stiffened at the injustice of this remark. 'I didn't ask you to tell me about your father's drinking problem, or your mother's death. You volunteered the information.'

He sighed and that bleakness was back in his eyes. 'So I did. Foolish of me. Could you forget I ever mentioned it? It's a rather depressing topic.'

Harriet wondered which one. His father's drinking problem or his mother's death? She suspected the latter. He must have loved his mother very much. Clearly, his way of coping initially with her death had been to run away from his life here in Australia by studying in England, making friends there and joining this Bachelor's Club.

'I only asked you about the Bachelor's Club, Alex,' she pointed out. 'If you don't want to tell me about it, then fine.'

Their meal arrived at that opportune moment, a simply huge platter full of the most delicious seafood. The tantalising smells wafted up to Harriet's nose, making her mouth water.

'Gosh, that looks good,' she said and the waiter smiled at her. So did Alex.

'Tuck in, then,' he said once the waiter had departed. 'I don't know about you, but I'm suddenly starving.'

They both tucked in, Harriet sampling a little bit of everything. Oysters, lobster, crab, scallops and fish pieces, along with side dishes of French fries and salad. They didn't talk much, and when they did, it was about the food. Alex ordered a second bottle of wine at one stage, though in the end they drank only half of it. He didn't mention the Bachelor's Club again and Harriet decided to let the matter drop. She could read between the lines, anyway. Unlike his sister and brother, Alex had decided that love and marriage were not for him. Maybe he was afraid of the responsibility that marriage entailed. And the emotion. Maybe he was afraid of falling in love. Or maybe he simply wasn't capable of falling in love, his mother's tragic death having killed off that particular part of him. Whatever, Alex obviously liked his life as a bachelor and had no intention of changing. Only a very foolish woman would start thinking—or hoping—that she would be the one to change him.

Harriet liked to think that she wasn't a very foolish woman.

Enjoy what you're doing whilst it lasts, she told herself as she wiped her fingers with her serviette. *Then do what Alex always does—move on!*

CHAPTER THIRTEEN

ALEX GLANCED ACROSS the table and wondered what was going on in Harry's mind. A somewhat defiant light had come into her eyes all of a sudden. Or was it determined? Whatever, he knew that his affair with her was not going to be like any affair he'd ever had before. How could it be? She was different from his usual choice of bed partner. Older, more intelligent and more difficult to control.

Not in bed, though. In a matter of minutes he'd torn down her defences and had her blindly surrendering to his wishes. Clearly, she was a passionate creature whose desire for sex easily matched his. That episode in the shower had been seriously hot. *She* was seriously hot. One night with her would definitely not be enough. One *month* seemed too inadequate as well. Which was a worry. He didn't want to want *any* woman too much. Harriet might start thinking he wanted more from her than just sex. Which he definitely didn't. He liked his life the way it was. He liked being a bachelor with no emotional ties.

It had been a mistake to confide in her the way he had. Big mistake. Like she'd said, confiding in people led to emotional involvement. Alex resolved not to do that again. Right. Time to finish up this meal and take her up to bed, where there would be very little talking.

Not on his part, anyway. His tongue would be otherwise occupied. By the time he finished with her tonight, asking him questions about his past life would be the last thing on her mind.

'Do you want dessert?' he asked, only out of sheer politeness.

'Heavens, no,' she replied. 'I've had more calories today than I usually eat in a week.'

'Rubbish. What about coffee?'

'No. I'd rather not sit here any longer, if you don't mind. I can always make us some coffee up in the apartment.'

Alex smiled. 'I do like a girl who knows what she wants.'

'I suppose you think I want you,' she said, her remark surprising him, then annoying him. Damn, but she was a difficult woman. A great PA, but a pain in the neck as a lover.

'That thought did cross my mind when you kissed me in the shower earlier,' he said in droll tones.

At least he had the satisfaction of seeing a guilty colour enter her cheeks.

'It's been some time since I've had any decent sex,' she said, defiance quickly back in her eyes. 'If I wasn't on the rebound from my relationship with Dwayne, you would never have made it to first base with me.'

The corners of his mouth tilted up into a sardonic smile. 'You honestly believe that?'

Harriet stifled a groan of dismay. What on earth had possessed her to start this type of tit-for-tat conversation? Not only was it dishonest of her, it was potentially humiliating. But, oh…how she'd hated seeing that smug look on his far-too-handsome face, as though it was a foregone conclusion that she would do whatever he wanted.

Her pathetic effort to pull his male ego down a peg or two was already in danger of backfiring on her; Alex's bedroom-blue eyes were glittering at her in a wickedly sexy fashion. Clearly, he meant to show her that she was talking rubbish. Which she was. That was the problem.

But she'd be darned if she was going to admit anything. Squaring her shoulders, she found a cool smile from somewhere.

'You do think you're irresistible, don't you?'

'Not at all, but I know what I know. You want me as much as I want you. I'm not afraid to admit it, but you are, for some reason. Silly, really. There's nothing to be gained from your pretending this has something to do with your breaking up with Dwayne. That was just the catalyst which threw us together. You've fallen in lust with me, Harry, and I with you. That's the cold, hard truth of it. Now, do stop putting obstacles in the way of our pleasure. And do stop wasting time. We should be in bed by now, doing what I do very well, and which you have already told me you like a lot. Come...'

When he stood up and reached out his hand towards her, Harriet gave up and gave in.

'You really are an arrogant bastard,' she muttered as she placed her hand in his and let him pull her up onto slightly unsteady feet. Possibly her light-headedness was due to the wine she had drunk, but Harriet doubted it. More likely it was due to the waves of desire that were currently washing through her body. Sweeping up her bag with her free hand, she let Alex steer her from the restaurant, leaving a forlorn-looking waiter in their wake. When she dared to say something, Alex just shrugged and said the charge for the meal would be added to his room account.

Alex didn't say a word to her during their lift ride

upwards, or during the short walk along the hallway, the silence only adding to the sexual tension which was gripping Harriet with cruelly frustrating tentacles. Every muscle in her body was tight with need. When she glanced over at Alex, she was taken aback at the tension she glimpsed in *his* face. He hadn't lied to her. He wanted her as much as she wanted him. It was a sinfully seductive thought.

Once they were alone, with the door locked behind them, he turned and yanked her into his arms.

'No more nonsense now,' he ground out after his ravaging kiss reduced them both to heavy breathing. 'You have five minutes to be naked in my bed.'

Alex's lack of sexual inhibition was overwhelming. Yet exciting at the same time.

'Well, what are you waiting for?' he asked, a dry amusement in his voice and eyes.

'You're not just an arrogant bastard,' she threw at him. 'You're a wicked devil as well!' And with that she whirled and flounced off, his laughter following her.

As Alex hurriedly stripped off in the bedroom, he smiled at the memory of the shock that had zoomed into her eyes. Harriet claimed to have been around, but he suspected that her idea of 'been around' was totally different from his. She wasn't even close to being the sophisticated woman of the world she liked to think she was. Not a *femme fatale*, either. But he liked that about her; liked that she could still be shocked.

He couldn't wait to shock her some more.

After a quick trip to the bathroom, Alex collected a new box of condoms from his gym bag, placed it on the bedside table, then climbed, naked, into the bed, his heart thudding with anticipation, his erection bordering on painful. He regretted now not jumping into a cold shower for a couple of minutes, scowling as he conceded he was not going to be able to last all that long the first time. Still, they had all night. He was not a once-a-night man; his sexual stamina was something he'd worked on over the years.

Where *was* that infernal woman? he thought, frustrated as he glared at the still-empty doorway. Five minutes had well and truly gone by now.

Harriet knew she'd passed her five-minute deadline, but she simply could not summon up the courage to walk stark naked into Alex's bedroom. She would have put on the white towelling bathrobe she'd worn earlier, except that it wasn't in her bathroom any more. It was out there somewhere. She hadn't packed a dressing gown, well aware that a five-star resort would provide one. In the end, she grabbed the PJs she'd brought with her and pulled them on. They were hardly the sexiest of outfits, the long pants and long sleeves covering almost every inch of her. And then there were the unfortunate little-girl colours. The bottom was pink-and-white stripes, the top plain white with little pink love hearts all over it. Emily had bought them for her for her birthday last year.

Thinking of Emily made Harriet groan. Her best friend would have a fit if she knew what she was doing at this moment. Which meant she would never tell her. By the time Emily got back from her holiday, her affair with Alex would probably be over. Taking a couple of deep breaths, Harriet turned and walked from the room with her chin held high. She was shaking inside when she thought of Alex's reaction. He liked to have his orders obeyed…

He was waiting for her on the bed, sitting up with just

a sheet over him, a mountain of pillows stuffed behind his head, his magnificent chest bare, his handsome face scowling. But not for long; major amusement rocketed into his eyes as they raked her up and down. He didn't laugh out loud, but he was close.

'I like your idea of naked,' he said, shooting her a heart-stopping smile.

Her stomach flipped right over. 'Sorry. I just couldn't do it.'

'You have no reason to be shy, Harry. You have a very beautiful body.'

Now her *heart* flipped over. *Oh, Harriet, Harriet. Be careful. You don't want to fall in love with this devil. He'll eat you alive.*

She gave him a long, considering look as she walked over to the side of the bed closest to where he was lying. 'I do *not* have a very beautiful body, Alex,' she denied quietly. 'It's nice enough, but not anything special. Please do not feel you have to flatter me. Trust me when I say it's not necessary—I'm a sure thing here.'

Now he laughed. 'That's good to know. When you came in wearing that, I thought you might have changed your mind.'

'Not at all.'

'Then perhaps you could take them off now,' he suggested.

'Is that an order?'

'Not at all,' he replied, cleverly echoing her own words. 'Would you like me to do it for you?'

Yes, she thought with a dizzying rush of desire. But it was imperative she keep some control in all this. Harriet already feared that once she was naked in his bed she might be lost for ever. It was one thing to have a couple of raunchy encounters out of bed, another thing entirely to spend the whole night in his arms.

Scooping in a steadying breath, she slipped off the bottom half of the PJs first, tossing it onto the armchair in the corner, before turning her attention to the top half. Crossing her arms, she lifted it up over her head, hotly aware of the way his eyes were glued to her. When at last she stood naked before him, it took all of her mental and physical strength not to tremble, or to flee. The raw hunger in his gaze was both seductive and terrifying. Had any man ever wanted her like this, and vice versa? Alex had said they'd fallen in lust with each other. Harriet hoped that was all it was.

'And you think you're not anything special,' he growled, shaking his head at her. Throwing back the sheet to reveal his own stunning nakedness, Alex stretched out his hand towards her. 'Now come here, you gorgeous thing, you. I can't wait another second.'

CHAPTER FOURTEEN

HARRIET WOKE IN the same position she'd fallen asleep, lying on her side with Alex's body wrapped around hers like two spoons. His arms were wrapped tightly around her waist, her bottom pressed up against his stomach. She didn't dare move, but whilst her body remained still, her brain was active, reliving their long night of lovemaking.

No, not lovemaking, she amended. *Your long night of sex, dummy. Don't start thinking of it as lovemaking.*

But it had *felt* like lovemaking at the time, she conceded, Alex proving to be a surprisingly tender lover. Imaginative, yes, and totally uninhibited—the things he did with his tongue!—but never had Harriet felt one second of disgust, or even embarrassment. He had a beguiling way about him which bypassed such feelings, caressing her at length between acts of actual intercourse, playing with her body with sometimes shocking intimacy. Yet she had never felt shock, only excitement and pleasure, along with the most amazing orgasms. So many that she had lost count.

Alex had been so right when he'd said she'd fallen in lust with him. She had. Totally.

Her sigh was the sigh of a thoroughly sated woman.

She should have been appalled with herself. But she wasn't. She wasn't even appalled with him. Yet she definitely should have been. If truth be told, Alex was nothing but an arrogant devil with the morals of an alley cat, who thought he could indulge in a strictly sexual affair with his PA, then just shrug her off when he grew bored with her in bed. Which he would. That was the nature of the beast. His admission that he'd always fancied her went some way to excusing his behaviour. But if that was the case, then he should never have hired her, damn him. His lust had become a time bomb waiting to happen.

I never stood a chance, she realised.

Her sigh this time had nothing to do with satisfaction.

'Will you stop all that sighing?' Alex muttered into her hair.

Harriet automatically stiffened, her buttocks tensing when her legs straightened.

He groaned, his hands lifting to cup her breasts as he rolled over onto his back, taking her with him. Panic filled Harriet as the evidence of his erection sent jabs of desire rocketing through her own infatuated flesh. She tried to wriggle away from him, but he held her tight.

'Hand me a condom, beautiful,' he purred into her ear. 'My hands are otherwise occupied.'

Which they were, his palms rubbing over her still-erect nipples, sending unnecessary messages to that part of her which seemed always to be ready for him. Her legs fell apart of their own volition, her belly tightening.

'Haven't you had enough?' Harriet protested, but weakly, her hand already reaching for the condom.

'Not even remotely,' he replied.

Alex had plenty of opportunity to think about that telling reply during the drive back to Sydney. Harry had refused to put off her Sunday lunch with her friend, despite his doing his best to persuade her over breakfast to stay another night. Whilst she was extremely compliant in bed—*and* in the spa bath this morning—she became a different woman once she was up and dressed, reverting to the difficult one who was not amenable to persuasion.

Alex's decision when he woke this morning to change the rules of their affair looked in danger of failing. When he'd suggested that they meet up at least one night during the week, she had been quick to say no, reminding him that that wasn't what they'd agreed on. She would come to his apartment next Friday night and not before.

Alex couldn't contemplate waiting that long before he made love to her again.

It came to Alex after he'd been driving in a somewhat frustrated silence for over two hours that his PA's hot-as-hell behaviour last night might be worrying her. In his experience, women weren't as pragmatic about sex as men. They read into things. They sometimes invented complications where there weren't any.

Slanting a quick glance her way, he saw that the set of her mouth was tight, her hands gripping her handbag in her lap with unnecessary force. Silly girl. Didn't she know that there was nothing wrong with what they'd done last night? They were consenting adults. Grown-ups. Yet she was sitting there, acting like some guilty schoolgirl or an adulterous wife. Okay, so the suddenness of their affair—and the fieriness of their passion for each other—was on the startling side. But why fight it? Why not just go with the flow and enjoy what they could share till the fire had burned out, after which they could call it quits and she could go back to the life she'd mapped out for herself?

Another reason for her grim mood suddenly crossed Alex's mind. Maybe she was worried that their affair might cost her her job.

He had to say something to reassure her.

'I would never fire you, Harry,' he said. 'If that's what's bothering you.'

Her head turned his way, but she was wearing sunglasses and he couldn't see what was going on in her eyes.

'I know that,' came her rather cool reply.

'Then what *is* bothering you? Are you regretting last night?'

He was taken aback when she laughed. 'Of course,' she said. 'Sleeping with the boss is never a good idea, even if he promises not to fire you when he grows bored with you in bed.'

'I can't see that happening in a hurry,' he muttered. And he meant it. Which was a first for him. Alex had a low boredom threshold at the best of times. He was always looking for new challenges, new goals and, yes, new girlfriends.

Of course, Harry would never be a proper girlfriend. She was going to be his secret mistress, one who would be at his sexual beck and call only at weekends. Stupid rule, that. He had been an idiot ever to suggest such a masochistic arrangement.

'I have no illusions,' came her firm pronouncement, 'about how this affair of ours will end.'

Maybe it will never end, Harry, came the unexpected thought. *Maybe I will keep you as my secret mistress for ever.*

It was a truly wicked thought. But a hell of an appealing one. People said you could never have your cake and eat it, too. But maybe he could. At least for a while. There was no hurry for her to get married, surely? She was only twenty-nine. Women got married later these days. And had children later. He would have to let her go eventually, he supposed. But till then he aimed to make her his. *Without* all these silly rules.

For the first time during this exasperating drive, Alex's black mood lifted. Knowing what you wanted in life was always a good thing, he accepted. And he wanted Harriet. Not just for a few weeks. For much, *much* longer than that.

'It's never a wise thing to think about endings, Harry,' he said, adopting his best salesman voice. 'Far better to live in the moment. The only assurance we have in life is the here and now. You like having sex with me, don't you?'

She sighed. 'You know I do.'

'Then stop stressing and just enjoy. We could be dead tomorrow.'

When he glanced over at her, he saw that she was frowning.

'I can't think like that,' she said. 'I have to plan. *You* plan. You plan all the time. So stop giving me this "live in the moment" nonsense, Alex. If you think you can persuade me to change my mind where the rules of our affair are concerned, then you can think again.'

Alex gritted his teeth. Lord, but she would try the patience of a saint. And he was no saint. He was, however, a man who rose to a challenge.

Relaxing the clenched muscles in his jaw took an effort, but he managed before shooting her a warmly amused smile. 'Can't blame a man for trying, Harry. Last night was so fabulous that I find it unbearable to wait another week to sample some more of your bewitching charms.'

'*You* were the one who claimed sex was better if you wait.'

He smiled with amusement at the cleverness of her

mind. And the sharpness of her wit. 'Yes, well, there's waiting and waiting. I was talking about a few hours on that occasion, not a whole week. I would imagine that by Friday night I'll be ready to explode.'

'Too much information,' she threw at him.

He laughed, then she laughed, breaking the tension that had been building since they'd set off.

'That's better,' he said.

'Better?' she echoed.

'I wasn't looking forward to sitting next to Miss Grumpy all the way back to Sydney.'

'I wasn't grumpy. I was just…thinking.'

'Thinking is almost as bad as planning. Or so Jeremy tells me. He doesn't believe in either.'

'Your best friend, Jeremy? The rake from London?'

'The one and the same.'

'He sounds very shallow.'

'Oh, he is. He admits it. But he's also intelligent and charming and the most wonderful friend I've ever had. Outside of Sergio, that is.'

'I presume it's Sergio, then, who's getting married.'

'Yes, the poor devil.'

'Why do you say it like that? What have you got against marriage?'

'Don't misunderstand me. I have nothing against marriage. It's the woman he's marrying that worries me.'

'What's wrong with her?'

For a split second, Alex hesitated. But then he told her. All about Sergio and Bella, detailing their past history and their current romance. She was taken aback at the identity of the bride-to-be, of course. Bella was very well known in Australia. But so was her reputation with men.

'I can understand why you're worried,' she said.

'Thank God someone agrees with me. Jeremy has

some doubts, but he believes that they're genuinely in love.'

'It does happen, you know. People do fall in love.'

'Not that quickly. It's nothing but lust. Which is not a recipe for marital happiness. You need to be best friends as well as lovers. Soul mates, for want of a better word.'

'In an idealistic world, perhaps. Life is not always quite so accommodating.'

'I suppose so. I have an awful feeling that Sergio loves Bella, but that she's only in it for the money. Being a billionaire is not always an advantage when it comes to finding true love.'

'Well, you don't have to worry about that, Alex. You're not interested in finding true love.'

'You are absolutely correct. That kind of love is not for me.'

Harriet wondered just *why* Alex was so against falling in love. He must have been badly hurt at one stage to feel so strongly about it. Before she could come to any conclusion, he turned and smiled at her.

'The turn-off for Taree is coming up. What say we get off the freeway and go have some lunch?'

CHAPTER FIFTEEN

IT WAS AFTER five before Alex pulled up outside her flat. Harriet was annoyed with herself when she asked him if he'd like to come up for a cup of coffee. What had happened to her resolve to keep some control over their affair and her own silly self? To invite him into her home was a foolish move. But it was done now.

Of course, he said yes, that big, bad wolf smile on his face.

At least he carried her bag up the stairs for her, her flat being on the second floor of the rather ancient red-brick building. There were eight units in all, hers at the front of the building facing east, though not with an ocean view, being a couple of streets back from the beach.

'Nice place you've got here, Harry,' Alex said even before she'd shown him inside. He knew she owned it. She'd said so when he'd interviewed her.

'I like it,' she replied, fishing out her key and opening the front door.

'*Very* nice,' he said once he went inside and glanced around.

His compliment pleased her, Harriet being on the house-proud side, something she'd learned from her mother, who had instilled in her daughter good habits when it came to keeping her home clean and tidy. Harriet's good taste in furniture and furnishings, however, was something she'd learned for herself after coming to Sydney. Selling expensive real estate did give one a yearning for having nice things around.

Her two-bedroomed flat wasn't overly large, but by painting all the walls and ceilings white, and not overfurnishing the rooms, she'd achieved the effect of making it look larger than it was. Both the kitchen and bathrooms were white, but that was not her doing. They'd been renovated shortly before she'd bought the place.

'Could you point me to the bathroom, Harry?' Alex asked.

She did, reminding him that the light in there wasn't working due to her poor DIY skills.

'Give me a bulb, then,' Alex said. 'I'll fix it while I'm here. You go make the coffee.'

He joined her in the kitchen a couple of minutes later. 'All fixed,' he said.

'Thank you,' she said. 'I didn't realise you would be such a good handyman.'

He laughed. Not a happy laugh. More a dry one. 'When you grow up living in government housing, you learn to do all minor repairs yourself. If there was one thing Dad did teach me growing up, it was how to change light bulbs and tap washers. I can also fix leaking toilets and blocked drains. So, if your kitchen sink ever gets blocked up...' he added, smiling wryly.

'I will call a plumber,' Harriet finished for him, at the same time wondering if Alex had called his dad today like he promised last night. She hadn't heard him do so. Still, it really wasn't her business to remind him. It wasn't like they were at work, when she often reminded him to do things. He could be forgetful at times. Oh, Lord, maybe she *should* say something...

'You're frowning,' he said. 'On top of that, you've stopped making the coffee. What gives?'

Harriet turned to look at him. 'I'm worried that you might have forgotten to ring your dad. You promised him last night that you would call him today.'

Alex shook his head at her. 'I should never have told you about him.'

'Well, you *did*,' she replied, feeling quite angry with his attitude. 'And I'm glad you did. Now at least I know that you're human, with personal problems like the rest of us.'

His eyebrows lifted. 'Wow, Harry, you have quite a temper on you, don't you? Something you've managed to keep hidden from me all these months.'

'A PA doesn't lose her temper with her boss. But a secret mistress is another thing entirely. Tamper with a woman's emotions and you have to pay the price.'

'I don't want to tamper with your emotions. Just your body.'

'Same thing, Alex. I'm a woman. Our bodies and our emotions are linked. Unlike men. It always amazes me how some men can compartmentalise their lives. Work over here and women over there. In the past, you've cleverly chosen to sleep with empty-headed young things who haven't given you any trouble. Let me warn you in advance, Alex, that I might give you trouble.'

His eyes narrowed on her. 'Are you warning me that you might fall in love with me?'

'I certainly hope not,' she said quite truthfully. 'But don't expect me to be entirely happy with this...relationship. Yes, I love having sex with you, and yes, I love working for you. But I'm going to find it increasingly hard to separate the two. Please appreciate that I might have to quit in the end.'

'Quit work or quit me?'

'Both.'

'I won't let you.'

A shiver of alarm ran down her spine at the sheer arrogance of him.

'You won't have any choice in the matter.'

'We'll see about that,' he ground out. 'Forget the coffee. I'm going home. But first a little taste of what you can expect next Friday night.'

Five minutes later, he was gone, leaving Harriet reeling with shock. She sagged back against the kitchen counter, her legs weak with desire. What a cruel devil he was, kissing her like that, then touching her like that, bringing her to the brink of release, then just abandoning her, his eyes glittering with a chilling resolve when his head finally lifted.

The week that stretched ahead of her would be unbearable. But of course Alex wanted it to be. That was why he'd just done what he'd done.

I should never have challenged him like that, Harriet conceded as she levered herself away from the kitchen counter, pulled her bra back into place, then did up her jeans. She'd known from the start that she was way out of her league, tangling with someone like Alex.

Try as she might, however, Harriet could not regret going to bed with him. How could she regret something which had brought her so much pleasure? Alex excited her as no man had ever excited her. He was a fabulous lover, with a way about him that was both seductive and oddly romantic. The compliments he'd made about her body last night were so sweet. Harriet knew she wouldn't be the one to call it quits. But *he* would one day, and this inevitability would happen sooner rather than later if she didn't lighten up a bit. She really had to stop acting the way she had earlier today. And just now. She had to start doing what Alex suggested. Live for the moment. Concentrate on just having fun!

It came to Harriet that she'd never been a 'just have fun' girl. She'd always been so serious. But it wasn't too late, surely? She could do fun, couldn't she? Not every relationship had to be about finding Mr Right. After the fiasco with Dwayne, that could definitely wait for a while. As for that stupid checklist of hers, that was definitely going to be thrown out the window.

Satisfied with her new resolve, Harriet made her way back into the living room, where Alex had left her bag. She had just picked it up when her phone rang. Dropping the bag, she walked over to where she'd placed her handbag on the dining table, retrieved her phone, then groaned. It was Emily. Oh, Lord. She had a sinking feeling that Emily might have found out about Dwayne.

'Hi, Em,' she said with false brightness. 'How's it going with the holiday?'

'Don't you say hi to me like that, Harriet McKenna. Why didn't you ring and tell me that you've broken up with Dwayne? All those text messages about work and not a single word about what's really important.'

Harriet scooped in a deep breath, then let it out slowly before answering.

'Why do you think?' she finally asked. 'I knew you wouldn't be on my side and I wasn't in the mood for a lecture.'

'Don't be silly. Of course I'm on your side. You're my best friend. Dwayne doesn't mean a thing to me. Okay, so I thought you and he were a good match, but it's what *you* think that really counts. Obviously, you decided he wasn't the right man for you.'

A huge lump had filled Harriet's throat at this unexpected show of support from Emily. She'd been so sure that she would be critical.

'No, he wasn't,' she choked out. 'I...I...' Her voice cut out as her whole chest filled with emotion, tears threatening. Silly, really, given she'd already realised she hadn't loved Dwayne.

'Oh, Harriet. Hon,' Emily said gently. 'I didn't mean to upset you.'

Harriet gulped, then cleared her throat. 'I thought you'd be mad at me.'

'Never. I just worry about you, that's all. I want you to be happy.'

'I want to be happy, too.'

'Then perhaps you should stop looking for Mr Perfect to marry and just have fun for a while,' Emily suggested. 'You're still young, Harriet. Plenty of time for you to get married yet.'

'You're so right, Em. I've been thinking exactly the same thing.'

CHAPTER SIXTEEN

'GOT ANYTHING SPECIAL planned for this weekend?' Audrey asked Harriet.

Friday night had finally arrived and the two women were sharing a bottle of white wine at the nearby hotel where the staff of Ark Properties gathered for drinks every Friday night after work. Audrey and Harriet were sitting at a quiet table in a dark corner, whilst the boys were gathered at the bar drinking beer and watching the Friday night football game. Alex was noticeably absent, as he'd been from the office most of the week, finding any and every excuse to go out—minus his PA—from business lunches to doing site-checks of all their current building projects. He'd claimed he had to have everything on track before leaving for Milan the following week, though Harriet suspected he just didn't want to be around her lest he be tempted to go back on his word.

When she'd arrived at work last Monday morning, a bagel already in hand, she'd made Alex coffee and taken both into his office, where she'd apologised for being so uptight the other night. She'd promised to lighten up in future, adding that she didn't want to live her life according to rules, and it would be all right with her if he wanted to see her before Friday night. He'd stared at her for a long moment, then told her that he would prefer to wait till Friday as they'd originally agreed upon. Although surprised and a little hurt, the new live-for-the-moment, just-have-fun Harriet simply smiled and said fine. Whatever.

But it had been a long, long week.

'No, nothing special,' Harriet told Audrey, hoping the lie didn't show in her eyes. 'I might try to catch up on housework. I usually give the flat a thorough clean on a Saturday, but I was away last Saturday.'

'That's right. You were up north with Alex. How did that go, by the way?'

Harriet shrugged. 'Okay. I think Alex was annoyed that the rain had delayed things so much. No way is that golf course going to be open by Christmas.'

'It's supposed to rain all next week, too,' Audrey said. 'Not just here in Sydney, but all the way up the coast.'

Harriet groaned. 'He's not going to be too thrilled with that.'

'Nothing you can do about the weather,' Audrey said. 'Where did you stay?'

'Oh, some place near Coffs Harbour. Quite nice, really. You know Alex. He wouldn't stay at a dump.'

'Why should he? I mean, he's seriously rich. And seriously sexy. I would watch yourself with him, if I were you.'

'What do you mean?'

'You know what I mean. Now that Dwayne's out of the picture...' Audrey shrugged, then took another sip of her wine.

No way did Harriet want any of the staff ever to know about her affair with Alex. Though they might twig after she resigned. But it wouldn't matter then.

'He's not really my type,' Harriet said. 'But I know

what you mean. He *is* handsome, but personally I don't like arrogant men.'

Audrey frowned at her over the rim of her glass. 'I thought you liked Alex.'

'Well, yes, I do. And to be fair, he's not all that arrogant. But he can be annoying at times.'

'Yes, I can see that. Rich bachelors like him are not used to considering other people's feelings. They don't mean to be selfish or self-centred, but they are.'

'You've got it in one,' Harriet stated, thinking that was Alex's biggest flaw. His selfishness. At the same time, however, he could be kind, generous and even rather sweet. She would never forget what he'd done for Romany.

But he should never have pursued *her*. That had not been kind, or sweet. It had been seriously selfish. He could have slept with just about any other woman in Sydney, but he had to pick her.

Such thinking suddenly annoyed Harriet, who'd determined to put aside the critical habits of her old, serious self and embrace a more easy-going attitude to life and men. So, instead of criticising Alex in her head, she focused on his good points. He gave oodles of money to charity, was a caring son and a fabulous lover. This last fact reminded her that in less than two hours she'd be in his arms again, being made love to in ways she'd only ever dreamt about. The anticipation of what was in store for her tonight had her shifting restlessly in her seat. Her phone suddenly ringing startled her, the identity of the caller startling her as well.

'Hi there,' she answered, careful not to say Alex's name.

'I presume you're still at the pub,' he ground out.

'Yes, I am.'

'Don't say my name,' he warned her sharply.

'I won't. What's up?' If he was calling to tell her not to come, she would just die.

'Is there any chance you can make it before nine?' he asked.

Nine was the time he'd designated before he'd left the office that morning, giving her a key-card at the same time so that she could access the building and the private lift to the penthouse.

'I'm going insane here,' he added thickly.

The passion and the urgency in his voice was both flattering and arousing. Not that Harriet needed arousing. She was already burning for him.

'Me, too,' she said quietly.

'Have you eaten?'

'Not yet.'

'Then don't. I've organised something for later. Can you come straight away?'

'I should be able to. I'll catch a taxi and meet you there ASAP. Bye.'

Putting her phone away, she rose and threw Audrey an apologetic smile. 'Sorry to abandon you so early, but I'm needed.'

'Oh?'

'A married girlfriend of mine has the chance of a rare night out while her husband minds the baby, so we're off to a movie together.'

'What are you going to see?'

'Have no idea. Have to go. See you on Monday.' And she bolted before Audrey could ask her any more awkward questions.

The hotel was within walking distance of the taxi rank down at the quay. Harriet didn't have to wait too long before she was climbing into the back seat and giving the driver Alex's address. But it was Friday night, of course, with Friday night traffic. Her level of frustration rose when it took ten minutes to go three blocks. She sent Alex a text message explaining she was on her way but the traffic was heavy.

No sweat, came his reply. I'll meet you downstairs.

He was standing on the pavement by the time she climbed out of the taxi, dressed in a black tracksuit with a white T-shirt underneath and white trainers. Harriet still had on the tailored black suit and white silk blouse that she'd worn to work, actually having planned to go home before coming here tonight to shower and change into something more feminine. She'd also planned to put on the new sexy black underwear that she'd bought this week.

During the ride in the taxi, she'd regretted not having the opportunity to dolly herself up for Alex, but at the sight of him she no longer cared. The way he was looking at her made her not care about anything but being here with him.

He didn't say a word, just took her arm and urged her through the revolving glass doors inside the foyer, which was modern and spacious with a large reception desk, behind which sat two burly security guards studying computer screens. They didn't even look up as Alex steered her across the vast expanse of marble tiled floor to an alcove which housed the lifts. There were four in all, Alex choosing the one marked for private use only. The doors opened immediately, Alex ushering her into the lavishly appointed lift that had lots of brass and glass, along with far too much lighting. Harriet could see her reflection everywhere, forcing her to note her flushed face and her over-bright eyes.

'How long have you lived here?' she asked him in an

effort to break the tension which was almost killing her. If her heart beat any faster, she was sure it would explode.

Alex pressed the button which had the lift doors closing with barely a sound before he turned and answered her.

'About three years. I bought it off-plan five years ago before it was even built and before the market went crazy. God, but it's been a long week. I have to kiss you, Harry. I simply can't wait.' He pulled her into his arms and kissed her right there in the lift. Even when it reached its destination, and the doors slid quietly open, the kissing didn't stop. By then he'd rammed her up against the mirrored back wall, the coldness of the glass seeping through her jacket. Not that she cared. She was way too hot to care about such a small discomfort. By then her handbag had fallen from numb fingers and her arms were wrapped tightly around his neck. His hands were much busier, hitching up her skirt, pushing aside her panties.

She moaned when his fingers found their target. God, she was close to coming. And she didn't care. She *needed* to come. *Yes, yes, just keep doing that*; all her muscles tensed in anticipation of release from the madness which was possessing her.

His taking his hand away brought a groan of despair, her eyes flying open when his head lifted. His expression was wry and knowing.

'Sorry, but I had to stop,' he said.

She just stared at him, her heartbeat still haywire. 'You're cruel,' she said shakily.

'Sometimes you have to be cruel to be kind. I didn't have a condom with me and I was close to losing control. For some reason kissing you does that to me,' he said and reached out to run a single fingertip over her still-burning mouth. 'I suspect you have some secret aphrodisiac in this red lipstick you always wear.'

She couldn't speak, all her attention on that tantalising fingertip.

His eyes darkened on her, aware no doubt of the extent of her desire.

'Come,' he said, this time taking her arm more gently.

Alex guided her across a wide entrance hall and into a huge living room which was beautifully appointed, filled with glass and white leather furniture which shouted money. The floors were all grey marble tiles, but the rugs were thick, soft and more colourful. The artwork on the walls were probably originals, not the framed prints which graced her own flat.

'This way,' he said, leading her past a semi-circular shaped alcove in which sat a circular glass dining table beautifully set for two, with elegant silver placemats and tall candles just waiting to be lit.

'That's for dinner later,' he told her, perhaps noting the direction of her eyes.

'It looks lovely.' She hadn't expected anything so romantic.

'I've ordered a meal to be delivered at ten from a local restaurant. And there's two bottles of chilled white wine waiting for you in the fridge.'

'You've thought of everything,' she said, taken aback by his thoughtful attention to detail.

'I try to please. I would have been showered and properly attired if my passion for you hadn't got the better of me. But while I was waiting for you to arrive, I realised I could kill two birds with one stone.'

'Sorry. I'm not following you.'

'You will. This way...'

He took her down a tiled hallway and into the master bedroom, which was large, spacious and thankfully nothing like a playboy's bedroom, other than the fact that the bed was king-sized. The floor was covered in a lush cream carpet, the furniture made in a dark wood, the furnishings in various shades of cream and brown. She loved the brass-based bedside lamps with their stylish cream shades and the gorgeous tapestry which hung above the bedhead. It was a park scene—Parisian, since it had the Eiffel Tower in the background. The colours were glorious.

'I love that tapestry,' she said as he led her past it.

'It's a recent purchase. An investment, really. I don't put my money in stock and shares. I prefer property. And art.'

Harriet couldn't afford to invest in art. But at least she did have her flat, which had already doubled in value since she'd bought it.

'In here,' he directed and guided her into an *en suite* bathroom which had to be seen to be believed. It was larger than her bedroom with a modern toilet and bidet, a sunken spa bath, a double vanity and a shower stall built for two. Or possibly three. But it wasn't any of those things which made her gasp. It was the candles which were dotted around the bath, all lit and giving out the most incredible vanilla fragrance.

'Did you do this for me?' she asked, amazed and touched.

His smile was warm, soft and faintly apologetic. 'I wanted to make it up to you for being a bit of a bastard last Monday. All I can say in my defence is that I knew I wouldn't be able to get all the work done that I needed to do before I went away if I started meeting up with you. And making love to you. And not getting any sleep. As it was, I didn't sleep all that well anyway, despite working my butt off in the gym every evening. All I could think about was you, Harry.'

'Oh…' she said, in danger of melting into a puddle. 'I…I didn't sleep very well, either.'

His smile was slow, sexy and incredibly arousing. 'That's nice to know,' he said as he turned on the bath taps, adjusted the temperature, then tipped in what looked like bubble bath. 'Can you wait a bit longer?' he asked her as he turned back to face her.

'What? Yes. No. Yes, I… I suppose so.'

'Good. Now I'm going to take off all your clothes.'

'What?'

'Don't think about it. Just let me do it.'

She didn't think about it, and she let him do it, dazed by the feeling of blissful helplessness which took possession of her as he slowly removed each item of clothing. First came her jacket, which he folded and placed on the vanity counter top. Her blouse followed, then her bra.

How weird it felt to be standing before Alex, naked to her waist. Weird, yet wickedly exciting. Her skirt came next, then her shoes, leaving her with nothing on but a black satin thong and a pair of lace-topped stay-up stockings.

Once she was naked, he took a step back and just looked at her.

'That's how I've been picturing you all week,' he said thickly, his eyes raking over her.

She'd done a lot of picturing of her own, her many erotic fantasies underlining just how much in lust with Alex she was. Lord, if he didn't make love to her soon, she was going to faint with desire. Her head was spinning, whilst the rest of her was on fire.

'Aren't you going to get undressed?' she asked him shakily.

'Of course. Do you want to watch?'

Oh, Lord, she was seriously out of her depth here.

He didn't strip slowly, but he didn't hurry, either. Once naked, he turned off the taps, then extracted a condom from a nearby drawer, ripping it open with his teeth before drawing it on with practised swiftness. She tried not to stare, but he was just so big and hard and ready. She wanted him inside her right now.

'I...I don't think I can wait much longer,' she told him shakily.

He smiled a wry smile. 'Me neither, beautiful.'

Taking her shoulders, he turned her to face the vanity mirror. Without his saying a word, she knew what he wanted her to do. She reached out to grip the edges of the marble bench top, moved her legs apart, then bent forward, dropping her head so that she couldn't see the wantonness in her eyes. She gasped when he stroked down the curve of her spine, caressing her bottom before taking a firm hold of her hips and doing what she was desperate for him to do.

Oh, God, she thought as her head spun and her body rocketed to a release that saw her crying out like some wild, wounded animal. He came soon after her, pulling her upright as his flesh shuddered within hers. When their eyes finally met in the mirror, his smile stunned her. For it was soft and sweet, making her heart lurch in a way that might have worried her at any other time. But her mind was on other things at that moment.

'I like the new you, Harry,' he said, a wicked twinkle in his eye. 'Now, let's go get in that bath.'

CHAPTER SEVENTEEN

I DON'T WANT her to go, Alex thought as he reluctantly followed Harry to the lift doors.

He'd never enjoyed a weekend so much in years. Never enjoyed a woman so much in years. It wasn't just the sex part—though that was fabulous—it was her company, her conversation, her intelligence. Alex hadn't realised till that weekend how much he craved being with a woman as smart as she was. And Harriet was smart. Perhaps not academically. She didn't have degrees to her name. But she had smarts of a different kind. She was quite well-read, too, he'd found out. Plus she was never at a loss for words. Or opinions. They hadn't spent the whole weekend having sex, though Friday night had been full on. Understandable, given they'd both been somewhat frustrated at the time.

After a long sleep-in on the Saturday, he'd driven her back to her place so that she could get a change of clothes. When he then suggested they drive out somewhere for lunch, she hadn't objected, so he'd headed west toward the Blue Mountains, showing her the parcels of land he'd bought near the proposed new airport at Badgery's Creek on the way. Her praise over his plan to build affordable housing for the people who would one day work at the airport had pleased him no end. He rarely told anyone about his charitable efforts, most people not being interested. But Harry had seemed genuinely impressed.

After lunch at a trendy café in Katoomba, they'd visited the Three Sisters, where Harry had taken heaps of photos of the iconic mountaintops, insisting he be in most of the shots. It had been a fun day. By the time they'd arrived back at his apartment, however, he'd been more than ready to take her to bed. He'd ordered Chinese that night and they'd eaten it whilst they watched a movie, their naked bodies wrapped in a mohair rug he kept on the sofa. Then it had been back to bed, where they'd stayed on and off for the whole of Sunday, only rising to shower and eat.

When Harry had said around five that she really had to go home, he'd tried to change her mind with some more lovemaking. But it had worked only temporarily. By five-thirty she was adamant that it was time for her to go. Sighing, he said he would drive her home. But he still hated the thought of her going. When the temptation arose to ask her to move in with him, he was totally taken aback. That was not what he wanted in life. Besides, he was pretty sure that Harry would say no. She just wanted to have fun with him, not live with him. Though he didn't abandon the idea altogether...

'Come with me,' he said when they stopped at a set of lights during the drive to her place. 'To Italy.'

Harriet's head whipped round, his offer clearly having thrown her. 'I can't do that,' she said at last. 'People at work will talk.'

'They don't have to know. I'll go into the office on Monday and say you've come down with a bad case of flu. I'll say I've given you the week off.'

He could see that she was tempted. Seriously tempted.

'I don't know, Alex,' she said slowly. 'I don't think it's a good idea.'

'Well, I do. You can come to the wedding with me, then afterwards I'll take you to Venice for a couple of days.'

'Venice,' she repeated, her eyes going all misty. 'I've always wanted to go to Venice.'

The lights went green and he drove on. 'Then let me take you there,' he said.

She shook her head at him. 'You are a wicked man, do you know that?'

'It has been said of me before. But I don't think it's wicked to offer to take you to Italy with me. You'll love Lake Como.'

'I dare say I will. I've heard it's very beautiful. But I won't go to the wedding with you. I wouldn't be comfortable doing that. They are *your* friends, Alex, not mine.'

Alex knew when he'd pushed things as far as he could.

'Very well. I'll book you into a nearby hotel on the lake whilst I'm doing my best man act. You can do a few touristy things by yourself that day. Then, after the wedding, I'll join you and we'll go to Venice together.'

'Won't that take longer than a week?'

He shrugged. 'Not much longer. Look, as things stand I won't be back by next weekend. I don't know about you, but I've enjoyed this weekend more than even I envisaged. I love your company, Harry, in bed *and* out. Come with me. Please…'

Harriet didn't speak again for a full minute. 'I should say no,' she said. But there was a smile in her voice.

He grinned. 'Possibly. But you're not going to. You're going to fly first class with me to Italy.'

'No,' she replied with a firmness which shocked him. 'I'm not.'

Before he could give vent to his frustration, she added, '*You* can fly first class, but *I'll* be in economy. I wouldn't feel comfortable having you pay that much money for my flight.'

'But I can afford it,' he told her.

'I don't care what you can afford. I will not be bought, Alex. I'm not that kind of girl.'

'Would you compromise by going business class?'

She heaved a resigned sigh. 'I suppose that would be all right. But I will be paying for my own ticket. I also want to pay half of all our hotel expenses. And before you object, I assure you, *I* can afford it. I'll just use the money I saved up for my wedding. I only lost the deposit on the reception venue when I broke up with Dwayne, so I have plenty left.'

Alex frowned. 'But surely your parents were going to pay for your wedding?'

Her laugh sounded bitter. 'My parents and I are estranged,' she told him. 'They wouldn't have come to my wedding even if I'd invited them. Which I had no intention of doing.'

Shock at this statement was quickly followed by curiosity.

'What on earth happened between you?'

'My father happened, that's what,' she stated with a bitterness which stunned him.

Alex recalled her telling him something at her interview about her father losing his job when she'd been a teenager, which was why she'd had to go out to work instead of studying. He'd been a miner up in the Singleton area. But that was all he knew about her family.

'He was a pig,' Harriet bit out. 'A male chauvinist pig.'

Whoa, Alex thought. They were pretty heavy words. 'What did he do?' Alex asked.

'What didn't he do?' she threw at him. 'First, he thought women were only put on this earth to wait on him hand and foot. Mum and I were treated like servants. Never with love or caring. My brothers were spoiled rotten, whilst I got nothing. He bought them everything they wanted, whereas I was given only the barest essentials. I lived in second-hand uniforms and clothes. If it hadn't been for gifts from relatives, I would never have had anything new.'

Alex could hardly believe what he was hearing. He'd been critical of his father at times, but he was still a loving parent. What little money he'd earned, he'd given to his children.

'I lied when I told you that Dad had lost his job,' Harriet went on. 'He never did. He always earned a good salary. But Mum and I never saw any of it. So, once I was old enough to get a job or three, I did so.' A small, very bitter smile curved her mouth. 'Naturally, Dad was furious when I refused to hand over any of my salaries.'

'He didn't hit you, did he?' Alex despised men who hit women.

'No. He wasn't a physically violent man, just verbally and emotionally abusive. I hated him.'

'Understandable. So I'm presuming you didn't have your parents' approval when you came to Sydney to pursue a career in real estate?'

'They had absolutely no idea of my plans. But I always knew what I was going to do. First, I saved up for a car. Not a new car, of course. But not bad, either. I also secretly went to college at night, doing an advanced computer course as well as getting my real-estate licence. Then, as soon as I turned twenty, I left home and drove the two hundred kilometres to Sydney.'

'That was brave of you,' he said, admiring her enormously.

'I didn't see it that way. I just knew I had to leave home and make a life for myself. I had enough money saved to survive for a few weeks till I got a job. And I booked into a backpackers' lodge till then as it was relatively cheap.'

'Did you tell your parents you were going or did you just up and leave?'

'Mum knew I was going, but Dad was at work when I left. I did ring home to tell Mum I'd arrived safely, but Dad answered and promptly disowned me, saying I was ungrateful and that he didn't want to set eyes on me ever again.'

'You're right. He is a pig. I hope you told him where to go.'

'I did indeed. In no uncertain terms. Then when I asked to speak to my mother, he hung up. I did ring again the next day when I knew he'd be at work, but Mum also hung up on me.'

Her sad sigh was very telling. 'Clearly, she'd been ordered not to talk to me, and she was too scared to defy him. I'd hoped I might be able to persuade her to leave him, but I soon saw that was never going to happen. I knew from that moment on that I was on my own. My life would be what *I* made it. No one was going to help me.'

Alex was beginning to understand exactly where that checklist had come from. It went a long way back.

'Well, you've done a very good job,' he complimented her. 'I was seriously impressed when I read your résumé, working your way up from being a receptionist to getting a job in sales. Not for any old company, either. For one of Sydney's top realtors. Frankly, I was a bit surprised when you applied for the job as my PA. You probably could have made more money staying in sales.'

'Life isn't all about money, Alex.'

'It's still nice to have it,' he replied.

'True. Right, we're nearly there. I suggest you just let me off outside my place, Alex. There'll be no parking in my street on a Sunday afternoon.'

She was right. There wasn't. 'Are you absolutely sure you have to go home?' he tried one last time. 'I could always turn around and take you back to my place for the night.'

'Alex, just stop it,' she said firmly. 'If I'm going to Italy with you on Tuesday, I have lots of things to do.'

'Give me a kiss before you go.'

She laughed. 'Good try, Alex.' And she was out of the car like a shot, leaning in to grab her overnight bag before waving and running inside.

Alex just sat there for a long moment, then drove slowly back to his place, feeling more alone than he ever had in his life before. Once there, he wandered around like a lost sheep for a while till in desperation he rang Sergio and talked for a good twenty minutes, unlike his previous congratulatory call, which had been rather brief. By the time he hung up, Alex saw what Jeremy meant about their friend being genuinely in love with Bella. He was utterly obsessed with the woman, unable to form a sentence without her name being in it. Alex hoped like hell that Sergio's love was returned. Falling that deeply in love could be dangerous enough. Even worse if it was one-sided.

Seeking more reassurance on the matter, he rang Jeremy, who clearly didn't appreciate being woken on a Sunday morning before noon.

'Alex,' he growled. 'Do you know what time it is?'

'I guess that depends on where you are. London or Lake Como?'

'Neither. I'm in Paris.'

'What are you doing in Paris?'

'What do you think I'm doing in Paris? Go back to sleep, *mon amie*,' he murmured to whoever was in bed beside him. 'So what drama is unfolding in your life that you feel you have to call me at this ungodly hour? It had better be life threatening, or you're a dead man.'

'No drama on my front,' he said, though his mind flew to a certain brunette who was definitely giving him grief. 'I've just been talking to Sergio. Hell, Jeremy, the poor man is seriously infatuated, isn't he?'

'Seriously in love, more like it. And Bella is, too, so you can stop worrying about their marriage. I'm beginning to think that it just might work.'

'How can you be sure? About *her* feelings, that is?'

'I can just tell. The way they look at each other and speak about each other. It's positively sickening. If I ever act like that around a woman, I want you to shoot me.'

Alex laughed. 'I don't have a gun.'

'I'll give you one. We have several in the gun room at the family's country estate.'

'Remind me not to go there with you any more.'

'Don't be ridiculous, you love it there. What say we pop down together for a few days after the wedding? It's lovely in Cornwall in the summer.'

At any other time, he would have said yes. But as much as he loved Jeremy's excellent company, it could not compare with being in Venice with Harriet. Not that he could say that.

'Sorry. No can do. I have to get back here ASAP. I'm up to my ears in work.'

Jeremy sighed. 'Truly, Alex, someone is going to have to take you in hand one day and teach you how to relax.'

Alex smiled as he thought about where Harry's hand had been earlier today. Not that he'd felt in any way relaxed at the time.

'Well, if anyone could teach me how to relax, it would be you,' he said. 'If R and R was a sport, you'd win the gold medal every four years.'

Jeremy chuckled. 'I'll take that as a compliment. But honestly, dear friend, all work and no play makes Alex a dull boy.'

'In that case, you'll be pleased to know I've been playing all weekend.' As soon as the bragging words were out of his mouth, he regretted them.

'*Really?* Do tell.'

'Sorry, mate, I'm not a kiss-and-tell kind of guy.'

'So, how old is this latest bimbo of yours?'

'I'll have you know she's in her late twenties. And no bimbo.'

'I'm impressed. What does she do for a crust?'

Alex had to think quickly. He could hardly say she was his PA. 'She's in real estate,' he said.

'Even better. Nothing worse than dating someone with very little between her ears.'

Alex had noticed over the years that Jeremy preferred intelligent girls, provided they were beautiful as well as brainy.

'So, who did you bring to Paris?' Alex asked.

'No one. Marlee lives in Paris. She's an editor. I'm going to put her in charge of my French office.'

'Combining business and pleasure is never a good idea,' Alex said with considerable irony.

'What rubbish. I've had some of my best sex by doing just that. Look, something's just come up. So I should go. Text me the details of your flight and I'll meet you at Milan airport. *Au revoir.*'

Alex had no time to open his mouth before Jeremy hung up. Smiling wryly over what it was that had come up, Alex put down his phone, then made his way out to the kitchen, where he poured himself a large glass of Scotch, added a few ice cubes, then returned to the living room, sipping slowly. Calling his two best friends hadn't helped all that much. He still missed Harriet and she'd been gone only an hour or so. The thought that he might be falling in love with her started worrying him. He didn't want to fall for her any more than she wanted to fall for him. They had different goals in life. Vastly different.

It was still just lust, he reassured himself. On both their parts. Still, to take her to Italy with him and romance her in Venice was playing with fire, especially when it came to *her* feelings. Women loved that kind of thing.

But it was no use. He wanted to do it. Wanted to see the pleasure in her eyes.

So he ignored the risk and sent her a text telling her to cancel his original first-class booking ASAP and to book two business-class seats for them on the same flight, or an equivalent one.

Will do, she texted back.

Ten minutes later, she texted him the details of their flight, at which point he gave in and rang her.

They talked for close to an hour.

CHAPTER EIGHTEEN

'OH, THIS IS HEAVENLY!' Harriet exclaimed once they settled into their business-class seats, Alex insisting Harriet have the window seat, with him right beside her.

It was early evening on the Monday, take-off in ten minutes. Only one brief stopover, in Dubai, then straight on to Malpensa airport, where they would arrive on Tuesday midmorning, Milan time.

'Thank you, Alex,' she said, turning her head to look over at him.

'For what? You paid for your own ticket.' He was still slightly exasperated with her over that. He'd wanted to spoil her. Make her feel special. Make up to her for what her mean and disgustingly unfair father had done. She'd told him a few more details about her father's appalling treatment last night. It had made him so angry, he'd felt like driving up to Singleton and teaching the man a lesson. When questioned about her mother, Harriet had also confessed that she sent her mother birthday and Mother's Day cards every year, with money enclosed, but never received a reply. How heartbreaking was that?

'Thank you for persuading me to come with you,' she said with the loveliest smile.

He reached over and took her hand in his. 'My pleasure,' he said softly.

* * *

Once again, Harriet's heart turned over and this time she noticed. For a split second she started worrying that she was falling in love with Alex, but just as quickly she decided to ignore any such worry. What would be, would be. She wasn't going to spoil this trip by stressing over future complications. She was going to have fun. And live in the moment.

A flight attendant materialised by their seats, with a tray holding glasses of champagne.

'Champagne, sir? Madam?' he asked.

'The lady doesn't drink champagne,' Alex replied.

'Can I get you anything else, sir? Some white wine, perhaps?'

'When will you be serving dinner?'

'About half an hour after take-off.'

'We'll have a bottle of wine with our meals. Perhaps some juice for now. What kind, Harriet?'

'I prefer orange,' she replied.

'Orange juice for two,' Alex relayed.

'Very good, sir. I'll be back shortly.'

Harriet loved the way Alex took command of situations. It had been sweet of him to remember about the champagne, and very sweet of him to insist on coming to pick her up today when it had been really out of his way. She could just have easily caught a taxi. She was glad she hadn't; his authoritative presence defused her tension over the trip, replacing anxiety with excitement, especially after he'd reassured her that everything was under control at the office. She had momentarily contemplated telling Emily about her affair with Alex. But only momentarily. She didn't want Emily to say anything negative or critical.

Of course, it was probably silly of her to have let Alex

persuade her to accompany him to Italy. Nothing could come of it. Nothing except…

Harriet brought herself up short before she could start thinking of the future again. Instead, she concentrated on the plusses of her affair with Alex. After all, how could she possibly regret having him as her lover? He was incredibly good in bed; last weekend had been the most amazing experience of her life. He was good out of bed, too, proving to be a fun companion, nothing at all like his often serious persona at work. As for this trip… Harriet vowed to enjoy every single moment. The prospect of spending more time alone with Alex was exciting enough, but to spend that time with him in stunning places like Lake Como and Venice was almost too good to be true. She had to keep glancing over at him to remind herself that it *was* true.

'Yes?' he queried after she'd probably looked at him one time too many.

'Nothing. Just checking that you're real.'

The steward arrived with the orange juice, relieving Harriet of having to explain her rather cryptic remark. It was freshly squeezed juice, and deliciously chilled, just the way she liked it. Harriet sipped it and sighed.

'I don't think I'll ever be able to fly anything but business class from now on,' she said.

'That can be arranged,' Alex said. 'I was thinking of taking you to Rio during our Christmas break.'

Harriet's heart skipped a beat at the thought that he was planning so far ahead. Christmas was five months away. As much as she was tempted just to say yes to anything he suggested, she could not afford to let him think she would settle for being his secret mistress for the rest of her life.

Her smile was light. 'What happened to the Alex who said I should just live for the here and now?'

'He was a fraud. And an opportunist. I've always been a planner, Harry. Just like you.'

'Well, that's a shame. Because I think that that particular Alex might have had the right idea. I've always worried too much about the future. Always planned too much. And where did it get me in the end? Nowhere.'

'I don't know about that, Harry. You have a nice flat near Bondi Beach, money in the bank, the best boss in the world and an even better lover.'

She had to laugh. 'You *are* an arrogant devil.' Not to mention so handsome that every woman on this plane had craned to look at him as they boarded. Harriet had felt so proud to be the woman by his side, resolving to wallow in the experience whilst it lasted.

It was the lasting part, however, that kept coming back to haunt her. Harriet knew in her heart that by Christmas this would all be over. Oh, dear, she was doing it again. Worrying about the future.

The thought sent a sad sigh escaping her lungs.

'You do that a lot, you know,' Alex said.

'Do what?'

'Sigh.'

'Sorry.'

'No need to apologise. It's just that I sometimes wonder what's behind the sigh.'

'Nothing serious. It's just a habit of mine, a way of relieving tension.'

'You're afraid of flying?'

Afraid of flying and dying and falling in love with the wrong man. Again.

'A little,' she admitted.

'Then here...take my hand. We're about to take off.'

* * *

Alex took her hand and squeezed it tight, feeling the tension in her as the jumbo airbus zoomed along the wet runway—it had started to rain—before lifting into the air slowly but safely. When the jet levelled off at God knew what height, she sighed again, then took her hand out of his. Alex wished she hadn't. He'd liked holding her hand.

When Alex sighed, Harriet leant over and poked him. '*You're* doing it now.'

He sent her a droll look. 'Maybe it's catching.'

'Maybe you're not the big, brave boy you pretend to be.'

'I never pretend, Harry. I don't like flying, but I'm not scared of it. What's the worst that can happen? The plane crashes and you die. There are worse ways to go.'

Harriet nodded, her big brown eyes turning soft. 'You're thinking of your mother, aren't you?'

Despite the sympathetic note in her voice, Alex could not stop his heart from hardening at the memory of what that wonderful woman had suffered. And so unnecessarily. It had blighted him, knowing he could do nothing to ease her pain. He'd been holding her hand when she'd taken her last breath. He could still see the look on his father's face when he realised she had gone. Poor bastard. Hopefully, this time he'd stick with the rehab and get his life back on track. When he'd rung him earlier today, he'd sounded good.

'Or is it your dad you're worrying about?' Harriet asked.

Her intuition touched him. 'Not really. You were right the first time. I was thinking of my mother.'

He glanced over at Harriet and smiled. 'But let's not

talk about sad things. We're off to Italy, to beautiful Lake Como and then on to amazing Venice, which, I might add, I have never seen.'

Harriet's eyes lit up with surprise. 'You haven't?'

'Nope. It will be the first time for both of us. I've been to Lake Como, of course. Jeremy and I holidayed with Sergio at his family villa quite a lot over the years.'

'You three are very close, aren't you?'

'Yep. Have been since our Oxford days.'

'Which is where you all joined that Bachelor's Club.'

'We didn't join it. We *formed* it. There were just the three of us. But that's ancient history now. In reality, the Bachelor's Club is no more. Once Sergio turned thirty-five, he decided to get married, so that was virtually the end of it.'

'What did his turning thirty-five have to do with it?'

'That was the age we vowed to stay bachelors till. And the age we aimed to become billionaires by.'

'Heavens. And did you? Become billionaires, I mean?'

Alex hesitated to tell her, out of habit. He'd always kept the extent of his wealth a secret, well aware that having heaps of money sometimes brought out the worst in people. Men envied and women grovelled. He quickly realised, however, that Harriet was not that type of woman. He'd never met a more independent, less grovelling female in his life.

'Yes, we did,' he admitted.

'*All* of you?'

Clearly, she was taken aback. Alex smiled, both at her and the memory of how their financial goals had finally been reached. Though just in time.

'It took many years, of course,' he explained. 'You don't become a billionaire overnight.'

'I would imagine not. So how *did* it happen?'

'Shortly after we started the Bachelor's Club, the three of us went into partnership in a wine bar. It was basically a dump, but the location was good. Very close to the university and between two restaurants. We worked hard to turn it into a hip and happening place. At least, Sergio and I worked hard. Jeremy provided the money. He was the wealthy one in our group. Anyway, to cut a long story short, we didn't stop at one wine bar. We eventually had several, all done out the same way. In the end, they were so successful that we formed a franchise. That was how we became billionaires. A little while ago, we sold the WOW franchise to an American company.'

'Oh, my goodness!' Harriet exclaimed. 'You owned the WOW wine bars? That's amazing! Emily and I go to the one in town all the time. They're so cool.'

'They are indeed. But we didn't own any of them in the end. We sold the ones we originally owned years ago. We just owned the franchise.'

'So, that's what you were doing in London recently? Selling the franchise?'

'Yes.'

'I did wonder what business interests you had over there.'

'Well, now you know.'

Harriet fell silent for a long moment before turning to look at him. 'Do you mind if I ask why you three boys decided to stay bachelors in the first place? I mean, I know most men these days don't rush to the altar, but they usually want to settle down eventually. It seems strange that all three of you wanted to stay single so much that you actually formed a club.'

'Look, it was just a bit of fun to begin with. We were all pretty sloshed at the time. Though underneath the fun we all had some serious reasons for embracing bachelor-hood. Sergio was still bitter over his father marrying a gold-digger. Jeremy was anti-marriage due to the number of divorces in his family. As for myself...I'd vowed on my mother's deathbed to spend my life making enough money to make sure no one had to suffer what my family did. Making that sort of money—and making a differ-ence—is hard. I didn't see myself ever having the time or the energy to marry and have children of my own. Remaining a bachelor suited my goals.'

Or, it *had*...

Alex could not ignore the fact that he'd reached his goals now. So maybe it was time to change his mind about staying a bachelor. Maybe it was time to face his inner demons and admit to himself that all he'd just said to Harriet was just rubbish. The truth was, he was afraid of falling in love. Afraid of ending up like his pathetic father.

It was a crazy fear. Irrational, really. Other than in looks, he was nothing like his father. But fear was not always logical.

He gazed into Harriet's lovely face and wished he could be more like Sergio. Fearless and brave when it came to matters of the heart. But he was more like Jer-emy, tainted by life's negative experiences, wary of feel-ing anything too deeply.

'What are you thinking?' she asked.

'Just how lovely you are,' he returned.

Her smile was wry. 'You shouldn't lie to me, Alex. You weren't thinking that at all.'

'You're right. I was thinking that it's rather sad that the Bachelor's Club is no longer relevant. It was a seri-ously fun club to belong to.'

'No doubt. But I think your Bachelor's Club is past its use-by date, Alex.'

'Only for one of us, Harry. Jeremy and I will soldier on.'

Her lips pursed. 'I have a feeling I won't like this Jeremy.'

Alex had to smile. 'Yes, you will. *Everyone* likes Jeremy.'

CHAPTER NINETEEN

THE CAPTAIN HAD just announced their descent into Milan when Alex turned to her.

'I didn't want to say anything earlier,' he said. 'I wanted you to enjoy the flight and not stress over anything, but Jeremy is going to meet me at the airport. Whilst I'm in Milan, I'm to be whisked off to some tailoring establishment to have a fitting for my suit for the wedding, after which we have to pick up Sergio at his factory, then drive down to Lake Como together.'

Harriet's heart sank. She didn't want to meet any of his rich friends, especially this Jeremy character.

'But won't that be awkward? How are you going to explain me?'

'I'm not,' he replied. 'We won't leave the plane together. You can go first. I know I said we were going to take the train down to Lake Como together, and I was going to see you safely booked into the hotel before I left you, but that was before Jeremy insisted on meeting me.'

Harriet could feel panic setting in. She was a confident girl travelling by train around Sydney, but to travel alone in a strange country was daunting.

'Stop worrying,' he said, seeing alarm in her face. 'I've booked you a hire car which will take you from the airport to the hotel door. The driver will be waiting for you in arrivals, holding up a card with your name on it. He'll help you with your luggage and so forth. I asked for a driver who spoke good English so that you wouldn't feel uncomfortable. Now, stop looking at me like that.'

'Like what?'

'Like I'm abandoning you in a strange land '

'Sorry. I know it's not your fault.'

'I'll ring you when I can. Or text you if I can't.'

'All right,' she said and sighed.

'And stop that damn sighing,' he snapped. 'You could have come to the wedding with me, but you refused.'

'I wouldn't have fitted in.'

'Rubbish. It's not too late to change your mind, you know. Come with me. Be with me.'

'But what about the hire car? And the booking at the hotel?'

'Nothing that can't be sorted out.'

'I don't know, Alex. Are you sure?'

Not even remotely, he thought. But he couldn't bear to see her go off alone, looking unhappy and worried. He'd brought her here. It was his job to look after her.

'Positive,' he said. 'Now, I don't want to hear another word about it. You're coming with me and that's that.'

Her smile did things to him that shouldn't be allowed. Dear God, if he didn't watch himself, he would fall in love with her. And that would never do.

'I'll just go along to the ladies' and freshen up,' she said.

'Better be quick. We'll be landing soon.'

'I'm always quick,' she told him with a wry smile. 'I have a boss who gives me five-minute deadlines all the time.'

'What a bastard.'

'He can be.'

'I'll have to have a word with him.'

'He won't listen. He never listens.'

'Stupid as well.'

She laughed, then left him. He watched her make her way down the aisle, her neat little backside encased in stylish black slacks. She wore black a lot, usually teaming it with white tops. Harriet's top today was a simple but expensive-looking white T-shirt. He watched her walk back towards him five minutes later, her dark hair swinging in a sleek curtain around her shoulders, her glossy red lipstick a perfect foil for her black-and-white outfit. Though not classically beautiful, Harriet's face was strikingly attractive, her big dark eyes her best feature.

'That's better,' she said as she sat down and clicked her seat belt into place. 'Can't have your best friends looking down their noses at me.'

'They'll love you,' he said, confident that neither Sergio nor Jeremy would make any girlfriend of his feel bad. Which was exactly how he would introduce Harriet. Not as his PA. As his new girlfriend. Jeremy wouldn't care that he was sleeping with one of his staff, but Sergio might.

Alex tried to remember if he'd ever told his friends his relatively new PA's name. He vaguely recalled saying something about her the last night they'd had dinner together a few weeks ago. Yes, he'd called her Harry, Jeremy having picked up that that was probably a nickname. Sergio, however, had been very distracted that night, his mind clearly on Bella. He was unlikely to remember what his PA was called.

Alex decided to clue Jeremy in on who Harriet really was, but he would keep Sergio in the dark. He wasn't in the mood for any lectures where his private life was concerned, especially from Sergio, who was stupidly about to marry a possible gold-digger!

The plane's landing was as smooth as silk, their disembarking just as trouble-free. They were whisked through Customs without a hitch, Alex collecting and loading their luggage on a trolley before proceeding to the arrivals area, an anxious-looking Harriet by his side.

Jeremy, as luck would have it, was standing not that far from a uniformed chauffeur who was holding up a card with Harriet's name on it. It wasn't till that moment that Alex thought of a way to soothe some of Harriet's nervousness over having to spend too much time with his friends.

'Jeremy! Mate!' he called out and steered Harriet in his direction.

CHAPTER TWENTY

JEREMY WASN'T ANYTHING like Harriet had been imagining. Since Alex virtually had described him as the best-dressed rake in London, she'd pictured a handsome but dissolute-looking man with slicked-back hair and heavy-lidded eyes, wearing a designer suit and sporting a lot of expensive jewellery.

The man who waved back at Alex *was* handsome, but he looked disgustingly healthy with a nice tan and sparkling blue eyes. His hair wasn't oily or slicked back. It was clearly freshly washed, brown and collar-length, with a boyish wave which fell across his high forehead. As for his clothes...they looked expensive but were very casual. Not a bit of jewellery, either, Harriet noted as they drew closer. No earrings or rings or even a watch.

When he threw his arms around Alex in a huge bear hug, Harriet was astounded, then oddly touched. It wasn't often that you saw grown men hug each other with such genuine warmth and affection.

'God, it's great to see you,' Jeremy said at the same time, astounding Harriet even more with the richness and depth of his voice, which seemed at odds with his size. Though far from short—he was only a couple of inches shorter than Alex—his frame was much leaner. His shoulders were broad enough, but the rest of his body was very slender. He could easily have made money as a model, or as a narrator, with that gorgeous voice of his.

Harriet couldn't remember what he did for a living. She didn't think Alex had actually told her. Just that he was a rich friend from Oxford and was a fellow member of their Bachelor's Club, which meant he, too, had recently become a billionaire. He *looked* rich; money had a way of clinging to a man like an invisible cloak.

When he cheekily winked at Harriet over Alex's shoulder, she got a glimpse of his much-vaunted charm.

'So, who's this gorgeous creature, Alex?' he asked as he stepped back to look her up and down, his blue eyes twinkling. 'You never mentioned you were bringing someone with you.'

'It was a last-minute decision. This is Harriet,' Alex introduced. 'My PA. And my new girlfriend,' he added before Harriet could be offended. 'I usually call her Harry, but in present company I think Harriet is called for.'

She saw the drily amused look Jeremy gave Alex. 'You sneaky devil,' he said, then grinned. 'And you had the hide to tell me that business and pleasure don't mix!'

'There are exceptions to every rule,' Alex said and smiled a wry smile at a slightly startled Harriet. 'I didn't say anything because I agreed to keep our affair a secret. But there's no need for secrets over here, though I think I might not tell Sergio she's my PA. Sergio isn't as much of a free spirit as you are, Jeremy. Without going into too many details, I have to speak to that chauffeur over there. He was going to drive Harriet down to a hotel at Lake Como, but I've persuaded her to change her plans and come to the wedding with me.'

'And rightly so,' Jeremy pronounced warmly as Alex walked off, leaving Harriet to fend alone in his friend's perversely bewitching company. It was simply impossible not to like him. She wasn't sexually attracted to him, but she could understand why lots of women had fallen under his spell over the years. He possessed a personal charisma which she imagined could be overpowering if he was also your physical type.

'It's wonderful to see Alex dating a real woman for a change,' he said. 'Though slightly disconcerting.'

'Disconcerting?'

'I don't want to be the only one left a bachelor in our Bachelor's Club. Oops. Maybe I shouldn't have said that. Has Alex told you about the Bachelor's Club?'

'Yes. I know all about it.'

'That's a relief. Thought I'd put my big foot in it just then. Sergio's broken ranks, but Alex and I are still committed bachelors. We both believe it's best for a girl to know the lie of the land before she gets in too deep. Or is it too late for that?' he added with a sudden searching look.

Oh, God. Why did she have to blush?

'I see,' he said, his brows drawing together.

'No, you don't,' she said quickly. 'Look, I know Alex isn't into love or marriage. I'm not a fool. I recently broke up with my fiancé and I'm not looking for love or commitment of any kind. I'm just having a much-needed fling. It won't last. When it's over, I'll move on and so will Alex.'

'Are you quite sure about that?'

'Quite sure,' she said coolly and glanced over at Alex, who was still talking to the chauffeur. Just then, he glanced back at her, smiled, then hurried over, the chauffeur in his wake.

'Right. All settled. Jeremy, am I right in guessing you didn't drive yourself to the airport? Knowing you, you either had Sergio drop you off or you took a taxi.'

154 THE BILLIONAIRE'S RUTHLESS AFFAIR

'I hate it when people know me that well,' he said, but without looking offended at all. 'Yes, Sergio dropped me off, then went on to his office. He's getting everything organised there before he and Bella fly off to New York.'

'Thought that might be the case,' Alex said. 'Anyway, I've organised for Lucca here to take us all to the tailor. After we're finished there, we'll drop you off back at Sergio's office, Jeremy, then I'll accompany Harriet down to the hotel I booked her into on Lake Como. Everyone, this is Lucca,' he finally introduced. 'Lucca, this is Harriet and Jeremy.'

Relief swamped Harriet at Alex not insisting that she stay at Sergio's villa on Lake Como. Now that she'd met Jeremy, she wasn't quite so nervous about meeting Sergio—whom she was sure would be nice to her as well—but she didn't want to spend every minute of the next two days in their company. Besides, it was only natural that the three friends would like to spend some time together. Clearly, that didn't happen too often these days.

'I'll tell you what,' Harriet butted in before he could put his plans into motion. 'Why don't you and Jeremy take a taxi to wherever it is you have to go and I'll have Lucca take me straight down to the hotel? To be honest,' she added, 'I feel seriously jet-lagged. You're an experienced traveller, Alex, but I'm not. I hardly slept a wink on that flight. Now, please, don't worry about me. I'll be fine. I'm going to go straight to bed once I check in, and sleep for hours, so don't go calling me for ages. Tonight'll be soon enough.'

'Are you sure?' Alex asked.

'Absolutely. I'm quite capable of looking after myself, like we originally planned. Go have some fun with your friends.'

He leant forward and gave her a peck on the cheek. 'You're a darling.'

His sweet words sent tears pricking at her eyes.

'Off you go,' she said hurriedly before she could embarrass herself totally. 'Lucca will look after me, won't you, Lucca?'

Lucca, who was a good-looking lad of no more than twenty, nodded enthusiastically. '*Si.* You will be safe with me.'

'Safe' was not quite the word Harriet would have used to describe Lucca's driving. Thankfully, the road from Milan to Lake Como was first class, but good God, didn't they have speed limits in Italy? If they did, Lucca was oblivious to them. Once off the freeway, fortunately he did slow down enough for Harriet to take in the sights. And what sights they were! Never had she seen such a beautiful spot as Lake Como, with its surrounding snow-capped mountains and magnificent villa-dotted shores.

The boutique hotel they were heading for was once a private villa, according to its website. The pictures of it looked beautiful, and the setting peaceful, which was why she'd booked it. But flat, one-dimensional photographs did not replicate the experience of seeing the place in real life, Harriet was soon to appreciate, especially on a warm summer's day with a clear blue sky.

When the hotel came into view, she was overwhelmed by the sheer grandeur of the ancient stone building gleaming a soft white in the sunshine. The magnificence of the grounds and the view of the lake were just as spellbinding. Harriet's eyes were everywhere as she followed Lucca into the grand foyer with its vaulted ceiling and spectacular marble staircase. She'd been in some nice hotels in Sydney over the years, but there was nothing at home like this. It was like stepping back in time to a world of splendour, elegance and opulent luxury, a feeling enhanced when she finally lay down on her antique four-poster bed in her exquisitely furnished room.

She didn't really want to go to sleep just yet. She wanted to wander in the garden and sit on the terrace which overlooked the lake. Instead, the excitement of the trip and the length of the flight finally caught up with her and she couldn't stop herself from drifting off, her last thought being that she hoped Alex was enjoying himself.

Alex finally became aware of the fact that Jeremy had been uncharacteristically quiet during their trip to the tailor. After the fitting was finished, Alex suggested they go have a spot of lunch somewhere. He was curious about what was bothering Jeremy. He suspected it was something to do with Harriet; Alex wondered what she'd said to him that had rendered him unusually taciturn.

They found a café nearby which wasn't too crowded. Summer in Milan was high tourist season, with all the cafés and restaurants doing excellent business. Alex had by then removed his suit jacket and rolled up his sleeves, but he was still on the warm side. Fortunately, the café was air-conditioned.

'Okay, so what's bugging you?' Alex asked after the waitress had departed with their order of wraps and coffee.

Jeremy widened ingenuous blue eyes. 'Why would you think something's bugging me?'

'Don't try to con me, Jeremy. I know you, remember?'

Jeremy shrugged. 'Okay, but you might not like what I have to say.'

'Let me be the judge of that.'

'Are you in love with this girl, Alex?'

His question stunned Alex. It was certainly not what he'd been expecting.

'No,' he said. 'I'm not.' Not yet, anyway.

'I see.' Jeremy began making circles on the table with his index finger, an old habit of his when he was thinking. Finally, he stopped and looked up at Alex. 'Harriet told me she's not interested in love or commitment from you. She says she's having a fling on the rebound.'

Alex only just contained his exasperation. 'I leave you with her for five minutes and she tells you her innermost thoughts and feelings. How on earth did you manage that?'

'It's a talent I inherited,' Jeremy said with a perfect poker face. 'All the Barker-Whittle males are born charmers. But that's beside the point.'

'And the point is?'

'I know you very well, Alex, the same way you know me. It's not like you to become involved with an employee, especially your PA. You're nothing like me. You have hidden depths. And a capacity for caring which I simply don't possess.'

'Don't undersell yourself, dear friend. You have a great capacity for caring. Look how you always remember everyone's birthdays.'

'Stop trying to be funny, Alex. This is serious.'

'What is?'

Jeremy's blue eyes turned a steely grey. 'I have this awful feeling that you're heading for an even worse disaster than Sergio's marriage.'

'In what way?'

'I'm worried you're going to fall in love with this girl and she's going to break your heart.'

Alex was taken aback. 'I can't see that happening.'

Jeremy shook his head. 'This is not going to end well, Alex.'

'Everything will work out fine, Jeremy. Harry and I are just having a bit of fun together. Lighten up, for pity's sake. It's not like you to worry so much.'

Jeremy heaved a frustrated sigh. 'You're right. I'm in danger of becoming a worrywart. And a workaholic. Ever since I bought my book business, I've changed.'

'I didn't notice much of a change when I rang you the other night,' Alex pointed out drily. 'You were happily bedding your French editor with your usual *laissez-faire* attitude. Ah…our wraps are here.'

Both men tucked into the food and didn't speak for a couple of minutes.

'I do know what you mean about changing, though,' Alex went on finally. 'I've changed, too, this past year. Possibly it's because we're getting older. Just think, both you and I will be thirty-five before the year is out. I hope we'll always stay friends, despite the tyranny of distance, but our lives are now taking different paths.'

'God, that sounds wretched. I already miss you and Sergio both. Terribly.'

Alex was touched by his words, but not surprised. Of the three friends, Jeremy had always been the softest, and the most sentimental. He *never* forgot birthdays. It came to Alex that Jeremy's *laissez-faire* attitude to life might hide a deep-seated loneliness. His upbringing, though privileged, had not been easy. He'd been sent to boarding school when he was eight, where his slight frame and pretty-boy looks had resulted in lots of bullying. It wasn't till puberty had hit that he'd found his feet, his voice breaking and his height shooting up to over six feet, putting paid to the bullying. But his less than positive experiences at school, plus his parents' constant divorcing and remarrying, had left lots of emotional scars.

'Who knows?' Alex said casually. 'Maybe *you'll* fall in love one day.'

'*What?*'

Alex laughed. 'You should see the look on your face.'

'Well, it isn't every day that one of my best friends says something to me so outrageous. I would possibly tolerate it from Sergio, now that he's about to embrace wedded bliss. But I expected better from a fellow dedicated bachelor.'

'I was only joking. Come on, finish up that coffee. Then we'll go pick up Sergio.'

Dragging Sergio away from work was not an easy task, but Jeremy managed it when he promised to tell Sergio some fascinating news, but only once they were on their way to Lake Como. Alex knew exactly what he had in mind, but went along with it. After all, if he was going to bring Harriet to the wedding, Sergio had to know about her.

'Okay, out with it!' an impatient Sergio demanded within thirty seconds of leaving the factory. Jeremy leant forward from where he was sitting in the back seat, kindly having given Alex the passenger seat.

'Alex brought a girl with him. No, no, strike that. He brought a *woman*.'

Sergio shot Alex a surprised look. 'A woman, eh? What happened?'

'I finally grew bored with dating dolly-birds whose IQs were smaller than their bra size.'

Jeremy chuckled. 'That's a good one, Alex.'

'So how did you meet this woman?' Sergio asked.

'Through work. She's in real estate.' He'd instructed Jeremy not to mention she was his PA.

'What's her name?' Sergio asked.

'Harriet.'

'Classy name.'

'She's a classy girl.'

'I thought she was a woman.'

'She is. But she's not that old. Late twenties.'

'Around Bella's age, then. I presume she's attractive.'

'*Very* attractive,' Jeremy jumped in. 'Brunette. Slim. She's also nicely independent. I met her at the airport.'

'So where the hell *is* she?' Sergio asked.

'By now she's settled in at the Villa Accorsi. You know it?'

'Of course. But why is she staying at a hotel when we have plenty of room at my place?'

'She didn't want to stay there. To be honest, she didn't even want to come to the wedding, but I talked her into it.'

'Are you serious about this Harriet?'

'Silly question, Sergio,' Jeremy intoned drily. 'Alex is never serious about *any* girl.'

'But it's clear this one is different. He wouldn't have brought her all this way if he didn't at least like her a hell of a lot.'

'I do like her a hell of a lot,' Alex confessed. 'But we've only been dating a short while. She's also just getting over a broken engagement. When Harry told me she'd always wanted to go to Italy, I impulsively asked her along—something I'll start to regret if my friends start harassing me over my intentions.'

When Sergio fell broodingly silent, Alex worried that he might have come down a bit heavy.

'Look, I'm sorry, I—'

'It's your PA you should apologise to,' Sergio broke in sharply. 'Did you honestly think I wouldn't remember? You called her Harry that night at dinner a few weeks back. The odds of both your new girlfriend and your PA being called Harry are at lotto-winning level, so let's cut the crap and tell the truth. You're having sex with your personal assistant—most likely on the sly—and you're using this trip as an excuse to have some more.'

Alex sighed heavily, whilst Jeremy remained conspicuously silent, both of them having been on the end of Sergio's disapproval more than once over the years.

'It's not like that,' Alex said defensively.

'Then what's it like?'

'We're just having some fun together. It's nothing serious.'

Jeremy's snort didn't help.

'Harry needs some fun right now,' Alex went on firmly. 'I would never hurt her.'

Now Sergio snorted.

Alex decided he'd heard enough. 'Hey, just cut it with the "high and mighty" stuff, buddy. From what I've heard, your intentions weren't exactly pure as the driven snow when you invited Bella to stay at your villa.'

Sergio had the grace to apologise.

'I was just thinking,' Jeremy piped up. 'We should have your stag party tonight. That way we won't be hung over for the wedding. What do you say, Sergio?'

'I say good thinking. I still have half a case of that gorgeous red you sent me last Christmas.'

'Great. And we'll order in some of those fantastic pizzas we ate last time. You like pizza, don't you, Alex?'

'I like good pizza.'

'These are the best. So that's settled. Another bonus is it leaves Alex free to spend tomorrow to do some sightseeing with Harriet. He could even stay the night with her. Then they can come to the wedding together the next morning.'

'You'd better watch it, Jeremy,' Alex said. 'You're turning into a planner.'

'You could be right,' he agreed. 'Like I told you, since I bought my book business I seem to have developed a strange compulsion for being organised. When I was working for the family bank, I didn't give a damn about nine-to-five, or even turning up at my desk at all. I did most of my business via my phone. Now I'm getting obsessed with marketing meetings and publishing deadlines and all sorts of weird things.'

Both Sergio and Alex laughed.

'We'll make a businessman out of him yet,' Alex said.

'Stranger things have happened, I suppose,' Jeremy remarked.

'About tomorrow night,' Sergio piped up. 'With the wedding at eleven, I'd be more comfortable if you spent that night with us at my place, Alex. I don't want anything going wrong.'

'Fair enough,' Alex said. 'How will Harriet get to the wedding, then?'

'I'll book her a water taxi to pick her up at the hotel around ten. They have their own jetty.'

'Okay.' Alex didn't mind. He would have all day with her, more than enough time to show her some sights *and* have late-afternoon delight in her hotel room. He wondered what Harriet was doing right at this moment. Hopefully, she was having a good rest and not feeling lonely or abandoned. He would call her later. Or perhaps he would just text her; tell her they were having their stag party tonight and that he would join her tomorrow morning. Yes, perhaps that would be better. He didn't want her thinking he simply *had* to hear the sound of her voice.

CHAPTER TWENTY-ONE

WHEN HARRIET WOKE, she wasn't sure where she was for a split second. But then she remembered. She was in Italy, in a gorgeous hotel on the shores of Lake Como.

Unfortunately, she was also alone. Harriet pulled a face. What she would not give to have Alex by her side at this moment.

Thinking of Alex had her rolling over, picking up her phone and turning it back on. Good Lord! It was almost seven o'clock. She'd slept for hours. She hoped he hadn't tried to ring her. She quickly checked. No. No missed calls, but one message, informing her that they were having Sergio's stag party that night so that they wouldn't be hung over for the wedding. This would also leave tomorrow free for him to spend with her.

Harriet's spirits immediately lifted.

'Ring me when you wake up,' he'd added before signing off.

She did so straight away, just the sound of his voice filling her with joy.

'Did you have a good sleep?' he asked.

'Very good.'

They talked for ages, Alex telling her of all the places he planned to take her the next day. Sergio had offered the use of his speedboat. It sounded wonderful. Still, she would enjoy going anywhere with Alex.

'Hey!' She heard a deep male voice call out. Jeremy, no doubt. He did have a distinctive voice.

'Girlfriends aren't allowed at stag parties,' he said. 'Not even via the phone.'

Harriet's heart turned over at the word 'girlfriend'. It sounded wonderful as well, though she'd better not get used to it. That would only be her title here, in this fantasy world, on this fantasy getaway. Once they got back to the real world at home, she would revert to being Alex's PA, plus his secret bit on the side.

It was a depressing thought.

Then don't think about that, Harriet, she lectured herself. *Live in the moment.* That was the order of the day.

'I'd better go,' Alex said. 'See you tomorrow morning around nine-thirty.'

'That early?'

'Don't worry. I won't be drinking too much. I'll leave that up to Sergio and Jeremy. I'll give you a call when I'm on my way. Bye, sweetheart.'

That evening seemed endless, despite the excellence of the meal she had in a local restaurant. She kept thinking about Alex, then about tomorrow. She could hardly wait.

She woke very early the next day, already excited. Unfortunately, it was still over three hours before Alex was due to join her. Showering, dressing and titivating took up a good hour and a half, and Harriet used up another hour having a leisurely breakfast out on the huge back terrace that overlooked the lake. The day promised to be warm again, but not too warm, with a smattering of cloud in the sky. She was lingering over a third cup of coffee when her phone pinged. Snatching it up, she read the message from Alex with a pounding heart.

I'm on my way, it said. Be on the lookout for the boat. It's red, so it should be easy to spot.

Harriet stood up and made her way over to stand at the stone railing that enclosed the terrace. Her eyes scanned the lake, looking for a red speedboat. There were myriad assorted craft on the water. Ferries, water taxis, sailing boats, jet skis and, yes, several speedboats, none of them red.

And then she saw it, cutting across the wake of a ferry, jumping the waves, Alex at the wheel, his fair hair glinting golden in the sunshine. He arrived like a hero from an action movie, Harriet only then noticing the hotel jetty at the bottom of some stone steps. Spotting her watching him from the terrace, he waved, jumped out of the boat, tied a rope around a post, then dashed up the steps towards her, dashingly handsome in white shorts and a navy polo. He gathered her to him and kissed her thoroughly, uncaring of the other guests sitting at tables nearby. When he finally let her come up for air, Harriet didn't care, either.

'You're looking good for a man who should have a hangover,' she said, cupping his face and pretending to inspect his eyes. Lord, but he had beautiful eyes, blue as the sky overhead, and with lashes that any woman would kill for.

'I told you I wouldn't drink much.'

'Have you had breakfast?'

'Would you believe that I have? Maria insisted on cooking an omelette.'

'Who's Maria?'

'Sergio's housekeeper. She wanted to pack me a picnic lunch, but I said no to that. So, are you ready to go? First, we're going over to Bellagio. You can't visit Lake Como without visiting the town of Bellagio. It's called "the pearl of Lake Como".'

'Sounds lovely.'

'It is. Very old, of course, but fascinating. Seeing all the main places of interest there will take us all morning. We'll have lunch there, too. Their restaurants are second to none. Then after lunch we'll motor down to Como. That's a beautiful town. After that I'll take you for a leisurely drive around the whole lake. You can see a lot from the water. I'll show you Sergio's villa, plus the one next door, the countess's. It's very grand. That's where they're having the wedding and the reception afterwards.'

'It's not going to be a big wedding, is it?'

Alex laughed. 'Hardly. Counting the celebrant and the photographer, there'll be just eleven of us. So don't start stressing that it's some huge celebrity shindig, because it isn't.'

Harriet had to admit she was relieved. She hadn't packed a dress suitable for a seriously formal do. But she *had* brought along her red cocktail dress, the one Alex had admired. That would do.

'Now, are you ready to go? You look ready. And you look very lovely, might I add. If I hadn't had our itinerary all worked out, I'd whisk you off upstairs for a quickie.'

'I don't much like quickies,' Harriet said, doing her best to ignore the wild jab of desire coursing through her veins.

He chuckled. 'You are such a little liar. I'm almost tempted to show you just how much. But I think I'll make you wait.'

'I can wait,' she told him. 'Provided you give me a little taster occasionally.'

'And what would that involve?'

'Nothing much. Just hold my hand and kiss me at regular intervals so that I don't go cold on you.'

'Done!'

* * *

Alex hadn't enjoyed himself so much in years. He'd been to Lake Como a few times as Sergio's guest, and he'd seen the various sights on offer, but there was something about seeing them through Harriet's delighted eyes which made the experience even more pleasurable, and infinitely more satisfying. Of course, it didn't hurt holding her hand or kissing her more times than he could count. By the time they docked at the hotel jetty in the late afternoon, he was more than ready to steer her up the amazing staircase to her room without further ado.

She made no objection to sharing a shower with him, or having what turned out to be a quickie under the jets of hot water, Alex coming with a speed that bothered him a bit, knowing that Harriet had been left panting and unsatisfied. Still, he made it up to her afterwards with an hour of leisurely love-play in bed, during which she came three times before he reached for a condom once more.

'Hate to love you and leave you,' he said afterwards, 'but I don't want to drive that boat across the lake at night. Sergio is a nervous enough bridegroom without my adding to his worries, so I promised I'd be back before dark.'

Harriet propped herself up on one elbow and watched him dress.

'How am I getting to the wedding?' she asked.

'Sergio's booked you a water taxi for ten. It'll bring you to his villa. I'll meet you down at his jetty and we'll all go over to the countess's place together.'

'I still can't believe how amazing her place is. I mean, Sergio's villa was grand enough, but hers is like a palace.'

'It *is* magnificent, but it's not as big as it looks. The setting up against the hillside makes it look larger.'

When Harriet reached for her phone and took a photo of him, he groaned. 'Will you stop doing that? You've already taken heaps of photos of me today.'

'Yes, but none with your shirt off.'

'I hope none of them shows up on social media,' he warned her.

Harriet shrugged. 'I'm not into social media on a personal basis. It has its uses, but I don't particularly want to give other people—even friends—a blow-by-blow description of my life.'

'Sensible girl. But, to be on the safe side, perhaps you'd better not take any snaps at the wedding tomorrow. Sergio has a passion for privacy.'

'In that case, he shouldn't be marrying Bella, should he?'

Alex laughed. 'You could be right there. Okay, I'll reassure Sergio that any photos you take are for your personal use only. They won't be gracing the glossies, or anywhere else.'

Harriet smiled. 'Good. Because I really want to take some photos. Not just of the bride. I especially want one of you and your two friends together.'

Alex bent down and gave her a kiss on the cheek. 'I'd like that. Have to go now, Harry. Sorry I wasn't able to take you out to dinner tonight.'

'No worries. I'll have room service, then read one of the books I downloaded onto my tablet back home before I left.'

'What kind of books?'

'Mostly thrillers, with a few romances thrown in. What do you suggest I try?'

'Not a romance. Romancing you is *my* job.'

'And you're very good at it, too. Lord knows what I'm going to do when you grow bored and don't want to have sex with me any more. I'm already seriously addicted to your unique brand of lovemaking.'

'I wouldn't worry about that, if I were you,' he said ruefully. 'There's no danger of my growing bored with you for a long time yet.' And wasn't that the truth!

It was actually a relief to hear that Harriet didn't envisage ending their affair any time soon. Alex couldn't bear the thought of her telling him one day that it was over between them. It would happen, of course. She didn't love him. Basically, she was just in it for the sex. Same as him.

Are you sure that's still true, Alex? questioned that inner voice that had been plaguing him ever since Jeremy had brought up the subject of love. *Are you sure that your feelings for her haven't already changed to something far deeper than a combination of liking and lust?*

Alex clenched his jaw down hard, refusing to listen to such rubbish. It was all Jeremy's fault, which was ironic, considering *his* attitude to love and marriage. Alex decided that it was the romantic setting that was making him feel things he didn't normally feel. Paris might be called the city of love, but Italy was the country of love. He would have to watch himself tomorrow at the wedding, and then in Venice. If he wasn't careful, before he knew it he'd be asking Harriet to marry him. Which was pretty stupid, considering he was the last man on earth she would marry. *So just put all these thoughts of love back into Pandora's box, Alex, and get yourself out of here. Pronto!*

'Must fly,' he told her, and with one last peck on the cheek he was gone.

CHAPTER TWENTY-TWO

HARRIET COULD NOT imagine a more perfect wedding. The lack of a church filled to the brim with guests didn't seem to matter, despite her own dream to have that kind of traditional wedding. Or it had been, till she witnessed this one. Admittedly, the setting for the ceremony was idyllic, on the wide stone terrace of a magnificent villa overlooking Lake Como. Plus the weather was beautiful, the skies blue overhead and the summer sun not too hot.

But it was the unique bridal party that dazzled Harriet the most. It wasn't often that there were no bridesmaids, just the bride, groom and two best men. She didn't know whose photograph to take first, they were all so good-looking. The bride, of course, was more than dazzling. Harriet had already known Bella was beautiful. She'd seen her on television and in the gossip magazines. Dressed as a bride, however, she was breathtaking. Yet her gown was simple, a sleek floor-length sheath in pearl satin which skimmed her figure rather than clung. She wore no veil. With that gorgeous mane of white-blonde hair, she didn't need a veil. Her jewellery was just as simple. A fine gold chain with a single pearl pendant, along with pearl-drop earrings.

She and Sergio looked brilliant standing together, his darkly handsome looks the perfect foil for Bella's exquisite blonde beauty. Harriet took heaps of photos, including several of the three friends together. She didn't have an opportunity to meet Bella before the actual ceremony, but Sergio had spoken to her at length as she'd walked with the men from Sergio's villa to the countess's. Such a nice man; a real gentleman. He'd made her feel so welcome, which was good of him, considering she was a wedding crasher.

The countess had been very sweet as well. Her name was Claudia and she was a widow. But a very merry one, Harriet deduced by her flashy clothes and flirtatious manner, especially towards Jeremy. Not that he seemed to mind. Alex had eventually confirmed her suspicions that the two of them might have been lovers at some stage, despite their age difference.

Which didn't surprise Harriet. Nothing would surprise Harriet about Jeremy's behaviour where women were concerned. She even caught him winking at the mother of the bride, who was still attractive and possibly younger than Claudia. The only other guests were Sergio's housekeeper, Maria, and her husband, Carlo, who obviously thought the marriage a marvellous idea, judging by the wide smiles on their faces.

By the time the celebrant—a portly and loquacious Italian named Giovanni—pronounced Sergio and Bella husband and wife, Claudia and the mother of the bride were dabbing at their eyes, though not enough to spoil their make-up.

Harriet felt teary herself, partly because she always cried at weddings, but mostly because she knew she would never marry the man *she* loved. Oh, dear God. She *did* love Alex, didn't she? There was no longer any doubt in her mind. She'd suspected as much yesterday but had pushed the dreaded thought away. When her eyes automatically went to him, more tears threatened. Fortunately, he didn't notice; the official photographer—a tall, thin woman in her forties—had pounced on the bridal party for more photos, leaving Harriet to battle her emotions in private.

Time to get a grip, girl, she lectured herself after slipping her phone back into her black clutch bag. *Go talk to the countess. Or Bella's mother. Whatever, just do something, and for pity's sake, no more silly crying!*

Alex felt impatient for the reception luncheon to be over, despite the happiness of the occasion and the quality of the food. They were sitting at the sumptuous table in Claudia's opulent dining room, being given course after mouth-watering course. Harriet was on his right side and Jeremy on his left, both of them obviously enjoying the lavish meal a lot more than he was. His mind was definitely elsewhere, his gaze drifting over the table to Sergio and Bella, who didn't seem to be eating much. They were too busy gazing adoringly into each other's eyes. Alex finally agreed with Jeremy that Bella did love Sergio; the way she looked at him was rather persuasive. But he would reserve judgment till their marriage had passed the hurdle of Sergio abandoning the family business in order to move to New York with her.

They were actually flying there later this evening, which was the reason for the morning wedding. Knowing this, Alex had booked a hire car to pick both himself and Harriet up at her hotel later that afternoon and take them straight to Venice, where he'd booked them into one of the city's most luxurious hotels. The suite he'd picked had cost a bomb, but he didn't care. He worked hard. Why shouldn't he spoil himself? Alex suspected, however, that it was Harriet whom he wanted to spoil.

He watched her out of the corner of his eye, thinking how lovely she looked today. She was wearing the same red cocktail dress she'd worn to the charity dinner earlier this year, the one which had given him wicked thoughts all that night. Or had they been jealous thoughts? He certainly hadn't liked the thought of her going home with that dullard Dwayne. She'd always deserved someone better.

But you're not better, that annoying voice piped up once again. *Except perhaps in bed. You're selfish and ruthless, and a total waste of time. She'd be better off without you in her life. Really, your behaviour has been quite shameless. So do the right thing, Alex, and once you get home let her go.*

But he didn't want to let her go. He couldn't. Not yet.

Harriet tried to pretend she was having a wonderful time, but she wasn't. The food was marvellous, yes, but there was way too much of it. The only reason she kept eating was that she didn't want to offend the countess, who'd obviously gone to a lot of trouble to make the wedding a success. She couldn't wait to get out of there and be alone with Alex once more; couldn't wait to go to Venice. Lake Como was lovely, but somehow seeing Sergio and Bella getting married here today had temporarily spoiled the place for her. Venice would be much better. Out of sight was out of mind, or so they said. She didn't want to think about love and marriage. She had to get her mind back to reality, which was that she was having a strictly sexual affair with Alex. Nothing more.

Before she'd left Sydney to come to Italy, Harriet had vowed to enjoy the trip for what it was. But somehow the enjoyment she'd experienced yesterday was in danger of disintegrating. Which was a shame. When she sighed, Alex gave her a nudge.

'None of that infernal sighing,' he muttered under his breath.

Harriet gave him a rueful smile. 'It's just that I'm full,' she whispered. 'I can't eat another bite.'

'Then don't.'

'I won't,' she said and put down her cutlery.

Jeremy leaned forward and shot a questioning glance down the table. 'You don't want your dessert?'

'I'm full,' Harriet answered.

'Pass it along to me. I need added fortification for the night ahead.'

'Don't even ask,' Alex informed her drily as he passed along her dessert.

'He really is very naughty,' Harriet said after Jeremy had dropped them back at the hotel in Sergio's speed-boat. The happy couple had by then departed, and Alex wasted no time in getting Jeremy to drive them across the lake. The hire car he'd booked was due to pick them up in less than an hour.

'But you can't help liking him,' she added as they hurried up the steps towards the hotel entrance.

'You don't fancy him, do you?' Alex said, his voice sharp.

'Don't be silly. He's not my type at all.'

'Why not?'

'He just isn't. You're my type, Alex, as you very well know. There's no need to be jealous.'

'I'm not jealous,' he denied. But he was. Fiercely jealous. The thought of Harriet even fancying another man brought a sour taste to his mouth. The thought of her having sex with another man didn't bear thinking about. The only man allowed to have sex with her was *him*!

'How long will it take you to pack?' he asked her.

'Not long. Why?'

He gave her a look which spoke a thousand words. Less than a minute later, Harriet was up against the bedroom door, her panties in tatters on the floor, her legs wrapped around Alex's waist while he pumped up into her with primal passion. As they both came, Alex thanked his lucky stars that he'd had enough foresight to put a condom in his jacket pocket that morning, perhaps anticipating a moment such as this. He shuddered at the thought of what he might have done if he hadn't.

Alex held her close, not wanting to let her go. But he really had to. Time was moving on.

Slowly, gently, he eased out of her, then headed for the bathroom. What he saw there brought a groan of dismay to his lips. Talk about life being cruel. After flushing the toilet, he adjusted his clothes, washed his hands and walked slowly back into the bedroom. Harriet was sitting on the side of the bed, looking slightly dishevelled.

'What is it?' she asked straight away on seeing worry stamped on his face.

'I hate having to tell you this,' he said, his heart sinking, 'but the condom broke.'

'Oh,' she said, then just sat there, silent and thoughtful. 'Is it a dangerous time of the month for you?'

CHAPTER TWENTY-THREE

HARRIET DIDN'T HAVE to think too long to know that it was. Extremely dangerous.

Her first reaction to the possibility of falling pregnant by Alex was despair. If it had been anyone else, she might have had a chance of being happy about having a baby. She'd always wanted to be a mother by the time she was thirty. But she knew having a child would be the last thing *he* wanted.

It took a while for Harriet to see the situation with a calmer mind, but she eventually came to a decision. If she had been unlucky enough to fall pregnant—or lucky enough, depending on how you looked at it—then the problem would be hers.

Finally, she looked up. 'I won't lie to you,' she said. 'There is a chance that I might fall pregnant. It's close to the middle of my cycle. But I also might not. Pregnancies don't always happen, even when people are trying to have a baby. We'll just have to wait and see.' She'd already decided not to tell him if she did. Still, whether she did or not, she was going to resign. She simply could not go on having wildly passionate sex with Alex and pretending it was just lust. She loved the man. But if she told him so, he would dump her cold. Even if it turned out that she wasn't pregnant, how could she continue to work for him under such circumstances? It had all become impossible. Going to Venice with him was impossible, too.

She smothered a sigh and made the hardest decision of her life.

'I'm sorry, Alex, but I can't go to Venice with you. Not now. I just want to go home.'

'But there's no need to do that. We could go buy you one of those morning-after pills. Then you won't have to worry.'

You mean you *won't have to worry*, Harriet thought unhappily. Still, she supposed it was a sensible suggestion and one which she hadn't thought of. Silly, really. It would solve the problem. Though not *all* of her problems.

'I still want to go home, Alex,' she said, the stark reality of their affair having finally sunk in. She simply could not go on pretending that she didn't love him; that all she cared about was fun and games. 'Look, I'll buy a morning-after pill at the airport. They always have pharmacies at airports. Then neither of us will have to worry. Now, please...just take me home.'

He stared at her for a long moment. 'All right,' he finally said, and Harriet let out a huge sigh of relief.

When they arrived at the airport, Harriet found a pharmacy and asked for the morning-after pill. But, as it turned out, the rules in Italy were different from some other parts of the world. You couldn't just buy one over the counter; you had to have a doctor's prescription to get the pill. She was told that the public health clinic in Milan would give her a prescription, but it wouldn't be open till the following morning, and there was often a several-hours wait to be seen.

Harriet decided fate was telling her something and they boarded their flight without said pill.

'But what if you *are* pregnant?' Alex asked, face grim.

'I'll cross that bridge when I come to it. But you don't have to worry, Alex. If I am pregnant, then I'll take care of it.'

'What do you mean by that?'

'I mean I'll take care of it,' she snapped. 'Now, if you don't mind, I don't want to talk about it any more.'

CHAPTER TWENTY-FOUR

ALEX WENT TO work extra early that Monday morning, mostly because he'd been awake for hours. Sleep had been elusive during the two and a half weeks since his return from Italy, something he wasn't used to. It had been especially elusive last night, knowing that Harriet had made a doctor's appointment for first thing this morning to find out if she was pregnant. She'd refused to use one of the home testing kits you can buy over the counter—despite being a few days late—claiming they weren't always accurate and she needed to be sure. She'd also refused to do other things, like talk to him more than strictly necessary. She wouldn't even have coffee with him.

The past two weeks at work had been sheer hell.

The moment Alex let himself into the office, the cat sauntered over to him, purring as he wound himself around his ankles.

'At least you still love me,' Alex muttered.

Not that Harriet had ever loved him. But she had liked him. And desired him. Now she couldn't seem to stand the sight of him, which really wasn't fair, in Alex's humble opinion. It wasn't *his* fault that the damned condom broke.

'Come on, Romany,' he said with a weary sigh. 'Let's go get you some food.'

That done, he made himself a mug of black coffee before taking it into his office and slumping down behind his desk. As he sat there, sipping slowly, he tried to work out exactly why Harriet was so angry with him. And she was. She tried to hide her antagonism towards him, but it had been there, in her body language, right from the time they'd had the disastrous news about the morning-after pill. Harriet had even looked perversely pleased when he'd informed her that the only seats left on the first available flight home were first class. Alex had soon twigged that this was because she would have her own space and not have to sit next to him. Or talk to him. From the moment they'd arrived back, she'd cut him dead, saying it was over between them and taking a taxi home.

Every day since, Alex had tried to work out what he would do and how he would feel if she *was* pregnant.

Clearly, Harriet had no intention of keeping the baby if she was. Her savage 'I'll take care of it' had indicated exactly what she would do. Alex knew that if he'd accidentally impregnated any other girl he'd been involved with over the years, he would not have objected to this course of action.

But you didn't love any of those girls. You love Harriet, he accepted at long last. *If she is going to have your baby, you will want her to keep it.*

Shock at this astonishing realisation propelled Alex forward in his chair, some coffee sloshing onto his tie and shirt front. Swearing, he banged the mug down on his desk and stood up, reefing his clothes off before the coffee burned his skin. Fortunately, there was a brand-new shirt and tie in the bottom drawer of his desk, courtesy of his brilliant PA, who thought of every eventuality before it had even happened.

What in God's name would he do without her? Alex's heart lurched at the very real possibility that Harriet would soon exit from his life altogether. She hadn't said anything yet, but he could *feel* it. She meant to move on, and there was absolutely nothing he could do to stop her. As time ticked away, he began to hope that she *wasn't* pregnant. Maybe then things might settle back to normal.

Not a very logical thought.

The next two and a half hours were agony. He couldn't think about work. Instead, he tried filling in the time till Harriet arrived by ringing his father and then Sarah. His father didn't want to talk. He was off to his morning exercise class, his perky voice actually irritating Alex, which was perverse. Sarah couldn't talk, either. She had to drive the kids to school, then go on to work, saying she would talk to him later. He contemplated calling Jeremy and confiding the situation to him. But it would be the middle of the night in London and no doubt Jeremy would not be alone.

In the end, Alex wandered downstairs into the café where he'd taken Harriet that fateful day not all that long ago. After ordering a bagel and another coffee, he sat down at the same table and stared through the window at the passing parade whilst his inner tension escalated to a level he'd never experienced before. By the time a pale-faced Harriet showed up for work shortly before eleven, Alex's temples were pounding and his shoulder blades ached.

At least she didn't keep him waiting. She came straight into his office, stood in front of his desk and said bluntly, 'I'm not pregnant. So you can breathe easier now.'

He actually did let out a huge breath, having found that his heartbeat had been temporarily suspended. He could not help but notice that she noticed, a small, rueful smile on her lips.

'The doctor said I'm late because I'm stressed,' she went on before he could say a single word. 'Which leads me to my next announcement. I'm resigning. Right now. I can't work for you any more, Alex. I'm sorry to leave you in the lurch like this, but you can get a temp till you can fill my position permanently. There are plenty of good agencies who specialise in excellent temps. I seem to recall you were working with a temp before you found me, so you'll know what to do. I'd take Romany with me, but animals still aren't allowed in my building. Besides, he'd miss this place now. It's his home. I'll ask Audrey to keep an extra eye on him on my way out.

'It's been a pleasure working for you, Alex,' she finished up while he just sat there, pole-axed. 'Up till recently, that is. Still, what happened was as much my fault as yours. You didn't force me to sleep with you, or do any of the other things we did together. As for a reference, I'm sure that when asked you will give me a good one. You might be a selfish man, but you're not a vindictive one. Goodbye, Alex. No, please don't say anything. I've made up my mind and you won't change it.'

So saying, she whirled and was gone, Alex staring at the empty doorway without moving a muscle till Audrey stormed in a couple of minutes later, looking outraged.

'Harriet's just left,' she informed him unnecessarily. 'She told me she'd quit, but she wouldn't tell me why. As if I can't guess!'

Alex suppressed a sigh as he snapped forward on his chair and adopted his firm 'boss face'. 'Why Harriet resigned is none of your business, Audrey. Please go back to Reception.'

'I always thought you were heartless where women

were concerned,' she spat at him. 'I just didn't realise how heartless. That girl's fallen in love with you. That's why she's quit. Blind Freddie could see how unhappy she's been these last couple of weeks. It's you! You seduced her that Friday you took her away with you, didn't you?'

'I did not seduce Harriet and she's not in love with me,' he stated, trying not to sound as shaken as he felt. 'So please don't go saying any of that to the others.'

'I wouldn't be bothered. But, just so you know in advance, I'll be looking around for another job. Even if you didn't do anything wrong with her, I don't want to work for a man who'd let a fantastic girl like Harriet just walk out without fighting to keep her. Don't you care how upset she is?'

'Of course I care. But she can be very stubborn.'

'But if she's not in love with you, then why did she leave?'

'I don't know, Audrey. Maybe it has something to do with her break-up with Dwayne. Maybe she just needs a change.'

'But she *loved* working for you.'

Alex was as close to weeping as he'd been in decades. 'Look, I'll give her a call later and see if I can change her mind.' Even as he said the placating words, he knew he wouldn't do any such thing. It was over.

'Go back to work, Audrey,' he said.

After she left, Alex sat there for ages, thinking about everything Audrey had said.

You seduced her. She's in love with you. If she's not in love with you, then why did she leave?

Could he be wrong in assuming she *didn't* love him? If she did love him, it would explain a lot, especially if she thought he didn't love her.

And why *wouldn't* she think that, when he'd gone to

such great lengths to make her understand that he didn't do love and marriage; that any relationship they had was strictly sexual?

God, but he was an idiot!

Jumping up, he pulled on his jacket, grabbed his keys and headed out, telling Audrey as he passed Reception that he was off to get Harriet back.

'Just as well,' she threw after him.

Ten minutes later, Alex was only a block from the office, stuck in traffic.

'Damn!' he swore. He thought about ringing Harriet but decided that wouldn't be good enough. He had to do this face-to-face. There was no option but to wait.

CHAPTER TWENTY-FIVE

HARRIET WAS CURLED up on her sofa, no longer crying but feeling terrible, when there was a knock on her flat door. It was a rather timid knock, so she knew it wasn't Alex come to demand she return to work. Not that he would. Alex wouldn't run after any woman.

Probably a neighbour, needing something.

It was Betty from next door, wanting to borrow an onion. She was a dear old love who found it hard enough to get up and down the stairs, let alone walk to the corner shop just to buy an onion. Harriet was happy to give her one.

'Thanks, pet,' she said. 'I saw you come home earlier. Not feeling well? You do look a little peaky.'

'I had a bad headache,' Harriet invented. 'But it's gone now. In fact, I was just about to go out for a walk along the beach.'

'Wish I could come with you, pet, but these old legs of mine won't cooperate. Thanks for the onion.'

After Betty left, Harriet forced herself to put on leggings, trainers and a light sweater, then set off for a power walk to the beach. Exercise always did her good, as did the sight of the sea. There was something calming about watching the waves roll into shore. Something…spiritual.

The first sight of the blue ocean lifted her spirits.

You will survive this, Harriet, she told herself. *And, just think, soon you'll have a baby to love.* How wonderful was that?

By the time Alex reached Harriet's address he was not a happy man, his frustration increasing when he couldn't find a parking spot in her street for love nor money. In the end, he parked in someone's driveway, knocked on their door and gave the startled woman a hundred dollars to let his SUV stay there for a couple of hours. Alex figured he might need a couple of hours to convince Harriet that he really, truly loved her. Lord knew what he was going to do if she didn't love him back and didn't give a damn.

It wasn't like Alex to entertain negative thinking, but it wasn't every day that he fell in love. He understood now why he'd been afraid of it. Because he had known, subconsciously, that when and if he fell in love it would be very deeply. Not to have his love returned would shatter him.

His tension increased as he hurried up the stairs of Harriet's block of flats, his heart pounding along with his feet. When he knocked loudly on her door, the sound echoed through the whole building. When she didn't answer, he knocked again. And again. And again.

A door opened along the way and an elderly lady peeped out. 'If you're looking for Harriet, she's gone for a walk along the beach.'

'Right. Thanks.'

Alex took off in the direction of nearby Bondi Beach, his long legs bringing him there in less than a minute. Thankfully, the beach wasn't all that crowded. He searched along the wide stretch of sand but didn't see her. And then she came into view, walking briskly along the promenade towards where he was standing in front of the Pavilion. She stopped as soon as she saw him, her body language not good. Her chin came up, her hands curling into fists by her sides. He couldn't see the expression in her eyes, as she was wearing sunglasses. But he got the impression of barely controlled anger and heaps of exasperation.

In the end, she covered the few metres which separated them, her hands finding her hips as she planted herself right in front of him.

'What are you doing here?' she bit out.

'I went to your flat, but you weren't there. Your neighbour told me where to find you.'

'That's not what I asked you. Look, you're wasting your time, Alex. I'm not coming back to work for you and that's that!'

'I haven't come to talk to you about work,' he returned in what he hoped was a calm voice. *Someone* had to be calm. Still, he took the level of her ongoing anger as a positive sign. She really didn't have that much reason to be angry with him. Not unless her emotions were involved.

'Neither am I going to keep sleeping with you!' she said in a voice loud enough to have passers-by stare over at them.

'Could we possibly have this discussion in private, Harry? I don't appreciate your telling the world about our personal business.'

At least she had the good grace to blush.

'Come on,' he said, taking her elbow and leading her away from several curious onlookers. 'We'll go back to your place and have things out there.'

'There are no things to have out,' she muttered.

'I beg to differ. We have lots of things to have out,

mostly concerning your misconception about my feelings for you.'

Her laugh was wry and bitter. 'I was *never* in any doubt over your feelings for me, Alex.'

'You could be wrong, you know.'

Harriet knew she wasn't wrong. The only reason Alex had come after her was because he didn't like being left in the lurch, either in his office or in his bed.

'If you think you can seduce me again, then you have another think coming.'

'I never seduced you in the first place, Harry. You came to my bed willingly.'

'You know what I mean. You engineered our being alone together so it would be harder for me to resist you.'

'I plead guilty to that one.'

Wrenching her arm out of his hold, she hurried ahead of him, not saying another word till she was standing by her front door fumbling with her keys.

'You can come in,' she threw over her shoulder at him. 'But not for long. It won't take long anyway, because there's nothing you can possibly say to make me change my mind on this. We're over, Alex. As hard as it might be for a man of your ego, I suggest you learn to take no for an answer.'

'Hell, but you don't make things easy on a man, do you?' he ground out as he strode after her into her living room. 'I almost pity poor old Dwayne.'

'I suggest you leave Dwayne out of this,' she snapped, banging the door after him and tossing her sunglasses onto the hall table. 'Now, just get on with what you have to say.'

'Okay, I will. The thing is, Harriet, that I love you.

Sorry if that's not the most romantic of declarations, but it's hard to be romantic when you're this angry.'

Harriet would wonder afterwards if she looked as shocked as she felt. All she could remember in hindsight was that her heart stopped beating and her body seemed to freeze on the spot. Nothing worked. Not her brain, her tongue or anything.

He started pacing, throwing snatches of words at her as he circumnavigated the room with long, angry strides.

'I know I said I didn't do love… And I don't…or I didn't… Till you came along. You changed everything… Loving you changed everything…'

He finally ground to a halt in front of her again, his handsome face all flushed and frustrated.

'I love you, Harriet. And I want to marry you. I even want to have babies with you, which believe me is such an astonishing concept that it took me a while to get my head around it. But once I did, I saw that it could be wonderful. You'd make a marvellous mother. When you told me this morning that you weren't pregnant, I actually felt disappointed. But I could hardly tell you that because at the time I thought you didn't love me back. But then Audrey stormed in and told me that you probably did. So then I got to thinking that maybe you did love me, that that was the reason for your anger. But now that I'm here, I'm not so sure.'

He took abrupt hold of her shoulders and dragged her close. 'Tell me that I'm not wrong, Harry,' he demanded in a passionate voice which fairly vibrated through the air. 'Tell me that you love me, because if you don't, I don't know what I'll do.'

Harriet's eyes swam with the impact of his declaration. He loved her. Alex loved her. He even wanted to marry her and have babies with her. Oh, God…

'Please don't cry,' he said, then gathered her to him. 'Just tell me that you love me.'

'I love you,' she choked out against his throat. 'Oh, Alex...'

His heart almost burst with happiness and relief. She loved him. She really loved him.

'And you'll marry me, even if I don't tick your check-boxes for a husband?'

'You tick the most important ones. But, Alex...'

His heart tightened at the sudden wariness in her voice. Holding her at arm's length, he looked deep into her still-teary eyes. 'What is it? What's wrong?'

'Nothing. I hope... It's just that I...I never imagined that you loved me. You were always so adamant that our relationship was about nothing but fun and sex. I honestly believed that if I was pregnant you'd try to talk me into having a termination. So I lied to you this morning. I lied and I...I'm sorry...'

His shock was evident. But it was quickly followed by delight. 'So you *are* pregnant?'

She nodded, still looking slightly guilty. 'I thought I was doing the right thing at the time.'

'I can understand that. So you were planning on raising our child all alone, were you?'

'I...I might have told you about it when it was too late for a termination.'

'I sincerely hope so. Still, you're going to *have* to marry me now,' he said, smiling.

'If you insist.'

'I insist.'

He kissed her then, the kissing leading to more than kissing. Lots more. Finally, they moved into her bedroom.

Afterwards, Harriet snuggled into Alex's arms, happier than she'd ever been in her life.

'I can't believe that you love me,' she murmured.

'Fishing for compliments, Harry?' he said softly and kissed the top of her head.

'Not really. But feel free to give them, if you like.'

He laughed. 'In that case, be assured that I love everything about you, including your obsessive sense of independence.'

'I'm not that bad. Surely?'

'You don't think it obsessively independent to not tell the father of your child that you're pregnant?'

'I would have told you. In the end.'

'I hope so. So when are we getting married?'

'Not too soon. I don't want a rushed wedding, Alex. How about we have the wedding in that little chapel you're building up at the golf resort?' she suggested, thinking it would be romantic to marry near where they'd first got together.

'But that won't be finished for months!' he protested.

'Does it matter?'

'Would you live with me in the meantime?'

'Of course. But I won't be selling this flat. It can be the beginning of my property portfolio.'

'Done!' he said. 'What about work? Will you come back to work for me?'

'I don't see why not.'

'Thank God for that. If you don't, I would never be able to show my face around there ever again. Audrey called me heartless. She even threatened to get another job. The only one who loves me there is Romany.'

'Don't be silly. Everyone there loves you. You're a great boss.'

'I don't care about everyone else. Just about you.'

'Oh, Alex…' The tears came hard and fast then, tears of happiness and relief, all the emotion and tension Harriet had been bottling up over the past month finally set free.

Alex drew her close, his heart squeezing tight at the thought that he might have lost her today. Lost her *and* his child. It had been a close call. Too close for comfort. Never again, he vowed, would he let her doubt his love for her. Never, ever again. And, as he held her even closer, he felt sure that his mother would be pleased that he'd finally found true love with a wonderful girl like Harriet. Being a philanthropist was all very well, but being a good husband and father was just as important.

'By the way,' he whispered into her hair. 'After the wedding, I'm taking you to Venice for our honeymoon.'

* * * * *

CIPRIANI'S INNOCENT CAPTIVE

CATHY WILLIAMS

CHAPTER ONE

'MR CIPRIANI IS ready for you now.'

Katy Brennan looked up at the middle-aged, angular woman who had earlier met her in the foyer of Cipriani Head Office and ushered her to the directors' floor, where she had now been waiting for over twenty minutes.

She didn't want to feel nervous but she did. She had been summoned from her office in Shoreditch, where she worked as an IT specialist in a small team of four, and informed that Lucas Cipriani, the ultimate god to whom everyone answered, requested her presence.

She had no idea why he might want to talk to her, but she suspected that it concerned the complex job she was currently working on and, whilst she told herself that he probably only wanted to go through some of the finer details with her, she was still...*nervous*.

Katy stood up, wishing that she had had some kind of advance warning of this meeting, because if she had she would have dressed in something more in keeping with the über-plush surroundings in which she now found herself.

As it was, she was in her usual casual uniform of jeans and a tee-shirt, with her backpack and a light-

weight bomber jacket, perfect for the cool spring
weather, but utterly inappropriate for this high-tech,
eight-storey glasshouse.

She took a deep breath and looked neither left
nor right as she followed his PA along the carpeted
corridor, past the hushed offices of executives and
the many boardrooms where deals worth millions
were closed, until the corridor ballooned out into a
seating area. At the back of this was a closed eight-
foot wooden door which was enough to send a chill
through any person who had been arbitrarily summoned by the head of her company—a man whose
ability to make deals and turn straw into gold was
legendary.

Katy took a deep breath and stood back as his PA
pushed open the door.

Staring absently through the floor-to-ceiling pane of
reinforced glass that separated him from the streets
below, Lucas Cipriani thought that this meeting was
the last thing he needed to kick off the day.

But it could not be avoided. Security had been
breached on the deal he had been working on for the
past eight months, and this woman was going to have
to take the consequences—pure and simple.

This was the deal of a lifetime and there was no
way he was going to allow it to be jeopardised.

As his PA knocked and entered his office, Lucas
slowly turned round, hand in trouser pocket, and
looked at the woman whose job was a thing of the
past, if only she knew it.

Eyes narrowed, it hit him that he really should
catch up on the people who actually worked for him,

because he hadn't expected this. He'd expected a nerd with heavy spectacles and an earnest manner, whilst the girl in front of him looked less like a computer whizz-kid and more like a hippy. Her clothes were generic: faded jeans and a tee-shirt with the name of a band he had never heard of. Her shoes were masculine black boots, suitable for heavy-duty construction work. She had a backpack slung over her shoulder, and stuffed into the top of it was some kind of jacket, which she had clearly just removed. Her entire dress code contradicted every single thing he associated with a woman, but she had the sort of multi-coloured coppery hair that would have had artists queuing up to commit it to canvas, and an elfin face with enormous bright-green eyes that held his gaze for reasons he couldn't begin to fathom.

'Miss Brennan.' He strolled towards his desk as Vicky, his secretary, clicked the heavy door to his office shut behind her. 'Sit, please.'

At the sound of that deep, dark, velvety voice, Katy started and realised that she had been holding her breath. When she had entered the office she'd thought that she more or less knew what to expect. She vaguely knew what her boss looked like because she had seen pictures of him in the company magazines that occasionally landed on her desk in Shoreditch, far away from the cutting-edge glass building that housed the great and the good in the company: from Lucas Cipriani, who sat at the very top like a god atop Mount Olympus, to his team of powerful executives who made sure that his empire ran without a hitch.

Those were people whose names appeared on letterheads and whose voices were occasionally heard down the end of phone lines, but who were never, ever seen. At least, not in Shoreditch, which was reserved for the small cogs in the machine.

But she still hadn't expected *this*. Lucas Cipriani was, simply put, beautiful. There was no other word to describe him. It wasn't just the arrangement of perfect features, or the burnished bronze of his skin, or even the dramatic masculinity of his physique: Lucas Cipriani's good looks went far beyond the physical. He exuded a certain power and charisma that made the breath catch in your throat and scrambled your ability to think in straight lines.

Which was why Katy was here now, in his office, drawing a blank where her thoughts should be and with her mouth so dry that she wouldn't have been able to say a word if she'd wanted to.

She vaguely recalled him saying something about sitting down, which she badly wanted to do, and she shuffled her way to the enormous leather chair that faced his desk and sank into it with some relief.

'You've been working on the Chinese deal,' Lucas stated without preamble.

'Yes.' She could talk about work, she could answer any question he might have, but she was unsettled by a dark, brooding, in-your-face sensuality she hadn't expected, and when she spoke her voice was jerky and nervous. 'I've been working on the legal side of the deal, dedicating all the details to a programme that will enable instant access to whatever is required, without having to sift through reams of documentation. I hope there isn't a problem. I'm running ahead of schedule, in actual fact. I'll be honest with you,

Mr Cipriani, it's one of the most exciting projects I've ever worked on. Complex, but really challenging.'

She cleared her throat and hazarded a smile, which was met with stony silence, and her already frayed nerves took a further battering. Stunning dark eyes, fringed with inky black, luxuriant lashes, pierced through the thin veneer of her self-confidence, leaving her breathless and red-faced.

Lucas positioned himself at his desk, an enormous chrome-and-glass affair that housed a computer with an over-sized screen, a metallic lamp and a small, very artfully designed bank of clocks that made sure he knew, at any given moment, what time it was in all the major cities in which his companies were located.

He lowered his eyes now and, saying nothing, swivelled his computer so that it was facing her.

'Recognise that man?'

Katy blanched. Her mouth fell open as she found herself staring at Duncan Powell, the guy she had fallen for three years previously. Floppy blond hair, blue eyes that crinkled when he grinned and boyish charm had combined to hook an innocent young girl barely out of her teens.

She had not expected this. Not in a million years. Confused, flustered and with a thousand alarm bells suddenly ringing in her head, Katy fixed bewildered green eyes on Lucas.

'I don't understand...'

'I'm not asking you to understand. I'm asking you whether you know this man.'

'Y-yes,' she stammered. 'I... Well, I knew him a few years ago...'

'And it would seem that you bypassed certain security systems and discovered that he is, these days, employed by the Chinese company I am in the process of finalising a deal with. Correct? No, don't bother answering that. I have a series of alerts on my computer and what I'm saying does not require verification.'

She felt dazed. Katy's thoughts had zoomed back in time to her disastrous relationship with Duncan.

She'd met him shortly after she had returned home to her parents' house in Yorkshire. Torn between staying where she was and facing the big, brave world of London, where the lights were bright and the job prospects were decidedly better, she had taken up a temporary post as an assistant teacher at one of the local schools to give herself some thinking time and to plan a strategy.

Duncan had worked at the bank on the high street, a stone's throw from the primary school.

In fairness, it had not been love at first sight. She had always liked a quirky guy; Duncan had been just the opposite. A snappy dresser, he had homed in on her with the single-minded focus of a heat-seeking missile with a pre-set target. Before she'd even decided whether she liked him or not, they had had coffee, then a meal, and then they were going out.

He'd been persistent and funny, and she'd started rethinking her London agenda when the whole thing had fallen apart because she'd discovered that the man who had stolen her heart wasn't the honest, sincere, single guy he had made himself out to be.

Nor had he even been a permanent resident in the little village where her parents lived. He'd been there on a one-year secondment, which was a minor detail he had cleverly kept under wraps. He had a wife and twin daughters keeping the fires warm in the house in Milton Keynes he shared with them.

She had been a diversion and, once she had discovered the truth about him, he had shrugged and held his hands up in rueful surrender and she had known, in a flash of pure gut instinct, that he had done that because she had refused to sleep with him. Duncan Powell had planned to have fun on his year out and, whilst he had been content to chase her for a few months, he hadn't been prepared to take the chase to a church and up an aisle, because he had been a fully committed family man.

'I don't understand.' Katy looked away from the reminder of her steep learning curve staring out at her from Lucas's computer screen. 'So Duncan works for their company. I honestly didn't go hunting for that information.' Although, she *had* done some basic background checks, just out of sheer curiosity, to see whether it was the same creep once she'd stumbled upon him. A couple of clicks of a button was all it had taken to confirm her suspicion.

Lucas leaned forward, his body language darkly, dangerously menacing. 'That's as may be,' he told her, 'but it does present certain problems.'

With cool, clear precision he presented those *certain problems* to her and she listened to him in ever-increasing alarm. A deal done in complete secrecy...a family company rooted in strong values of tradition... a variable stock market that hinged on nothing being leaked and the threat her connection to Duncan posed at a delicate time in the negotiations.

Katy was brilliant with computers, but the mysteries of high finance were lost on her. The race for money had never interested her. From an early age, her parents had impressed upon her the importance of recognising value in the things that money couldn't buy. Her father was a parish priest and both her parents lived a life that was rooted in the fundamental importance of putting the needs of other people first. Katy didn't care who earned what or how much money anyone had. She had been brought up with a different set of values. For better or for worse, she occasionally thought.

'I don't care about any of that,' she said unevenly, when there was a brief lull in his cold tabulation of her transgressions. It seemed a good moment to set him straight because she was beginning to have a nasty feeling that he was circling her like a predator, preparing to attack.

Was he going to sack her? She would survive. The bottom line was that that was the very worst he could do. He wasn't some kind of mediaeval war lord who could have her hung, drawn and quartered because she'd disobeyed him.

'Whether you care about a deal that isn't going to impact on you or not is immaterial. Either by design or incompetence, you're now in possession of information that could unravel nearly a year and a half of intense negotiation.'

'To start with, I'm obviously very sorry about what happened. It's been a very complex job and, if I accidentally happened upon information I shouldn't have, then I apologise. I didn't mean to. In fact, I'm not at all interested in your deal, Mr Cipriani. You gave me a job to do and I was doing it to the best of my ability.'

'Which clearly wasn't up to the promised standard, because an error of the magnitude of the one you made is inexcusable.'

'But that's not fair!'

'Remind me to give you a life lesson about what's fair and what isn't. I'm not interested in your excuses, Miss Brennan. I'm interested in working out a solution to bypass the headache you created.'

Katy's mind had stung at his criticism of her ability. She was good at what she did. Brilliant, even. To have her competence called into question attacked the very heart of her.

'If you look at the quality of what I've done, sir, you'll find that I've done an excellent job. I realise that I may have stumbled upon information that should have not been available to me, but you have my word that anything I've uncovered stays right here with me.'

'And I'm to believe you because…?'

'Because I'm telling you the truth!'

'I'm sorry to drag you into the world of reality, Miss Brennan, but taking things at face value, including other people's *sincerely meant promises*, is something I don't do.' He leaned back into his chair and looked at her.

Without trying, Lucas was capable of exuding the sort of lethal cool that made grown men quake in their shoes. A chit of a girl who was destined for the scrapheap should have been a breeze but for some reason he was finding some of his formidable focus diluted by her arresting good looks.

He went for tall, career-driven brunettes who were rarely seen without their armour of high-end designer suits and killer heels. He enjoyed the back and forth of intellectual repartee and had oftentimes found himself embroiled in heated debates about work-related issues.

His women knew the difference between a bear market and a bull market and would have sneered at anyone who didn't.

They were alpha females and that was the way he liked it.

He had seen the damage caused to rich men by airheads and bimbos. His fun-loving, amiable father had had ten good years of marriage to Lucas's mother and then, when Annabel Cipriani had died, he had promptly lost himself in a succession of stunningly sexy blondes, intelligence not a prerequisite.

He had been taken to the cleaners three times and it was a miracle that any family money, of which there had been a considerable sum at the starting block, had been left in the coffers.

But far worse than the nuisance of having his bank accounts bled by rapacious gold-diggers was the *hope* his father stupidly had always invested in the women he ended up marrying. Hope that they would be there for him, would somehow give him the emotional support he had had with his first wife. He had been looking for love and that weakness had opened him up to being used over and over again.

Lucas had absorbed all this from the side lines and had learned the necessary lessons: avoid emotional investment and you'd never end up getting hurt. Indeed, bimbos he could handle, though they repulsed him. At least they were a known quantity. What he really didn't do were women who demanded anything from him he knew he was incapable of giving, which was why he always went for women as emotionally and financially independent as him. They obeyed the same rules that he did and were as dismissive of emotional, overblown scenes as he was.

The fact was that, if you didn't let anyone in, then you were protected from disappointment, and not just the superficial disappointment of discovering that some replaceable woman was more interested in your bank account than she was in *you*.

He had learned more valuable lessons about the sort of weaknesses that could permanently scar and so he had locked his heart away and thrown away the key and, in truth, he had never had a moment's doubt that he had done the right thing.

'Are you still in contact with the man?' he murmured, watching her like a hawk.

'No! I am *not*!' Heated colour made her face burn. She found that she was gripping the arms of the chair for dear life, her whole body rigid with affront that he would even ask her such a personal question. 'Are you going to sack me, Mr Cipriani? Because, if you are, then perhaps you could just get on with it.'

Her temples were beginning to throb painfully. Of course she was going to be sacked. This wasn't going to be a ticking off before being dismissed back to Shoreditch to resume her duties as normal, nor was she simply going to be removed from the task at which inadvertently she had blundered.

She had been hauled in here like a common criminal so that she could be fired. No one-month's notice, no final warning, and there was no way that she could even consider a plea of unfair dismissal. She would be left without her main source of income and that was something she would just have to deal with.

And the guy sitting in front of her having fun being judge, jury and executioner didn't give a hoot as to whether she was telling the truth or not, or whether her life would be affected by an abrupt sacking or not.

'Regrettably, it's not quite so straightforward—'

'Why not?' Katy interrupted feverishly. 'You obviously don't believe a word I've told you and I know I certainly wouldn't be allowed anywhere near the project again. If you just wanted me off it, you would have probably told Tim, my manager, and let him pass the message on to me. The fact that I've been summoned here tells me that you're going to give me the boot, but not before you make sure I know why. Will you at the very least give me a reference, Mr Cipriani? I've worked extremely hard for your company for the past year and a half and I've had nothing but glowing reports on the work I've done. I think I deserve some credit for that.'

Lucas marvelled that she could think, for a minute, that he had so much time on his hands that he would personally call her in just to sack her. She was looking at him with an urgent expression, her green eyes defiant.

Again distracted, he found himself saying, 'I noticed on your file that you only work two days a week for my company. Why is that?'

'Sorry?' Katy's eyes narrowed suspiciously.

'It's unusual for someone of your age to be a part-time employee. That's generally the domain of women with children of school age who want to earn a little money but can't afford the demands of a full-time job.'

'I… I have another job,' she admitted, wondering where this was heading and whether she needed to be on her guard. 'I work as an IT teacher at one of the secondary schools near where I live.'

Lucas was reluctantly fascinated by the ebb and flow of colour that stained her cheeks. Her face was as transparent as glass and that in itself was an unusual enough quality to hold his attention. The tough career women he dated knew how to school their expressions because, the higher up the ladder they climbed, the faster they learned that blushing like virginal maidens did nothing when it came to career advancement.

'Can't pay well,' he murmured.

'That's not the point!'

Lucas had turned his attention to his computer and was very quickly pulling up the file he had on her, which he had only briefly scanned before he had scheduled his meeting with her. The list of favourable references was impressively long.

'So,' he mused, sitting back and giving her his undivided attention. 'You work for me for the pay and you work as a teacher for the enjoyment.'

'That's right.' She was disconcerted at how quickly he had reached the right conclusions.

'So the loss of your job at my company would presumably have a serious impact on your finances.'

'I would find another job to take its place.'

'Look around the market, Miss Brennan. Well paid part-time work is thin on the ground. I make it my duty to pay my employees over the odds. I find that tends to engender commitment and loyalty to the company. You'd be hard pressed to find the equivalent anywhere in London.'

Lucas had planned on a simple solution to this unexpected problem. Now, he was pressed to find out a bit more about her. As a part-time worker, it seemed she contributed beyond the call of duty, and both the people she answered to within the company and external clients couldn't praise her enough. She'd pleaded her innocence, and he wasn't gullible enough to wipe the slate clean, but a more detailed hearing might be in order. His initial impressions weren't of a thief who might be attracted to the lure of insider trading but, on the other hand, someone with a part-time job might find it irresistible to take advantage of an unexpected opportunity, and Duncan Powell represented that unexpected opportunity.

'Money doesn't mean that much to me, Mr Cipriani.' Katy was confused as to how a man whose values were so different from hers could make her go hot and cold and draw her attention in a way that left her feeling helpless and exposed. She was finding it hard to string simple sentences together. 'I have a place to myself but, if I had to share with other people, then it wouldn't be the end of the world.'

The thought of sharing space with a bunch of strangers was only slightly less appalling to Lucas than incarceration with the key thrown away.

Besides, how much did she mean that? he wondered with grim practicality, dark eyes drifting over her full, stubborn mouth and challenging angle of her head. What had been behind that situation with Powell, a married man? It wasn't often that Lucas found himself questioning his own judgements but in this instance he did wonder whether it was just a simple tale of a woman who had been prepared to overlook the fact that her lover was a married man because of the financial benefits he could bring to the table. Although, he'd seen enough of that to know that it was the oldest story in the world.

Maybe he would test the waters and see what came out in the wash. If this had been a case of hire and fire, then she would have been clearing out her desk eighteen hours ago, but it wasn't, because he couldn't sack her just yet, and it paid to know your quarry. He would not allow any misjudgements to wreck his deal.

'You never thought about packing in the teaching and taking up the job at my company full time?'

'No.' The silence stretched between them while Katy frantically tried to work out where this sudden interest was leading. 'Some people aren't motivated by money.' She finally broke the silence because she was beginning to perspire with discomfort. 'I wasn't raised to put any value on material things.'

'Interesting. Unique.'

'Maybe in *your* world, Mr Cipriani.'

'Money, Miss Brennan, is the engine that makes everything go, and not just in my world. In everyone's world. The best things in life are not, as rumour would have it, free.'

'Maybe not for you,' Katy said with frank disapproval. She knew that she was treading on thin ice. She sensed that Lucas Cipriani was not a man who enjoyed other people airing too many contradictory opinions. He'd hauled her in to sack her and was now subjecting her to the Spanish Inquisition because he was cold, arrogant and because *he could*.

But what was the point of tiptoeing around him when she was on her way out for a crime she hadn't committed?

'That's why you don't believe what I'm saying,'

she expanded. 'That's why you don't trust me. You probably don't trust anyone, which is sad, when you think about it. I'd hate to go through life never knowing my friends from my enemies. When your whole world is about money, then you lose sight of the things that really matter.'

Lucas's lips thinned disapprovingly at her directness. She was right when she said that he didn't trust anyone but that was exactly the way he liked it.

'Let me be perfectly clear with you, Miss Brennan.' He leaned forward and looked at her coolly. 'You haven't been brought here for a candid exchange of views. I appreciate you are probably tense and nervous, which is doubtless why you're cavalier about overstepping the mark, but I suggest it's time to get down from your moral high ground and take a long, hard look at the choices you have made that have landed you in my office.'

Katy flushed. 'I made a mistake with Duncan,' she muttered. 'We all make mistakes.'

'You slept with a married man,' Lucas corrected her bluntly, startling her with the revelation that he'd discovered what he clearly thought was the whole, shameful truth. 'So, while you're waxing lyrical about my tragic, money-orientated life, you might want to consider that, whatever the extent of my greed and arrogance, I would no more sleep with a married woman than I would jump into the ocean with anchors secured to my feet.'

'I...'

Lucas held up one hand. 'No one speaks to me the way you do.' He felt a twinge of discomfort because that one sentence seemed to prove the arrogance of which he had been accused. Since when had he become so *pompous*? He scowled. 'I've done the maths, Miss Brennan and, however much you look at me with those big, green eyes, I should tell you that taking the word of an adulterer is something of a tall order.'

Buffeted by Lucas's freezing contempt and outrageous accusations, Katy rose on shaky legs to direct the full force of her anger at him.

'How *dare you*?' But even in the midst of her anger she was swamped by the oddest sensation of vulnerability as his dark eyes swept coolly over her, electrifying every inch of her heated body.

'With remarkable ease.' Lucas didn't bat an eyelid. 'I'm staring the facts in the face and the facts are telling me a very clear story. You want me to believe that you have nothing to do with the man. Unfortunately, your lack of principles in having anything to do with him in the first place tells a tale of its own.'

The colour had drained away from her face. She hated this man. She didn't think it would be possible to hate anyone more.

'I don't have to stay here and listen to this.' But uneasily she was aware that, without her laying bare her sex life, understandably he would have jumped to the wrong conclusions. Without her confession that she had never slept with Duncan, he would have assumed the obvious. Girls her age had flings and slept with men. Maybe he would be persuaded into believing her if she told him the truth, which was that she had ended their brief relationship as soon as she had found out about his wife and kids. But even if he believed that he certainly wouldn't believe that she hadn't *slept* with the man.

Which would lead to a whole other conversation and it was one she had no intention of having. How would a man like Lucas Cipriani believe that the hussy who slept with married guys was in fact a virgin?

Even Katy didn't like thinking about that. She had never had the urge to rush into sex. Her parents hadn't stamped their values on her but the drip, drip, drip of their gentle advice, and the example she had seen on the doorstep of the vicarage of broken-hearted, often pregnant young girls abandoned by men they had fallen for, had made her realise that when it came to love it paid to be careful.

In fairness, had temptation knocked on the door, then perhaps she might have questioned her old-fashioned take on sex but, whilst she had always got along just fine with the opposite sex, no one had ever grabbed her attention until Duncan had come along with his charm, his overblown flattery and his *persistence*. She had been unsure of where her future lay, and in that brief window of uncertainty and apprehension he had burrowed in and stolen her heart. She had been ripe for the picking and his betrayal had been devastating.

Her virginity was a millstone now, a reminder of the biggest mistake she had ever made. Whilst she hoped that one day she would find the guy for her, she was resigned to the possibility that she might never do so, because somehow she was just out of sync with men and what they wanted.

They wanted sex, first and foremost. To get to the prince, you seemed to have to sleep with hundreds of frogs, and there was no way she would do that. The thought that she might have slept with *one* frog was bad enough.

So what would Lucas Cipriani make of her story?

She pictured the sneer on his face and shuddered.

Disturbed at the direction of her thoughts, she tilted her chin and looked at him with equal cool. 'I expect, after all this, I'm being given the sack and that Personnel will be in touch—so there can't be any reason for me to still be here. And you can't stop me leaving. You'll just have to trust me that I won't be saying anything to anyone about your deal.'

CHAPTER TWO

SHE DIDN'T GET FAR.

'You leave this office, Miss Brennan, and regrettably I will have to commence legal proceedings against you on the assumption that you have used insider information to adversely influence the outcome of my company's business dealings.'

Katy stopped and slowly turned to look at him.

His dark eyes were flat, hard and expressionless and he was looking right back at her with just the mildest of interest. His absolute calm was what informed her that he wasn't cracking some kind of sick joke at her expense.

Katy knew a lot about the workings of computers. She could create programs that no one else could and was downright gifted when it came to sorting out the nuts and bolts of intricate problems when those programs began to get a little temperamental. It was why she had been carefully headhunted by Lucas's company and why they'd so willingly accommodated her request for a part-time job only.

In the field of advanced technology, she was reasonably well-known.

She didn't, however, know a thing about law. What

was he going on about? She didn't really understand what he was saying but she understood enough to know that it was a threat.

Lucas watched the colour flood her face. Her skin was satiny smooth and flawless. She had the burnished copper-coloured hair of a redhead, yet her creamy complexion was free of any corresponding freckles. The net result was an unusual, absurdly striking prettiness that was all the more dramatic because she seemed so unaware of it.

But then, his cynical brain told him, she was hardly a shrinking violet with no clue of her pulling power, because she *had* had an affair with a married guy with kids.

He wondered whether she thought that she could turn those wide, emerald-green eyes on him and get away scot-free.

If she did, then she had no idea with whom she was dealing. He'd had a lifetime's worth of training when it came to spotting women who felt that their looks were a passport to getting whatever they wanted. He'd spent his formative years watching them do their numbers on his father. This woman might not be an airhead like them, but she was still driven by the sort of emotionalism he steered well clear of.

'Of course—' he shrugged '—my deal would be blown sky-high out of the water, but have you any idea how much damage you would do to yourself in the process? Litigation is something that takes its time. Naturally, your services would be no longer required at my company and your pay would cease immediately. And then there would be the small question of your legal costs. Considerable.'

Her expression was easy to read and Lucas found that he was enjoying the show.

'That's—that's ridiculous,' Katy stuttered. 'You'd find out that I haven't been in touch with...with Duncan for years. In fact, since we broke up. Plus, you'd *also* find out that I haven't breathed a word about the Chinese deal to...well, to anybody.'

'I only have your word for it. Like I said, discovering whether you're telling the truth or not would take time, and all the while you would naturally be without a penny to your name, defending your reputation against the juggernaut of my company's legal department.'

'I have another job.'

'And we've already established that teaching won't pay the rent. And who knows how willing a school would be to employ someone with a potential criminal record?'

Katy flushed. Bit by bit, he was trapping her in a corner and, with a feeling of surrendering to the inexorable advance of a steamroller, she finally said, 'What do you want me to do?'

Lucas stood up and strolled towards the wall of glass that separated him from the city below, before turning to look at her thoughtfully.

'I told you that this was not a straightforward situation, Miss Brennan. I meant it. It isn't a simple case of throwing you out of my company when you can hurt me with privileged information.' He paced the enormous office, obliging her to follow his progress, and all the time she found herself thinking, *he's almost too beautiful to bear looking at*. He was very tall and very lean, and somehow the finely cut, expensive suit did little to conceal something raw and elemental in his physique.

She had to keep dragging her brain back to what he was telling her. She had to keep frowning so that she could give the appearance of not looking like a complete nitwit. She didn't like the man, but did he have this effect on *all* the women he met?

She wondered what sort of women he met anyway, and then chastised herself for losing the thread when her future was at stake.

'The deal is near completion and a fortnight at most should see a satisfactory conclusion. Now, let's just say that I believe you when you tell me that you haven't been gossiping with your boyfriend...'

'I told you that Duncan and I haven't spoken for years! And, for your information, we broke up because *I found out that he was married.* I'm not the sort of person who would ever dream of going out with a married guy—!'

Lucas stopped her in mid-speech. 'Not interested. All I'm interested in is how this situation is dealt with satisfactorily for me. As far as I am concerned, you could spend all your free time hopping in and out of beds with married men.'

Katy opened her mouth and then thought better of defending herself, because it wasn't going to get her anywhere. He seemed ready to hand down her sentence.

'It is imperative that any sensitive information you may have acquired is not shared, and the only way that that can be achieved is if you are incommunicado to the outside world. Ergo that is how it is going to be for the next fortnight, until my deal is concluded.'

'Sorry, Mr Cipriani, but I'm not following you.'

'Which bit, exactly, Miss Brennan, are you not following?'

'The *fortnight* bit. What are you talking about?'

'It's crystal clear, Miss Brennan. You're not going to be talking to anyone, and I mean *anyone*, for the next two weeks until I have all the signatures right where I want them, at which point you may or may not return to your desk in Shoreditch and we can both forget that this unfortunate business ever happened. Can I get any clearer than that? And by "incommunicado", I mean no mobile phone and no computer. To be blunt, you will be under watch until you can no longer be a danger to me.'

'But you can't be serious!'

'Do I look as though I'm doing a stand-up routine?'

No, he didn't. In fact, without her even realising it, he had been pacing the office in ever decreasing circles and he was now towering right in front of her; the last thing he resembled was a man doing a stand-up routine.

Indeed, he looked about as humorous as an executioner; she quailed inside.

Mentally, she added 'bully' to the growing list of things she loathed about him.

'Under watch? What does that even mean? You can't just…just *kidnap* me for weeks on end because you have a deal to complete! That's a crime!'

'Incendiary words, Miss Brennan.' He leaned over and placed both hands on either side of her chair, caging her in so that she automatically cringed back. The power of his personality was so suffocating that she had to make an effort to remember how to breathe. 'I won't be kidnapping you. Far from it. You can walk out of here, but you know the consequences of that if you do. The simple process of consulting a lawyer would start racking up bills you could ill afford, I'm sure. Not to mention the whiff of unemployability that would be attached to you at the end of the long-winded and costly business. I am an extremely powerful man, for my sins. Please do us both a favour by not crossing me.'

'Arrogant.' Katy's green eyes narrowed in a display of bravado she was inwardly far from feeling. 'That's what you are, Mr Cipriani! You're an arrogant, domineering bully!' She collided with eyes that burned with the heat of molten lava, and for a terrifying moment her anger was eclipsed by a dragging sensation that made her breathing sluggish and laborious.

Lucas's eyes drifted to her full lips and for a second he was overwhelmed by a powerful, crazy urge to crush them under his mouth. He drew back, straightened and resumed his seat behind his desk.

'I'm guessing that you're beginning to see sense,' he commented drily.

'It's not ethical,' Katy muttered under her breath. She eyed him with mutinous hostility.

'It's perfectly ethical, if a little unusual, but then again I've never been in the position of harbouring suspicions about the loyalties of any of my employees before. I pay them way above market price and that usually works. This is a first for me, Miss Brennan.'

'I can't just be *kept under watch* for *two weeks*. I'm not a specimen in a jam jar! Plus, I have responsibilities at the school!'

'And a simple phone call should sort that out. If

you want, I can handle the call myself. You just need to inform them that personal circumstances will prevent you from attending for the next fortnight. Same goes for any relatives, boyfriends and random pets that might need sorting out.'

'I can't believe this is happening. How is it going to work?'

'It's simple.' He leaned forward, the very essence of practicality. 'You will be accommodated without benefit of your phone or personal computer for a fortnight. You can consider it a pleasant holiday without the nuisance of having your time interrupted by gadgets.'

'A *pleasant holiday*?' Her breathing was ragged and her imagination, released to run wild, was coming up with all sorts of giddying scenarios.

Lucas had the grace to flush before shrugging. 'I assure you that your accommodation will be of the highest quality. All you need bring with you are your clothes. You will be permitted to return to your house or flat, or wherever it is you live, so that you can pack what you need.'

'Where on earth will I be going? This is mad.'

'I've put the alternative on the table.' Lucas shrugged elegantly.

'But where will I be *put*?'

'To be decided. There are a number of options. Suffice to say that you won't need to bring winter gear.' In truth, he hadn't given this a great deal of thought. His plan had been to delegate to someone else the responsibility of babysitting the headache that had arisen.

Now, however, babysitting her himself was looking good.

Why send a boy to do a man's job? She was lippy, argumentative, stubborn, in short as unpredictable as a keg of dynamite, and he couldn't trust any of his guys to know how to handle her.

She was also dangerously pretty and had no qualms when it came to having fun with a married guy. She said otherwise, but the jury was out on that one.

Dangerously pretty, rebellious and lacking in a moral compass was a recipe for disaster. Lucas looked at her with veiled, brooding speculation. He frankly couldn't think of anyone who would be able to handle this. He had planned to disappear for a week or so to consolidate the finer details of the deal, without fear of constant interruption, and this had become even more pressing since the breach in security. He could easily kill two birds with one stone, rather than delegating the job and then wasting his time wondering whether the task would go belly up.

'So, to cut to the chase, Miss Brennan…' He buzzed and was connected through to his PA. In a fog of sick confusion, and with the distinct feeling of being chucked into a tumble drier with the cycle turned to maximum spin, Katy was aware of him instructing the woman who had escorted her to his office to join them in fifteen minutes.

'Yes?' she said weakly.

'Vicky, my secretary, is going to accompany you back to…wherever you live…and she will supervise your immediate packing of clothes to take with you. Likewise, she will oversee whatever phone calls you feel you have to make to your friends. Needless to say, these will have to be cleared with her.'

'This is ridiculous. I feel as though I'm starring in a low-grade spy movie.'

'Don't be dramatic, Miss Brennan. I'm taking some simple precautions to safeguard my business interests. Carrying on; once you have your bags packed and you've made a couple of calls, you will be chauffeured back here.'

'Can I ask you something?'

'Feel free.'

'Are you always this...*cold*?'

'Are you always this outspoken?' Eyes as black as night clashed with emerald-green. Katy felt something shiver inside her and suddenly, inexplicably, she was aware of her body in a way she had never been in her life before. It felt heavy yet acutely sensitive, tingly and hot, aching as though her limbs had turned to lead.

Her mouth went dry and for a few seconds her mind actually went completely blank. 'I think that, if I have something to say, then why shouldn't I? As long as I'm not being offensive to anyone, we're all entitled to our opinions.' She paused and tilted her chin at a challenging angle. 'To answer your question.'

Lucas grunted. Not even the high-powered women who entered and exited his life made a habit of disagreeing with him, and they certainly never criticised. No one did.

'And to answer yours,' he said coolly, 'I'm cold when the occasion demands. You're not here on a social visit. You're here because a situation has arisen that requires to be dealt with and you're the root cause of the situation. Trust me, Miss Brennan, I'm the opposite of cold, given the right circumstances.'

And then he smiled, a long, slow, lazy smile and her senses shot into frantic overdrive. She licked her lips and her body stiffened as she leant forward in the chair, clutching the sides like a drowning person clutches a lifebelt.

That smile.

It seemed to insinuate into parts of her that she hadn't known existed, and it took a lot of effort actually to remember that the man was frankly insulting her and that sexy smile was not directed at her. Whoever he was thinking of—his current girlfriend, no doubt—had instigated that smile.

Were he to direct a smile at her, it would probably turn her to stone.

'So you stuff me away somewhere...' She finally found her voice and thankfully sounded as composed as he did. 'On a two week *holiday*, probably with those bodyguards of yours who brought me from the office, where I won't be allowed to do anything at all because I'll be minus my mobile phone and minus my computer. And, when you're done with your deal, you might just pop back and collect me, provided I've survived the experience.'

Lucas clicked his tongue impatiently. 'There's no need to be so dramatic.' He raked his fingers through his hair and debated whether he should have taken a slightly different approach.

Nope. He had taken the only possible approach. It just so happened that he was dealing with someone whose feet were not planted on the ground the way his were.

'The bodyguards won't be there.'

'No, I suppose it would be a little *chancy* to stuff

me away with men I don't know. Not that it'll make a
scrap of difference whether your henchmen are male
or female. I'll still be locked away like a prisoner in
a cell with the key thrown away.'

Lucas inhaled deeply and slowly, and hung on to
a temper that was never, ever lost. 'No henchmen,'
he intoned through gritted teeth. 'You're going to be
with me. I wouldn't trust anyone else to keep an eye
on you.'

Not without being mauled to death in the process.

'With *you*?' Shot through with an electrifying
awareness of him, her heart sped up, sending the
blood pulsing hotly through her veins and making it
difficult to catch her breath. *Trapped somewhere with
him?* And yet the thought, which should have filled
her with unremitting horror, kick-started a dark, in-
surgent curiosity that frankly terrified her.

'I have no intention of having any interaction with
you at all. You will simply be my responsibility for a
fortnight and I will make sure that no contact is made
with any outside parties until the deal is signed, sealed
and delivered. And please don't tell me the prospect
of being without a mobile phone or computer for a
handful of days amounts to nothing short of torture,
an experience which you may or may not survive!
It *is* possible to live without gadgets for a fortnight.'

'Could *you*?' But her rebellious mind was somewhere else, somewhere she felt it shouldn't be.

'This isn't about me. Bring whatever books you
want, or embroidery, or whatever you might enjoy
doing, and think about it positively as an unexpected
time out for which you will continue to be paid. If
you're finding it difficult to kick back and enjoy the

experience, then you can always consider the alternative: litigation, legal bills and no job.'

Katy clenched her fists and wanted to say something back in retaliation, even though she was dimly aware of the fact that this was the last person on the planet she wanted to have a scrap with, and not just because he was a man who would have no trouble in making good on his threats. However, the door was opening and through the haze of her anger she heard herself being discussed in a low voice, as if she wasn't in the room at all.

'Right.'

She blinked and Lucas was staring down at her, hands shoved in his trouser pockets. Awkwardly she stood up and instinctively smiled politely at his secretary, who smiled back.

He'd rattled off a chain of events, but she'd only been half listening, and now she didn't honestly know what would happen next.

'I'll have to phone my mum and dad,' she said a little numbly and Lucas inclined his head to one side with a frown.

'Of course.'

'I talk with them every evening.'

His frown deepened, because that seemed a little excessive for someone in her twenties. It didn't tally with the image of a raunchy young woman indulging in a steamy affair with a married man, not that the details of that were his business, unless the steamy affair was ongoing.

'And I don't have any pets.' She gathered her backpack from the ground and headed towards the door in the same daze that had begun settling over her the second his secretary had walked into the room.

'Miss Brennan…'

'Huh?' She blinked and looked up at him.

She was only five-three and wearing flats, so she had to crane her neck up. Her hair tumbled down her back in a riot of colour. Lucas was a big man and he felt as though he could fit her into his pocket. She was delicate, her features fine, her body slender under the oversized white shirt. Was that why he suddenly felt himself soften after the gruelling experience he had put her through? He had never in his life done anything that disturbed his conscience, had always acted fairly and decently towards other people. Yes, undeniably he could be ruthless, but never unjustly so. He felt a little guilty now.

'Don't get worked up about this.' His voice was clipped because this was as close as he was going to get to putting her mind at ease. By nature, he was distrustful, and certainly the situation in which he had encountered her showed all the hallmarks of being dangerous, as she only had to advertise what she knew to her ex. Yet something about her fuelled an unexpected response in him.

Her eyes, he noted as he stared down into them, were a beguiling mix of green and turquoise. 'This isn't a trial by torture. It's just the only way I can deal with a potential problem. You won't spend the fortnight suffering, nor is there any need to fear that I'm going to be following you around every waking moment like a bad conscience. Indeed, you will hardly notice my presence. I will be working all day and you'll be free to do as you like. Without the tools for communicating with the outside world, you can't get up to any mischief.'

'But I don't even know where I'm going!' Katy cried, latching on to that window of empathy before it vanished out of sight.

Lucas raised his eyebrows, and there was that smile again, although the empathy was still there and it was tinged with a certain amount of cool amusement. 'Consider it a surprise,' he murmured. 'A bit like winning the lottery which, incidentally, pretty much sums it up when you think about the alternative.' He nodded to his secretary and glanced at his watch. 'Two hours, Vicky. Think that will do it?'

'I think so.'

'In that case, I will see you both shortly. And, Miss Brennan...don't even think about doing a runner.'

Over the next hour and a half Katy experienced what it felt like to be kidnapped. Oh, he could call it what he liked, but she was going to be held prisoner. She was relieved of her mobile phone by Lucas's secretary, who was brisk but warm, and seemed to see nothing amiss in following her boss's high-handed instructions. It would be delivered to Lucas and held in safekeeping for her.

She packed a bunch of clothes, not knowing where she was going. Outside, it was still, but spring was making way for summer, so the clothes she crammed into her duffel bag were light, with one cardigan in case she ended up somewhere cold.

Although how would she know what the weather was up to when she would probably be locked in a room somewhere with views of the outside world through bars?

And yet, for all her frustration and downright *anger,* she could sort of see why he had reacted the way he had. Obviously the only thing that mattered to Lucas Cipriani was making money and closing deals. If this was to be the biggest deal of his career—and dipping his corporate toes into the Far East would be—then he would be more than happy to do what it took to safeguard his interest.

She was a dispensable little fish in the very big pond in which he was the marauding king of the water.

And the fact that she knew someone at the company he was about to take over, someone who was so far ignorant of what was going on, meant she had the power to pass on highly sensitive and potentially explosive information.

Lucas Cipriani, being the sort of man he was, would never believe that she had no ongoing situation with Duncan Powell because he was suspicious, distrustful, power hungry, arrogant, and would happily feed her to the sharks if it suited him, because he was also ice-cold and utterly emotionless.

'Where am I being taken?' she asked Vicky as they stepped back into the chauffeur-driven car that had delivered her to her flat. 'Or am I going to find myself blindfolded before we get there?'

'To a field on the outskirts of London.' She smiled. 'Mr Cipriani has his own private mode of transport there. And, no, you won't be blindfolded for any of the journey.'

Katy subsided into silence and stared at the scenery

passing by as the silent car left London and expertly took a route with which she was unfamiliar. She seldom left the capital unless it was to take the train up to Yorkshire to see her parents and her friends who still lived in the area. She didn't own a car, so escaping London was rarely an option, although, on a couple of occasions, she *had* gone with Tim and some of the others to Brighton for a holiday, five of them crammed like sardines into his second-hand car.

She hadn't thought about the dynamics of being trapped in a room with just Lucas acting as gaoler outside, but now she did, and she felt that frightening, forbidding tingle again.

Would other people be around? Or would there just be the two of them?

She hated him. She loathed his arrogance and the way he had of assuming that the world should fall in line with whatever he wanted. He was the boss who never made an effort to interact with those employees he felt were beneath him. He paid well not because he was a considerate and fair-minded guy who believed in rewarding hard work, but because he knew that money bought loyalty, and a loyal employee was more likely to do exactly what he demanded without asking questions. Pay an employee enough, and they lost the right to vote.

She hoped that he'd been telling the truth when he'd said that there would be no interaction between them because she couldn't think that they would have anything to talk about.

Then Katy thought about seeing him away from the confines of office walls. Something inside trembled and she had that whooshing feeling again, as if she

had been sitting quietly on a chair, only to find that
the chair was attached to a rollercoaster and the switch
had suddenly been turned on. Her tummy flipped
over; she didn't get it, because she really and truly
didn't like the guy.

She surfaced from her thoughts to find that they
had left the main roads behind and were pulling into
a huge parking lot where a long, covered building
opened onto an air field.

'I give you Lucas's transport...' Vicky murmured.
'If you look to the right, you'll see his private jet. It's
the black one. But today you'll be taking the helicopter.'

Jet? Helicopter?

Katy did a double-take. Her eyes swivelled from
private jet to helicopter and, sure enough, there he
was, leaning indolently against a black and silver helicopter, dark shades shielding his eyes from the early-
afternoon glare.

Her mouth ran dry. He was watching her from behind those shades. Her breathing picked up and her
heart began to beat fast as she wondered what the heck
she had got herself into, and all because she had stumbled across information she didn't even care about.

She didn't have time to dwell on the quicksand
gathering at her feet, however, because with the sort
of efficiency that spoke of experience the driver was
pulling the car to a stop and she was being offloaded,
the driver hurrying towards the helicopter with her
bag just as the rotary blades of the aircraft began to
whop, whop, whop in preparation for taking off, sending a whirlwind of flying dust beneath it.

Lucas had vanished into the helicopter.

Katy wished that she could vanish to the other side of the world.

She was harried, panic-stricken and grubby, because she hadn't had a chance to shower, and her jeans and shirt were sticking to her like glue. When she'd spoken to her mother on the phone, under the eagle eye of Vicky, she had waffled on with some lame excuse about being whipped off to a country house to do an important job, where the reception might be a bit dodgy, so they weren't to worry if contact was sporadic. She had made it sound like an exciting adventure because her parents were prone to worrying about her.

She hadn't thought that she really *would* end up being whipped off to anywhere.

She had envisaged a laborious drive to a poky holding pen in the middle of nowhere, with Internet access cruelly denied her. She hadn't believed him when he had told her to the contrary, and she certainly had not been able to get her head around any concept of an unplanned holiday unless you could call *incarceration* a holiday.

She was floored by what seemed to be a far bigger than average helicopter, but she was still scowling as she battled against the downdraft from the blades to climb aboard.

Lucas had to shout to be heard. As the small craft spun up, up and away, he called out, 'Small bag, Miss Brennan. Where have you stashed the books, the sketch pads and the tin of paints?'

Katy gritted her pearly teeth together but didn't say anything, and he laughed, eyebrows raised.

'Or did you decide to go down the route of being

a good little martyr while being held in captivity against your will? No books…no sketch pads…no tin of paints…and just the slightest temptation to stage a hunger strike to prove a point?'

Clenched fists joined gritted teeth and she glared at him, but he had already looked away and was flicking through the papers on his lap. He only glanced up when, leaning forward and voice raised to be heard above the din, she said, 'Where are you taking me?'

Aggravatingly seeming to read her mind, privy to every dark leap of imagination that had whirled through her head in a series of colourful images, Lucas replied, 'I'm sure that you've already conjured up dire destinations. So, instead of telling you, I'll leave you to carry on with your fictitious scenarios because I suspect that where you subsequently end up can only be better than what you've wasted your time imagining. But to set your mind at rest…'

He patted the pocket of the linen jacket which was dumped on the seat next to him. 'Your mobile phone is safe and sound right there. As soon as we land, you can tell me your password so that I can check every so often: make sure there are no urgent messages from the parents you're in the habit of calling on a daily basis…'

'Or from a married ex-boyfriend?' She couldn't resist prodding the sleeping tiger and he gave her a long, cool look from under the dark fringe of his lashes.

'Or from a married ex-boyfriend,' he drawled. 'Always pays to be careful, in my opinion. Now why don't you let me work and why don't you…enjoy the ride?'

CHAPTER THREE

THE RIDE PROBABLY TOOK HOURS, and felt even longer, with Katy doing her best to pretend that Lucas wasn't sitting within touching distance. When the helicopter began descending, swinging in a loop as it got lower, all she could see was the broad expanse of blue ocean.

Panicked and bewildered, she gazed at Lucas, who hadn't looked up from his papers and, when eventually he did, he certainly didn't glance in her direction.

After a brief hovering, the helicopter delicately landed and then she could see what she had earlier missed.

This wasn't a shabby holding pen.

Lucas was unclicking himself from his seat belt and then he patiently waited for her to do the same. This was all in a day's work for him. He turned to talk to the pilot, a low, clipped, polite exchange of words, then he stood back to allow her through the door and onto the super-yacht on which the helicopter had landed.

It was much, much warmer here and the dying rays of the sun revealed that the yacht was anchored at some distance from land. No intrusive boats huddled anywhere near it. She was standing on a yacht that was almost big enough to be classified as a small liner—sleek, sharp and so impressive that every single left wing thought about money not mattering was temporarily wiped away under a tidal wave of shameless awe.

The dark bank of land rose in the distance, revealing just some pinpricks of light peeping out between the trees and dense foliage that climbed up the side of the island's incline.

She found herself following Lucas as behind them the helicopter swung away and the deafening roar of the rotary blades faded into an ever-diminishing wasp-like whine. And then she couldn't hear it at all because they had left the helipad on the upper deck of the yacht and were moving inside.

'How does it feel to be a prisoner held against your will in a shabby cell?' Lucas drawled, not looking at her at all but heading straight through a vast expanse of polished wood and expensive cream leather furniture. A short, plump lady was hurrying to meet them, her face wreathed in smiles, and they spoke in rapid Italian.

Katy was dimly aware of being introduced to the woman, who was Signora Maria, the resident chef when on board.

Frankly, all she could take in was the breath-taking, obscene splendour of her surroundings. She was on board a billionaire's toy and, in a way, it made her feel more nervous and jumpy than if she had been dumped in that holding pen she had created in her fevered, over-imaginative head.

She'd known the guy was rich but when you were

as rich as this, rich enough to own a yacht of this calibre, then you could do whatever you wanted.

When he'd threatened her with legal proceedings, it hadn't been an empty threat.

Katy decided that she wasn't going to let herself be cowed by this display. She wasn't guilty of anything and she wasn't going to be treated like a criminal because Lucas Cipriani was suspicious by nature.

She had always been encouraged by her parents to speak her mind and she wasn't going to be turned into a rag doll because she was overwhelmed by her surroundings.

'Maria will show you to your suite.' He turned to her, his dark eyes roving up and down her body without expression. 'In it you will find everything you need, including an *en suite* bathroom. You'll be pleased to hear that there is no lock on the outside of your room, so you're free to come and go at will.'

'There's no need to be sarcastic,' Katy told him, mouth set in a sullen line. Her eyes flicked to him and skittered away just as fast before they could dwell for too long on the dark, dramatic beauty of his lean face because, once there, it was stupidly hard to tear her gaze away.

'Correction—there's *every* need to be sarcastic after you've bandied around terms such as *kidnapped*. I told you that you should look on the bright side and see this as a fully paid two-week vacation.' He dismissed Maria with a brief nod, because this looked as though it was shaping up to be another one of *those* conversations, then he shoved his hands in his pockets and stared down at her. She looked irritatingly unrepentant. 'In the absence of your books, you'll find that there is a private home cinema space with a comprehensive selection of movies. There are also two swimming pools—one indoor, one on the upper deck. And of course a library, should you decide that reading is a worthwhile option in the absence of your computer.'

'You're not very nice, are you?'

'Nice people finish last so, yes, that's an accolade I've been more than happy to pass up, which is something you'd do well to remember.'

Katy's eyes narrowed at the bitterness in his voice. Was he speaking from experience? What experience? She didn't want to be curious about him, but she suddenly was. Just for a moment, she realised that underneath the ruthless, cool veneer there would be all sorts of reasons for him being the man he was.

'Nice people don't always finish last,' she murmured sincerely.

'Oh, but they do.' Lucas's voice was cool and he was staring at her, his head at an angle, as if examining something weird he wasn't quite sure about. 'They get wrapped up in pointless sentimentality and emotion and open themselves up to getting exploited, so please don't think I'll be falling victim to that trait while we're out here.'

'Get exploited?' Katy found that she was holding her breath as she waited for his answer.

'Is that the sound of a woman trying to find out what makes me tick?' Lucas raised his eyebrows with wry amusement and began walking. 'Many have tried and failed in that venture, so I shouldn't bother if I were you.'

'It's very arrogant of you to assume that I want

to find out about you,' Katy huffed. 'But, as you've reminded me, we're going to be stuck here together for the next two weeks. I was just trying to have a conversation.'

'Like I said, I don't intend to be around much. When we do converse, we can keep it light.'

'I'm sorry.' She sighed, reaching to loop her long hair over one shoulder. 'Believe it or not, I can almost understand why you dragged me out here.'

'Well, at least *drag* is an improvement on *kidnap*,' Lucas conceded.

'I'm hot, tired and sticky, and sitting quietly at my desk working on my computer feels like a lifetime ago. I'm not in the best of moods.'

'I can't picture you sitting quietly anywhere. Maybe I've been remiss in not getting out and seeing what my employees are doing. What do you think? Should I have left my ivory tower and had a look at which of my employees were sitting and meekly doing their jobs and which ones were pushing the envelope?'

Katy reddened. His voice was suddenly lazy and teasing and her pulses quickened in response. How could he be so ruthless and arrogant one minute and then, in a heartbeat, make the blood rush to her head because of the way he was able to laugh at himself unexpectedly?

She didn't know whether it was because she had been yanked out of her comfort zone, but he was turning her off and on like a tap, and it unsettled her.

After Duncan, she had got her act together; she had looked for the silver lining and realised that he had pointed her in the right direction of what to look for in a man: someone down-to-earth, good-natured, genuine. Someone *normal*. When she found that man, everything else would fall into place, and she was horrified that a guy like Lucas Cipriani could have the sort of effect on her that he did. It didn't make sense and she didn't like it.

'I think my opinion doesn't count one way or another,' she said lightly. 'I can't speak for other people, but no one in my office actually expects you to swoop down and pay a visit.'

'You certainly know how to hit below the belt,' Lucas imparted drily. 'This your normal style when you're with a man?'

'You're not a man.'

Lucas laughed, a rich, throaty laugh that set her senses alight and had her pulses racing. 'Oh, no,' he murmured seriously. 'And here I was thinking that I was...'

'You know what I mean.' Rattled, Katy's gaze slid sideways and skittered away in confusion.

'Do I? Explain.' This wasn't the light conversation he had had in mind, but that wasn't to say that he wasn't enjoying himself, because he was. 'If I'm not a man, then what am I?'

'You're...you're my *captor*.'

Lucas grinned. 'That's a non-answer if ever there was one, but I'll let it go. Besides, I thought we'd got past the kidnap analogy.'

Katy didn't answer. He was being nice to her, teasing her. She knew that he still probably didn't trust her as far as he could throw her, but he was worldly wise and sophisticated, and knew the benefits of smoothing tensions and getting her onside. Constant sniping would bore him. He had been forced into a situation he hadn't banked on, just as she had, but he wasn't throwing temper tantrums. He wasn't interested in having meaningful conversations, because he wasn't interested in her and had no desire to find out anything about her, except what might impact on his business deal; but he would be civil now that he had told her in no uncertain terms what the lay of the land was. He had laughed about being called her captor, but he was, and he called the shots.

Instead of getting hot and bothered around him, she would have to step up to the plate and respond in kind.

They had reached the kitchen and she turned her attention away from him and looked around her. 'This is wonderful.' She ran her fingers over the counter. 'Where is Maria, your...chef?' She remained where she was, watching as he strolled to an over-sized fridge, one of two, and extracted a bottle of wine.

He poured them both a glass and nodded to one of the grey upholstered chairs tucked neatly under the metal kitchen table. Katy sat and sipped the wine very slowly, because she wasn't accustomed to drinking.

'Has her own quarters on the lower deck. I dismissed her rather than let her hang around listening to...a conversation she would have found puzzling. She might not have understood the meaning but she would have got the gist without too much trouble.'

Lucas sat opposite her. 'It is rare for me to be on this yacht with just one other person. It's generally used for client entertaining and occasionally for social gatherings. Under normal circumstances, there would be more than just one member of staff present, but there seemed little need to have an abundance of crew for two people. So, while we're here, Maria will clean and prepare meals.'

'Does she know why I'm here?'

'Why would she?' Lucas sounded genuinely surprised. 'It's none of her business. She's paid handsomely to do a job, no questions asked.'

'But wouldn't she be curious?' Katy couldn't help asking.

Lucas shrugged. 'Do I care?'

'*You* might not care,' she said tartly. 'But maybe *I* do. I don't want her thinking that I'm... I'm...'

'What?'

'I wouldn't want her thinking that I'm one of your women you've brought here to have a bit of fun with.'

Lucas burst out laughing. When he'd sobered up, he stared at her coolly.

'Why does it matter to you what my chef thinks of you? You'll never lay eyes on her again once this two-week stint is over. Besides...' he sipped his wine and looked at her over the rim of his glass '...I often fly Maria over to my place in London and occasionally to New York. She has seen enough of my women over the years to know that you don't fit the mould.'

Katy stared at him, mortified and embarrassed, because somehow she had ended up giving him the impression that...*what*? That she thought he might fancy her? That she thought her precious virtue might be *compromised* by being alone with him on this yacht, when she was only here because of circumstances? The surroundings were luxurious but this wasn't a five-star hotel with the man of her dreams. This was a prison in all but name and he was her gaoler...and since when did gaolers fancy their captives?

'Don't fit the mould?' she heard herself parrot in a jerky voice, and Lucas appeared to give that some consideration before nodding.

'Maria has been with me for a very long time,' he said without a shade of discomfort. 'She's met many of my women over the years. I won't deny that you have a certain appeal, but you're not my type, and she's savvy enough to know that. Whatever she thinks, it won't be that you're here for any reasons other than work. Indeed, I have occasionally used this as a work space with colleagues when I've needed extreme privacy in my transactions, so I wouldn't be a bit surprised if she puts that spin on your presence here.' He tried and failed to think of the woman sitting opposite him in the capacity of *work colleague*.

You have a certain appeal. Katy's brain had clunked to a stop at that throwaway remark and was refusing to budge. Why did it make her feel so flustered; hadn't she, two seconds ago, resolved not to let him get to her? She wanted to be as composed and collected as he was but she was all over the place.

Why was that? Was it the unsettling circumstances that had thrown them together? Lucas was sexy and powerful, but he was still just a man, and male attention, in the wake of Duncan, left her cold. So why did half a sentence from a man who wasn't interested in her make her skin prickle and tingle?

She forced her brain to take a few steps forward and said faintly, 'I didn't realise men had a type.' Which wasn't what she had really wanted to say. What she had *really* wanted to say was '*what's your type?*'

Rich men were always in the tabloids with women dripping from their arms and clinging to them like limpets. Rich men led lives that were always under the microscope, because the public loved reading about the lifestyles of the rich and famous, but she couldn't recall ever having seen Lucas Cipriani in any scandal sheets.

'All men have a *type*,' Lucas informed her. He had a type and he was clever enough to know *why* he had that particular type. As far as he was concerned, knowledge in that particular area was power. He would never fall victim to the type of manipulative women that his father had. He would always be in control of his emotional destiny. He had never had this sort of conversation with a woman in his life before, but then again his association with women ran along two tracks and only two. Either there was a sexual connection or else they were work associates.

Katy was neither. Yes, she worked for him, but she was not his equal in any way, shape or form.

And there was certainly no sexual connection there.

On cue, he gazed away from her face to the small jut of her breasts and the slender fragility of her arms. She really was tiny. A strong wind would knock her off her feet. She was the sort of woman that men instinctively felt the need to protect.

It seemed as good a time as any to remember just the sort of women he went for and, he told himself, keeping in the practical vein, to tell *her,* because, work or no work, aside from his chef there were only the two of them on board his yacht and he didn't want her to start getting any ideas.

She was a nobody suddenly plunged into a world of extreme luxury. He'd had sufficient experience over the years with women whose brains became scrambled in the presence of wealth.

'Here's *my* type,' he murmured, refilling both their glasses and leaning towards her, noting the way she reflexively edged back, amused by it. 'I don't do clingy. I don't do gold-diggers, airheads or any women who think that they can simper and preen their way to my bank balance—but, more than that, I don't care for women who demand more than I am capable of giving them. I lead an extremely pressurised working life. When it comes to my private life, I like women to be soothing and compliant. I enjoy the company of high fliers, career women whose independence matches my own. They know the rules of my game and there are never any unpleasant misunderstandings.'

He thought of the last woman in his life, a raven-haired beauty who was a leading light in the field of international law. In the end their mutually busy schedules had put paid to anything more than a six-month dalliance although, in fairness, he hadn't wanted more. Even the most highly intelligent and ferociously independent woman had a sell-by date in his life.

Katy was trying to imagine these high-flying, saintly paragons who didn't demand and who were also soothing and compliant. 'What would constitute them demanding more than you're capable of giving them?' she asked impulsively and Lucas frowned.

'Come again?'

'You said that you didn't like women who demanded more than you were capable of giving them. Do you mean *love and commitment*?'

'Nicely put,' Lucas drawled. 'Those two things are

off the agenda. An intellectually challenging relationship—with, of course, ample doses of fun—is what
I look for and, fortunately, the women I go out with
are happy with the arrangement.'

'How do you know?'

'How do I know what?'

'That they're happy. Maybe they really want more
but they're too scared to say that because you tell
them that you don't want a committed relationship.'

'Maybe. Who knows? We're getting into another
one of those deep and meaningful conversations
again.' He stood up and stretched, flexing muscles
that rippled under his hand-tailored clothes. 'I've
told you this,' he said, leaning down, hands planted
squarely on the table, 'Because we're here and I
wouldn't want any *wow* moments to go to your head.'

'I beg your pardon?'

'You're here because I need to keep an eye on you
and make sure you don't do anything that could jeopardise a deal I've been working on for the past year
and a half,' he said bluntly, although his voice wasn't
unkind. He was unwillingly fascinated by the way
her face could transmit what she was thinking, like
a shining beacon advertising the lay of the land. 'I
know you're out of your comfort zone but I wouldn't
want you to get any ideas.'

Comprehension came in an angry rush…although,
a little voice whispered treacherously in her head,
hadn't she been looking at him? Had he spotted that
and decided to nip any awkwardness in the bud by
putting down 'no trespass' signs? She wasn't his type
and he was gently but firmly telling her not to start
thinking that she might be. 'You're right.' Katy sat

back and folded her arms. 'I *am* out of my comfort zone and I *am* impressed. Who wouldn't be? But it takes more than a big boat with lots of fancy gadgets to suddenly turn its owner into someone I could *ever* be attracted to.'

'Is that a fact?'

'Yes, it is. I know my place and I'm perfectly happy there. You asked me why do I continue to work in a school? Because I enjoy giving back. I only work for your company, Mr Cipriani, because the pay enables me to afford my rent. If I could somehow be paid more as a teacher, then I would ditch your job in a heartbeat.' Katy thought that, at the rate she was going, she wouldn't have to ditch his job because *it* would be ditching *her*. 'You don't have to warn me off you and you don't have to be afraid that I'm going to start suddenly wanting to have a big boat like this of my own...'

'For goodness' sake, it's a *yacht*, not a *boat*.' And the guy who had overseen its unique construction and charged mightily for the privilege would be incandescent at her condescending referral to it as a boat. Although, Lucas thought, his lips twitching as he fought off a grin, it would certainly be worth seeing. The man, if memory served him right, had embodied all the worst traits of someone happy to suck up to the rich while stamping down hard on the poor.

Katy shrugged. 'You know what I mean. At any rate, Mr Cipriani, you don't want to be stuck here with me and I don't want to be stuck here with you either.'

'Lucas.'

'Sorry?'

'I think it's appropriate that we move onto first names. The name is Lucas.'

Flustered, Katy stared at him. 'I wouldn't feel right calling you by your first name,' she muttered, bright red. 'You're my boss.'

'I'll break the ice. Are you hungry, Katy? Maria will have prepared food and she will be unreasonably insulted if we don't eat what she has cooked. I'll call her up to serve us, after which she'll show you to your quarters.'

'Call her up?'

'The food won't magically appear on our plates.'

'I don't feel comfortable being waited on as though I'm royalty,' Katy told him honestly. 'If you direct me, I'm sure I can do whatever needs doing.'

'You're not the hired help, Katy.'

Katy shivered at the use of her name. It felt...*intimate*. She resolved to avoid calling him by his name unless absolutely necessary: perhaps if she fell overboard and was in the process of drowning. Even then she knew she would be tempted to stick to Mr Cipriani.

'That's not the point.' She stood up and looked at him, waiting to be directed, then she realised that he genuinely had no idea in which direction he should point her. She clicked her tongue and began rustling through the drawers, being nosy in the fridge before finding casserole dishes in the oven.

She could feel his dark, watchful eyes following her every movement, but she was relieved that he hadn't decided to fetch Maria, because this was taking away some of her jitters. Instead of sitting in front of him, perspiring with nerves and with nowhere to rest her eyes except on *him,* which was the least rest-ful place they could ever land, busying herself like this at least occupied her, and it gave her time to get her thoughts together and forgive herself for behav-ing out of character.

It was understandable. Twenty-four hours ago, she'd been doing her job and going through all the usual daily routines. Suddenly she'd been thrown blindfolded into the deep end of a swimming pool and it was only natural for her to flounder before she found her footing.

She could learn something from this because, after Duncan, being kind to herself had come hard. She had blamed herself for her misjudgements. How could she have gone so wrong when she had spent a lifetime being so careful and knowing just what she wanted? She had spent months beating herself up for her mistake in not spotting the kind of man he had been. She had been raised by two loving parents who had instilled the right values in her, so how had she been sucked into a relationship with a man who had no values at all?

So here she was, acting out of character and going all hot and cold in the company of a man she had just met five seconds ago. It didn't mean anything and she wasn't going to beat herself up over it. There was nothing wrong with her. It was all a very natural re-action to unforeseen circumstances.

Watching her, Lucas thought that this was just the sort of domestic scene he had spent a lifetime avoid-ing. He also thought that, despite what he had said about his high-flying career women wanting no more than he was willing to give them, many of them had tentatively broached the subject of a relationship that would be more than simply a series of fun one-night stands. He had always shot those makings of uncomfortable conversations down in flames. But looking at the way Katy was pottering in this kitchen, making herself at home, he fancied that many an ex would have been thrilled to do the same.

'I like cooking,' she told him, bringing the food to the table and guilt-tripping him into giving her a hand because, as he had pointed out with spot-on accuracy, she *wasn't* the hired help. 'It's not just because it feels wrong to summon Maria here to do what I could easily do, but I honestly enjoy playing around with food. This smells wonderful. Is she a qualified chef?'

'She's an experienced one,' Lucas murmured.

'Tell me where we're anchored,' Katy encouraged. 'I noticed an island. How big is it? Do you have a house there?'

'The island is big enough for essentials and, although there is some tourism, it's very exclusive, which is the beauty of the place. And, yes, I have a villa there. In fact, I had planned on spending a little time there on my own, working flat-out on finalising my deal without interruptions, but plans changed.'

He didn't dwell on that. He talked, instead, about the island and then, as soon as he was finished eating, he stood up and took his plate to the sink. Katy followed his lead, noticing that his little foray into domesticity didn't last long, because he remained by the sink, leaning against it with his arms folded. She couldn't help but be amused. Just like the perplexed frown when he had first entered the kitchen, his obvious lack of interest in anything domestic was something that came across as ridiculously macho yet curiously endearing. If a man like Lucas Cipriani could ever be *endearing,* she thought drily.

'You can leave that,' was his contribution. 'Maria will take care of it in the morning.'

Katy paused and looked up at him with a half-smile. Looking down at her, he had an insane urge to…to *what?*

She had a mouth that was lush, soft and ripe for kissing. Full, pink lips that settled into a natural, sexy pout. He wondered whether they were the same colour as her nipples, and he inhaled sharply because bringing her here was one thing, but getting ideas into his head about what she might feel like was another.

'I'll show you to your cabin,' he said abruptly, heading off without waiting while she hurriedly stacked the plates into the sink before tripping along behind him.

Let this be a lesson in not overstepping the mark, she thought firmly. They'd had some light conversation, as per his ground rules, but it would help to remember that they weren't pals and his tolerance levels when it came to polite chit chat would only go so far. Right now, he'd used up his day's quota, judging from the sprint in his step as he headed away from the kitchen.

'Have you brought swimsuits?' he threw over his shoulder.

'No.' She didn't even know what had happened to her bag.

Maria, as it turned out, had taken it and delivered it to the cabin she had been assigned. Lucas pushed open the door and Katy stood for a few seconds, looking at the luxurious bedroom suite, complete with a proper king-sized bed and a view of the blue ocean, visible through trendy oversized port holes. Lucas showed her a door that opened out onto a balcony and she followed him and stood outside in a setting that was impossibly romantic. Balmy air blew gently through her hair and, looking down, she saw dark waves slapping lazily against the side of the yacht. She was so conscious of him leaning against the railing next to her that she could scarcely breathe.

'In that case, there's an ample supply of laundered swimsuits and other items of clothing in the walk-in wardrobe in the cabin alongside yours. Feel free to help yourself.'

'Why would that be?'

'People forget things. Maria digs her heels in at throwing them out. I've stopped trying to convince her.' He raked his fingers through his hair and watched as she half-opened her mouth, and that intensely physical charge rushed through him again.

'Okay.'

'You have the freedom of my yacht. I'll work while I'm here and the time will fly past, just as long as we don't get in one another's way...'

CHAPTER FOUR

LUCAS LOOKED AT the document he had been editing for half an hour, only to realise that he had hardly moved past the first two lines.

At this point in time, and after three days of enforced isolation on his yacht, he should have been powering through the intense backlog of work he had brought with him. Instead, he had been wasting time thinking about the woman sharing his space on his yacht.

Frustrated, he stood up, strolled towards the window and stared out, frowning, at a panoramic view of open sea. Every shade of blue and turquoise combined, in the distance, into a dark-blue line where the sea met the skyline. At a little after three, it was still very hot and very still, with almost no breeze at all rippling the glassy surface of the water.

He'd looked at this very skyline a hundred times in the past, stared through this very window of his office on the lower deck, and had never been tempted to leave it for the paradise beckoning outside. He'd never been good at relaxing, and indeed had often found himself succumbing to it more through necessity than anything else. Sitting around in the sun doing nothing was a waste of valuable time, as far as he was concerned; and on the few occasions he had been on weekend breaks with a woman he had found himself enduring the time spent playing tourist with a certain amount of barely concealed impatience.

He was a workaholic and the joys of doing nothing held zero appeal for him.

Yet, he was finding it difficult to concentrate. If he had noticed Katy's delicate, ridiculous prettiness on day one, and thought he could studiously file it away as something he wasn't going to allow to distract him, then he'd made a big mistake because the effect she was having on him was increasing with every second spent in her company.

He'd done his best to limit the time they were together. He'd reminded himself that, were it not for an unfortunate series of events, the woman wouldn't even be on his yacht now, but for all his well-constructed, logical reasons for avoiding her his body remained stubbornly recalcitrant.

Perversely, the more uptight he felt in her company, the more relaxed she seemed to be in his.

Since when had the natural order of things been rearranged? For the first time in his life, he wasn't calling the shots, and *that* was what was responsible for his lack of focus.

Being stuck on the yacht with Katy had made him realise that the sassy, independent career women he dated had not been as challenging as he had always liked to think they were. They'd all been as subservient and eager to please as any vacuous airhead keen to burn a hole in his bank account. In contrast, Katy didn't seem to have a single filter when it came to telling him what she thought about…anything and everything.

So far, he had been regaled with her opinions on money, including his own. She had scoffed at the fool-ishness of racing towards power and status, without bothering to hide the fact that he was top of her list as a shining example of someone leading the race. She had quizzed him on what he did in his spare time, and demanded to know whether he ever did anything that was actually *ordinary*. She seemed to think that his lack of knowledge of the layout of his own private yacht's kitchen was a shocking crime against human-ity, and had then opined that there was such a thing as more money than sense.

In short, she had managed to be as offensive as any human being was capable of being and, to his as-tonishment, he had done nothing to redress the bal-ance by exerting the sort of authority that would have stalled her mid-sentence.

He had the power in his hands to ruin her career but the thought had not crossed his mind.

She might have been in his company for all the wrong reasons, but he was no longer suspicious of her motives, especially when she had no ability to contact anyone at all, and her openness was strangely engaging.

It was also an uncomfortable reminder as to how far he normally went when it came to getting exactly what he wanted, and that he had surrounded himself with people who had forgotten how to contradict him.

Without giving himself a chance to back out, he headed to his quarters and did the unthinkable: he swapped his khakis for a pair of swimming trunks that hadn't seen the light of day in months, if not years, and a tee-shirt.

Barefoot, grabbing a towel on the way, he headed up to the pool area where he knew Katy was going to be.

She had been oddly reticent about using the swimming pool and, chin tilted at the mutinous angle he was fast becoming accustomed to, she had finally confessed that she didn't like using stuff that didn't belong to her.

'Would you rather the swimsuits all sit unused in cupboards until it's time for the lot to be thrown away?'

'Would you throw away perfectly good clothes?'

'I would if it was cluttering up my space. You wouldn't have to borrow them if you'd thought ahead and brought a few of your own.'

'I had no idea I would be anywhere near a pool,' she had been quick to point out, and he had dealt her a slashing grin, enjoying the way the colour had rushed into her cheeks.

'And now you are. Roll with the punches, would be my advice.'

His cabin was air-conditioned, and as he headed up towards the pool on the upper deck he was assailed by heat. It occurred to him that she might not be there, that she might have gone against her original plan of reading in the afternoon and working on ideas for an app to help the kids in her class with their homework, something he had discovered after some probing. If she wasn't there, he'd be bloody disappointed, and that nearly stopped him in his tracks because disappointment wasn't something he associated with the opposite sex.

He enjoyed the company of women. He wasn't promiscuous but the truth was that no woman had ever had the power to hold his attention for any sustained length of time, so he had always been the first to do the dispatching. By which point, he was always guiltily relieved to put the relationship behind him. In that scenario, disappointment wasn't something that had ever featured.

Katy, with her quirky ways and forthright manner, was yanking him along by some sort of invisible chain and he was uneasily aware that it was something he should really put a stop to.

Indeed, he paused, considering that option. It would take him less than a minute to make it back down to his office where he could resume work.

Except...would he be able to? Or would he sit at his desk allowing his mind idly to drift off to the taboo subject of his sexy captive?

Lucas had no idea what he hoped to gain by hitting the upper deck and joining her by the pool. So what if she was attractive? The world was full of attractive women and he knew, without a shred of vanity, that he could have pretty much any of them he wanted.

Playing with his reluctant prisoner wasn't on the cards. He'd warned her off getting any ideas into her head so there was no way he was going to try to get her into his bed now.

Just thinking about that, even as he was fast shoving it out of his head, conjured up a series of images that sent his pulses racing and fired up his libido as though reacting to a gun at the starting post.

He reached out one hand and supported himself heavily against the wall, allowing his breathing to settle. His common sense was fighting a losing battle with temptation, telling him to hot foot it back to the office and slam the metaphorical door on the siren lure of a woman who most definitely wasn't his sort.

He continued on, passing Maria in the kitchen preparing supper, and giving a brief nod before heading up. Then the sun was beating down on him as he took a few seconds to appreciate the sight of the woman reclining on a deck chair, eyes closed, arms hanging loosely over the sides of the chair, one leg bent at the knee, the other outstretched.

She had tied her long, vibrant hair into some kind of rough bun and a book lay open on the ground next to her.

Lucas walked softly towards her. He hadn't seen her like this, only just about decently clothed, and his breathing became sluggish as he took in the slender daintiness of her body: flat stomach, long, smooth legs, small breasts.

He cleared his throat and wondered whether he would be able to get his vocal cords to operate. 'Good job I decided to come up here…' He was inordinately thankful for the dark sunglasses that shielded his expression. 'You're going pink. Where's your sunblock? With your skin colouring, too much sun and you'll end up resembling a lobster—and your two-week prison sentence might well end up being longer than you'd bargained for. Sun burn can be a serious condition.'

'What are you *doing* here?' Katy jack-knifed into a sitting position and drew her knees up to her chest, hugging herself and glowering from a position of disadvantage as he towered over her, all six-foot-something of bronzed, rippling muscle.

Her eyes darted down to his legs and darted away again just as fast. Something about the dark, silky hair shadowing his calves and thighs brought her out in a sweat.

She licked her lips and steadied her racing pulse. She'd kept up a barrage of easy chatter for the past few days, had striven to project the careless, outspoken insouciance that she hoped would indicate to him that she wasn't affected by him, *not at all,* and she wasn't going to ruin the impression now.

He'd warned her not to go getting any ideas and that had been the trigger for her to stop gaping and allowing him to get under her skin. She was sure that the only reason he had issued that warning was because he had noticed her reaction to him and, from that moment onwards, she had striven to subdue any wayward reactions under a never-ending stream of small talk.

To start with, she'd aimed to keep the small talk *very* small, anything to break the silence as they had shared meals. In the evenings, before he left to return to the bowels of the yacht, they'd found themselves continuing to talk over coffee and wine.

Her aim had been harder to stick to than she'd thought because something about him fired her up. Whilst she managed to contain her body's natural impulse to be disobedient—by making sure she was physically as far away from him as possible without being too obvious—she'd been seduced into provoking him, enjoying the way he looked at her when she said something incendiary, head to one side, his dark eyes veiled and assessing.

It was a subtle form of intellectual arousal that

kept her on a permanent high and it was as addictive as a drug.

In Lucas's presence, Duncan no longer existed.

In fact, thanks to Lucas's all-consuming and wholly irrational ability to rivet her attention, Katy had reluctantly become aware of just how affected she had been by Duncan's betrayal. Even when she had thought she'd moved on, he had still been there in the background, a troubling spectre that had moulded her relationships with the opposite sex.

'I own the yacht,' Lucas reminded her lazily. He began stripping off the tee-shirt and tossed it onto a deckchair, which he pulled over with his foot so that it was right next to her. 'Do you think I should have asked your permission before I decided to come up here and use the pool?'

'No, of course not,' Katy replied, flustered. 'I just thought that you had your afternoon routine and you worked until seven in the evening...'

'Routines are made to be broken.' He settled down onto the deck chair and turned so that he was looking at her, still from behind the dark shades that gave him a distinct advantage. 'Haven't you been lecturing me daily on my evil workaholic ways?'

'I never said that they were *evil*.'

'But you were so persuasive in convincing me that I was destined for an early grave that I decided to follow your advice and take some time out.' He grinned and tilted his shades up to look at her. 'You're not reacting with the sort of smug satisfaction I might have expected.'

'I didn't think that you would actually listen to

what I said,' Katy muttered, her whole body as rigid as a plank of wood.

She wanted to look away but her greedy eyes kept skittering back to him. He was just so unbelievably perfect. More perfect than anything she had conjured up in her fevered imaginings. His chest was broad and muscular, with just the right dusting of dark hair that made her draw her breath in sharply, and the line of dark hair running down from his belly button electrified her senses like a live wire. How was it possible for a man to be so sexy? So sinfully, darkly and *dangerously* sexy?

Every inch of him eclipsed her painful memories of Duncan and she was shocked that those memories had lingered for as long as they had.

Watching him, her imagination took flight. She thought of those long, clever fingers stroking her, touching her breasts, lingering to circle her nipples. She felt faint. Her nipples were tight and pinched, and between her legs liquid heat was pooling and dampening her bikini bottoms.

She realised that she had been fantasising about this man since they had stepped foot on the yacht, but those fantasies had been vague and hazy compared to the force of the graphic images filling her head as she looked away with a tight, determined expression.

It was his body, she thought. Seeing him like that, in nothing but a pair of black trunks, was like fodder for her already fevered imagination.

Under normal circumstances, she might have looked at him and appreciated him for the drop-dead, gorgeous guy that he was, but actually she wouldn't have turned that very natural appreciation into a full-on mental sexual striptease that had him parading naked in her head.

But these weren't normal circumstances and *that* was why her pragmatic, easy-going and level-headed approach to the opposite sex had suddenly deserted her.

'Tell me about the deal.' She launched weakly into the first topic of conversation that came into her head, and Lucas flung himself back into the deck chair and stared up at a faultlessly blue, cloudless sky.

He was usually more than happy to discuss work-related issues, except right now and right here that was the last thing he wanted to do. 'Persuade me that you give a damn about it.' He slanted a sideways look at her and then kept looking as delicate colour tinged her cheeks.

'Of course I do.' Katy cleared her throat. 'I'm here *because* of it, aren't I?'

'Are you enjoying yourself?' He folded his arms behind his head and stared at her. 'You're only here because of the deal but, now that you *are* here, are you having a good time?'

Katy opened her mouth to ask him what kind of question that was, because how on earth could she be having a good time when life as she knew it had been turned upside down? Except she blinked and thought that she *was* having a good time. 'I've never been anywhere like this before,' she told him. 'When I was a kid, holidays were a week in a freezing-cold British seaside town. Don't get me wrong, I adored my holidays, but this is...out of this world.'

She looked around her and breathed in the warm breeze, rich with the salty smell of the sea. 'It's a different kind of life having a father who's the local parish priest,' she confided honestly. 'On the one hand, it was brilliant, because I never lacked love and support from both my parents, especially as I was an only child. They wanted more but couldn't have them. My mum once told me that she had to restrain herself from lavishing gifts on me, but of course there was always a limit to what they could afford. And besides, as I've told you, they always made sure to tell me that money wasn't the be-all and end-all.' She looked at Lucas and smiled, somewhat surprised that she was telling him all this, not that any of it was a secret.

Never one to encourage confidences from women, Lucas was oddly touched by her confession because she was usually so outspoken in a tomboyish, challenging way.

'Hence your entrenched disregard for money,' he suggested drily. 'Tell me about the down sides of life in a vicarage. I'll be honest with you, you're the first daughter of a man of the cloth I've ever met.'

The image of the happy family stuck in his mind and, in a rare bout of introspection, he thought back to his own troubled youth after his mother had died. His father had had the love, but he had just not quite known how to deliver it and, caught up in his own grief and his never-ending quest to find a substitute for the loss of his wife, he had left a young Lucas to find his own way. The independence Lucas was now so proud of, the mastery over his own emotions and his talent for self-control, suddenly seemed a little tarnished at the edges, too hard-won to be of any real value.

He dismissed the worrying train of thought and

encouraged her to keep talking. She had a very melodic voice and he enjoyed the sound of it as much as he enjoyed the animation that lit up her ravishingly pretty, heart-shaped face.

'Down sides... Well, now, let me have a think...!' She smiled and lay down on the deck chair so that they were now both side by side, faces upturned to the brilliant blue sky above. She glanced across at him, expecting to see amusement and polite interest, just a couple of people chatting about nothing in particular. Certainly nothing that would hold the interest of a man like Lucas Cipriani. But his dark, fathomless eyes were strangely serious as he caught her gaze and held it for a few seconds, and she shivered, mouth going dry, ensnared by the gravity of his expression.

'So?' Lucas murmured, closing his eyes and enjoying the warmth and the rarity of not doing anything.

'So...you end up always knowing that you have to set a good example because your parents are pillars of the community. I could never afford to be a rebel.'

Even when she had gone to university her background had followed her. She'd been able to have a good time, and stay out late and drink with the best of them, but she had never slept around or even come close to it. Maybe if she hadn't had so many morals drilled into her from an early age she would have just got sex out of the way and then would have been relaxed when it came to finding relationships. Maybe she would have accepted that not all relationships were serious, that some were destined to fall by the wayside, but that didn't mean they weren't worthwhile.

It was a new way of thinking for Katy and she gave

it some thought because she had always assumed,
post-Duncan, that she would hang on to her virginity, would have learned her lesson, would be better
equipped to make the right judgement calls.

Thinking that she could deviate from that path
gave her a little frisson of excitement.

'Not that I was ever tempted,' she hurriedly expanded. 'I had too much experience of seeing where
drugs and drink and casual sex could lead a person.
My dad is very active in the community and does a
lot outside the village for down-and-outs. A lot of
them ended up where they did because of poor choices
along the way.'

'I feel like I'm talking to someone from another
planet.'

'Why?'

'Because your life is so vastly different from anything I've come across.'

Katy laughed. Lying side by side made it easier
to talk to him. If they'd been sitting opposite one another at the table in the kitchen, with the yacht rocking softly as they ate, she wasn't sure she would have
been able to open up like this. She could spar with
him and provoke him until she could see him gritting
his teeth in frustration—in fact, she got a kick out of
that—but this was different.

She couldn't even remember having a conversation
like this with Duncan, who had split his time talking about himself and flirting relentlessly with her.

'What do you come across?' she asked lightly,
dropping her hands to either side of the deck chair
and tracing little circles on the wooden decking.

'Tough career women who don't make a habit of

getting too close to down-and-outs,' Lucas told her wryly. 'Unless, in the case of at least a couple of them who were top barristers, a crime had been committed and they happened to be confronted with one of those down-and-outs in a court of law.'

'I remember you telling me,' Katy murmured, 'About those tough career women who never wanted more than you were prepared to give them and were always soothing and agreeable.'

Lucas laughed. That had been when he'd been warning her off him, just in case she got ideas into her head. On cue, he inclined his head slightly and looked at her. She was staring up at the sky, eyes closed. Her long, dark lashes cast shadows on her cheeks and her mouth, in repose, was a full, pink pout. The sun had turned her a pale biscuit-gold colour and brought out shades of strawberry blonde amidst the deep russets and copper of her hair. Eyes drifting down, he followed the line of her shoulders and the swell of her breasts under the bikini, which he had not really been able to appreciate when she had been hugging her knees to herself, making sure that as little of her body was on show as humanly possible.

The bikini was black and modest by any modern standard but nothing could conceal the tempting swell of her pert, small breasts, the barely there cleavage, the jut of her hip bones and the silky smoothness of her thighs.

Lucas didn't bother to give in to consternation at the hot, pulsing swell of his arousal which, had she only opened her big green eyes and cast a sideways glance at him, she'd have noticed was distorting his swimming trunks.

He'd acknowledged her appeal from day one, from the very second she had walked into his office. No red-blooded male could have failed to. He'd also noted her belligerence and lack of filter when it came to speaking her mind, which was why he had decided to take on babysitting duties personally until his deal was safely in the bag. When you took into account that she had shimmered into his line of vision as a woman not averse to sleeping with married men, one who could not be trusted, it had seemed the obvious course of action.

But he knew, deep down, that even though he had dismissed any notion of going anywhere near Katy the prospect of bcing holed up with her for a fortnight had not exactly filled him with distaste.

He wondered whether he had even played with the forbidden thought of doing what his body wanted against the wishes of his brain. Or maybe he had been invigorated just by the novelty of having that mental tussle at all. In his well-ordered life, getting what he wanted had never posed a challenge, and internal debates about what he should or shouldn't do rarely featured, especially when it came to women.

He thought that if she had lived down to expectations and proved herself to be the sort of girl who had no morals, and really *might* have tried her luck with him, he would have had no trouble in eating, breathing and sleeping work. However, she hadn't, and the more his curiosity about her had been piqued the more he had been drawn to her like a wanderer hearing the call of a siren.

Which was so not him *at all* that he almost didn't know how to deal with it.

Except, his body was dealing with it in the time-honoured way, he thought, and then hard on the heels of that thought he wondered what she would do if she looked and saw the kind of response she'd awakened in him.

Katy wasn't sure whether it was the sudden silence, or just something thick and electric in the air, but she opened her eyes and turned her head, her mouth already opening to say something bland and chirpy to dispel the sudden tension.

His eyes caught hers and she stopped breathing. She had a drowning sensation as she was swallowed up in the deep, dark, quiet depths of his eyes. Those eyes were telegraphing a message to her, or they seemed to be. Was she imagining it? She had no experience of a man like him. That cool, brooding, speculative expression seemed to be inviting a response, but was it? Flustered and confused, her eyes dipped...

And then there was no doubt exactly what message was being telegraphed.

For a few seconds, Katy froze while her mind went into free fall. He was *turned on*. Did he think that he could try it on and she would fall in line because she was easy? Who knew, he probably still believed that she was the sort who had affairs with married men, even though he surely should know better, because she had shared stuff with him, told him about her childhood and her parents and the morals they had instilled in her. Maybe he hadn't believed her. Maybe he had taken it all with a pinch of salt because he was suspicious and mistrustful.

She *wasn't* easy. And yet, unleashed desire flooded through her in an unwanted torrent, crashing through common sense and good intentions. *She wanted this man, this unsuitable man, and she wanted him with a craving that was as powerful as a depth charge.*

The shocking intensity of a physical response she had never, *ever* felt towards any man, including Duncan, scared the living daylights out of her. Mumbling something under her breath, she leapt to her feet, the glittering blue of the infinity pool beckoning like an oasis of safety away from the onslaught of confusion overwhelming her.

Heart hammering in her chest, she scrambled forward, missed the step that gave down to the smooth wood around the pool and found herself flying forward.

She landed with a painful thump, her knees stinging where she had grazed them after her airborne flight.

Clutching her leg, she watched in fascinated slow motion as Lucas strode towards her, every lean muscle of his body intent.

'What were you thinking?' he asked urgently, scooping her up and ignoring her protests that he put her down because she was *absolutely fine.* 'You took off like a bat out of hell. Something I said?'

He was striding away from the pool area, carrying her as easily as he would carry a couple of cushions. Katy clutched his broad shoulders, horribly aware that in this semi-folded position there were bits of her on view that made her want to die an early death from embarrassment.

One glance down and he would practically be able to see the shadow of one of her nipples.

'Where are you taking me?' she croaked. 'This is ridiculous. I tripped and fell!'

'You could have broken something.'

'I haven't broken *anything*!' Katy practically sobbed.

'How do you know?'

'Because if I had I wouldn't be able to walk!'

'You're not walking. I'm carrying you. How much do you weigh, by the way? You're as light as a feather. If I didn't see how much food you're capable of putting away, I'd be worried.'

'I've always been thin,' Katy said faintly, barely noticing where they were going because she was concentrating very hard on making sure no more of her bikini-clad body went on show. She felt she might be on the verge of passing out. 'Please just take me to my cabin. That would be fine. I can clean my knee up and I'll be as right as rain.'

'Nonsense. How could I live with myself if I didn't do the gentlemanly thing and make sure you're all right? I wasn't brought up to ignore damsels in distress.'

'I'm not one of those!'

'Here we are,' Lucas intoned with satisfaction. He kicked open the door and, when Katy tore her focus away from her excruciating attempts to keep her body safely tucked away in the swimsuit, she realised where he had taken her.

Away from the safety of the pool and straight into the hellfire of his private quarters.

CHAPTER FIVE

LUCAS'S CABIN WAS different from hers insofar as it was twice the size and unnervingly masculine: dark-grey silky throw on the bed, dark-grey pillows, built-in furniture in rich walnut that matched the wooden flooring. He laid her on the bed and she immediately wriggled into a sitting position, wishing that she had something to tug down to cover herself, but instead having to make do with arranging herself into the most modest position possible, back upright, legs rammed close together and hands primly folded on her lap.

Sick with tension, she watched him disappear into an adjoining bathroom, that made hers look like a shower cubicle, to return a minute later with a first-aid kit.

'This really isn't necessary…er… Lucas.'

'You managed the first name. Congratulations. I wondered whether you would.'

'I have a few grazes, that's all.'

He was kneeling in front of her and he began to feel her ankle with surprisingly gently fingers. 'Tell me if anything hurts.'

'Nothing,' Katy stated firmly. She gave a trial tug

of her leg so that Lucas could get the hint that this was all pretty ridiculous and overblown but he wasn't having it.

Relax, she told herself sternly; *relax and it'll be over and done with in a second and you can bolt back to your cabin.* But how could she even begin to relax when those fingers were doing all sorts of things to her body?

The feathery delicacy of his touch was stirring her up, making her breathing quicken and sending tingling, delicious sensations racing through her body like little lightning sparks. She looked at his down-bent head, the raven-black hair, and had to stop herself from reaching out and touching it just to see what it felt like between her fingers.

Then she thought of the bulge of his arousal and felt faint all over again.

'I'm surprised you have a first-aid kit to hand,' she said breathlessly, tearing her fascinated gaze away from him and focusing hard on trying to normalise the situation with pointless conversation.

'Why?' Lucas glanced up briefly before continuing with his exceedingly slow exploration of her foot.

'Because you don't seem to be the type to do this sort of thing,' Katy said honestly.

'It's essential to have a first-aid kit on board a sailing vessel. In fact, this is just one of many. There's a comprehensive supply of medical equipment in a store room on the middle deck. You would be surprised at the sort of unexpected accidents that can happen when you're out at sea, and there's no ambulance available to make a five-minute dash to collect and take you to the nearest hospital.' He was working his way gently up her calf, which was smooth, slender and sprinkled with golden hair. Her skin was like satin and still warm from the sun.

'And you know how to deal with all those unexpected accidents?' Lucas's long, clever fingers were getting higher and, with each encroaching inch, her body lit up like a Christmas tree just a tiny bit more. Any higher and she would go up in flames.

'You'd be surprised,' Lucas drawled. 'Your knees are in a pretty terrible state, but after I've cleaned them up you should be fine. You'll be pleased to know that nothing's been broken.'

'I told you that,' Katy reminded him. 'Why would I be surprised?'

He was now gently swabbing her raw, torn skin and she winced as he patted the area with some over-sized alcohol wipes, making sure to get rid of every last bit of dirt.

'Because,' Lucas said wryly, not looking at her, 'I get the feeling you've pigeonholed me as the sort of money-hungry, ambitious businessman who hasn't got time for anything other than getting richer and richer and richer, probably at the expense of everyone around him. Am I right?'

'I never said that,' Katy told him faintly.

'It's hard not to join the dots when your opening words to me were to accuse me of being capable of kidnapping you.'

'You *were* kidnapping me, in a manner of speaking!'

'Tell me how it feels to be a kidnap victim.' His voice was light and teasing as he continued to tend to her knee, now applying some kind of transparent ointment, before laboriously bandaging it and then turning his attention to foot number two. 'I always wanted to be a doctor,' he surprised her and himself by saying.

'What happened?' For the first time since she had been deposited on his bed, Katy felt herself begin to relax, the nervous tension temporarily driven away by a piercing curiosity. Lucas could be many things, as she had discovered over the past few days. He could be witty, amusing, arrogant and always, always wildly, extravagantly intelligent. But confiding? No.

'My father's various wives happened,' Lucas said drily. 'One after each other. They looked alike and they certainly were all cut from the same cloth. They had their eyes on the main prize and, when their tenure ran out, my father's fortune was vastly diminished. By the time I hit sixteen, I realised that, left to his own devices, he would end up with nothing to live on. It would have killed my father to have seen the empire his grandfather had built dwindle away in a series of lawsuits and maintenance payments to greedy ex-wives.

'I knew my father had planned on my inheriting the business and taking over, and I had always thought that I'd talk to him about that change of plan when the time was right; but, as it turned out, the time never became right because without me the company would have ended up subdivided amongst a string of gold-diggers and that would have been that.'

'So you gave up your hopes and dreams?'

'Don't get too heavy on the pity card.' Lucas laughed, sitting back on his heels to inspect his work, head tilted to one side. He looked at her and her mouth went dry as their eyes tangled. 'I enjoy my life.'

'But it's a far cry from being a doctor.' She had never imagined him having anything to do with the caring profession and something else was added to the swirling mix of complex responses she was stockpiling towards him. She thought that the medical profession had lost something pretty big when he had decided to pursue a career in finance because, knowing the determination and drive he brought to his chosen field of work, he surely would have brought tenfold to the field of medicine.

'So it is,' Lucas concurred. 'Hence the fact that I actually enjoy being hands-on when it comes to dealing with situations like this.'

'And have you had to deal with many of them?' She thought of him touching another woman, one of the skinny, leggy ones to whom those thong swimsuits forgotten on the yacht belonged, carefully stored just in case someone like her might come along and need to borrow one of them.

'No.' He stood up. 'Like I said, my time on this yacht is limited, and no one to date has obliged me by requiring mouth-to-mouth resuscitation whilst out to sea.' He disappeared back into the bathroom with the kit and, instead of taking the opportunity to stand up and prepare herself for a speedy exit, Katy remained on the bed, gently flexing both her legs and getting accustomed to the stiffness where the bandages had been applied expertly over her wounds.

'So I'm your first patient?'

Lucas remained by the door to the bathroom, lounging against the doorframe.

Katy was riveted at the sight. He was still wearing his bathing trunks although, without her even noticing when he had done it, he had slung on his tee-shirt. He was barefoot and he exuded a raw, animal sexiness that took her breath away.

'Cuts and grazes don't honestly count.' Lucas grinned and strolled towards her, holding her spellbound with his easy, graceful strides across the room. He moved to stand by the window which, as did hers, looked out on the blue of an ocean that was as placid as the deepest of lakes. His quarters were air-conditioned, as were hers, but you could almost feel the heat outside because the sun was so bright and the sky was so blue and cloudless.

'I'm sorry if I ruined your down time.'

'You never told me why you leapt off your deck-chair and raced for the pool as though the hounds of hell were after you,' Lucas murmured.

She was in his bedroom and touching her had ignited a fire inside him, the same fire that had been burning steadily ever since they had been on his yacht. He knew why she had leapt off that deck chair. He had enough experience of the opposite sex to register when a woman wanted him, and it tickled him to think that she wasn't doing what every other woman would have done and flirting with him. Was that because she worked for him? Was that holding her back? Maybe she thought that he would sack her if she was too obvious. Or maybe she had paid attention to the speech he had given her at the start when he had told her not to get any crazy ideas about a relationship developing between them.

He almost wished that he hadn't bothered with that

speech because it turned him on to imagine her making a pass at him.

Lucas enjoyed a couple of seconds wondering what it would feel like to have her begin to touch him, blushing and awkward, but then his innate pragmatism kicked in and he knew that she was probably playing hard to get, which was the oldest game in the world when it came to women. She had revealed all sorts of sides to her that he hadn't expected, but the reality was that she *had* had an affair with a married man. She'd denied that she'd known about the wife and kiddies, and maybe she hadn't. Certainly there was an honesty about her that he found quite charming but, even so, he wasn't going to be putting any money on her so-called innocence any time soon.

'It was very hot out there,' Katy muttered awkwardly, heating up as she recalled the pivotal moment when raging, uncontrolled desire had taken her over like a fast-moving virus and she had just *had to escape*. 'I just fancied a dip in the pool and unfortunately I didn't really look where I was going. I should head back to my room now. I think I'll give my legs a rest just while I have these bandages on—and, by the way, thank you very much for sorting it out. There was no need, but thanks anyway.'

'How long do you think we should carry on pretending that there's nothing happening between us?' Which, frankly, was a question Lucas had never had to address to any other women because other women had never needed persuading into his bed. Actually, it was a question he had not envisaged having to ask *her,* considering the circumstances that had brought them together. But he wanted her and there was no

point having a mental tussle over the whys and where-
fores or asking himself whether it made sense or not.

On this occasion, self-denial probably made sense,
but Lucas knew himself and he knew that, given the
option of going down the route of what made sense
or the less sensible route of scratching an itch, then
the less sensible route was going to win the day hands
down every time.

He also knew that he wasn't a man who was into
breaking down barriers and jumping obstacles in
order to get any woman between the sheets—and
why would he do that anyway? This wasn't a game
of courtship that was going anywhere. It was a case
of two adults who fancied one another marooned on
a yacht for a couple of weeks..

In receipt of this blunt question, presented to her
without the benefit of any pretty packaging, Katy's
eyes opened wide and her mouth fell open.

'I beg your pardon?'

'I've seen the way you look at me,' Lucas murmured, moving to sit on the bed right next to her, and
depressing the mattress with his weight so that Katy
had to shift to adjust her body and stop herself from
sliding against him.

She should have bolted. His lazy, dark eyes on her
were like lasers burning a hole right through the good,
old-fashioned, grounded common sense that had dictated her behaviour all through her life—with the exception of those few disastrous months when she had
fallen for Duncan.

The slow burning heat that had been coursing
through her, the exciting tingle between her legs and
the tender pinching of her sensitive nipples—all re-

sponses activated by being in his presence and feeling his cool fingers on her—were fast disappearing under a tidal wave of building anger.

'The way I *look at you*?'

'Don't be embarrassed. Believe me, it isn't usually my style to force anyone's hand, but we're here and there's a sexual chemistry between us. Are you going to dispute that? It's in the air like an invisible electric charge.' He laughed with some incredulity. 'You're not going to believe this, but it's something I can't remember feeling in a very long time, if ever.'

'And you think I should be *flattered*?'

Lucas frowned because this wasn't the reaction he had been expecting. 'Frankly, yes,' he told her with complete honesty.

Katy gaped, even though she knew very well why a woman would be flattered to be the object of attention from Lucas Cipriani. He was drop-dead gorgeous and a billionaire to boot. If he made a pass at a woman, then what woman was going to stalk off in the opposite direction and slam the door in his face? He probably had a queue of them waiting to be picked.

Her lips tightened because what he saw as a flattering, complimentary approach was, to her, downright insulting.

At least the creep Duncan had had the wit to approach her a little less like a bull stampeding through a china shop.

But then, Katy concluded sourly, time wasn't on Lucas's side. They were here for a limited duration, so why waste any precious time trying to seduce her into bed the old-fashioned way?

'That's the most egotistical, arrogant thing I have ever heard *in my entire life*!'

'Because I've been honest?' But Lucas flushed darkly. 'I thought you were all in favour of the honest approach?'

'Who do you think I am?'

'I have no idea where you're going with this.'

'You think that you just have to snap your fingers and someone like me will dump all her principles and come running, don't you?'

'Someone like you?' But she had scored a direct hit, and he was guiltily aware that he *had* indeed compartmentalised her, however much he had seen evidence to the contrary.

'The sort of person,' Katy informed him with scathing distaste, 'Who needs a good, long lecture on making sure her little head doesn't get turned by being on a big, expensive boat—oh, sorry, *super-yacht*— with the great Lucas Cipriani! The sort of person,' she added for good measure, 'Who comes with a dubious reputation as someone who thinks it's okay to hop into bed with a married guy!' It made her even madder to think that she had fallen into the trap of forgetting who he really was, won over by his charm and the random confidences he had thrown her way which she had sucked up with lamentable enthusiasm.

And what made her even madder *still* was the fact that he had managed to read her so correctly! She thought she'd been the model of politeness, but he'd seen right through that and homed in laser-like on the fevered core of her that was attracted to him.

'You're over-analysing.' Lucas raked his fingers

through his hair and sprang to his feet to pace the cabin before standing by the window to look at her.

'I am *not* over-analysing,' Katy told him fiercely. 'I know what you think of me.'

'You don't.' Unaccustomed to apologising for anything he said or did, Lucas now felt...like a cad. He couldn't credit how she had taken his interest in her and transformed it into an insult, yet he had to admit to himself that his approach had hardly been handled with finesse. He'd been clumsy, and in no one's wildest imagination could it have passed for *honesty*.

'I know exactly what you think of me! And you've got a damned cheek to imagine that I would be so easy that I'd just fall into bed with you because you happened to extend the invite.'

'I... I apologise,' Lucas said heavily, and that apology was so unexpected that Katy could only stare at him with her mouth open. He looked at her with a roughened sincerity and she fought against relenting.

Glaring, she stood up. Her good intentions of sweeping out of his cabin with her head held high, now that she had roundly given him a piece of her mind, were undermined by the fact that she was wearing next to nothing and had to hobble a bit because the grazes on her knees were killing her.

'Katy,' he murmured huskily, stopping her in her tracks. He reached out to stay her and the pressure on her arm where his fingers circled her skin was as powerful as a branding iron. She had to try not to flinch. Awareness shot through her, rooting her to the spot. 'I don't, actually, think that you're easy and I certainly don't take it for granted that you're going to fall into bed with me because that's the kind of person you are. And,' he continued with grudging sincerity, 'If there's a part of me that is still wary, it's because it's my nature to be suspicious. The bottom line is that I want you, and I might be wrong but I think it's mutual. So tell me...is it?'

He took half a step closer to her, looked down and suppressed a groan at the delicious sight of her delicate breasts encased in stretchy fabric. 'If I've misread the signals,' he told her, 'Then tell me now and I'll back off. You have my word. Nor will I let it affect whatever lies down the line in terms of your position in my company. Say no, and this is never mentioned again. It will never have happened.'

Katy hesitated. She so badly wanted to tell him that, no, she most certainly was *not* interested in him *that* way, but then she thought of him backing away and leaving her alone and she realised with a jolt how much she enjoyed spending time in his company when they were tossing ideas around and sparring with one another. She also now realised that underneath that sparring had been the very thread of sexual attraction which he had picked up with his highly developed antennae.

'That's not the point,' she dodged feebly.

'What do you mean?'

'I mean...' Katy muttered *sotto voce*, red-faced and uncomfortable, 'It doesn't matter whether we're attracted to one another or not. It would be mad for us to do anything about it. Not that I would,' she continued at speed, face as red as a beetroot. 'After Duncan, I swore to myself that I would never make the mistake of throwing myself into anything with someone unless I really felt that they were perfect for me.'

'I've never heard such nonsense in my entire life,' Lucas said bluntly, and, feathers ruffled, Katy tensed and bristled.

'What's wrong with wanting the best?' she demanded, folding her arms, neither leaving the room nor returning to the bed, instead just standing in the middle as awkward as anything. He, on the other hand, looked totally at ease even though he was as scantily clad as she was. But then, he obviously wasn't the sort who gave a jot if his body was on display.

'Nothing's wrong with wanting the best,' Lucas concurred. 'But tell me, how do you intend to find it? Are you going to present each and every candidate with a questionnaire which they will be obliged to fill out before proceeding? I'm going to take a leap of faith here and assume that you didn't know about Powell's marital status. You went out with the man and presumably you believed that he was the right one for you.'

'I made a mistake,' Katy said defensively.

'And mistakes happen. Even if you're not being deliberately misled by a guy, you could both go out in good faith, thinking that it will go somewhere, only to discover that you hit obstacles along the way that make it impossible for you both to consider a life together.'

'And you're an expert because...?' Katy asked sarcastically.

'People are fond of self-deception,' Lucas delivered with all-knowing cool. 'I should know because I witnessed it first-hand with my father. You want something badly enough and you try and make it work and, if it all makes sense on paper, then you try all the harder to make it work. In a worst case scenario, you might actually walk up the aisle and then into a maternity ward, still kidding yourself that you've got the real deal, only to be forced to concede defeat, then cutting the ties is a thousand times more complicated.'

'You're so cynical…about *everything*.' She harked back to the lack of trust that had made him think that the only solution to saving his deal was to isolate her just in case.

'There's no such thing as the perfect man, Katy. With Powell, you got someone who deliberately set out to deceive you.' He shrugged. 'You might think I'm cynical but I'm also honest. I have never in my life set out to deceive anyone. I've never promised a bed of roses or a walk up the aisle.' He looked at her thoughtfully. 'You had a crap time with some guy who strung you along…'

'Which is why you should have believed me when I told you that I'd rather have walked on a bed of hot coals than have anything to do with him in my life again.'

'That's beside the point. At the time, I looked at the facts and evaluated them accordingly. What I'm trying to tell you is this: the world is full of men who will do whatever it takes to get a woman into bed, and that includes making promises they have no intention of keeping. With me, what you see is what you get. We're here, we're attracted to one another and that's all there is to it.'

'Sex for the sake of sex.' That was something she had never considered and surely *would* never consider. It contravened pretty much everything she had been taught to believe in. Didn't it? It was what Duncan had been after and that had repulsed her. Sex and love were entwined and to disentangle them was to reduce the value of both.

Lucas laughed at the disapproving, tight-lipped expression on her face. 'It could be worse,' he drawled. 'It could be sex for the sake of a happy-ever-after that is never going to be delivered.'

The air sizzled between them. Katy was mesmerised by the dark glitter in his eyes and could feel herself being seduced by opinions that were so far removed from her own. Yet he made them sound so plausible. Instead of giving her the freedom to enjoy a healthy and varied sex life, to take her time finding the right man for her, her experience with Duncan had propelled her ever further into a mind-set that rigidly refused to countenance anything but the guy who ticked all the boxes.

Wasn't Lucas right in many ways? How could you ever be sure of finding Mr Right unless you were prepared to bravely face down the probability that you might have to risk some Mr Wrongs first?

And who was to say that all Mr Wrongs were going to be creeps like Duncan? Some Mr Wrongs might actually be *fun*. Not marriage material, but *fun*.

Like Lucas Cipriani. He had Mr Wrong stamped all over him and yet...wouldn't he be fun?

For the first time in her life, Katy wondered when and how she had become so protective of her emotions and so incapable of enjoying herself in the way all other girls of her age would. Her parents had never laid down any hard and fast rules but she suspected now, looking back down the years, that she had picked things up in overheard conversations about some of the young women in distress they had helped. She had seen how unwanted pregnancies and careless emotional choices could destroy lives and she had consigned those lessons to the back of her mind, little knowing how much they would influence her later decisions.

Lucas could see the range of conflicting emotions shadowing her expression.

The man had really done a number on her, he thought, and along with that thought came another, which was that the first thing he would do, provided the deal went through, was to sling Powell out on his backside.

Whatever experiences she had had before the guy, he had clearly been the one she had set her sights on for a permanent relationship, and throwing herself into something only to find it was built on lies and deceit would have hit her hard.

For all her feisty, strong-willed, argumentative personality, she was a romantic at heart and that probably stemmed from her background. Sure she would have enjoyed herself as a girl, would have had the usual sexual experiences, but she would have kept her heart intact for the man she hoped to spend the rest of her life with, and it was unfortunate that that man happened to have been a married guy with a penchant for playing away.

'You may think that I don't have the sort of high moral code that you look for,' Lucas told her seriously. 'But I have my own code. It's based on honesty. I'm not in search of involvement and I don't pretend to be. You were hurt by Powell but you could never be hurt by me because emotions wouldn't enter the equation.'

Katy looked at him dubiously. She was surprised that she was even bothering to listen but a Pandora's box had been opened and all sorts of doubts and misgivings about that high moral code he had mentioned were flying around like angry, buzzing wasps.

'I'm not the type you would ever go for.' Lucas had never thought he'd see the day he actually uttered those words to a woman. 'And quite honestly, I second that, because I would be no good for you. This isn't a relationship where two people are exploring one another in the hope of taking things to the next level. This is about sex.'

'You're confusing me.'

'I'm taking you out of your comfort zone,' Lucas murmured, yearning to touch her, only just managing to keep his hands under lock and key. 'I'm giving you food for thought. That can't be a bad thing.'

Katy looked at him and collided with eyes the colour of the deepest, darkest night. Her heart did a series of somersaults inside her chest. He was temptation in a form she was finding irresistible. Every word he had said and every argument he had proffered combined to produce a battering ram that rendered her defenceless.

'You're just bored,' she ventured feebly, a last-ditch attempt to stave off the crashing ache to grab hold of what he was offering and hold on tight. 'Stuck here without a playmate.'

'How shallow do you think I am?' Lucas grinned, his expression lightening, his eyes rich with open amusement. 'Do you think I need to satisfy my raging libido every other hour or risk exploding? I'm tired of talking. I don't think I've ever spent this much time trying to persuade a woman into bed with me.'

'Should I be flattered?'

'Most definitely,' Lucas returned, without the slightest hesitation.

Then he reached out, trailed a long finger against her cheek and tucked some strands of coppery hair behind one ear. When he should have stopped and given her time to gather herself, because she was all over the place, he devastated her instead by feathering his touch along her collarbone then dipping it down to her cleavage.

Gaze welded to his darkly handsome face, Katy remained rooted to the spot. Her nipples were pinched buds straining against the bikini top. If she looked down she knew that she would see their roused imprint against the fabric. Her eyelids fluttered and then she breathed in sharply as he stepped closer to her and placed both of his big hands on her rib cage.

He had been backing her towards the bed without her even noticing and suddenly she tumbled back against the mattress and lay there, staring up at him.

She was about to break all her rules for a one-night stand and she wasn't going to waste any more time trying to tell herself not to.

CHAPTER SIX

EXCEPT KATY WASN'T entirely sure how she was going to initiate breaking all those rules. She'd never done so before and she was dealing with a man who had probably cut his teeth breaking rules. He'd made no bones about being experienced. Was he expecting a similar level of experience? Of course he was!

She quailed. Mouth dry, she stared at him in silence as he whipped off his shirt in one fluid movement and then stood there, a bronzed god, staring down at her. She greedily ate him up with her eyes, from his broad shoulders to his six-pack and the dark line of hair that disappeared under the low-slung swimming trunks.

Lucas hooked his fingers under the waistband of the trunks and Katy shot up onto her elbows, fired with a heady mixture of thrilling excitement and crippling apprehension.

What would he do if she were to tell him that she was a virgin? *Run a mile*, was the first thought that sprang to mind. Katy didn't want him to run a mile. She wanted him near her and against her and inside her. It made her feel giddy just thinking about it.

In the spirit of trying to be someone who might actually know what to do in a situation like this, she reached behind her to fumble unsuccessfully with the almost non-existent spaghetti strings that kept the bikini top in position.

Lucas couldn't have been more turned on. He liked that shyness. It wasn't something with which he was familiar. He leant over her, caging her in.

'You smell of the sun,' he murmured. 'And I don't think I've ever wanted any woman as much as I want you right now.'

'I want you too,' Katy replied huskily. She tentatively traced the column of his neck then, emboldened, his firm jawline and then the bunched muscles of his shoulder blades. Her heart was thumping hard and every jerky breath she took threatened to turn into a groan.

He eased her lips apart and flicked his tongue inside her mouth, exploring and tasting her, and setting off a dizzying series of reactions that galvanised every part of her body into furious response. Her small hands tightened on his shoulders and she rubbed her thighs together, frantic to ease the tingling between them.

Lucas nudged her with his bulging erection, gently prising her legs apart and settling himself between them, then moving slowly as he continued to kiss her.

He tugged at her lower lip with his teeth, teasing her until she was holding her breath, closing her eyes and trembling like a leaf.

Katy didn't think that anything in the world could have tasted as good as his mouth on her and she pulled him against her with urgent hands.

She wished she'd rid herself of her bikini because now it was an encumbrance, separating their bodies.

She wriggled under him, reaching behind herself and, knowing what she wanted to do, Lucas obliged, urging her up so that he could tug free the ties. Then he rose up to straddle her and looked down, his dark eyes slumberous with desire.

Katy had never thought about sex without thinking about love and she had never thought about love without painting a tableau of the whole big deal, from marriage to babies in a thirty-second fast-forward film reel in her head.

Big mistake. In all those imaginings, her body had just been something all tied up with the bigger picture and not something needing fulfilment in its own right. The fact she had never been tempted had only consolidated in her head that sex was not at all what everyone shouted about.

Even the momentous decision that desire had propelled her into making, to ditch her hard and fast principles and sleep with him, had been made with no real prior knowledge of just how wonderfully liberating it would feel for her.

Yes, she had imagined it.

In practice, it was all oh, so wildly different. She felt joyously free and absolutely certain that what she was doing was the right thing for her to do.

Burning up, she watched Lucas as he looked at her. He was so big, so dangerously, *sinfully* handsome, and he was gazing at her as though she was something priceless. The open hunger in his eyes drove away all her inhibitions and she closed her eyes on a whimper as he leaned back down to trail his tongue against her collarbone.

Then he pinned her hands to her sides, turning her

into a willing captive so that he could fasten his mouth on one nipple. He suckled, pulling it into his mouth while grazing the stiffened bud with his tongue.

This was sex as Katy had never imagined it. Wild, raw and basic, carrying her away on a tide of passion that was as forceful as a tsunami. This wasn't the physical connection from a kind, considerate and thoughtful guy who had wooed her with flowers and talked about a happy-ever-after future. This was the physical connection from a guy who had promised nothing but sex and would walk away from her the minute their stay on his yacht had come to an end.

His mouth and tongue against her nipple were sending piercing arrows of sensation through her body. She was on fire when he drew back to rid himself of his swimming trunks. The bulge she had felt pressing against her was impressively big, big enough for her to feel a moment of sheer panic, because how on earth could something so big fit inside her and actually feel good?

But that fear wasn't allowed to take root because desire was smothering it. He settled back on the bed and then tugged down the bikini bottoms.

Katy closed her eyes and heard him laugh softly.

'Don't you like what you see?' Lucas teased and she cautiously looked at him. 'Because I very much like what *I* see.'

'Do you?' Katy whispered, very much out of her depth and feverishly making all sorts of comparisons in her head between her boyish figure and the women he probably took to his bed. She wasn't going to dwell on it, but she wasn't an idiot. Lucas Cipriani could have any woman he wanted and, whilst she was confident enough about her looks, that confidence took a very understandable beating when she considered that the man in bed with her was every woman's dream guy. 'Sexy' didn't get more outrageous.

Lucas felt a spurt of pure rage against Powell, a man whose existence he had known nothing about a week ago. Not only had he destroyed Katy's faith in the opposite sex, but he had also pummelled her self-esteem. Any human being with functioning eyesight could have told her that she was a show-stopper.

He bent over to taste her pouting mouth whilst at the same time gently inserting his hand between her thighs.

She wasn't clean-shaven down there and he liked that; he enjoyed the feel of her soft, downy fluff against his fingers. He liked playing with it before inserting one long finger into her.

It was electrifying. He slid his finger lazily in long strokes, finding the core of her and the tight little bud that throbbed as he zeroed in on it. In the grip of sensations she had never known before, Katy whimpered and clutched him, all frantic need and craving. She was desperate to ride the crest of a building wave and her whimpers turned into soft, hitched moans as she began to arch her spine, pushing her slight breasts up, inviting him to tease a nipple with his tongue.

He released her briefly to fetch a condom from his wallet then he was over her, nudging her legs apart with his thigh and settling between them. Nerves firmly back in place, Katy smoothed exploratory hands along his back, tracing the hardness of muscle and sinew.

Her coppery hair was in tangles over her shoulders,

spread like flames across the pillows. Lucas stroked some of the tangles back and kissed her.

'I want you,' Katy muttered into his mouth, and she felt him smile. Desire was a raging force inside her, ripping all control out of her grasp and stripping her of her ability to think straight, or even to think at all.

She felt his impatience and his need matching hers as he pushed into her, a deep, long thrust that made her cry out. He stilled and frowned.

'Don't stop,' she begged him, rising up so that he could sink deeper into her. She was so wet for him and so ready for this.

'You're so tight,' Lucas murmured huskily in a driven undertone. 'I can't describe the sensation, *mia bella*.'

'Don't talk!' Katy gasped, urging him on until he was thrusting hard, and the tight pain gave way to a soaring sense of pleasure as he carried her higher and higher until, at last, she came...and it was the most out-of-body experience she could ever have imagined. Wracked with shudders, she let herself fly until she weakly descended back down to planet Earth. Then, all she wanted to do was wrap her arms around him and hold him tightly against her.

Lucas was amused when she hugged him. He wasn't one for hugs, but there was something extraordinarily disingenuous about her and he found that appealing.

He gently moved off her and then looked down and frowned, his brain only slowly making connections that began to form into a complete picture, one that he could scarcely credit.

There wasn't much blood, just a few drops, enough

for him to work out that none of that shyness and hesitancy had been put on. She'd blushed like a virgin because that was exactly what she was. He looked at her as the colour drained from her face.

'This is your first time, isn't it?'

For Katy, that was the equivalent of a bucket of cold water being poured over her. She hadn't thought that he would find out. She had vaguely assumed that if she didn't say anything then Lucas would never know that she had lost her virginity to him. She hadn't wanted him to know because she had sensed, with every pore of her being, that he wouldn't be thrilled.

For a man who didn't do commitment, and who gave warnings about the perils of involvement, a virgin would represent the last word in unacceptable.

She quailed and clenched her fists because making love to Lucas had been the most wonderful thing in her life, just the most beautiful, *right* thing she had ever done, and now it was going to be spoiled because, quite rightly, he was going to hit the roof.

She wriggled and tried to yank some of the covers up because there was no way she was going to have an argument with him in the nude.

'So what?' She eyed him mutinously under the thick fringe of her lashes and glowered. 'It's really no big deal.'

'No big deal?' Lucas parroted incredulously. 'Why didn't you tell me?'

'Because I know how you would have reacted,' Katy muttered, hugging her knees to her chest and refusing to meet his eyes for fear of the message she would read there.

'You know, do you?'

Katy sneaked a glance at him, and just as fast her eyes skittered away. He was sprawled indolently on the bed, an in-your-face reminder of the intimacy they had just shared. She was covering up for all she was worth but he was carelessly oblivious to his nakedness.

'I wanted to do it.' She stuck her chin up and challenged him to argue with that. 'And I knew that if I told you that I'd never slept with anyone before you'd have run a mile. Wouldn't you?'

Lucas grimaced. 'I probably would have been a little cautious,' he conceded.

'Run a mile.'

'But I would have been flattered,' he admitted with even more honesty. 'I would also have been more gentle and taken my time.' He raked his fingers through his hair and vaulted out of the bed to pace the floor, before snatching a towel which was slung over the back of a chair and loosely settling it around his waist. Then he circled to sit on the bed next to her. 'It *is* a big deal,' he said gently. He took her hands in his and stroked her wrists until her clenched fists relaxed. 'And if I was a little rough for you, then I apologise.'

'Please don't apologise.' She smiled cautiously and stroked his face, and it was such an intimate gesture that she almost yanked her hand back, but he didn't seem to mind; indeed he caught her hand and turned it over so that he could place a very tender kiss on the underside of her wrist.

'You're beautiful, *cara*. I don't understand how it is that you've remained a virgin. Surely there must have been other men before Powell?'

Katy winced at the reminder of the man who had

been responsible for landing them here together on this yacht. It was fair to say that, however hateful her memories of him were, they seemed a lot less hateful now. Maybe one day she might even mentally thank him because she couldn't see how she could ever regret having slept with Lucas.

'That was another of those down sides to having parents who were pillars of the community.' Katy let loose a laugh. 'There were always expectations. And especially in a tiny place, when you're growing up, everyone knows everyone else. Reputations are lost in the snap of a finger. I didn't really think about that, though,' she said thoughtfully. 'I just knew that I wanted the whole love and marriage thing, so my standards were maybe a bit on the high side.'

She sighed and smiled ruefully at Lucas, who was looking at her with such sizzling interest that every pulse in her body raced into overdrive.

'When Duncan came along, I'd just returned from university and I wasn't quite sure what direction my life was going to take. I remember my mother and I talking about the social scene at university, and my mum asking me about the boys, and something must have registered that I needed to take the next step, which was finding someone special.' She gazed at Lucas. 'I slept with you because I really wanted to. You said a lot of stuff…basically about seizing the day…'

'I had no idea I was addressing a girl who had no experience.'

'But, you see, that's not the point.' Katy was keen to impress this on him. 'The point is that you made me think about things differently. I know this isn't going anywhere but at least you were honest about that and you gave me a choice.' Duncan had denied her the truth about himself and, even if this was just a one night stand, which was something she had always promised herself she would never do, was it really worse to lose her virginity to Lucas than to a liar like Duncan?

She gazed up at him earnestly and Lucas lowered his head and very tenderly kissed her on the lips. He could have taken her again, right then, but she would be sore. Next time, he intended to make it up to her, to take his time. It blew his mind to think that she had come to him as a virgin. It was a precious gift and he knew that, even though he couldn't fully understand what had led her to give it to him.

'Yes, *cara,* there will be no "for ever after" with us but believe me when I tell you that, for the time we're together, I will take you to paradise and back. But before that...can I interest you in a shower?' He stood up and looked down at her slender perfection.

'With you?'

'Why not?' Lucas raised his eyebrows. 'You'd be surprised how different an experience it can be when you're in a shower with your lover.'

Katy shivered pleasurably at that word...*lover.* She shook her head and laughed. 'I think I'm going to relax here for a bit, then I'll go back to my cabin.'

Of course there would be no 'for ever after'...and she was tempted to tell him that she understood that well enough without having to be reminded of it.

'Why?' Lucas frowned and then heard himself inviting her to stay with him, which was astonishing, because he had always relished his privacy, even when

he was involved with someone. Sex was a great outlet, and his appetite for it was as healthy as the next
man's, but when the sex was over his craving for his
own space always took precedence over post-coital
closeness. He'd never spent the night with a woman.

'Because I need to be on my own for a bit.'

Right then, Lucas felt that by the time they were
ready to leave this yacht he would have introduced
her to the joys of sharing showers and shown her how
rewarding it could be to spend the night in his bed…

Katy had fallen into something of a sleep when she
heard the bang on the door to her cabin. For the first
time since she had arrived on Lucas's cruiser, she had
retired to bed without anything to eat, but then it had
been late by the time she had eventually left his cabin.

Having intended to sneak out while he was showering, she had remained where she was and they had
spent the next few hours in one another's arms. To his
credit, he had not tried to initiate sex again.

'I can show you a lot of other ways we can satisfy
one another,' he had murmured, and he had proceeded
to do just that.

In the end, *she* had been the one whose body had
demanded more than just the touch of his mouth and
the feel of his long, skilful fingers. *She* had been the
one to guide him into her and to demand that he come
inside her.

It had been a marathon session and she had made
her way back to her cabin exhaustedly, still determined not to stay the night in his room, because if
she slept in her own bed then she would somehow be
able to keep control of the situation.

'Katy! Open up!'

Katy jerked up with a start at the sound of Lucas's voice bellowing at her through the locked door. She leapt out of the bed, half-drugged with sleep, and yanked open the door, every fibre in her body responding with panic to the urgency in his voice.

She looked at him in consternation. He was in a pair of jeans and a black, figure-hugging tee-shirt. Not the sort of clothes anyone would consider wearing for a good night's sleep. Her already panicked antennae went into overdrive.

'Lucas! What time is it?'

'You need to get dressed immediately. It's a little after five in the morning.'

'But why?'

'Don't ask questions, Katy. Just do it.' He forged into the room and began opening drawers, yanking out a pair of jeans, quickly followed by the first tee-shirt that came to hand. Even at that hour in the morning, it would be balmy outside. 'Maria is sick.' He looked at his watch. 'Very sick. It has all the makings of acute appendicitis. Any delay and peritonitis will kick in, so you need to dress and you need to dress fast. I can't leave you on this yacht alone.'

Katy dashed into the bathroom and began stripping off the oversized tee-shirt she slept in, replacing it with the jeans and tee-shirt she had grabbed from his outstretched hand.

'Do you think I might get up to no good if you're not around to keep an eye on me?' she asked breathlessly, only half-joking because that deeply intimate step she had taken with him had clearly not been a deeply intimate step for him. He was a man who could detach, as he had made perfectly clear.

'Not now, Katy.'

'How will we get her to the hospital?' She flushed, ashamed that her thoughts had not been one hundred percent on the woman of whom she had grown fond during the short time she had been on the yacht.

'Not by helicopter,' Lucas told her, his every movement invested with speed as he took her arm and began leading her hurriedly out of the bedroom. 'Too long to get my pilot here and nowhere to land near the hospital.'

They were walking quickly to a part of the yacht Katy hadn't known existed, somewhere in the bowels of the massive cruiser.

'Fortunately, I am equipped to deal with any emergency. And to answer your earlier question...' He briefly glanced down at her, rosy, tousled and so utterly adorable that she literally took his breath away. 'I'm not taking you with me because I think you might get up to no good in my absence. I'm taking you with me because if something happened to you and I wasn't around I would never forgive myself.'

Something flared inside her and she felt a lump in her throat, then she quickly told herself not to be an idiot, because that wasn't a declaration of caring; it was a simple statement of fact. If she was left alone on the yacht and she needed help of any sort, she would be unable to swim to shore and unable to contact him. How would he, or anyone in his position, be able to live with that?

Things were happening at the speed of light now. In a move she thought was as impressive as a master magician's sleight of hand, the side of the yacht opened up to reveal a speedboat, an expensive toy within an expensive toy. Maria, clearly in a great deal of pain but smiling bravely, was waiting for them and was soon ensconced, to be taken to the island.

Dawn was breaking as they hit the island, a rosy, blushing dawn that revealed lush trees and flowers and narrow, winding roads disappearing up sloping hills.

A car was waiting for them, a four-wheel drive with an elderly man behind the wheel. They reached the town in under half an hour and then Maria was met in Accident and Emergency and whizzed through in a wheelchair, everything moving as though orchestrated.

Katy had barely had time to draw breath. Only when the older woman had been wheeled into the operating theatre, and they were sitting in the small hospital café with a cup of coffee in front of them, did she begin to pay attention to her surroundings… and then it registered.

'Your name is all over this hospital…'

Lucas shifted uncomfortably and glanced around him. 'So it would seem.'

'But why?'

'My money went towards building most of it.' He shrugged, as though that was the most natural response in the world. 'My father's family owned a villa here and he spent his holidays on the island with my mother and me when I was very young. It's about the only thing my father didn't end up giving away to one of the ex-wives who fleeced him in their divorce proceedings. I expect he had strong sentimental attachments to it. There was a prolonged period when the villa got very little use but, as soon as I was able, I began the process of renovation. I have the money, so when the head of the hospital came to me for help it was only natural for me to offer it.'

It felt odd to be offering her this slither of personal information and for a few seconds he was uncomfortable with what felt like a loss of his prized self-control.

What was it about this woman that made him behave out of character? Not in ways that should be disconcerting, because she neither said nor did anything that raised red flags, but still...

He was intensely private, not given to sharing. However, this was the first time he had been on the island with any woman. He rarely came here but, when he did, he came on his own, relishing the feeling of being swept back to happier times. Was Katy's necessary presence here the reason why he was opening up? And why was he making a big deal of it anyway? he thought with prosaic irony. She couldn't help but have noticed his name on some of the wards, just as she couldn't have failed to notice how eager the staff were to please.

'The old hospital, which was frankly far from perfect, was largely destroyed some time ago in a storm. I made sure that it was rebuilt to the highest specification. The infrastructure here is not complex but it is essential it all works. The locals depend on exporting produce, and naturally on some tourism. The tourists, in particular, are the wealthy sort who expect things to run like clockwork. Including the hospital, should one of them decide to take ill.' He grinned. 'There's nothing more obnoxious than a rich tourist who finds himself inconvenienced.'

'And I'm guessing you don't include yourself in that category?' Katy teased. Their eyes met; butterflies fluttered in her tummy and her heart lurched. They hadn't had a chance to talk about what had happened because she had disappeared off to her own quarters, and here they were now, caught up in unexpected circumstances.

She had no idea whether this was something that would be more than a one-night stand. She hoped it was. She had connected with him and she would feel lost if the connection were abruptly to be cut. It panicked her to think like that but she had to be honest with herself and admit that Lucas was not the man she had originally thought he was. He still remained the last person on earth she could ever contemplate having an emotional relationship with, but he had shown her the power of a sexual relationship and, like a starving person suddenly led to a banquet, she didn't want the experience to end. Just yet.

But nothing had been said and she wasn't going to engineer round to the conversation.

'Do *you* think I'm obnoxious?' Lucas questioned softly and she blushed and squirmed, so very aware of those dark eyes fastened to her face.

'My opinion of you *has* changed,' Katy admitted, thinking back to the ice-cold man who had forced her hand for the sake of a deal. She thought that her opinion also *kept* changing. She didn't want to dwell on that, so instead she changed the subject. 'What about Maria? When will we find out what the outcome is?'

'There's every chance it will be a positive one.'

Lucas glanced at his watch. 'I personally know the surgeon and there's no one better. I've contacted her family, who will be in the waiting area, and as soon as the operation is over I've asked to be called. I don't anticipate any problems at all. However...'

'However?'

'It does mean that there will be a small change of plan.'

'How do you mean?'

'We will no longer be based on the yacht. For a start, without Maria around, there will be no one to attend to the cooking and all the other little things she takes care of, and it's too late to find a replacement who can stay on board. So we'll have to relocate to my villa. I can get someone to come in on a daily basis and, furthermore, I will be on hand in case there are any complications following surgery.'

He paused. 'Maria worked for my father before he...began steadily going off the rails. My mother was very fond of her, so I've made sure to look out for her and her family, and also made sure to carry on employing her in some capacity when my father's various wives decided that they would rather have somewhat smarter people holding the fort in the various properties.'

His mobile phone buzzed and he held up one hand as he spoke in rapid Italian to the consultant, the concerned lines on his face quickly smoothing over in reaction to whatever was being said on the other end.

'All's gone according to plan,' he said. 'But, had she not reached the hospital when she did, then it would have been quite a different story. Now, why don't you wait here while I have a word with some of her family? I won't be long. I'll also arrange for your clothes and possessions to be transported to the villa.' He looked at her, head tilted to one side, then he patted his pocket. 'You can call your parents, if you like,' he said gruffly. 'I've been checking your phone, and I see that they've taken you at your word and not texted, but I expect they'd like to hear from you.'

He handed over the phone and her eyes shone, because more than anything else this demonstrated that he finally trusted her, and she found that that meant a great deal to her.

'What can I say to them?' she asked, riding high on the fact that she was no longer under suspicion. A barrier between them had been crossed and that felt good in the wake of what they had shared.

'Use your discretion,' Lucas told her drily. 'But it might be as well not to mention too many names, not that I think anything can go wrong with the deal at this stage. It's a hair's breadth away from being signed.' He stood up, leaving her with her mobile phone, and it felt like the greatest honour bestowed on her possible. 'I'll see you shortly and then we'll be on our way.'

CHAPTER SEVEN

LYING ON THE wooden deckchair by the side of the infinity pool that graced the lush grounds of his villa and overlooked the distant turquoise of the ocean, Lucas looked at Katy as she scythed through the water with the gracefulness of a fish.

The finalising of the deal had taken slightly longer than Lucas had anticipated, but he wasn't complaining. Indeed, he had encouraged his Chinese counterparts to take their time in sorting out all the essential details on which the takeover pivoted. In the meantime…

Katy swam to the side of the pool and gazed at him with a smile.

Up above, the sun had burnt through the early-morning clouds to leave a perfectly clear, milky, blue sky. Around them, the villa afforded absolute isolation. It was ringed with trees and perched atop a hill commanding views of the sea. Lucas had always valued his privacy and never more so than now, when he didn't want a single second of his time with her interrupted by so much as a passing tradesman. Not that any passing tradesman would be able to make it past the imposing wrought-iron gates that guarded the property.

He had dismissed all help, ensuring that the villa was stocked with sufficient food for their stay.

Just him…and her…

Right now, she was naked. He had half-expected, after that tentative surrender four days ago when she had placed her small hand on his thigh and sent his blood pressure through the roof, that a three-steps-forward, one-step-back game might ensue. He had predicted a tussle with her virtuous conscience, with lust holding the trump card, but in fact she had given herself to him without a trace of doubt or hesitation. He had admired her for that. Whatever inner battles she had fought, she had put them behind her and given generously.

'It's beautiful in here.' She grinned. 'Stop being so lazy and come and swim.'

'I hope that's not the sound of a challenge,' Lucas drawled, standing up, as naked as she was. He couldn't see her without his libido reacting like a lit rocket and now was no exception.

'Is sex *all* you ever think about, Lucas?' But she was laughing as she stepped out of the pool, the water streaming off her slick body.

'Are you complaining?' His eyes darkened and he balled his hands into fists. The urge to take her was so powerful it made him feel faint. He wanted to settle her on a towel on the ground and have her hard and fast, like a teenager in the grip of too much testosterone. Around her he lost his cool.

'Not at the moment,' Katy said breathlessly, walking straight into his arms. They had a lot of sex but, in fact, they also talked as well, and laughed, and enjoyed a level of compatibility she would never have thought possible when she had first met him.

He was still the most arrogant man she had ever met but there was so much more to him as well. She had no idea what was going to happen when they returned to London and she didn't think about it. Maybe they would carry on seeing one another...although how that would work out when she was his employee she couldn't quite fathom. The gossip would be out of control and he would loathe that.

For the first time in her life, Katy was living in the moment, and she wasn't going to let fear of what might or might not lie round the corner destroy her happiness.

Lucas cupped her pert bottom, which was wet from swimming, and kneaded it between his hands, driving her closer to him so that his rock-hard erection pushed against her belly.

She held him, played with him, felt the way his breathing changed and his body stiffened. She couldn't stop loving the way he reacted to her. It made her feel powerful and sexy and very, very feminine.

'I'm too big for deck-chair sex,' Lucas murmured.

'Who said anything about scx?' Katy breathed. 'We could just...you know...'

'I think I'm getting the picture.' He emitted a low, husky laugh and settled her on the cushioned deck chair, arranging her as carefully as an artist arranging a model he was about to paint, lying her in just the right place with her legs parted, hanging over either side of the chair, leaving her open for his attentive ministrations.

Then, sitting at the foot of the chair on his over-sized beach towel, he tugged her gently down towards his mouth and began tasting her. He slid his tongue into her, found the bud of her clitoris and licked it delicately, feathering little explosions of sensation through her, and he continued licking and teasing, knowing at which point she would begin to buck against his mouth as those little explosions became more and more impossible to control.

When he glanced up, he could see her small breasts, pointed and crowned with the dusky pink of her nipples, which were pinched from the water cooling on them. Her lips were parted, her nostrils flared as she breathed laboriously and her eyes were closed.

A thought flashed through his head. His condoms were nowhere to hand. What would happen if he were to sweep her up right now, hoist her onto him and let her ride them both to one of the body-shattering orgasms that they seemed strangely adept at giving one another? What if he were to feel himself in her without the barrier of a condom? Would it be such a bad thing? It wasn't as if pregnancy would be a certainty.

Shock at even thinking such a thing stilled him for a second. He'd never had thoughts like that in his life before and it implied a lack of self-control he found disturbing.

He killed the wayward thought that had sprung from nowhere and drove a finger into her, rousing her deep inside, and feeling her begin to spasm as she began to soar towards a climax.

She came against his mouth, arching up with an

abandoned cry of intense satisfaction, and then and only then did he allow her to touch him, with her mouth and with her hands.

The errant desire to take her without protection had been ruthlessly banished from his head but it left a lingering taste of unease in his mouth as they both subsided and flopped back into the pool to cool off.

Katy swam to Lucas but he stiffened and turned away, striking out into the water and rapidly swimming four lengths, barely surfacing for air as she watched from the side. He'd rejected her just then. Or maybe she'd been imagining it. Had she? He certainly hadn't done the usual and held her against him, coming down from a high with his body still pressed up against hers.

Sensitive to the fact that this was not a normal situation, that it was the equivalent of a one-night stand stretched out for slightly longer than the one night, Katy got out of the pool and walked over to her towel, anchoring it firmly around her so that she was covered up. Then she watched him as he continued swimming, his strong, brown body slicing through the water with speed and efficiency.

He didn't spare her a glance and after five minutes she retired to the villa and to the *en suite* bathroom which had been designated for her but rarely used, now she and Lucas were lovers.

The villa was magnificent, interestingly laid out with lots of nooks and crannies in which to relax, and huge, open windows through which breezes could circulate freely through the house. It lacked the slick sophistication of his yacht and was rather colonial in style with a stunning mixture of wood, billowing muslin at the windows, shutters and overhead fans. Katy loved it. She settled with her book into a rocking chair on the wide veranda that fronted the villa.

She kept waiting for Lucas to show up but eventually she gave up and nodded off. It was a little after four but still baking hot and, as always, cloudless.

Allowing her mind to drift, yanking it back every time it tried to break the leash and worry away at Lucas's reaction earlier on, she was scarcely aware of time going by, and it was only when she noticed the tell-tale signs of the sun beginning to dip that she realised that several hours must have passed.

In a panic, she scrambled to her feet and turned round, to find the object of her feverish imaginings standing framed in the doorway…and he wasn't smiling. Indeed, the humorous, sexy guy she had spent the past week with was noticeably absent.

'Lucas!' She plastered a smile on her face. 'How long have you been standing there? I was reading… er… I must have nodded off…'

Lucas saw the hurt beneath the bright smile and he knew that he had put it there. He had turned his back on her and swam off, and he had carried on swimming because he had needed to clear his head. When he'd finally stopped, she was gone and he had fought against the desire to seek her out because he was not going to allow a simple sexual liaison to get out of control. When they returned to London, this would finish and his life would return to normal, which was exactly as it should be. So he'd kept his distance and that would have upset her. He clenched his jaw and focused on what really mattered now, which was a turn of events that neither of them could have predicted.

'You've been talking to your parents. What, exactly, have you told them?'

'Lucas, I have no idea what you're talking about.'

'Just try and think.' He moved to stand in front of her, the beautiful lines of his handsome face taut and forbidding. 'Did you tell either of them where you were? What you were doing here? Who you were with?'

'I...you're making me nervous, Lucas. Let me think...no; *no*. I just told Mum that I was in Italy and that it was lovely and warm and that I was fine and having a good time...'

'I have just spent the past hour on the phone with the Chinese company. It seems that they were told by Powell that I was the wrong kind of person to be doing business with—that I was the sort of guy who seduces innocent girls and shouldn't be trusted as far as I can be thrown. It would seem that news travelled and connections were made. Someone, somewhere, figured out that we're here together and social media has taken the information right into Powell's hands and given the man ammunition to blow my deal sky-high at the last minute.'

The colour drained from Katy's face. When he said that 'connections were made', it was easy to see how. They had been into the little town several times over the past few days, checking on Maria and doing all sorts of touristy things. He could have been recognised and, whilst *she* wouldn't have been, someone could have sneakily taken a picture of them together and tagged them in something they posted online. The mind boggled.

'This is *not* my fault, Lucas. You know how pervasive social media is.' But it *was* her fault. She was the one with the connection to Duncan and, if gossip had been spread, then who knew what her mum might have mentioned to anyone in the village? Someone might be friends with Duncan on Facebook or whatever. Guilt pinked her cheeks, but before she could go on the defensive he held up one imperious hand to close down her protest.

'I'm not going to waste time going back and forth with this.' He frowned down at her and sighed. 'I'm not playing blame games here, Katy, and you're right: there's no privacy left anywhere. If anyone is to blame, then it's me, because I should have been more circumspect in my movements here. The place is small, I'm a well-known face, it's close to the busiest time of year for tourists and they have smart phones. But the fact remains that I have now been left with a considerable problem.

'No, perhaps I should amend that: when I say that *I* have a considerable problem, it might be fairer to say that we *both* have a considerable problem. Your ex approached Ken Huang and told him a story, and there's an underlying threat to go to the press and take public this sordid tale of a young, innocent girl being taken advantage of by an unscrupulous billionaire womaniser.'

Katy paled. 'Duncan wouldn't...'

But he would.

'He's played up your innocence to the hilt.'

'He knew...' Katy swallowed painfully. 'He knew

that I was inexperienced. I never thought that he would use the information against me. I trusted him when I confided in him.'

In the midst of an unfolding nightmare, Lucas discovered that the deal which should have been uppermost in his mind was overshadowed by a gut-wrenching sympathy for her vulnerability, which Powell had thoroughly taken advantage of.

Lucas dragged over a chair to join hers and sat heavily, closing his eyes for a few seconds while he sifted through the possibilities for damage limitation. Then he looked at her.

'The man has an axe to grind,' Lucas stated flatly. 'Tell me why.'

'Does it matter?'

'In this instance, everything matters. If I need to use leverage, then I need to know where to apply it. I don't play dirty but I'm willing to make an exception in this case.'

'It ended really badly between me and Duncan.' She shot him a guilty, sidelong look before lowering her eyes. 'As you may have gathered. It wouldn't have been so bad if I'd found out about his wife and children *after* I'd slept with him, but I think he was doubly enraged that, not only did I find out that he was married, but he hadn't even succeeded in getting me into bed *before* I'd had a chance to find out.'

'Some men are bastards,' Lucas told her in a matter-of-fact voice. 'It has to be said that some women leave a lot to be desired as well. It's life.'

'You mean those women your father married,' Katy murmured, distracted, thinking that on some level their approaches to life had been similarly tarnished by unfortunate experiences with the opposite sex. It was easy to think that, because you came from a wildly different background from someone, the things that affected the decisions you made had to be different, but that wasn't always the case. Money and privilege had been no more guarantee of a smooth ride in his case than a stable family background had been in hers.

Lucas shrugged. 'I have no more time for the gold-diggers,' he gritted. 'At least a guy with his head screwed on has a fighting chance of recognising them for what they are and can take the necessary precautions. You, I'm guessing, had no chance against a skilled predator. Continue.'

'I'd confided in my best friend,' Katy said, with a grimace. 'I felt such a fool. Claire was far more experienced than me, and she was livid when I told her about the messages I'd accidentally seen on his phone from his wife. He'd made a mistake in leaving it on the table while he vanished off to the toilet when we'd been having a meal out. Up popped a reminder to phone the kids to say good night and to remember some party they were going to on the weekend. He'd told me he was going to be away on business. Weekends, he'd always said, were tricky for him because he was trying to kick-start a photography business and they were the only times he could do whatever he had to do—networking and the like—because he was at the bank during the week.'

'A skilled excuse,' Lucas said drily. 'The man obviously came with form.'

'That was what Claire said. She told me that I was

probably not the first, which needless to say didn't make me feel at all better.'

'It was as though she was looking at a very young, very naïve stranger from the advantageous position of someone who was much older and wiser. And she had Lucas to thank for that.

'Anyway, she started doing a little digging around. The world's a small place these days.' Katy grimaced. 'She found that he was a serial womaniser and she went to see his wife.'

'Ah.'

'I had no idea at the time that that was her plan, and afterwards she confessed that she didn't quite know what had prompted her to take such drastic action. But she was upset on my behalf and, in a weird way, upset on behalf of all the other girls he had conned into sleeping with him. His marriage fell apart on the back of that, so...'

'I'm getting the picture loud and clear. The ex who hates you and holds you responsible for the breakdown of his marriage now has the perfect vehicle for revenge put into his hands.'

'If I had told you the whole story in the first place, you would have realised that there was no chance I could have been any kind of mole. Then we wouldn't have ended up here and none of this would be happening now.'

Lucas smiled wryly. 'Really think that would have been how it would have worked?'

'No,' Katy answered honestly. 'You wouldn't have believed me. I would have been guilty until proven innocent.' At that point in time, he'd been a one-dimensional autocrat—ruthless, suspicious, arrogant. At this point in time…

She didn't know what he was and she didn't want to think too hard about it. They had a situation and she began to see all the nooks and crannies of it. If Duncan decided to take his revenge by publicising a tale of some sordid love tryst between Lucas and herself, not only would Lucas's deal be ruined but he would have to face the horror of the world gossiping about him behind his back. His reputation would be in tatters because, however much a lie could be disproved, mud inevitably stuck. He was the sort of guy who would claim to shrug off the opinions of other people, but that would be a heck of a lot to shrug off.

And it would all have been *her* fault.

Could she allow that to happen?

And then, aside from Lucas, there was the matter of her and her parents. They would never live it down. She felt sick thinking about their disappointment and the whispers that would circulate around the village like a raging forest fire blazing out of control. When she returned to see them, people would stare at her. Her parents would shy away from discussing it but she would see the sadness in their eyes.

She would be at the heart of a tabloid scandal: 'desperate virgin in sordid tryst with billionaire happy to use her for a few days before discarding her'. 'Sad and gullible innocent lured to a villa for sex, too stupid to appreciate her own idiocy'.

'Marry me!' she blurted out and then looked at him with wide-eyed dismay.

She jumped to her feet and began pacing the veranda, before curling onto the three-seater wicker sofa and drawing her knees up.

'Forget I said that.'

'Forget that I've received a marriage proposal?' Lucas drawled, strolling over to the sofa and sitting down, body angled towards her. 'It's the first I ever have...'

'It wasn't a marriage proposal,' Katy muttered, eyeing him with a glower, her cheeks tinged with heated colour.

'Sure about that? Because I distinctly heard the words "marry me".'

'It wasn't a *real* marriage proposal,' Katy clarified, hot all over. 'It just seemed that...if Duncan does what he's threatening to do—and I guess he will, if he's already started dropping hints to your client—then it's not just that your deal will be jeopardised—'

'Ruined,' Lucas elaborated for good measure. 'Shot down in flames...dead in the water and beyond salvation...'

'All those things,' Katy mumbled, guilt washing over her with tidal force. She breathed in deeply and looked him directly in the eyes. 'It's not even a marriage proposal,' she qualified. 'It's an *engagement* proposal. If we're engaged then Duncan can't spread any rumours about sordid trysts and he can't take your reputation away from you by implying that you're the sort of womaniser who's happy to take advantage of... of...an inexperienced young girl...'

He wasn't saying anything and she wished he would. In fact, she couldn't even read what he was thinking because his expression was so shuttered.

'Your deal can go ahead,' she plunged on. 'And you

won't have to worry about people gossiping about you behind your back.'

'That sort of thing has never bothered me.'

Katy almost smiled, because that was just *such* a predictable response, then she thought about people gossiping about him and her heart clenched.

'What's in it for you?' Lucas asked softly.

'Firstly,' Katy told him with absolute honesty, 'You're here because of me, so this is pretty much my fault. Secondly, I know how much this deal means to you. Thirdly, it's not just about you. It's also about me. My parents would be devastated and I can't bear the thought of that. And *you* might not care about what other people think of you, but *I* care what other people think of me. I wouldn't be able to stay on at either of my jobs because of the shame, and I would find it really hard to face people at home who have known me all my life.'

It was slowly dawning on her that there had been something in his softly spoken words when he had asked her what would be in it for her, something she hadn't registered immediately but which she was registering fast enough now.

'It would work.' She tilted her chin at a defiant angle to rebut the hidden insinuation she had read behind his words. She might have been wrong in her interpretation but she didn't think so. 'And it would work brilliantly because there's no emotional bond between us. I mean, there's no danger that I would get it into my head that I was doing anything but role-playing. You could get your deal done, we could defuse a potential disaster and I would be able to live with myself.'

'You're presenting me with a business proposition, Katy?' He dealt her a slashing smile that threatened to knock her sideways. 'You, the ultimate romantic, are presenting me with a business proposition that involves a phoney engagement?'

'It makes sense,' she defended.

'So it does,' Lucas murmured. 'And tell me, how long is this phoney engagement supposed to last?' He couldn't help but be amused by this from the girl who typified everything that smacked of flowers, chocolates, soul mates and walks up the aisle in a frothy, meringue wedding dress. Then he sobered up as he was struck by another, less amusing thought.

Had he changed her into something she was never meant to be? He had shown Katy the marvels of sex without strings because it was something that worked for him, but had he, in the process, somehow *changed* her? For reasons he couldn't explain, he didn't like the thought of that, but he pushed those uneasy reservations to one side, choosing instead to go for the straightforward explanation she had given, which was that it was a solution that would work for her as well as it would work for him.

Katy shrugged. 'You still haven't said whether you think it's a good idea or not.'

'I couldn't have come up with something better myself.' Lucas grinned, then looked at her seriously. 'But you should know that I wouldn't ask you to do anything you feel uncomfortable about.'

Katy's heart did that weird, clenching thing again. 'I feel very comfortable about this and, as for how long it would last, I haven't given much thought to that side of things.'

'You'd be deceiving your parents,' Lucas pointed out bluntly.

'I realise that.' She sighed and fiddled with the ends of her long hair, frowning slightly. 'I never thought that the ends justified the means, and I hate the thought of deception, but, between the devil and the deep blue sea, this seems the less hurtful option.'

Lucas looked at her long and hard. 'So we're a loved-up couple,' he murmured, his dark eyes veiled. 'And in fact, so irresistibly in love with one another that we escaped for some heady time to my yacht where we could be together free from interruption from the outside world. Your colleagues at work might find it a little hard to swallow.'

'You'd be shocked at how many people believe in love at first sight.' Katy smiled. 'You know, just because *you're* such a miserable cynic when it comes to love, doesn't mean that the rest of us are as well…'

'So now I'm a miserable cynic,' Lucas drawled, reaching out to tug her towards him. 'Tell me how likely it is that you would fall head over heels for a miserable cynic?'

'Not likely at all!' Katy laughed, looking up at him, and her heart did that funny thing again, skipping a beat, which made her feel as though she'd been cruising along quite nicely only to hit a sudden patch of violent turbulence. 'I'm afraid what you have is a girl who could only fall head over heels for someone as romantic as she is!' She frowned and tried to visualise this special person but the only face to fill her head was Lucas's dark and devastatingly handsome one.

'If we're going to be engaged, then we need to get

to know one another a whole lot better,' Lucas told her, still admiring the very practical streak which had led her to propose this very practical solution. Although, why should he be that surprised? She was a whizz at IT and that, surely, indicated a practical side to her that she herself was probably not even aware of.

He stood up, his fingers still linked with hers, and led her back through the villa and in the direction of his bedroom.

'What are you going to do with me once the engagement is over?' he murmured, toeing open his bedroom door, and then propelling her backwards to his bed while she tried to contain her laughter. 'I mean...' he lowered his head and kissed her, flicking his tongue into her mouth and igniting a series of fireworks inside her '... I'm assuming that, since you are the one with the clever plan to stage a fake engagement, you'll likewise be the one with the clever plan when it comes to wriggling out of it. So how will you dispose of me?'

He slid his hand under her tee-shirt and the warmth of her skin sent his body immediately into outer orbit. She wasn't wearing a bra, and he curved his big hand over her breast and gently teased her nipple until it was ripe and throbbing between his skilful fingers. They tumbled onto the bed, he settled her under him and straddled her so that he could see her face as he continued to tease her.

As usual, Katy's brain was losing the ability to fire on all cylinders, especially when he pushed up the tee-shirt and lowered himself to suckle her nipple. He looked up and caught her eyes, then flicked his tongue over the stiffened bud before devoting his attention to her pouting lips, kissing her again until she felt as though she was coming apart at the seams.

'Well?' He nuzzled the side of her neck and she wriggled and squirmed underneath him, hands on his waist, pushing into the waistband of his trousers and feeling his buttocks.

'Oh, I think we'll just drift apart,' Katy murmured. 'You know the sort of thing. You'll be working far too hard and you'll be spending most of your time in the Far East because of the deal you've managed to secure. I'll grow lonely and...who knows?...maybe I'll find some hunky guy to help me deal with my loneliness...'

'Not if I have any say in the matter,' Lucas growled, cupping her between her legs and rubbing until the pressure of his hand did all sorts of things through the barrier of her clothes.

'No,' Katy panted, bucking against his hand as she felt the stirrings of an orgasm building. 'I have to admit,' she gasped, her fingers digging into his shoulders, 'That finding another man wouldn't work, so perhaps you'll have to tire of me not being around and find someone else instead...'

And how she hated the thought of that although, she laughed shakily to herself, in the game of make-believe, what was the big deal? 'Let's not talk about this.' She tugged apart the button on his trousers and awkwardly tried to pull down the zipper. She looked at him and met his eyes. 'We can be engaged...for two months. Long enough to find out that we're not really compatible and short enough for no lasting damage.'

'You're the one calling the shots.' Lucas nipped her

neck, reared up and yanked off his shirt, before proceeding to undress her very, very slowly and, when she was completely naked, pushing apart her thighs and gazing down for a few charged seconds at her stupendous nudity. 'And I like it... Now, stop talking. It's time for action, my wife-to-be...'

CHAPTER EIGHT

KATY HAD A week to think about what would happen when they arrived back in London. The surprise announcement of their engagement had hit the headlines with the fanfare of a royal proclamation. Sitting in the little square in the island's town, whilst they sipped coffees in the sunshine, she had scrolled through the newspapers on her phone and read out loud some of the more outrageous descriptions of the 'love at first sight' scenario which Lucas had vaguely hinted at when he had called, firstly, the anxious Ken Huang and then his personal assistant, who had been instructed to inform various elements of the press.

Lucas had been amused at her reaction to what, for him, was not entirely surprising, considering the extent of his wealth and eligibility.

Now, finally on the way back to London, with the helicopter that had delivered them to his super-yacht due to land in under half an hour, the events of the past few days no longer felt like a surreal dream that wasn't quite happening.

It was one thing to read the centre pages of the tabloids and marvel that she was actually reading about herself. It was quite another to be heading straight into the eye of the hurricane where, she had been warned by Lucas, there might still be some lingering press attention.

'At least there's been some time for the story to calm down a bit,' he had told her. 'Although there's nothing the public loves more than a good, old-fashioned tale of romance.'

'Except,' Katy had quipped, 'A good, old-fashioned tale of a break-up.'

Lucas had laughed but, now that the story was out in the open, now that her parents had been told and had doubtless told every single person in the village and beyond, Katy was beginning to visualise the fall-out when the phoney engagement came to an end. In short, her theory about the end justifying the means was beginning to look a little frayed at the edges.

She had spoken to her parents every single day since the announcement and had played fast and loose with fairy stories about the way her heart had whooshed the minute she had clapped eyes on Lucas, the second she had *known* that it was the real thing. They had wanted details and she had given them details.

Katy knew that she would have to face all sorts of awkward questions when this charade was over. No doubt, she would be an object of pity. Her parents would be mortified that yet again she had been short-sighted enough to go for the wrong guy. If they ever happened to meet Lucas in the flesh, then they would probably suss that he was the wrong guy before the fairy tale even had time to come crashing down.

The world would feel sorry for her. Her friends would shake their heads and wonder if there was something wrong with her. And, inevitably, there would be malicious swipes at her stupidity in thinking that she could ever have thought that a relationship with someone like Lucas Cipriani could ever last the distance.

Who did she think she was?

And yet she was happy to close the door on reality because the thrill of living for the moment was so intense. It ate everything up. All her incipient doubts, and all her darkest imaginings about what lay beyond that two-month time line they had agreed upon, were swept aside and devoured by the intensity of appreciating every single second she had with him.

The timer had been set and every feeling, every sensation and every response was heightened to an excruciating pitch.

'I have something to tell you.' Lucas pulled her towards him. It still surprised him the way he couldn't get enough of her. 'Tonight we will be the main event at a black-tie ball.'

Katy stared at him in consternation. 'Tonight?'

'The Chinese company's throwing it. It seems that Ken Huang is keen to meet you, as are all the members of his family—and, in all events, with signatures now being put to paper, it's a fitting chance to celebrate our engagement publicly as well as the closing of the deal. Your parents, naturally have been invited to attend, as have your friends and other family members. Have you got any other family, as a matter of interest?'

Katy laughed. 'Shouldn't you know that?'

'I should,' Lucas said gravely, 'But these things sometimes get overlooked in a hectic whirlwind romance.' She was wearing a little blue top and some faded cut-off jeans and, if they had been anywhere remotely private, he would have enjoyed nothing better than getting her out of both items of clothing.

'I've never been to a ball in my life before,' Katy confided, brushing aside her unease because not only would she have to mix with people she had no experience of mixing with but she would also be *on show*. 'It would be nice if Mum and Dad came, but honestly, I doubt they will. It wouldn't be their thing at all, and my dad's calendar is so packed with community stuff that he will struggle to free up the time without more advance warning.' She sighed and looked at him a little worriedly.

Lucas was overwhelmed by a sudden surge of protectiveness that came from nowhere and left him winded. He drew back slightly, confused by an emotion that had no place within his vocabulary. 'It's no big deal.'

'It's no big deal *for you*,' Katy told him gently. 'It's a huge deal *for me*.'

Lucas frowned. 'I thought everyone liked that sort of thing,' he admitted. 'There'll be a host of well-known faces there.'

Katy laughed because his self-assurance was so deeply ingrained that it beggared belief. 'Part of me didn't really think about how this would play out when we returned to London,' she admitted. 'It felt very… unreal when we were in Italy.'

'Yes it did,' Lucas agreed. 'Yet surely you would have expected a certain amount of outside attention focused on us…?'

He knew that this very naivety was something he

found intensely attractive about her. Having experienced all the trappings of extreme wealth for the past fortnight, she still hadn't joined the dots to work out what came as part and parcel of that extreme wealth, and intrusive media coverage at a time like this was one of those things. Not to mention a very necessary and unfortunately inevitable black-tie event. He decided that it would be unwise to mention just how much attention would be focused on her, and not just from reporters waiting outside the venue.

'You're going to tell me I'm an idiot.'

'I've discovered I quite like idiots.' He touched her thigh with his finger and Katy shivered and came close to forgetting all her apprehensions and doubts. They might be acting out a charade when it came to an emotional involvement with one another, or at least the sort of emotional involvement that came under the heading of 'love', but when it came to physical involvement there was no reporter who wouldn't be convinced that what they had was the real deal.

'When we get to the airfield, don't be surprised if there are one or two reporters waiting and just follow my lead. Don't say anything. I've given them enough fodder to be getting on with. They can take a couple of pictures and that'll have to do. In a week, we'll be yesterday's salacious gossip. And don't worry—you'll be fine. You never run yourself down, and you're the only woman I've ever met who gets a kick out of telling me exactly what she thinks of me. Don't be intimidated by the occasion.' He laughed and said, only partly in jest, 'If you're not intimidated by me, then you can handle anything.'

Buoyed up by Lucas's vote of confidence, Katy

watched as the door of the helicopter was pushed open to blue sky, a cooler temperature than they had left behind and a fleet of reporters who flocked towards them like a pack of wolves scenting a fresh kill.

Katy automatically cringed back and felt his arm loop through hers, gently squeezing her reassuringly as he batted aside questions and guided her towards the black car waiting for them.

A reporter yelled out asking to see the engagement ring. Katy gazed in alarm at her ring-free finger and began stumbling out something vague when Lucas cut into her stammering non-answer, drawing briefly to a halt and smoothly explaining that the jeweller's was going to be their first stop as soon as they were back in the city.

'But it won't be, will it?' she asked as soon as they were settled into the back of the car with the glass partition firmly shut between the driver and them.

'Do you think you're going to be able to get away without a ring on your finger at the ball?' Lucas said wryly. 'Brace yourself for a lot more attention than you got from those reporters back there at the air field.' He settled against the door, inclining his big body towards her.

She was waking up to life in *his world*. Not the bubble they had shared in the villa, and even more so on his yacht, where they'd been secluded and tucked away from prying eyes, but the real world in which he moved. She was going to be thrown into the deep end and it couldn't be helped. Would she be able to swim or would she flounder?

He had told her that she would be fine and again he felt it—that strong streak of protectiveness when he thought about her lost and trying to find her way in a world that was probably alien to her. He knew from experience that the people who occupied his world could be harsh and critical. He disliked the thought of seeing her hurt, even though the practical side of him knew that the disingenuousness that he found so intensely appealing would be a possible weakness under the harsh glare of real life, away from the pleasant bubble in which they had been cocooned.

'We can stop for a bite to eat, get freshened up at my place and then head out to the jeweller's, or else we can go directly there. And, on the subject of things to be bought, there'll be a small matter of something for you to wear this evening.'

'Something to wear…'

'Fancy. Long.' He shrugged. 'Naturally you won't be expected to foot the bill for whatever you get, Katy.' He wondered whether he should go with her, hold her hand.

Katy stilled and wondered how the insertion of money into the conversation could make the hairs on the back of her neck stand on end. It felt as though something was shifting between them, although she couldn't quite put her finger on what that *something* was.

'Of course.' Politeness had crept into her voice where before there had only been teasing warmth, and she didn't like it. But how could she pretend that things hadn't changed between them? They had embarked on a course of action that wasn't *real* and perhaps that was shaping her reactions towards him, making her prickly and on edge.

Yes, she was free to touch, but there were now in-built constraints to their relationship. They were supposed to project a certain image, and that image would require her to step out of her comfort zone and do things she wasn't accustomed to doing. She was going to be on show and Lucas was right—she wasn't in the habit of running herself down and she wasn't going to start now. If she was hesitant and apprehensive, then that was understandable, but she wasn't going to let sudden insecurities dictate how she behaved.

'I think I'd rather get the ring and the outfit out of the way, then at least I can spend the afternoon relaxing, although I don't suppose I'll have much time to put my feet up.' She sighed and said with heartfelt honesty, 'I never thought I'd be getting an engagement ring under these circumstances.' She looked at her finger and tried to think back to those days when she had stupidly believed that Duncan was the man for her. Then she glanced across at Lucas and shivered. He was so ridiculously handsome, so madly self-assured. He oozed sex appeal and her body wasn't her own when she was around him. When she was around him, her body wanted to be his and only his.

What if this were a real engagement, not some crazy charade to appease other people?

She was suddenly filled with a deep, shattering yearning for a real relationship and for everything that came with it. This time it wasn't just for a relationship to rescue her from making decisions about her future, which had been the reason she'd allowed herself to be swept away by fantasies about tying the knot with Duncan.

Time slowed. It felt so right with Lucas and yet he was so wrong. How was that possible? She had proposed a course of action that had made sense, and she had imagined she could handle it with cool and aplomb because what she felt for Lucas was lust and lust was a passing fever. But looking at him now, feeling his living, breathing warmth next to her... The time they had spent together flickered like a slow-motion movie in her head: the laughter they had shared; the conversations they had had; their lazy love-making and the soaring happiness that had engulfed her when she had lain, warm and sated, in his arms.

Katy was overcome with *wanting more*. She transferred her gaze blindly down to her finger and pictured that ring on it, and then her imagination took flight and she thought of so much more. She imagined him on bended knee...smiling up at her...wanting her to be his wife *for real* and not a pretend fiancée for two months...

She loved him. She loved him and he certainly didn't love her. Sick panic filled her at the horror that she might have opened the door for hurt, and on a far bigger scale than Duncan had delivered. Indeed, next to Lucas, Duncan was a pale, ineffectual ghost and obviously one who had not taught her any lessons at all.

Lucas noted the emotions flickering across her face and instantly barriers that had been carefully crafted over many years fell back into place. He didn't do emotion. Emotions made you lose focus, sapped your strength, made you vulnerable in ways that were destructive. Gold-diggers had come close to destroying his business, but it had been his father's own emotions that had finally let him down. Lucas could feel himself mentally stepping back and he had the oddest feeling that just for a while there he had been standing too close to an inferno, the existence of which he had been unaware.

He leaned forward, slid the glass partition to one side and instructed the driver to deliver them to a jeweller Katy had never heard of but which, she guessed, would be the sort of place to deal with very, very exclusive clients.

'Where are we?' she asked forty-five minutes later, during which time Lucas had worked on his computer, catching up on transactions he had largely ignored while they had been in Italy, he'd told her without glancing at her.

'Jeweller's,' he said. 'Stop number one.'

'It doesn't look like a jeweller's...'

'We wealthy folk like to think that we don't frequent the sort of obvious places every other normal person does,' Lucas said, back in his comfort zone, back in control.

'Interesting story here,' he expanded as the car drew to a smooth halt and the driver stepped out to open the door for her. 'The woman who owns the place, Vanessa Bart, inherited it from her father and employed a young girl to work here—Abigail Christie. Long story but, to summarise, it turned out that she had a child from my friend Leandro, unbeknown to him, and like star-crossed lovers they ended up meeting again quite by chance, falling in love and getting married a while back.'

'The fairy tale,' Katy said wistfully as they were allowed into a shop that was as wonderful as Aladdin's cave. 'It's nice that it happens now and again.' She smiled and whispered, 'There's hope for me yet.'

'Wrong sentiment for a woman on the verge of wearing an engagement ring from the man of her dreams.' Lucas's voice was less amused than he would have liked. He laughed shortly and then they were being ushered into the wonderful den of exquisite gems and jewels, tray after tray of diamond rings being brought out for her to inspect, none of them bearing anything so trashy as a price tag.

Lucas watched her down-bent head as she looked at the offerings. He was a man on the verge of an engagement and, whether it was phoney or not, he suddenly had that dangerous, destabilising feeling again…the sensation of getting close to a raging inferno, an inferno he couldn't see and therefore could not protect himself against. He shifted uneasily and was relieved when she finally chose the smallest, yet as it turned out one of the dearest, of the rings.

'Rest assured,' Katy said quietly as they were once again passengers in the back seat of the car, 'That I won't be taking the ring with me when this is all over.'

'Let's just live a day at a time.' Lucas was still unsettled and frankly eager now to get to his office where he wouldn't be inconvenienced by feelings he couldn't explain. 'Before we start deciding who gets what when we're dividing the spoils.'

'Where do we go for the dress?'

'Selfridges. I've already got my PA to arrange a personal shopper for you.'

'A personal shopper…'

'I have to get to my office, so will be unable to accompany you.'

As their eyes tangled, Katy felt the thrill of being

here next to him, even if that thrill was underlain with the presence of danger and the prospect of unhappiness ahead. 'I wouldn't expect you to come with me. I don't need you to hold my hand. If you let me have the name of the person I'm supposed to meet, then I can take it from there. And, after I've done all the other stuff I'm supposed to do, then I think I'm going to head back to my place and get changed there.'

Begin stepping away, she thought sadly. *Begin a process of detachment. Protect yourself.*

Lucas was already putting the romance of Italy behind him. There would be a ring on her finger, but he wasn't going to be hankering for all that undiluted time in each other's company they had had at his villa. He was slipping back to his reality and that involved distancing himself from her; Katy could sense that.

'Why?' Lucas realised that he didn't want her not to be around when he returned to his apartment. He wanted her to be there for him and he was irritated with himself for the ridiculous gap in his self-control.

'Because I want to check on my place, make sure everything's in order. So I'll meet you at the venue. You can text me the details.' She sounded a lot brisker than she felt inside. Inside, she wanted so much more, wanted to take without consequence, just as she wanted to give without thought. She wanted him to love her back and she wanted to shove that feeling into a box and lock it away to protect her fragile heart.

'You'll be nervous.' Lucas raked his fingers through his hair, for once on the back foot with his legendary self-control. 'There'll be reporters there.

You won't know what to do. You'll need me to be there with you, by your side.'

Where had that come from?

'But...' His voice as smooth as silk, he regained his footing. 'I see that you might want to check your place and check your mail.' He was back on familiar ground and he relaxed. 'We've got our lives to be getting on with.' He smiled wryly. 'Why kid ourselves otherwise? Don't worry. In a few weeks' time, this will be little more than something you will one day laugh about with your kids.'

'Quite,' Katy responded faintly, sick with heartache, for which she knew that she had only herself to blame. 'I'll see you later.' She forced herself to smile and marvelled that he could be so beautiful, so cool, so composed when she was breaking up inside. But then, he hadn't crossed the lines that she had.

Katy had no idea where to start when it came to looking for something to wear to a black-tie event because she had never been to one in her life before, and certainly, in her wildest imagination, had never dreamt that she would be cast in the starring role at one. She had phoned her mother but, as predicted, it had been impossible at short notice, what with her father's community duties. She had promised that she would send lots of pictures. Now, suddenly, she felt quite alone as she waited for her personal shopper to arrive.

It took over two hours for a dress to be chosen and, no matter how much she told herself that this was all an act, she couldn't help wondering what it would feel like to be trying these clothes on for real, to parade for a man who returned her love, at an event that would celebrate a union that wasn't a charade.

The dress she chose was slim-fitting to the waist, with a back scooped so low that wearing a bra was out of the question, but with an alluringly modest top half that fell in graceful layers to the floor. When she moved, it swirled around her like a cloud, and, staring at the vision looking back in the mirror, she felt the way Cinderella might have felt when the wand had been waved and the rags had been replaced with the ball gown that would later knock Prince Charming off his feet.

Prince Charming, however, had left her thoroughly to her own devices. He was back in the real world and already distancing himself from her without even realising it.

The Fairy Godmother would have to come up with more from her little bag of tricks than ever to turn Lucas into anything more than a guy who had fancied her and had talked her into having sex with him. He would happily sleep with her until the designated time was over, and then he would shove her back into the nearest pumpkin and head straight back to the women he was accustomed to dating, the women who slotted into his lifestyle without causing too many ripples.

She had expected the car from earlier to collect her but when the driver called for her at home, punctual to the last second, and when she went outside, it was to find that a stretch limo was waiting for her.

She felt like a princess. It didn't matter what was real or what was fake, she was floating on a cloud. But that sensation lasted just until they arrived at the hotel and she spotted the hordes of reporters, the beautiful people stopping to smile and pose for photos and the crowds milling around and gaping, as though they were being treated to a live cabaret. The limo pulled to a slow stop and nerves kicked in like a rush of adrenaline injected straight into her blood system. She feared that she wouldn't be able to push her way through the throng of people.

Then, like magic, the crowd parted and she was looking at Lucas as she had never seen him before. Her eyes weren't the only ones on him. As one, everyone turned. He had emerged from the hotel and was impeccably dressed in his white dress shirt and black trousers, everything fitting like a dream. He was so breathtakingly beautiful that Katy could scarcely bring herself to move.

The scene was borderline chaos, with guests arriving, cameras snapping, reporters jostling for prime position, but all of that faded into the background for Lucas as his eyes zeroed in on the open door of the limo and the vision that was Katy stepping out, blinking but holding her own as cameras flashed all around her.

Lucas felt a surge of hot blood rush through him. Of course she was beautiful. He knew that. He had known it from the very first minute he had set eyes on her in his office, but this Katy was a feast for sore eyes, and she held him captive. Their eyes met and he was barely aware of walking towards her, hand outstretched, gently squeezing her small hand as she placed it in his.

'You look amazing, *cara*,' he murmured with gruff honesty.

Nerves threatening to spill over, and frantically aware of the popping of camera bulbs and the rapt attention of people who were so far removed from her world that they could have been from another planet, Katy serenely gazed up at him and smiled in her most confident manner.

'Thank you, and so do you. Shall we go in?'

CHAPTER NINE

KATY HAD TO call upon every ounce of showmanship and self-confidence acquired down the years to deal with the evening.

Blinded by the flash of cameras, which was only slightly more uncomfortable than the inquisitive eyes of the hundred or so people who had been selectively invited to celebrate the engagement of the year, she held on to Lucas's hand and her fixed, glassy smile didn't waver as she was led like a queen into the hotel.

Lucas had told her that she looked amazing, and that buoyed her up, but her heart was still hammering like a drum beating against her ribcage as she took in the flamboyant décor of the five-star hotel.

It was exquisite. She had no idea how something of this calibre could be rustled up at a moment's notice, but then money could move mountains, and Lucas had oodles of it.

In a daze, she took in the acres of pale marble, the impeccable line of waiting staff in attendance, the dazzling glitter of chandeliers and an informal bar area dominated by an impressive ice sculpture, around which was an even more impressive array of canapés for those who couldn't wait for the waitresses to swing by. There was a buzz of interest and curiosity all around them.

'You'll be fine,' Lucas bent to murmur into her ear. 'After an hour, you'll probably be bored stiff and we'll make our departure.'

'How can we?' Katy queried, genuinely bewildered. 'Aren't *we* the leading actors in the production?'

'I can do whatever I like.' Lucas didn't crack a smile but she could hear the rich amusement in his lowered voice. 'And, if you feel nervous, rest assured that you outshine every other woman here.'

'You're just saying that…they'll all be wondering how on earth you and I have ended up engaged.'

'Then we'd better provide them with an explanation, hadn't we?' He lowered his head and kissed her. His hand was placed protectively on the small of her back and his mouth on hers was warm, fleeting and, oh, so good. Everything and everyone disappeared and Katy surfaced, blinking, ensnared by his dark gaze, her body keening towards his.

She wanted to cling and carry on clinging. Instead, she stroked his cheek briefly with her fingers and then stepped back, recalling the way he had reminded her earlier that what was happening here was just a show.

'Perhaps you could introduce me to the man you're doing the deal with.' She smiled, looking around her and doing her best to blank out the sea of beautiful faces. 'And thanks,' she added in a low voice, while her body continued to sizzle in the aftermath of that kiss. 'That was an inspired way to provide an explanation. I think you're going to be far better at this than I could ever hope to be.'

'I'll take that as a compliment,' Lucas drawled, wanting nothing more than to escort her right back into his limo and take her to his bed. 'Although I'm not entirely sure whether it was meant to be. Now, shall we get this party started?'

Having been introduced to Ken Huang, who was there with his family and two men who looked very much like bodyguards, Katy gradually edged away from the protective zone around Lucas.

Curiosity warred with nerves and won. She was surrounded by the beautiful people you saw in the gossip magazines and, after a while, she found that she was actually enjoying the experience of talking to some of those famous faces, discovering that they were either more normal than she had thought or far less so.

Every so often she would find herself drifting back towards Lucas but, even when she wasn't by his side, she was very much aware of his dark gaze on her, following her movements, and that made her tingle all over. There was something wonderfully possessive about that gaze and she had to constantly stop herself from luxuriating in the fallacy that it was heartfelt rather than a deliberate show of what was expected from a man supposedly in love with the woman wearing his ring.

Katy longed to glue herself to his side but she knew that circulating would not only remind Lucas that she was independent and happy to get on with the business of putting on a good show for the assembled crowd, just as he was, but would also shore up the barriers she knew she should mentally be erecting between them.

Everything had been so straightforward when she had been living with the illusion that what she felt for him was desire and nothing more.

With that illusion stripped away, she felt achingly vulnerable, and more than once she wondered how she was going to hold on to this so-called relationship for the period of time they had allotted to it.

In theory, she would have her window, during which she could allow herself to really enjoy him, even if she knew that her enjoyment was going to be short-lived.

In practice, she was already quailing at the prospect of walking away from him. He would probably pat her on the back and tell her that they could remain good friends. The truth was that she wasn't built to live in the moment, to heck with what happened next. Investing in a future was a by-product of her upbringing and, even though she could admit to the down side of that approach, she still feverishly wondered whether she would be able to adopt the right attitude, an attitude that would allow her to live from one moment to the next.

Thoughts buzzing in her head like a horde of hornets released from their nest, she swirled the champagne in her glass and stared down at the golden liquid while she pictured that last conversation between them. She dearly wished that she had the experience and the temperament to enjoy what she had now, instead of succumbing to dark thoughts about a future that was never going to be.

From across the crowded room, Lucas found his fiancée with the unerring accuracy of a heat-seeking missile. No matter where she was, he seemed to possess the uncanny ability to locate her. She wasn't taller than everyone else, and her outfit didn't stand out as being materially different from every other fancy long, designer dress, but somehow she emanated a light that beckoned to him from wherever she was. It was as if he was tuned into her on a wave length that was inaudible to everyone except him.

Right now, and for the first time that evening, she was on her own, thoughtfully staring down into a flute of champagne as though looking for answers to something in the liquid.

Abruptly bringing his conversation with two top financiers to an end, Lucas weaved his way towards her, approaching her from behind.

'You're thinking,' he murmured, leaning down so that he could whisper into her ear.

Katy started and spun round, and her heart began to beat faster. *Thud, thud, thud.*

She had shyly told the three colleagues who'd been invited to the ball about Lucas, glossing over how they had met and focusing instead on how they had been irresistibly drawn towards one another.

'You know how it is,' she had laughed coquettishly, knowing that she was telling nothing but the absolute truth, 'Sometimes you get hit by something and, before you know it, you're going along for the ride and nothing else matters.'

Lucas's stunning eyes on her now really did make her feel as though she had been hit head-on by a speeding train and she had to look down just in case he caught the ghost of an expression that might alert him to the way she really felt about him.

'Tired?' Lucas asked, drawing her towards the dance floor.

A jazz band had been playing for the past forty-five minutes, the music forming a perfect backdrop to the sound of voices and laughter. The musicians were on a podium, in classic coat and tails, and they very much looked as though they had stepped straight out of a twenties movie set.

'A little,' Katy admitted. His fingers were linked through hers and his thumb was absently stroking the side of hers. It made her whole body feel hot and she was conscious of her bare nipples rubbing against the silky fabric of her dress. The tips were stiff and sensitive and, the more his thumb idly stroked hers, the more her body went into melt down.

This was what he did to her and she knew that if she had any sense at all she would enjoy it while she had it. Instead of tormenting herself with thoughts of what life would be like when he disappeared from it, she should be relishing the prospect of climbing into bed with him later and making love until she was too exhausted to move a muscle.

'It's really tiring talking to loads of people you don't know,' she added breathlessly as he drew her to the side of the dance floor and turned her to face him.

The lighting had been dimmed and his gorgeous face was all shadows and angles.

'But you've been doing a pretty good job of it,' Lucas assured her with a wry smile. 'And here I was imagining that you would be a little out of your depth.'

Katy laughed, eyes dancing as she looked up at him. 'That must have been a blessed relief for you.'

'What makes you say that?' After spending the

past hour or so doing the rounds, Lucas felt relaxed for the first time that evening. No one had dared ask him any direct questions about the engagement that had sprung from nowhere, and he had not enlightened anyone, aside from offering a measured explanation to Ken Huang and his wife, both of whom, he had been amused to note, were full of praise for the romance of the situation. He had thought them far too contained for flowery congratulations but he'd been wrong on that point.

Under normal circumstances, he would have used the time to talk business. There were a number of influential financiers there, as well as several political figures with whom interesting conversations could have been initiated. However, his attention had been far too taken up with Katy and following her progress through the room.

People were keen to talk to her; he had no idea what she'd told them, but whatever it was, she had obviously struck the right note.

With women and men alike. Indeed, he hadn't failed to notice that some of the men had seemed a lot busier sizing her up than listening to whatever she had had to say. From a distance, Lucas had had to swallow down the urge to muscle in on the scene and claim his property—because she wasn't his and that was exactly how it ought to be. Possessiveness was a trait he had no time for and he refused to allow it to enter into the arrangement they had between them.

But several times he had felt his jaw tighten at the way her personal space had been invaded by men who probably had wives or girlfriends somewhere in the room, creeps with fancy jobs and flash cars who figured that they could do what they wanted with whomever they chose. Arrangement or no arrangement, Lucas had been quite prepared to land a punch if need be, but he knew that not a single man in the room would dare cross him by overstepping the mark.

Still.

Had she even noticed the over-familiarity of some of those guys? Should he have warned her that she might encounter the sort of men who made her odious ex pale in comparison?

'I can't imagine you would have wanted to spend the evening holding my hand,' she teased with a catch in her voice. 'That kiss of yours did the trick, and I have to say no one expressed any doubt about the fact that the most unlikely two people in the world decided to get engaged.'

'Even the men who had their eyes on stalks when they were talking to you?'

Katy looked at him, startled. 'What on earth are you talking about?'

'Forget it,' Lucas muttered gruffly, flushing.

'Are you *jealous*?'

'I'm not the jealous type.' He downed his whisky in one long swallow and dumped the empty glass, along with her champagne flute, on a tray carried by one of the glamorous waitresses who seemed to know just where to be at the right time to relieve important guests of their empty glasses.

'No.' Katy was forced to agree because he really wasn't, and anyway, jealousy was the domain of the person who actually *felt* something. She smiled but it was strained. 'No need to point out the obvious!'

Lucas frowned even though she was actually saying all the right things. 'That kiss, by the way,' he murmured, shifting his hand to cup the nape of her neck, keen to get off a subject that was going nowhere, 'Wasn't just about making the right impression.'

'It wasn't?'

'Have you stopped to consider that I might actually have wanted to kiss you?'

Katy blushed and said with genuine honesty, 'I thought it was more of a tactical gesture.'

'Then you obviously underestimated the impact of your dress,' Lucas delivered huskily. 'When I saw you get out of the back of my limo, my basic instinct was to get in with you, slam the door and get my driver to take us back to my apartment.'

'I don't think your guests would have been too impressed.' But every word sent a powerful charge of awareness racing through her already heated body. He was just talking about sex, she told herself weakly. Okay, so he was looking at her as though she was a feast for the eyes, but that had nothing to do with anything other than desire.

Lucas was excellent when it came to sex. He was just lousy when it came to emotion. Not only was he uninterested in exploring anything at all beyond the physical, but he was proud of his control in that arena. If he had foresworn involvement on an emotional level because of one bad experience with a woman, then Katy knew that somehow she would have tried to find a way of making herself indispensable to him. A bad experience left scars, just as Duncan had left her with scars, but scars healed over, because time moved on and one poor experience would always end up buried under layers of day-to-day life.

But Lucas wasn't like that. He wasn't a guy who had had one bad experience but was essentially still interested in having a meaningful relationship with a woman. He wasn't a guy who, even deep down, had faith in the power of love.

Lucas's cynicism stemmed from a darker place and it had been formed at so young an age that it was now an embedded part of his personality.

'Do I look like the kind of man who lives his life to impress other people?' he asked, libido kicking fast into gear as his eyes drifted down to her breasts. Knowing what those breasts looked like and tasted like added to the pulsing ache in his groin. 'Quite honestly, I can't think of anything I'd rather do than leave this room right now and head back to my apartment. Failing that, rent a bloody room in the hotel and use it for an hour.'

'That would be rude.' But her eyes were slumberous as she looked at him from under her lashes. 'We should dance instead.'

'You think that dancing is a good substitute for having mind-blowing sex?'

'Stop that!' She pulled him onto the dance floor. The music's tempo had slowed and the couples who were dancing in the half-light were entwined with one another.

It was almost midnight. Where on earth had the time gone? Lucas pulled Katy onto the dance floor and then held her so close to him that she could feel the steady beat of his heart and the pressure of his body, warm and so, so tempting.

She rested her head on his chest and he curled his fingers into her hair and leant into her.

This was heaven. For the duration of this dance, with his arms around her, she could forget that she wasn't living the dream.

Lucas looked down and saw the glitter of the diamond on her finger. The ring had fitted her perfectly, no need to be altered. He had slipped it onto her finger and it had belonged there.

Except, it didn't. Did it?

They had started something in full knowledge of how and when it would end. Katy had proposed a course of action that had been beneficial to them both and at the time, which was only a matter of days ago, Lucas had admired the utter practicality of the proposal.

She had assured him that involvement was not an issue for either of them because they were little more than two people from different planets who had collided because of the peculiar circumstances that had hurled them into the same orbit.

They had an arrangement and it was an arrangement that both of them had under control.

Except, was it?

Lucas didn't want to give house room to doubt, but that ring quietly glittering on her finger was posing questions that left him feeling uneasy and a little panicked, if truth be known.

The song came to an end and he drew away from her.

'We should go and say goodbye to Huang and his family. I've spotted them out of the corner of my eye and they've gathered by the exit. Mission accomplished, I think.'

Katy blinked, abruptly yanked out of the pleasant little cloud in which she had been nestled.

For all that common sense was telling her to be wary of this beautiful man who had stolen her heart like a thief in the night, her heart was rebelling at every practical step forward she tried to take.

She should pull back, yet here she was, wanting nothing more than to linger in his arms and for the music to never end.

She should remember Duncan and the hurt he had caused because, however upset she had been—and she now realised it had been on the mild end of the scale—whatever she had thought at the time, it would be nothing compared to what she would suffer when Lucas walked away from her. But nothing could have been less important in that moment than her cheating ex. In fact, she could barely remember what he looked like, and it had been that way for ages.

She had weeks of this farce to go through! She should steel herself against her own cowardly emotions and do what her head was telling her made sense—which was appreciate him while she could; which was gorge herself on everything he had to offer and look for no more than that.

But her own silly romanticism undermined her at every turn.

She gazed up at him helplessly. 'Mission accomplished?'

'We did what we set out to do,' Lucas said flatly. 'You only spent a short while with Ken Huang and his family, but let me tell you that he was charmed by our tale of love at first sight.'

'Oh, good.' He had already turned away and she

followed him, hearing herself say all the right things to the businessman while sifting through her conflicting emotions to try and find a path she could follow. In a show of unity, Lucas had his arm around her waist lovingly, and she could see how thrilled Ken Huang and his wife were by the romance.

Mission accomplished, indeed.

'Time to go, I think.' Lucas turned to her the second Huang had departed.

'Where?'

'Where do you think? We're engaged, Katy. Getting my driver to deliver you back to your flat is a sure-fire way of getting loose tongues wagging.'

'We're going back to your place?'

'Unless you have a better idea?' He shot her a wolfish smile but this time her blood didn't sizzle as it would have normally. This time she didn't give that soft, yielding sigh as her body took over and her ability to think disappeared like water down a plughole.

Mission accomplished. It was back to business for Lucas, and for that read 'sex'. They would go to his apartment, like the madly in love couple they weren't, and he would take her to his bed and do what he did so very, very well. He would send her pliant body into the stratosphere but would leave her heart untouched.

'We need to talk.' Nerves poured through her. She couldn't do this. She'd admitted how she felt about Lucas to herself and now she couldn't see a way of continuing what they had, pretending that nothing had changed.

'What about?'

'Us,' Katy told him quietly, and Lucas stilled.

'Follow me.'

'Where are we going? I mean, I'd rather not have this conversation in your apartment.'

'I'm on nodding acquaintance with the manager of this hotel. I will ensure we have privacy for whatever it is you feel you need to talk about.'

The shutters had dropped. Katy could feel it in his body language. Gone was the easy warmth and the sexy teasing. She followed him away from the ball room, leaving behind the remaining guests. He had said his goodbyes to the people who mattered and, where she would have at least tried to circulate and make some polite noises before leaving, Lucas had no such concerns.

She hung back as he had a word with the manager, who appeared from nowhere, as though his entire evening had been spent waiting to see if there was anything he could do for Lucas. There was and he did it, leading them to a quiet seating area and assuring them that they would have perfect privacy.

'Will I need something stiff for this *talk*?' Lucas asked once the door was closed quietly behind them. On the antique desk by the open fireplace, there was an assortment of drinks, along with glasses and an ice bucket. Without waiting for an answer, he helped himself to a whisky and then remained where he was, perched against the desk, his dark eyes resting on her without any expression at all.

Katy gazed helplessly at him for a few seconds then took a deep, steadying breath.

'I can't do this.' She hadn't thought out what she was going to say but, now the words had left her mouth, she felt very calm.

'You can't do what?'

'This. *Us.*' She spread her arms wide in a gesture of frustration. His lack of expression was like an invisible force field between them and it added strength to the decision she had taken impulsively to tell him how she felt.

'This is as far as I can go,' she told him quietly. 'I've done the public appearance thing and I've had the photos taken and I… I can't continue this charade for any longer. I can't pretend that…that…'

Lucas wasn't going to help her out. He knew what she was saying, he knew why she was saying it and he also knew that it was something he had recognised over time but had chosen to ignore because it suited him.

'You love me.'

Those three words dropped like stones into still water, sending out ripples that grew bigger and bigger until they filled the space between them.

Stressed out, stricken and totally unable to tell an outright lie, Katy stared at him, her face white, her arms folded.

'I wish I could tell you that that wasn't true, but I can't. I'm sorry.'

'You knew how I felt about commitment…'

'Yes, I knew! But sometimes the heart doesn't manage to listen to the head!'

'I told you I wasn't in the market for love and commitment.' He recalled what he had felt when he had seen other men looking at her and then later, when his gaze had dropped to that perfect diamond on her finger, and something close to fear gripped him. 'I will *never* love you the way you want to be loved and the way you deserve to be loved, *cara.* I can desire you but I am incapable of anything more.'

'Surely you can't say that?' she heard herself plead in a low, driven voice, hating herself, because she should have had a bit more pride.

Lucas's mouth twisted. In the midst of heightened emotions, he could still grudgingly appreciate her bravery in having a conversation that was only ever going to go in a pre-ordained direction. But then she *was* brave, wasn't she? In the way she always spoke her mind, the way she would dig her heels in and de-fend what she believed in even if he was giving her a hard time. In the way she acted, as she had at an event which would have stretched her to the limits and taken her far out of her comfort zone.

'I can't feel the way you do,' Lucas said, turning away from her wide, green, honest eyes and feeling a cad. But it wasn't his fault that he just couldn't give her what she wanted, and it was better for him to be upfront about that right now!

And maybe this was a positive outcome. What would the alternative have been—that a charade born of necessity dragged on and on until he was forced to prise her away from him? She had taken the bull by the horns and was doing the walking away herself. She was rescuing him from an awkward situation and he wondered why he wasn't feeling better about that.

He hated 'clingy' and he didn't do 'needy' and a woman who was bold enough to declare her love was both. He should be feeling relieved!

'I've seen how destructive love can be,' he told her harshly. 'And I've sworn to myself that I would never allow it to enter my life, never allow it to destroy me.' He held up one hand, as though she had interrupted him in mid-flow when in fact she hadn't said a word.

'You're going to tell me that you can change me. I can't change. This is who I am—a man with far too many limitations for someone as romantic and idealistic as you.'

'I realise that,' Katy told him simply. 'I'm not asking you to change.'

Suddenly restless, Lucas pushed himself away from the desk to pace the room. He felt caged and trapped—two very good indications that this was a situation that should be ended without delay because, for a man who valued the freedom of having complete control over his life, *caged and trapped* didn't work.

'You'll meet someone…who can give you what you want and need,' he rasped, his normally graceful movements jerky as he continued to pace the room, only stopping now and again to look at her where she had remained standing as still as a statue. 'And of course, you'll be compensated,' he told her gruffly.

'I'm not following you.'

'Compensated. For what you've done. I'll make sure that you have enough money so that you can build your life wherever you see fit. Rest assured that you will never want for anything. You will be able to buy any house you want in any part of London, and naturally I will ensure that you have enough of a comfort blanket financially so that you need not rush to find another job. In fact, you will be able to teach full-time, and you won't have to worry about finding something alongside the teaching because you won't have to pay rent.'

'You're offering me money,' Katy said numbly, frozen to the spot and stripped bare of all her defences. Had he any idea how humiliating this was for her—

to be told that she would be *paid off* for services rendered? She wanted the ground to open up and swallow her. She was still wearing the princess dress but she could have been clothed in rags because she certainly didn't feel like Cinderella at the ball.

'I want to make sure that you're all right at the end of this,' Lucas murmured huskily, dimly unsettled by her lack of expression and the fact that she didn't seem to hear what he was saying. The colour had drained from her face. Her hair, in contrast, was shockingly vibrant, hanging over her shoulders in a torrent of silken copper.

'And of course, you can keep the ring,' he continued in the lengthening silence. 'In fact, I insist you do.'

'As a reminder?' Katy asked quietly. 'Of the good old days?'

The muscles in her legs finally remembered how to function and she walked towards him stiffly.

For one crazy, wild moment, Lucas envisaged her arms around him, but the moment didn't last long, because she paused to meet his eyes squarely and directly.

'Oh, Lucas. I don't want your money.' She felt the engagement ring with her finger, enjoying the forbidden thought of what it would feel like for the ring to be hers for real, and then she gently pulled it off her finger and held it out towards him. 'And I don't want your ring either.'

Then she turned and left the room, noiselessly shutting the door behind her.

CHAPTER TEN

BEHIND THE WHEEL of his black sports car, Lucas was forced to cut his speed and to slow down to accommodate the network of winding roads that circled the village where Katy's parents lived like a complex spider's web.

Since leaving the motorway, where he had rediscovered the freedom of not being driven by someone else, he had found himself surrounded on all sides by the alien landscape of rural Britain.

He should be somewhere else. In fact, he should be on the other side of the world. Instead, however, he had sent his next in command to do the honours and finalise work on the deal that had been a game changer.

Lucas didn't know when or how the thing he had spent the better part of a year and a half consolidating had faded into insignificance. He just knew that two days ago Katy had walked out of his life and, from that moment on, the deal that had once upon a long time ago commandeered all his attention no longer mattered.

The only thing that had mattered was the driving need to get her back and, for two days, he had fought that need with every tool at his disposal. For two days, Lucas had told himself that Katy was the very epitome of what he had spent a lifetime avoiding. She lived and breathed a belief in a romantic ideal that he had always scorned. Despite her poor experience, she nurtured a faith in love that should have been buried under the weight of disappointment. She was the sort of woman who terrified men like him.

And, more than all of that put together, she had come right out and spoken words that she surely must have known would be taboo for him.

After everything he had told her.

She had fallen in love with him. She had blatantly ignored all the 'do not trespass' signs he had erected around himself and fallen in love with him. He should have been thankful that she had not wept and begged him to return her love. He should have been grateful that, as soon as she had made that announcement, she had removed the engagement ring and handed it back to him.

He should have thanked his lucky stars that she had then proceeded to exit his life without any fuss or fanfare.

There would be a little untidiness when it came to the engagement that had lasted five seconds before imploding, and the press would have a field day for a week or so, but that hadn't bothered him. Ken Huang would doubtless be disappointed, but he would already be moving on to enjoy his family life without the stress of a company he had been keen to sell to the right bidder, and would not lose sleep over it because it was a done deal.

Life as Lucas knew it could be returned to its state of normality.

Everything was positive, but Katy had left him and, stubborn, blind idiot that he was, it was only when that door had shut behind her that he had realised how much of his heart she was taking with her.

He had spent two days trying to convince himself that he shouldn't follow her, before caving in, because he just hadn't been able to envisage life without her in it, at which point he had abandoned all hope of being able to control his destiny. Along with his heart, that was something else she had taken with her.

And now here he was, desperately hoping that he hadn't left everything too late.

His satnav was telling him to veer off onto a country lane that promised a dead end, but he obeyed the instructions and, five minutes later, with the sun fading fast, the vicarage she had told him about came into view, as picturesque as something lifted from the lid of a box of chocolates.

Wisteria clambered over faded yellow stone. The vicarage was a solid, substantial building behind which stretched endless acres of fields, on which grazing sheep were blobs of white, barely moving against the backdrop of a pink-and-orange twilit sky. The drive leading to the vicarage was long, straight and bordered by neat lawns and flower beds that had obviously taken thought in the planting stage.

For the first time in his life, Lucas was in a position of not knowing what would happen next. He'd never had to beg for anyone before and he felt that he might have to beg now. He wondered whether she had decided that replacing him immediately would be a cure for the pain of confessing her love to a guy who had sent her on her way with the very consider-ate offer of financial compensation for any inconve-nience. When Lucas thought about the way he had responded to her, he shuddered in horror.

He honestly wouldn't blame her if she refused to set eyes on him.

He drove slowly up the drive and curled his car to the side of the vicarage, then killed the engine, qui-etly opened the door and got out.

'Darling, will you get that?'

Propped in front of the newspaper where she had been scouring ads for local jobs for the past hour and a half, Katy looked up. Sarah Brennan was at the range stirring something. Conversation was thin on the ground because her parents were both so busy tiptoeing around her, making sure they didn't say the wrong thing.

Her father was sitting opposite her with a glass of wine in his hand, and every so often Katy would purposefully ignore the look of concern he gave her, because he was worried about her.

She had shown up, burst into tears and confessed everything. She had wanted lots of tea and sympathy, and she had got it from her parents, who had put on a brave face and said all the right things about time being a great healer, rainbows round corners and sil-ver linings on clouds, but they had been distraught on her behalf. She had seen it in the worried looks they gave one another when they didn't think she was looking, and it was there in the silences, where before there would have been lots and lots of chat and laughter.

'I should have known better,' Katy had conceded the evening before when she had finally stopped crying. 'He was very honest. He wasn't into marriage, and the engagement was just something that served a purpose.'

'To spare us thinking you were...were...' Her mother had stumbled as she had tried to find a polite way of saying *easy*. 'Do you honestly think we would have thought that, when we know you so very well, my darling?'

Katy could have told them that sparing them had only been part of the story. The other part had been her concern for Lucas's reputation. Even then, she must have been madly in love with him, because she had cared more about his reputation than he had.

She also didn't mention the money he had offered her. She felt cheapened just thinking about that and her parents would have been horrified. Even with Lucas firmly behind her, she still loved him so much that she couldn't bear to have her parents drill that final nail in his coffin.

The doorbell rang again and Katy blinked, focused and realised that her mother was looking at her oddly, waiting for her actually to do something about getting the door.

Her father was already rising to his feet and Katy waved him down with an apologetic smile. She wondered who would be calling at this time but then, for a small place it was remarkably full of people who urgently needed to talk to her parents about something or other. Just as soon as the cat was out of the bag, the hot topic of conversation would actually be *her*, and she grimaced when she thought about that.

She was distracted as she opened the door. The biggest bunch of red roses was staring her in the face. Someone would have to have wreaked havoc in a rose garden to have gathered so many. Katy stared down, mind blank, her thoughts only beginning to sift through possibilities and come up with the right answer when she noted the expensive leather shoes.

Face drained of colour, she raised her eyes slowly, and there he was, the man whose image had not been out of her head for the past two agonising days since they had gone their separate ways.

'Can I come in?' Unfamiliar nerves turned the question into an aggressive statement of fact. Lucas wasn't sure whether flowers were the right gesture. Should he have gone for something more substantial? But then, Katy hated ostentatious displays of wealth. Uncertainty gripped him, and he was so unfamiliar with the sensation that he barely recognised it for what it was.

'What are you doing here?' Katy was too shocked to expand on that but she folded her arms, stiffened her spine and recollected what it had felt like when he had offered to pay her off. That was enough to ignite her anger, and she planted herself squarely in front of him, because there was no way she was going to let him into the house.

'I've come to see you.'

'What for?' she asked coldly.

'Please let me in, Katy. I don't want to have this conversation with you on your doorstep.'

'My parents are inside.'

'Yes, I thought they might be here.'

'Why have you come here, Lucas? We have nothing to say to one another. I don't want your flowers. I don't want you coming into this house and I don't want you meeting my parents. I've told them everything, and now I just want to get on with my life and pretend that I never met you.'

'You don't mean that.'

'Yes. I do.'

Her voice was cold and composed but she was a mess inside. She badly wanted her body to do what her brain was urgently telling it to do, but like a runaway train it was veering out of control, responding to him with frightening ferocity. More than anything in the world, she wanted to creep into his arms, rest her head against his chest and pretend that her life wasn't cracking up underneath her; she hated herself for that weakness and hated him for showing up and exposing her to it.

She glanced anxiously over her shoulder. In a minute, she knew her father would probably appear behind her, curious as to who had rung the doorbell. Lucas followed her gaze and knew exactly what she was thinking. He was here and he was going to say what he had come to say and, if forcing his way in and flagrantly taking advantage of the fact that she wouldn't be able to do a thing about it because it would create a scene in front of her parents was what it took, then so be it.

What was the point of an opportunity presenting itself if you didn't take advantage of it?

So he did just that. Hand flat against the door, he stepped forward and pushed it open and, caught unawares, Katy fell back with a look that was part surprise, part horror and part incandescent rage.

'I need to talk to you, Katy. I need you to listen to me.'

'And you think that gives you the right to barge into my house?'

'If it's the only way of getting you to listen to me...'

'I told you, I'm not interested in anything you have to say, and if you think that you can sweet talk your way back into my bed then you can forget it!' Her voice was a low, angry hiss and her colour was high.

His body was so familiar to her that she was responding to him like an engine that had been turned on and was idling, ready to accelerate.

From behind, Katy heard her mother calling out to her and she furiously stepped aside as Lucas entered the house, *her sanctuary,* with his blasted red roses, on a mission to wreck her life all over again. No way was she going to allow her parents to think that a bunch of flowers meant anything, and she took them from him and unceremoniously dumped them in an umbrella stand that was empty of umbrellas.

'I should have bought you the sports car,' Lucas murmured and Katy glared at him. 'That wouldn't have fitted into an umbrella stand.'

'You wouldn't have dared.'

'When it comes to getting what I want, there's nothing I won't do.'

Katy didn't have the opportunity to rebut that contentious statement because her mother appeared, and then shortly after her father, and there they stood in the doorway of the kitchen, mouths round with surprise, eyes like saucers and brains conjuring up heaven only knew what. Katy shuddered to think.

And, if she had anticipated Lucas being on the back foot, the wretched man managed, in the space of forty-five minutes, to achieve the impossible.

After *everything* she had told her parents—after she had filled them in on her hopeless situation, told them that she was in love with a man who could never return her love, a man whose only loyal companion would ever be his work—she seethed and fumed from the sidelines as her parents were won over by a display of charm worthy of an acting award.

Why had Lucas come? Shouldn't he have been in China working on the deal that had ended up changing *her* life more than it had changed his?

He didn't love her and, by a process of common sense and elimination, she worked out the only thing that could possibly have brought him to her parents' house would be an offer to continue their fling. Lucas was motivated by sex, so sex had to be the reason he was here.

The more Katy thought about that, the angrier she became, and by the time her parents began making noises about going out for supper so that she and Lucas could talk she was fit to explode.

'How *dare* you?' That was the first thing she said as soon as they were on their own in the comfortable sitting room, with its worn flowered sofas, framed family photos on the mantelpiece and low coffee table groaning under the weight of the magazines her mother was addicted to. 'How *dare you* waltz into my life here and try and *take over*? Do you think for a moment that if you manage to get to my parents that you'll get to me as well?'

She was standing on the opposite side of the room to him, her arms folded, the blood running hot in her veins as she tried her hardest not to be moved by the dark, sinful beauty that could get to her every time.

It infuriated her that he could just *stand there,* watching her with eyes that cloaked his thoughts, leaning indolently against the wall and not saying anything, which had the effect of propelling her into hysterical, attacking speech. She was being precisely the sort of person she didn't want to be. If she wasn't careful, she would start throwing things in a minute, and she definitely wasn't going to sink to that level.

Lucas watched her and genuinely wasn't sure how to proceed. Where did you start when it came to talking about feelings? He didn't know because he'd never been there before. But she was furious, and he didn't blame her, and standing in silence wasn't going to progress anything.

'I really like your parents,' Lucas said, a propos of nothing, and she glared at him as though he had taken leave of his senses.

'You've wasted your time,' she told him flatly. 'I'm not interested in having another fling with you, Lucas. I don't care whether my parents fell in love with you. I want you to leave and I don't want to see you ever again. I just want to be left in peace to get on with my life.'

'How can you get on with your life when you're in love with me?'

Mortification and anger coursed through her, because just like that he had cut her down at the knees. He had taken her confession and used it against her.

'How can *I* get on with my life when I'm in love with *you*?' Lucas realised that he was perspiring. Sealing multi-million-pound deals were a walk in the park compared to this.

Thrown into instant confusion, Katy gaped, unwilling to believe him. If he'd loved her, he wouldn't have let her go, she thought painfully. He would have tried to stop her. He wouldn't have offered her money to compensate for all the other things he couldn't provide.

Lucas noted the rampant disbelief on her face, and again he couldn't blame her.

'You don't believe me and I understand that.' His voice was unsteady and he raked his fingers through his hair in an unusually clumsy gesture. 'I'd made it clear that I could never be interested in having the sort of relationship I knew you wanted. You were so…so *different* that I couldn't get my head around ever falling for you. I'll be honest—I could never get my head around falling for *anyone*. I'd always equated love with vulnerability, and vulnerability with being hurt.'

'Why are you telling me this?' Katy cried jerkily. 'Don't you think I don't know all that?' But the uncertainty on his face was throwing her off-balance, and hope was unfurling and blossoming fast, yanking the ground from under her feet and setting up a drumbeat inside her that was stronger than all the caution she was desperate to impose on herself.

'What you *don't* know is that you came along and everything changed for me. You made me feel…different. When I was around you, life was in Technicolor. I put it down to the incredible sex. I put it down to the fact that I was in a state of suspended animation, far from the daily demands of my office. I never put it down to the truth, which was that I was falling for you. I was blind, but then I'd never expected to fall in love. Not with you, not with any woman.'

'You mean it? Please don't say anything you don't mean. I couldn't bear it.' Was this some ploy to try and talk her into bed? He was right, the sex *had* been incredible. Was he working up to an encore by flattering her? But, when she looked at him, the discomfort on his face was palpable and it made her breathing shallow and laborious.

'You confused me. There were times when I felt disorientated, as though the world had suddenly been turned upside down, and when that happened I just told myself that it was because you were a novelty, nothing like what I was used to. But I behaved differently when I was around you. You made me say things I've never said to anyone else and I felt comfortable doing it.'

'But you didn't try and stop me,' Katy whispered. 'I told you how I felt and you…you let me walk away. No, worse than that, you offered me money.'

'Please don't remind me,' Lucas said quietly. Somehow, he had closed the gap between them, but he was still hesitant to reach out and touch her even though he badly wanted to do just that.

'You have to understand that money is the currency I'm familiar with, not love. My father was derailed after my mother's death. I grew up watching him get carried along on emotional riptides that stripped him of his ability to function, and that taught me about the importance of self-control and the need to focus on things that were constant. Relationships, in my head, were associated with frightening inconsistency and I wanted no part of that. The only relationship I would ever consider would be one that didn't impact on the quality of my life. A relationship with a woman who wanted the same sort of thing that I did.' He smiled wryly. 'Not an emotional, outspoken and utterly adorable firebrand like you.'

Katy liked all of those descriptions. She liked the expression on his face even more, and just like that her caution faded away and her heart leapt and danced and made her want to grin stupidly at him.

'Keep talking,' she whispered, and he raised his eyebrows and smiled at her.

'So here I am,' Lucas said simply. 'I'd worked like the devil for a deal that, in the end, won't mean anything if you aren't by my side. I think that was when I was forced to accept that the only thing that mattered to me was *you*. I should have guessed when I realised how protective you made me feel and how possessive. You make me the best person I could be, and that means someone who can be hurt, who has feelings, who's willing to wear his heart on his sleeve.' He pulled her towards him and Katy sighed as she was enveloped in a hug that was so fierce that she could feel the beating of his heart. He curled his fingers into her hair and tilted her face to deliver a gentle kiss on her lips.

'I never expected to fall in love with you either,' she admitted softly. 'I was so certain that I knew the sort of guy I should end up with, and it wasn't a guy like you. But it's like you fill in the missing pieces of me and make me complete. It's weird, but when I met Duncan I was looking for love, looking for that *something else*, but I wasn't looking for anything at all when I met you—yet love found me.'

'I know what you mean. I was comfortable *wanting* you because I understood the dynamics of desire. Strangely, loving you has made me understand how my father ended up becoming entangled in a series of inappropriate relationships. He was deeply in love with my mother and he wanted to replicate that. Before I met you, I just didn't get it, but then I never understood how powerful love could be and how it can turn a black-and-white life into something filled with colour and light.'

'And when I returned home,' Katy admitted, 'And I saw the interaction between my parents, I knew that I could never settle for anything less than what they have. I was so upset when you showed up because I thought you'd come to try and persuade me into carrying on with what we had. Maybe because of the deal, or maybe because you still fancied me, even though you didn't love me.'

'Now you know the real reason I turned up with those flowers that you dumped out of sight—you want the fairy-tale romance and I want to be the lucky person who gives it to you. Will you do me the honour of marrying me, my darling? For real and for ever?'

'Just try and stop me...'

EPILOGUE

KATY PAUSED AND looked at Lucas, who was standing staring out to the sea, half-naked because he enjoyed swimming at night, something he had yet to
convince her to try.

There was a full moon and the light threw his magnificent body into shadow. To think that a little over a
year ago she had come aboard this very yacht, kicking
and screaming and accusing him of kidnapping her.

She smiled because that felt like a lifetime ago and
so much had happened since then. The engagement
that wasn't an engagement had turned into the real
thing and they had been married, not once, but *twice*.
There was a lavish affair, held a week after the actual
wedding, where reporters had jostled for prime position and celebrities had emerged from limos dressed
to kill for the event of the century. But first had come
something altogether smaller, in her home village,
where they had married at a ceremony officiated by
her father at the picturesque local church. The reception there had been warm, small and cosy.

Lavish or cosy, Katy just knew that she was the
happiest person in the world.

They had had their honeymoon in Italy, where they

had stayed with Lucas's father for a few days. Katy knew that she would be seeing a great deal more of Marco Cipriani, because he had got along with her parents like a house on fire, and plans were already afoot for him to discover the joys of the northern countryside at its finest at Christmas.

And she knew that during the festive season there would certainly be reason for a great deal of celebration.

'Lucas...'

Lucas turned, and his heart stopped just for a second as he watched the woman who had so taken over his life that contemplating an existence without her was unthinkable. He smiled, held his hand out and watched her walk towards him, glorious in a casual, long dress which he knew he would be removing later.

Katy walked straight into his open arms and then looked up at him with a smile. 'I have something to say... We both have eight months to start thinking of some names...'

'Names?'

'For our baby, my darling. I'm pregnant.' She tiptoed to plant a kiss on his very sexy mouth.

'My darling, perfect wife.' Lucas closed his eyes and allowed himself to be swept away in the moment before looking down at her with love. 'I never thought that life could get any better, but I do believe it has...'

* * * * *

DESERVING OF HIS DIAMONDS?

MELANIE MILBURNE

To Carol Marinelli – not just a fellow author but also a fabulous and fun friend. XX

CHAPTER ONE

EMILIO was sitting in a café in Rome not far from his office when he finally found out the truth. His chest seized as he read the article about twin girls who had been separated at birth due to an illegal adoption. The article was journalism at its best: an intriguing and poignant account of how identical twins had finally been reunited, quite by chance, after a shop attendant mistook one for the other in a Sydney department store.

One mistaken for the other...

Emilio ignored his coffee and sat back in his chair and looked out at the bustling city crowds wandering past. Tourists and workers, young and old, married and single—everyone going about their business, totally unaware of the shock that was consuming him until he could scarcely breathe.

It hadn't been Gisele in the sex tape.

His throat felt as if a spanner were going down sideways. He had been so adamant about it, so stubborn. He had not listened to Gisele's protestations of innocence. He had *refused* to listen. She had begged and pleaded with him to believe in her, but he had not.

He had got it wrong.

She had cried. She had screamed. She had pummelled

at his chest with tears pouring down her face, and yet he had walked away. He had cut all contact with her. He had sworn on his life he would never see or speak to her again.

He had got it wrong.

Emilio's company had almost folded over the scandal. He'd had to work so hard to get back to where he was today. Eighteen-hour, sometimes twenty-four-hour days, sleepless nights, endless travel, jet lag so bad he didn't sleep properly any more, no matter how utterly exhausted he was. He went from project to project like an automaton, putting in the hours, signing up the deals, paying off the debts and then finally banking the millions, his drive to succeed knowing no bounds.

And for all this time he had blamed Gisele.

He had fuelled his hatred of her every day since. It had festered inside him like a gangrenous wound. He had felt it in every pore of his body. Every time he had thought of her the temperature of his wrath had risen. It had burned like a roaring furnace deep inside him. It had blazed like wild flames through his veins. Some days it had almost consumed him. It had been like a fever he could not control.

His gut clenched with a fist of guilt. He had always prided himself on never making an error of judgement. He aimed—some would say ruthlessly—for perfection in every area of his life. Failure was anathema to him.

And yet with Gisele he had got it wrong.

Emilio looked at his phone. He still had her number in his contacts. He had left it there as a reminder to trust no one, to let no one under his guard. He had never thought of himself as the sentimental type, but when he brought her details to the screen his fingers shook slightly as they hovered over her name. Somehow calling out of the blue to say sorry didn't seem the right way to handle things. He owed her a face-to-face apology. It was the least he could do. He wanted to erase that mistake, to draw a line through it and move on with his life.

He clicked on his phone's rapid dial instead and called his secretary. 'Carla, cancel all of my appointments for the next week and get me a flight to Sydney as soon as you can,' he said. 'I have some urgent business to see to there.'

Gisele was showing a first time mother the handmade christening gown she had embroidered when Emilio Andreoni came in. Seeing him standing there, so tall, so out of place in her baby clothes boutique made her heart leap to her throat like a gymnast on an overused trampoline.

She had practised this day over in her head just in case he took it upon himself to apologise once he found out about her long-lost identical twin. She had imagined how vindicated she would feel that he would have to admit he had got it wrong about her. She had imagined she would look at him and feel nothing, nothing but the bitter hatred of him for his cruel and ruthless rejection and his inexcusable lack of trust.

And yet that first glimpse of him sent a shockwave through her that made her feel as if the floor beneath her feet were suddenly shifting. Emotions she had bolted down with bitter determination suddenly popped against their restraints. One by one she could feel them spreading through her, making her chest ache with the weight of them. How could it physically hurt to see someone face to face? How could her heart feel pain like a stab wound at seeing his tall, imposing frame standing there? How could her insides clench and twist when his coal-black eyes met hers?

Gisele had seen him in the press several times since their break-up and although each time it had made her feel a tight sort of ache, it had felt nothing like the raw, claw-scraping pain of this.

He still had the same darkly tanned olive skin. The same Roman nose, the same penetrating dark brown eyes, the same intractable jaw that right now looked as if it hadn't seen a razor in the last thirty-six hours. The slightly wavy black hair was a little longer than the last time she had seen him—it was curling around the collar of his shirt and it looked as if his fingers had been the last thing that had moved through it. There were bruiselike shadows beneath his thickly lashed bloodshot eyes, no doubt put there by yet another sleepless night out with one of his one-night stand bimbo bedmates, she imagined.

'Excuse me...' she said to the young mother. 'I won't be a minute.'

Gisele walked over to where he was standing next to the premature baby clothes. He had one of his hands on a tiny vest that had a pink rosebud with little green leaves embroidered at the neck. The vest looked so tiny against his hand and it occurred to her then that Lily would have been too small for it when she had been born.

'Can I help you with something?' she asked with a brittle look.

Emilio's eyes meshed with hers, holding them captive. 'I think you know why I am here, Gisele,' he said in that deep, rich voice she had missed so much. It moved along her skin like a caress, settling at the base of her spine like a warm pool of slowly spreading honey.

Gisele had to fight hard to keep her emotions in check. This was not the time to show him she was still affected by him, even if it was only physically. She had to be strong, to show him he hadn't destroyed her life with his lack of trust. She had to show him she had moved on, that she was self-sufficient and successful. She had to show him he meant *nothing* to her now. She drew in a breath and lifted her chin, keeping her voice cool and composed. 'Of course.' She gave him an impersonal on-off movement of her lips that was nowhere near a smile. 'How could I forget? The two-for-one sale on all-in-one suits we have on at the moment. You can have blue, pink or yellow. I'm afraid we're all out of the white.'

His gaze never once wavered from hers; it was as dark and mesmerising as ever. 'Is there somewhere we could talk in private?' he asked.

Gisele straightened her shoulders. 'As you can see I have customers to see to,' she said, indicating with a waft of her hand the young woman browsing along the racks.

'Are you free for lunch?' he asked, still watching her steadily.

Gisele wondered if he was studying her for flaws. Could he see the way her once creamy skin had lost its glow? Could he see the shadows below and in her eyes that no amount of make-up could disguise? He had always prized perfection. Not just in his work but in every facet of his life. He would find her sadly lacking now, she thought, in spite of her name and reputation finally being cleared. 'I own and run this business,' she said with more than a hint of pride. 'I don't take a lunch break.'

Gisele saw his dark critical gaze sweep over the baby wear boutique she had bought a few weeks after he had cut her from his life just days before their wedding. Building it up from yet another struggling suburban retail outlet to the successful exclusive affair it was now had been the only thing that had got her through the heartbreak of the past two years.

Some well meaning friends, along with her mother, had suggested it would have been better to have sold the business as soon as she had been told Lily wasn't going to make it, but somehow, in her mind, holding on to the shop was a way to hold on to her fragile little daughter for just that little bit longer. She felt close to Lily here, surrounded by the handmade blankets and bonnets and booties she made for other babies to wear. It was her only connection now with motherhood and she wasn't going to relinquish it in spite of the pain it caused to see those brand-new prams being pushed through the door day after day. No one knew how hard it was for her to look and not touch those precious little bundles inside. No one knew how long at night she clung to the bunny blanket she had made for Lily's tiny body to be wrapped in during those few short hours of her life.

Emilio's eyes came back to connect with hers. 'Dinner then,' he said. 'You don't work past six, do you?'

Gisele watched in irritation as the young mother left

the shop, no doubt put off by Emilio's brooding presence. She sent him a glare. 'Dinner is out of the question,' she said. 'I have another engagement.'

'Are you involved with someone?' he asked, pinning her with his eyes.

She worked hard at keeping her composure. Did he really think she would have dived headfirst into another relationship after what he had done to her? She often wondered if she would ever feel safe in a relationship again. But she daren't admit to her singleton status. She had a feeling he wasn't just here to apologise and to clear the air between them. She could see it in the dark magnetic pull of his gaze. She could sense it in the atmosphere, the way the air she shared with him thickened with each breath she took into her lungs. Damn it, she could even feel it in her traitorous body as it reacted to his dark, disturbing presence the way it had always done in the past. Her senses went on full alert, her legs giving a little tremble as she thought of how he had taught her all she knew about physical intimacy, how it had been his body and his alone that had shown her what hers had been capable of in giving and receiving pleasure. 'I can't see how that is any of your business,' she said with a hoist of her chin.

A muscle flexed beside his mouth. 'I know this is hard for you, Gisele,' he said. 'It's hard for me too.'

'Meaning you never thought you'd ever have to apologise to me for getting it wrong?' she asked with a cutting look. 'Hate to say I told you so.'

His expression immediately became shuttered, closed off, remote. 'I'm not proud of how I ended things,' he said. 'But you would have done the same if things were the other way around.'

'You're wrong, Emilio,' she said. 'I would have looked high and low for an alternative explanation for how that tape came about.'

'For God's sake, Gisele,' he said roughly. 'Do you think I didn't look for an explanation? You told me you were an only child. *You* didn't even know you had a twin. How was I supposed to come up with something as bizarre as that? I looked at that tape and I saw you. I saw the same silver-blonde hair, the same grey-blue eyes, even the same mannerisms. I had no choice but to believe what I was seeing.'

'You *did* have a choice,' Gisele said, shooting him a blistering glare. 'You could have believed me in spite of, not because of, the evidence. But you didn't love me enough to trust me. You didn't love me at all. You just wanted a perfect wife to hang off your arm. That wretched tape tarnished me so I was of no further use to you. It wouldn't have mattered if the truth had come out in two minutes or two hours instead of two years. Your business was always going to be the priority. You put it before everything.'

'I put my business on hold to come out here to see you,' he said, frowning at her broodingly.

'You've seen me, so now you can jump back on your private jet and fly all the way back,' she said, sending him a haughty look as she spun on her heel.

'Damn it, Gisele,' he said, snagging one of her arms to stall her.

Gisele felt the steely grip of his long, strong fingers on her bare arm as he turned her back to face him. His touch was like a flame. It seared her skin like a brand. Every nerve flinched beneath her skin. She felt her stomach go hollow as his eyes locked on hers. She didn't want to lose herself in that glittering dark gaze. Not again. Once was enough. It had been her downfall, falling for a man with the inability to love and trust.

She didn't want him this close.

She could smell the heat of him, the sharp and heady cocktail of musk and male and lemon-based aftershave that made her nostrils flare and tingle. She could see the black pepper of the stubble on his jaw and her fingers suddenly itched to feel that sexy rasp under the soft pads of her fingertips. She could see the grim line of his beautifully sculptured mouth. The mouth that had wreaked such havoc on her senses from the very first time he had kissed her. She only had to close her eyes to remember how it felt to have those hard, insistent lips press down on hers…

She snapped out of her reverie like an elastic band that had been stretched too far. That same mouth had vilified her cruelly. Her ears still rang with his hateful, unforgettable, unforgivable words. There was no way she was going to let him off lightly, if at all. Her life had come undone the day he had cut her adrift. She had been so devastated and alone. Her happy future had suddenly been ripped away from her without warning. She had been shattered by his accusations. She had been left so raw with pain she had barely been able to drag herself through each agonising day.

Finding out she was pregnant a couple of months after she had returned to Sydney had been her only glimmer of hope in that very dark place she had found herself in.

But then that hope had been cruelly dashed a few weeks later at the second ultrasound. She had always wondered if that was her punishment for not telling Emilio about the pregnancy. He had forbidden all contact after their break-up, but she had been too devastated and hurt to even try.

And too angry.

She had wanted to punish him for not believing in her. She still wanted to punish him. It was like a rod of steel inside her. The only thing holding her upright was her fury and resentment and hatred towards him. Nothing was going to melt it.

'Why are you making this harder than it already is?' Emilio asked.

Gisele needed the trench of her anger to hide in and the deeper and dirtier the better. 'You think you can breeze in here and issue some half-hearted apology and I'll forgive you?' she asked. 'I'll *never* forgive you. Do you hear me? *Never.*'

The line of his mouth was grim. 'I don't expect you to forgive me,' he said. 'I do, however, expect you to act like an adult and hear me out.'

'I'll act like an adult when you stop restraining me like an out of control child,' she said, shooting him a livid look. 'Let go of my arm.'

His fingers softened their hold but he didn't release her. Gisele felt her heart give a nervous flutter as the broad pad of his thumb slid down to her pulse. Could he feel the thud of those hit-and-miss beats? She surreptitiously moistened her mouth but his gaze caught the movement. His eyes darkened, the pupils disappearing into the chocolate-brown of his irises. She knew that look so well. It triggered a visceral reaction in her body. The pulse of longing was like a lightning strike to that secret place between her thighs. Every erotically sensual moment they had ever shared flashed through her brain like a film on fast-forward. Those sensually provocative images made a mockery of every paltry attempt she had made to keep herself immune. What hope of immunity when one look from those dark eyes made her blood rush through her veins at breakneck speed?

'Have dinner with me tonight,' he said.

'I told you I already have an engagement,' she said, not quite meeting his eyes.

Emilio tipped up her chin with his other hand, his eyes dark and penetrating as they held hers. 'And I know you are lying,' he said.

'What a pity you weren't such a hotshot detective two years ago,' she threw back resentfully as she finally managed to break free. She stood and pointedly rubbed at her wrist, still glaring at him.

'I'll pick you up at seven,' he said. 'Where do you live?'

Gisele felt a bolt of panic rush through her. She didn't want him at her flat. That was her private sanctuary, the one place she felt safe enough to let out her grief. Besides, how would she explain all the photos of Lily? It was much better to leave him ignorant of their baby's short life. She wasn't ready to tell him. She would *never* be ready to tell him. How could she cope with the pain of him telling her she should have had a termination as she had been advised? It had been hard enough hearing it from her mother and some of her friends. Emilio wouldn't have wanted a child who wasn't perfect. It wouldn't have suited his plan for a perfectly ordered life.

'You don't seem to be getting the message, Emilio,' she said with a defiant look. 'I don't want to see you again. Not tonight. Not tomorrow night. Not ever. You've apologised. End of story. Now, please leave before I have you evicted by Security.'

His expression was faintly mocking. 'What Security?' he asked. 'Anyone could walk in here and empty your cash register while your back was turned and you wouldn't be able to do a single thing to stop them. You don't even have CCTV cameras installed.'

Gisele pressed her lips together, hating him for pointing out what he obviously perceived as a flaw in her personality. Her mother…*her adoptive mother*, she corrected herself, had communicated much the same thing only a few days ago, saying she was far too trusting with her customers. It didn't come naturally to Gisele to mistrust people, but then wasn't that why her life had ended up the way it had? She had been so naive and trusting with Emilio and it had backfired spectacularly.

Emilio continued to study her for a lengthy moment. 'Have you been ill recently?' he asked.

Gisele suddenly froze, caught off guard by that dark penetrating gaze that refused to let hers go. 'Um…why do you ask that?'

'You look pale and much thinner than when we were together,' he said.

'Not quite up to your impeccable standards any more?' she said, giving him a hardened look. 'What a lucky escape you had in calling off our wedding. It wouldn't suit your image to be married to a frump, now, would it?'

Another heavy frown appeared between his brows. 'You misunderstand me,' he said. 'I was simply commenting on your pallor, not your lack of beauty. You are still one of the most beautiful women I have ever seen.'

It was amazing how easily cynicism came to Gisele now. In the past she would have blushed and felt incredibly flattered by such a compliment. Now all she felt was a simmering fury that he was trying to charm her into forgiving him. He was wasting his time and hers. *Forgiveness* was a word she had long ago deleted from her vocabulary.

She walked over to the shop service counter and barricaded herself behind it. 'You can save your shallow compliments for someone who will believe them enough to fall into your bed,' she said. 'It's not going to work with me.'

'Is that why you think I am here?' he asked.

Gisele felt herself being swallowed by that charcoal-black unreadable gaze. The air seemed to be charged with an erotic energy she had no control over. Her hands gripped the edge of the counter for support, her heart beating too hard and too fast as his hooded gaze slipped to her mouth.

She held her breath in that infinitesimal moment as his gaze rested on her lips.

His gaze was like a touch. It burned her with its intent. She felt the tingle of her lips as if he had reached across the counter and pressed his mouth to hers…

But her best friend cynicism came to her rescue just in time. 'I think you are here to clear your conscience,' she said. 'You're not here because of me. You're here because of you.'

His expression gave no clue to what was going on behind the screen of his dark eyes, but a tiny nerve twitched at the edge of his mouth as if it were being tugged by an invisible needle and thread.

It seemed a very long time before he spoke.

'I am here for both of us,' he said. 'I want to wipe the slate clean. Neither of us can truly move on with our lives with this lying like a festering sore between us.'

Gisele put up her chin with cool hauteur. 'I *have* moved on with my life,' she said.

His eyes challenged hers for endless seconds, but when he finally spoke his voice was gruff. 'Have you, *cara*? Have you really?'

Was it his unexpectedly gentle tone or his use of an all too familiar endearment that made her throat suddenly close over as if someone had gripped it and cruelly squeezed? She blinked against the sting of tears, once, twice, three times before she was confident they were not going to break through. 'Of course,' she said coldly. 'Or would you rather I said I'd been pining for you forlornly ever since you cut me from your life?'

'That would indeed be a punishment I would not like to have inflicted on me,' he said with a rueful movement of his lips. 'It would make the guilt I feel all the harder to bear.'

Gisele looked at him standing there, so tall, so assured, the master of all he controlled. Was he really feeling guilty or just annoyed at being wrong for once in his life? He was a fiercely proud man. She had met no one prouder or more stubborn. 'You can sleep easy,

Emilio,' she said. 'After the way you treated me I put you out of my mind as soon as I stepped off the plane. I haven't thought of you in months.'

He held her look for a heartbeat longer than she would have liked. 'I'll be in town for the rest of the week,' he said, handing her a business card. 'If you change your mind about meeting with me, please feel free to call me at any time.'

Gisele took the silver-embossed card with a hand that trembled slightly as it came in contact with his. She curled her fingers around the card until its edges bit into her palm. 'I won't change my mind,' she said with steely determination wrapped around each and every word.

She waited until he had left before she let out her breath in a long ragged stream. She looked at the card she had crushed in her hand. A sharp corner had broken the skin of her palm; a very timely reminder that if she allowed Emilio Andreoni too close again she would be the only one to get hurt.

CHAPTER TWO

A COUPLE of days later Gisele received a visit from her landlord, Keith Patterson. For a heart-stopping moment she wondered if she had somehow overlooked paying her rent, but then she remembered she had seen the electronic transfer of the funds on her accounts profile page only the week before.

'I know this is short notice, Miss Carter,' Keith said after the usual polite exchange of greetings, 'but I've decided to sell the building to a developer. I got an offer too good to refuse. The wife and I lost a fair bit in the global financial crisis and we need to refinance ourselves for our retirement. This offer couldn't have come at a better time.'

Gisele blinked at him in alarm. While her profit turnover was good and her bank overdraft manageable, finding other premises would no doubt involve a rise in rent. She didn't want to overstretch herself, especially as she had only recently employed an assistant. So many small businesses folded due to having too many overheads and not enough income. She didn't want to become another statistic of economic disaster. 'Does that mean I have to move out?' she asked.

'That will depend on the new owner,' Keith said.

'He'll have to get council approval before he does any alterations. That could take weeks or a couple of months. He gave me his card for you to contact him to discuss the lease.' He handed her a silver-embossed card across the counter.

Gisele's heart dropped like a stone inside her chest even before she saw the name on the card. 'Emilio Andreoni bought the building?' she asked in a shocked gasp.

'You've heard of him?' Keith asked.

She felt her face grow warm. 'Yes…I've heard of him,' she said. 'But he's an architect, not a property developer.'

'Maybe he's diversifying his interests,' Keith said. 'I've heard he's won numerous awards for his designs. He seemed mighty keen to buy the place.'

'Did he give you a reason for his enthusiasm?' Gisele asked, boiling with anger inside.

'Yes, he said it held sentimental value,' Keith said. 'Maybe a relative of his owned it in the past. Some Italians used to have a fruit shop here in the fifties. I can't remember their name.'

Gisele ground her teeth. Sentimental value indeed! She knew for a fact Emilio had no living relatives, or at least none he wanted to associate with. He had told her very little about his background, but she sensed it hadn't been much like hers. She had often wondered if that was another reason he had wanted to marry her. Her blue-blooded pedigree had appealed to him. How ironic that it turned out she and her twin were the products of an illicit affair their father had had with a housekeeper while he and his wife were living in London.

Once Keith Patterson had gone Gisele looked at the business card lying on the counter. She drummed her fingers on the glass surface, her teeth almost going to powder as she considered her options. She could tear up the card into tiny little pieces as she had a couple of days ago, or she could call the mobile number on it and arrange a showdown. If she tore up the card he would surely come in to see her and she would be caught off guard just as she had been before.

She decided it would be better to see him on her terms this time around. She picked up the phone and started dialling.

'Emilio Andreoni.'

'You bastard!' Gisele spat before she could stop herself.

She heard the sound of a leather chair squeaking as he shifted position. She imagined him with his feet up on the desk, his ankles crossed casually, his head laid back against the headrest and a self-satisfied smile on his mouth.

'Nice to hear from you, Gisele,' he said smoothly. 'Have you changed your mind yet about meeting with me one last time before I leave?'

Gisele almost broke the phone with the pressure of her fingers as she gripped it in her hand. 'I can't believe how ruthless you're prepared to be in getting your own way,' she hissed at him. 'Do you really think by charging me an exorbitant rent it will make me hate you less?'

'You're assuming I'm going to charge you rent,' he said. 'Maybe I'll lease the premises to you without charging a cent.'

Gisele's heart clanged against her rib cage. 'Wh-what did you say?'

'I'm offering you a business proposition,' he said. 'Meet with me and we'll discuss it.'

She felt a shiver of apprehension trickle down her spine like a single drop of icy water. 'I'd rather turn tricks on the nearest street corner than have anything to do with you,' she threw back.

'Before you reject an offer you really should discuss the terms and conditions more thoroughly,' he said. 'You might be surprised at some of the benefits.'

'I can just imagine some of the benefits,' Gisele said, her voice liberally laced with scorn. 'A rent-free premises in exchange for my body and my self-respect. No thanks.'

'You really should consider my proposal, Gisele,' he said. 'It wouldn't do to put at risk everything you've worked so hard for, now, would it?'

'I've lost everything before and survived,' she said, throwing a verbal punch.

She heard it land with a sharp intake of his breath. 'Don't make me play dirty, Gisele,' he gritted. 'I can and I will if I have to.'

Gisele felt that icy shiver again. She knew just how ruthless he could be. She knew he had ways and means to make things very difficult for her, even more difficult than when he had thrown her out of his life so callously just days before the wedding she had planned with such excitement and anticipation. She still remembered the horror of that moment. She couldn't even look at a wedding gown now without feeling that gut-wrenching sense of despair. But she was not going to roll over for him. 'I don't want or need your help,' she said. 'I don't care if I have to beg on the streets. I will not accept anything from you.'

'I recently designed a holiday retreat for one of Europe's largest retail giants,' Emilio said. 'With a click of a computer mouse I could make your business expand exponentially. Your shop will not just be a local enterprise. It will instantly become a global brand.'

Gisele thought of the expansion she had planned over the next few years. How she had imagined building her business to spread to other suburban outlets and to the larger department stores and, more importantly, increasing her online presence. The only things that had been holding her back were secure finance and the right contacts.

She fought with her resolve. She wanted to say no. She wanted to slam the phone down in his ear. But turning her back on him would mean turning her back on the sort of success most people could only dream about. But then, doing any sort of business deal with Emilio would mean contact with him.

Contact she didn't want, wouldn't *allow* herself to want.

Her stomach slipped like a cat's claws on a highly polished surface.

Maybe even intimate contact...

'Think about it, Gisele,' he said. 'You have a lot to gain by allowing me back in your life, even if it's only temporarily.'

'What do you mean, temporarily?' she asked warily.

'I would like you to spend the next month with me in Italy,' Emilio said. 'It will give us a chance to see if we can still make things work between us. I will, of course, pay you an allowance for the time we spend together.'

'I'm not spending the next minute with you,' Gisele said with a fresh upsurge of resolve. 'I'm hanging up right now so don't bother call—'

'It will also be the perfect opportunity for me to introduce you to the right contacts,' he said. 'How does a million dollars for the month sound?'

Gisele's mouth opened and closed. She couldn't seem to get her voice to work. Her heart was pumping so hard and so fast she felt as if it were going to explode out from between her breasts and land on the floor in front of her.

A million dollars.

Could she do it? Could she survive a month living with Emilio? She had shared his bed with love in the past. How could she do it this time with hatred?

Would he *want* her to share his bed?

A shiver ran over her skin. Of course he would want her to. Hadn't she seen his desire for her burning in his dark eyes when he came into the shop? Couldn't she hear the spine-tingling rumble of it in his voice now? 'I...I need some time to think about this,' she said.

'What's to think about?' he asked. 'You win either way, Gisele. If after a month we both feel there's no point in carrying on any further, you will be free to go. No strings. You can take the money and leave.'

She chewed at her bottom lip for a moment. 'And you're happy to have me back in your life, hating you the way I do?' she asked.

'I understand your feelings,' he said. 'But I feel we both need to be sure we're not making the biggest mistake of our lives by not exploring the possibility of a future together.'

Gisele frowned. 'Why are you doing this?' she asked. 'Why not leave things as they are?'

'Because as soon as I saw you the other day I knew we had unfinished business,' he said. 'I felt it and I know you did too. You can deny it but it won't make it any less real. You might hate me but I felt your body react to mine. You still want me just as much as I still want you.'

Gisele hated that he knew her body so well that he could read its most subtle of signals. What hope did she have of coming out of this with her pride intact? 'I want another day or two to think it over,' she said. 'And if I agree, I won't accept less than two million.'

'I can see why you have done so well for yourself in the time we've been apart,' Emilio said musingly. 'You drive a hard bargain. Two million is a lot of money.'

'I have a lot of hate,' she shot back.

'I will look forward to dismantling it,' he said.

Gisele felt her insides clench with unruly desire. 'You haven't got a hope, Emilio,' she said. 'You can pay all you like for my body but you will never have my heart.'

'Your body will do for now,' he said with smouldering intensity. 'I will send a car for you on Friday evening. Pack your passport and some clothes if it is a yes.' And with that the phone line went dead.

As Emilio's driver pulled up in front of her block of flats Gisele told herself she was saying yes for one reason and one reason only. She wanted to make Emilio's life as miserable as she could for the next month. She would enjoy every minute of making him regret the way he had treated her. He would not find her such an easy conquest this time around. She was not the sweet, shy, rather naive virgin he had met and swept off her feet two years ago. She was older and wiser, harder and more cynical. More battle scarred and dangerously, scarily angry.

Also, being in Europe for a month might give her the opportunity to get to know the sister she had never met until a couple of weeks ago. Sienna was currently living in London, which was a whole lot closer to Rome than Sydney.

Gisele felt her chest tighten as she thought of all the lost years, all the lost confidences and closeness she and Sienna should have had together. Selfish adults who had not stopped to think of the long-term consequences of such a reckless and self-serving deception had stolen it from them.

She was still coming to terms with the heartbreak of finding out the truth. It wasn't just about the sex tape scandal mix-up, although that was heartbreaking enough. She felt her whole life had been a lie. She didn't know who she was any more. It was as if Gisele Carter, the Sydney born and bred only child of Richard and Hilary Carter, had suddenly vanished, vaporised into thin air.

Who was she now?

She was not her mother's daughter. And yet she was not her biological mother's daughter either as she had never felt her mother's arms or ever felt the brush of her lips on her skin, or if she had in those first early days after birth she had no memory of it now.

She had been handed over like a package, a one-way delivery, never to be returned to sender. How had her mother, Nell Baker, chosen which baby to keep and which one to give away? Had she done it willingly or had she done it for the money?

A little dagger of guilt pierced Gisele as she thought of what she had led Emilio to believe *she* would do for money. He thought he could pay any amount to have her back in his life and back in his bed but he was in for a big surprise. She gave a grimly determined smile as she pressed down on the suitcase to snap the locks closed. Once the month was up Emilio would be just as glad to see the back of her as he had been the last time.

She would make sure of it.

Emilio was waiting in the hotel bar when Gisele came. He felt the jolt of awareness hit him like a punch to his abdomen. He had met hundreds of beautiful women but no one had that powerful physical effect on him just by walking into the room. And yet she hardly seemed to be aware of how every male head turned and looked at her.

Her simple but elegant cream dress was nipped in at the waist with a black bow at the front that drew attention to how slim she was. He suspected he could now span her waist with his hands. Her silver-blonde hair was pulled back in a smooth knot at the back of her head, showcasing the swanlike grace of her neck. She was wearing make-up but it was so skilfully applied it looked entirely natural. She had subtly highlighted the grey-blue of her eyes with eyeliner and a brush of smoky eyeshadow, and her lush lips were shiny with pink-tinted lipgloss. It made him want to lean down and press his lips to hers to see if she still tasted the same. He could smell her perfume, her signature summery honeysuckle scent that had clung to his skin for hours after making love with her. He had missed that fragrance. It never smelled quite the same on anyone else.

He stood to greet her, and even though she was wearing shiny patent black killer heels he still towered over her. 'Did you bring your passport?' he asked.

She gave him a churlish look from beneath her lashes. 'I almost didn't, but the thought of two million reasons why I should made me see reason.'

Emilio allowed himself a small smile of satisfaction. She was here under duress but at least she was here. He led her to a quiet corner in the bar with a gentle hand at her elbow. He felt her bare skin shiver in response to his touch and an arrow of need staked him in his groin. Her skin was so soft and creamy, like silk against his fingers. 'What would you like to drink?' he asked. 'Champagne?'

She shook her head. 'I'm not celebrating anything,' she said, shooting him another look. 'White wine will do.'

Emilio ordered their drinks and, once they had been served, he leaned back in his seat to study her icemaiden features. He knew he deserved her ire. He had thrown her out of his life with a callous and ruthless disregard for her feelings. He had been so convinced she had betrayed him. The red mist of anger he had felt had blinded him to anything but what he believed she had done. The image of her with that man taunted him and had done so until he had found out about the discovery of her identical twin.

Seeing her in the flesh again had brought back all the

reasons he had wanted to marry her in the first place. It wasn't just her natural beauty or grace or poise. It wasn't just her softly spoken voice and the way she nibbled at her bottom lip when she was feeling uncertain, or the way she sometimes twirled a loose strand of hair around one of her fingers when she was concentrating on something. It was something in her eyes, those incredible were-they-grey-were-they-blue eyes that had warmed and softened the first time she'd looked at him. What man didn't want the woman he had chosen to be his wife to look at him like that?

As far as he had been concerned, Gisele had been perfect wife material, sweet and gentle, biddable and loving. The fact that he hadn't been in love with her was irrelevant. For his whole life love had been an emotion he had never been able to rely on. In his experience, people used the words so freely but their actions rarely backed them up. The sex tape scandal had reinforced to him how pointless it was to love someone, for people *always* let you down. But in the end he had been the one to let *her* down. He had destroyed her love with his lack of trust in her. But he was determined to get her back. He would make it up to her in a thousand different ways. He couldn't allow a failure like this to blot his life. It felt like a giant ink stain on his soul. He had made the error and it was up to him to do whatever it took to fix it.

And he would do *whatever* it took.

He knew she still wanted him. He had seen it that first day in her shop, the way her body spoke to him in its own private language. His own intensely visceral response to her had sideswiped him. He had thought he had put his desire for her behind him, but it was back with a vengeance as soon as he had laid eyes on her. It was an aching, pulsing need to feel her in his arms again. He couldn't wait to take her upstairs and prove to her they still had a future, that the past could be permanently put aside, erased as if it hadn't happened. She was playing coy with him but he was sure once he kissed her she would melt, just as she always had in the past. He could not tolerate any other outcome.

Failure was not an option.

'I have arranged a flight for tomorrow,' he said. 'We leave at 10:00 a.m.'

Gisele gave him a brittle look. 'You were that certain I'd come?'

He returned her look with measured calm. 'Let's say I know you well enough to be quietly confident,' he said.

'You don't know me any more, Emilio,' she said with another hardened look. 'I'm not the same person I was two years ago.'

'I don't believe that,' Emilio said. 'I know we all change a bit over time but you can't really change who you are deep inside.'

She lifted a slim shoulder in a devil-may-care manner. 'Maybe in a month you'll change your mind,' she said and took a sip of her drink.

'Is your sister still here in Sydney?' Emilio asked.

'No, she flew back to London ten days ago,' she said, looking into the contents of her glass with a little frown. 'The press were hounding her. They were hounding us both. I found it a little scary...' She bit her lip and drained her glass as if she wanted to stop any more words coming out of her mouth.

'It must have been a very difficult time for you both,' he said.

She lifted her gaze to his; her eyes were like stormy grey-blue ice cubes, hard, cold and resentful. 'I'd rather not talk about it if you don't mind,' she said. 'I'm still trying to sort it out in my head. So is Sienna.'

'Perhaps you can invite her to stay at my villa for a few days,' Emilio said. 'I would like to meet her.'

She gave another shrug of indifference. 'Whatever.'

Emilio signalled for the waiter to refresh their drinks. He sat back in his seat and observed Gisele as she tucked an imaginary strand of hair behind her ear, another one of her I'm-out-of-my-depth-and-trying-not-to-show-it mannerisms. She was not as immune to him as she tried to make out. He had seen the flare of female interest in her gaze. He had felt the shiver of reaction on her skin when he had touched her. One kiss would prove he could have her back where he wanted her.

'Tell me about your shop,' he said. 'How did you come about buying the business?'

She dropped her gaze to the drink the waiter had just set before her. 'When I came back…from Italy I…I wanted a secure base,' she said. 'I liked the idea of working for myself. Having more control, that sort of thing. I'd sold some items to the owner in the past and she gave me the first option of buying.'

'It's a big commitment for a young woman of just twenty-five, or twenty-three as you were then,' Emilio said. 'Did your parents help you?'

Gisele put her glass down. 'At first, but then things got a bit tricky after my father got sick. He had a few debts we didn't know about until after he'd died. Bad business decisions, a bit of gambling with the stock market that didn't pay off as well as he'd hoped. I had to help my mother...I mean Hilary out.'

Emilio put his drink down on the coaster on the table between them. 'I'm sorry I didn't send a card,' he said. 'I'd heard he was terminally ill. I should have made contact to offer my condolences. It must have been a very difficult time for you and your mother.'

She looked back at the contents of her glass; the grip of her fingers was so tight around the stem he wondered if it would snap. 'He took eight and a half miserable months to die,' she said. 'Not once in all that time did he ever say anything about me having a twin sister.' She looked at him at that point, her grey-blue gaze blazing with anger. 'Both my parents knew our relationship had broken up because of that sex tape but still neither he nor my mother said a word. I can never forgive them for that.'

Emilio carefully removed the wineglass from her stiff fingers and put it to one side. 'I can understand your anger towards them but our relationship broke up because I didn't trust you,' he said. 'If anyone is to blame it is me.'

Gisele met his gaze in the long silence that ensued. 'You know what really upsets me?' she asked.

'Tell me,' he said, still holding her gaze.

'How did they choose?' she asked.

'You mean who got which twin?' he asked.

Gisele blew out a hissing breath. 'I can't get it out of my mind,' she said. 'How did they do it? How could my mother, my biological mother, give me up? And how could my father ask it of her? And not only that, what was my adoptive mother thinking by agreeing to bring up her husband's love child? Did she have no self-respect?'

Emilio bent his forearms on his thighs so he could reach Gisele's tightly knotted hands. He took them both in one of his, stroking the tension away as best he could. 'Have you asked her about it?' he said.

She looked at him with flashing eyes. 'Of course I've asked her,' she said. 'She said she did it to keep my father happy. She spent their whole married life trying to make him happy but it never worked.'

'From what you told me, your family always seemed so perfect to me,' Emilio said, still stroking her hands. 'You never said anything about them being unhappy together.'

Gisele looked down at their joined hands and hastily pulled hers away. She sat straighter in her seat, ramrod straight, angry straight, keep-away-from-me straight. 'I never liked admitting it to anyone but I always felt I wasn't good enough for either of my parents,' she said. 'I tried my best but nothing I did or achieved seemed to please them. My mother wasn't the maternal type. She never liked cuddling me or playing with me. She employed a nanny to do that. Now I understand why. I wasn't her child.' She drew in another painful-sounding breath and continued, 'My father was just as bad. Deep down, I think he really wanted a son. My mother certainly couldn't give him one, but then his mistress gave him two daughters so he chose one. But I've often wondered if he thought he'd chosen the wrong one or whether he wished he had just walked away from both of us. He was stuck in a loveless marriage until the day he died, out of guilt presumably. All of those long stone-walling silences between him and my mother over the years suddenly made a whole lot of sense.'

Emilio frowned. He had never heard Gisele talk so honestly about her childhood. He had thought she had come from a reasonably happy and stable home. He had envied her background, given the bleak misery of his. It made him realise how little he had known her, even though he'd been days off marrying her. He had been struck by her beauty but had given little thought to who she was, what she valued and how she wanted her life to run. He had swept her off her feet, dazzled her with his wealth and charm, and yet had not known for a moment how deeply insecure she really was. It was like look-ing at her for the first time. The same beauty was there but so too was a fragility that he had not seen the first time around. But then she had been devastatingly hurt and he, to his shame, had done that to her, even more so than her parents. He wasn't sure how he could ever fix that terrible mistake but he was determined to try. 'How is your sister dealing with this?' he asked.

Gisele let her stiff shoulders drop. 'She's a lot more chilled about it than me,' she said. 'I guess growing up with a single mother who was known to be a bit of a tear-away has toughened her up rather a lot. It sounded like Sienna was the parent rather than the child most of the time. She told me there were always a lot of men com-ing and going in her mother's life. It can't have been an easy childhood but she just made the best of it.'

'Is she disappointed she didn't get to meet your fa-ther?'

'Yes and no, I suppose,' Gisele said, frowning a little. 'I think she would've given him a serve for what he did. She's a bit of a straight shooter. I think I could do with some lessons from her, actually. It's about time I learned to speak up for myself.'

'I think you're doing rather a good job of it,' Emilio said with a crooked smile. 'Perhaps I am wrong after all. Maybe you have changed.'

Her eyes glittered as they held his. 'You'd better believe it.'

Emilio allowed a little silence to pass before he spoke. 'Did you give the keys and all the relevant paperwork for your shop to the driver?'

'Yes.'

'Good,' he said. 'Your new assistant will hold the fort until you decide what course of action to take. I've already spoken to her about it.'

She frowned at him. 'What do you mean?'

He held her look for a moment. 'You might decide to stay on in Italy,' he said. 'It would be imprudent not to prepare for that possibility.'

She gave him a disdainful look. 'You must get really exhausted carrying that monumental ego around. Do you really think I will step back into your life as if nothing has changed? You're paying for a month and that's all you're going to get.'

Emilio fought back his temper. He was not used to her being so obstructive and defiant. In the past she had been so willing to fit in with his plans. Where was the sweet young woman he had chosen as his bride?

'Would you like another drink?' he asked after a tense pause.

'No... Thank you.' She pushed the glass away with another little frown pulling at her brow.

'I thought we could have dinner in my suite,' he said.

She looked at him with startled eyes. 'Why not in a restaurant?' she asked.

'I thought it might be more private.'

Her eyes narrowed. 'You can quit it with the whole seduction routine, Emilio,' she said. 'It won't work.'

Emilio felt his groin tighten as she threw the challenge down with her flashing gaze. 'You think not?' he asked.

'I know not,' she said with a lift of her chin.

He held her gaze, hot, hungry desire leaping like flames in his body. This new feisty Gisele was turning him on. There was something about her newfound defiance that thrilled him. It stirred his blood, making it surge through his system like rocket fuel. There was one thing he loved more than anything and that was a challenge. He had left his dirt-poor background behind with the same gritty determination to succeed no matter what it cost. He had put himself through school and then university, working day and night to cover the expense. He had made his fortune by rising to the demands of difficult clients and completing next to impossible projects. He had nearly lost it all after the scandal, but he had clawed his way back.

Gisele was another next to impossible project but, just like all the rest, he was determined to succeed.

Nothing and no one was going to stand in his way.

CHAPTER THREE

GISELE stood like a statue of marble as Emilio escorted her up to his suite. She could smell his aftershave; it stirred deep memories she tried desperately to suppress. She felt as if she were stepping back in time. How many times had she stepped into an elevator to accompany him up to his penthouse suite in hotels all over Europe? The erotic images that thought triggered made her skin prickle all over and she had to bite her lip until it hurt to block them from her mind.

Back then she had been so eager to please him. She knew right from the moment she had met him that he was a proud and strong-willed man but she had never questioned him, never stood up to him and never challenged him. She had just loved him, completely and desperately. How had she allowed herself to become so vulnerable? The power balance of their relationship had been wrong. She had loved him too much and he hadn't loved her at all.

It was only his pride that wanted her back now. She knew it wasn't about her as a person. He wanted the world to know he was setting the record straight. His offer of a one-month trial seemed to prove it. A man with his high profile could not afford to be seen as act-

ing unfairly. The press had gone wild with the story of
Sienna and her being reunited. She was surprised he
hadn't already informed the media of his intention to
resume his relationship with her.

The elevator stopped and Emilio held the doors back
for her with an outstretched arm. Gisele moved past him,
determined not to show how unsettled she was. Her
stomach was twitching with nerves. Everything about
him unsettled her. He seemed to see much more than
she wanted him to see. What if he sensed she was hiding something from him? How long before he guessed
the pain in her eyes had been put there, not just by him,
but also by the loss of their child? The child whose soft
pink bunny blanket that still held a faint trace of her
sweet baby smell was folded inside her suitcase? She
hadn't been able to leave that final link with Lily behind.
Her mother...*Hilary*, she quickly amended, had said it
was unhealthy to keep holding on. She had said Gisele
should put it all behind her, pack the blanket away so
she could finally move on.

Gisele wasn't ready to move on.

She didn't think she would ever be ready to move on.
What would Hilary know anyway? She hadn't physically given birth to a child only to have that child's life
snatched away. She didn't know, *couldn't* possibly know
what it felt like...

'Relax, *cara*,' Emilio said as he opened the door to
his suite. 'You look like you're about to be devoured by
a wild beast.'

Gisele stalked past him. 'I have a headache,' she said
and it wasn't a lie. The pain behind her eyeballs had gone
from a dull ache to a pounding that felt as if a team of

jackhammers on steroids had taken up residence inside her skull.

His brows moved together. 'Why didn't you say something earlier?' he asked.

'I'll be fine,' she said, licking her lips to give them some much-needed moisture. 'I probably shouldn't have had that second drink. I don't have a good head for alcohol.'

'When was the last time you ate?' he asked.

The fact that she had to think about it didn't go unnoticed by him, Gisele thought as she saw that dark frown deepen across his brow. 'I can't remember,' she said. 'It wasn't a priority. I had to get things sorted at my flat and at the shop.' She threw him a resentful scowl. 'You didn't give me much time.'

'I'm sorry but I have to get back to Rome for a project I'm working on,' he said. 'The client is a big one. I had to work hard to get the contract. It's worth several million.'

Gisele thought of all the money he earned from his designs. She suspected he hadn't come by it easily. He was a prime example of the adage that anyone could do anything if they had enough determination. And the one thing Emilio had in spades was determination. She could see it in the glittering depths of his dark eyes and the strong lines of his jaw, both hinting at the implacability of his nature. In the days and weeks ahead she would be going head to head with that intransigent personality. Who would eventually come out on top? She gave a little involuntary shiver. It was a nerve-jangling thought.

'I'll have dinner sent up immediately,' he said. 'The porter brought up your things earlier,' he said. 'Would you like me to get a housemaid to unpack it for you? I should have thought of it before.'

'No,' Gisele said, perhaps a little too quickly. She saw his eyebrows lift. *Yes, definitely too quickly.* 'We're… um…leaving tomorrow, in any case.'

He held her gaze for an infinitesimal moment. 'Would you prefer the guest suite tonight?' he asked.

Gisele gave him a flinty look. 'Where else did you expect me to sleep?'

He came up close and brushed her hot cheek with the backs of his bent knuckles. 'Do you really think you'll be sleeping in the spare room for the entire month?' he asked.

She brushed his hand away as if it were an annoying fly. 'I haven't signed anything that requires me to sleep with you.'

'That reminds me.' He moved away from her and opened a briefcase that was lying on a table near the window. He took out a document and brought it over. 'You should read it before you sign it,' he said, his expression now inscrutable. 'The full amount we agreed on will be transferred to your account on the completion of your stay.'

Gisele looked at the sheaf of papers, wishing she could walk away. But two million dollars was not the sort of money she could turn her back on right now. She took pride in her success so far; it had helped her cope. How much better would she feel if her baby wear became even more successful? What else did she have in her life other than her shop? It wasn't as if she was ever going to get married and have a family now. That dream was long gone.

She took the papers and sank to the nearest chair, casting her eyes over the words printed there. She read it in detail but it was as straightforward as he had said. After the month was up she would be two million dollars richer and would owe him nothing. She signed it with a hand that wasn't quite steady. 'There,' she said, shoving the papers at his chest.

He put them to one side before he faced her again. 'So, it looks like we have a deal.'

She lifted her chin. 'Yes,' she said. 'You just signed away two million dollars.' *For nothing.*

His lips moved up in a curl that had a hint of mockery about it. 'How long do you think you will hold out, mmm? A week? Two?'

She glared at him fiercely. 'If you want a bedmate then you'll have to look elsewhere. I'm not interested.'

'You're planning your own little payback, aren't you?' he asked, still with that sardonic half smile.

Gisele felt a betraying flush stain her cheeks. 'I don't know what you're talking about,' she said.

'You think I don't know how your mind works?' he asked. 'You plan to make me suffer every minute of the time we spend together. But do you really think that by snipping and snarling at me it will make me want you less? Don't fool yourself, Gisele. You will sleep with me again, not because I paid you, but because you just can't help yourself.'

Gisele thought she couldn't hate him more than at that moment. She wanted to slap his arrogant face for assuming she had no self-control, no discipline and no self-respect. 'I hate you with every cell in my body,' she snarled at him like a cornered cat, all claws and bared teeth. 'Do you realise that? I *hate* you.'

Emilio's calmness riled her even further. 'The fact that you feel something for me is good,' he said. 'I can handle anger. It is far better than cold indifference.'

Gisele was determined she would show him just how cold and indifferent she could be. 'OK then.' She kicked off her heels and began to unzip her dress. 'You want me to sleep with you? Then let's get it out of the way right here and now.'

He stood there watching her silently, hardly a muscle moving, apart from his eyes. She saw the flare of his pupils, the primal signal of male attraction as she stepped out of her dress, leaving it in a puddle of fabric on the floor. She was standing in just her bra and knickers before him. She had stood in a whole lot less before him two years ago. But suddenly she felt naked in a way she had never felt before. A shiver broke out over her skin and her stomach curdled at the thought of going any further with this.

She put her hands behind her back to unhook her bra but her fingers were suddenly fumbling and useless. She felt as if she was going to cry. The emotions were like a fountain inside her that had been blocked. The pressure was building and building. She could feel it behind her eyes; she could feel it inside her chest, a tight ache that burned like fire.

'Get dressed,' Emilio said curtly as he turned away.

Gisele felt as if he had ripped the ankle-deep carpet out from under her feet. She had been prepared to play him at his own game but he had somehow turned the tables on her. He wanted her but on his terms, not hers.

She felt foolish.

She felt uncertain.

She felt *rejected*.

She watched as he walked over to the bar and poured himself a drink. He tipped back his head and drained his glass and then set in down on the bar with a thump. His shoulders looked tense; the muscles were bunched beneath the fine cotton of his shirt. She remembered how those muscles felt under the soft pads of her fingertips, how she used to massage away those tight knots, how she used to press her mouth to that hot, salty male skin...

Gisele ran the tip of her tongue over her bone-dry lips. 'So,' she said, summoning up what was left of her paltry attempt at cold indifference, 'I take it you no longer require my services this evening?'

Emilio turned to look at her but his expression was difficult to read. 'I will have a meal sent up to you presently,' he said. 'Please make yourself at home. I'm going out.'

'Where are you going?' The question was out before she could stop it and, to her shame, it sounded scarily close to one a jealous wife might have asked.

He turned from the door and raked her with his cold indifferent gaze. 'Don't wait up,' he said and then he was gone.

Gisele picked up one of her shoes and threw it at the door, angry tears spilling from her eyes. 'Damn you,' she said. 'Damn you to hell.'

Emilio entered the penthouse at two in the morning. He had walked the streets of Sydney for hours, determined not to return until Gisele was safely out of his range. His body had ached to take what she was offering so defiantly but he was not going to give her any more reasons to hate him. He would bide his time, waiting for her to come to him, as he knew she would. One night would not be enough for either of them. He was counting on that. He knew as soon as she gave in to the sexual chemistry that sizzled between them she would want more. She was bitter and angry but he knew she would get over it. Time was a great healer and a month was surely long enough to see if what they had shared together before could be resurrected.

The meal he had sent up to the suite looked as if it had been barely touched. He frowned as he looked at the selection of dishes and the undrunk wine sitting on the dining table. Her lack of appetite could have been because of her headache, but he suspected it was more to do with her current I'll-show-you attitude.

He admired her for standing up to him. Not many people did. He had learned on the filthy backstreets of Rome how to intimidate people. Those skills had come in handy in his professional life. What he said went. People didn't argue with him. They didn't challenge or defy him. The women in his life—and there had been plenty—never argued with him. They played by his rules. He always made sure of that. And Gisele had been no different during their time together. She had been biddable and gracious, the perfect companion, the perfect hostess, the perfect woman to be his wife.

Emilio frowned as he wandered over to the windows to look at the harbour view below. Some would say he had selected a trophy wife but he had never thought of Gisele like that. He had genuinely liked having her around. She had been easy company, at ease with him and with others. He was proud to have her on his arm. She moved with such poise and grace, with such natural elegance.

He let out a sigh that pulled on something deep inside his chest. If it hadn't been for the scandal they would have celebrated their second wedding anniversary a couple of weeks ago. Perhaps they might have even had a child by now. They had talked about it. That was another of the reasons he had wanted her as his wife. She had been keen to have a large family, having grown up as an only child. And he had been just as keen. All those years in and out of ill-run foster homes or begging on the streets had made him envious of all those warm, well-lit homes he had wandered past, with their close-knit family units inside.

His envy of other people's homes had been his primary motivation to become an architect. He had been barely ten years old when he had made the decision. He had thought by designing hundreds of dream homes that he would be satisfied, but it hadn't had the effect he'd imagined. He suspected that having his own family would be the only thing that would truly satisfy him. That and that alone would be able to soothe the raw sore of loneliness that constantly oozed deep inside his soul.

He felt it now, the never-ending sense of something missing from his life, of being incomplete. Was that why he had been drawn to Gisele, because of her own previously unspoken of loneliness?

Emilio turned from the window when he heard a

sound behind him. 'You didn't eat your dinner,' he said, just as Gisele was searching for the light switch.

She put a hand up to her throat, her eyes wide with shock. 'I didn't see you there,' she gasped. 'You scared me half to death. Why didn't you put the lights on?'

'Maybe I prefer the dark.'

She clutched the edges of her wrap together close to her chest. 'You could have said something,' she said with an accusing glare.

'I did,' he said. 'I said you didn't eat your dinner.'

She gave him a testy look. 'Maybe I wasn't hungry.'

'You need to eat,' he said. 'You're too thin.'

'You need to keep your opinions to yourself,' she shot back.

Emilio came over to where she was standing. 'Weren't you able to sleep?' he asked.

She flicked some hair back off her face and gave him a defiant stare. 'What's it to you?'

'I'm concerned about you,' he said. 'You look like you haven't slept properly in months.'

'Concerned, are you?' She flashed her eyes at him like blue lightning. 'What a pity you weren't so concerned about my welfare when you tossed me out on the street two years ago.'

Emilio ground his teeth together to stop himself saying something he might regret later. He had always prided himself on his self-control but Gisele's stubborn refusal to meet him halfway was testing his limits. How long was she going to persist with this game of payback? He had made amends. Wasn't it time to move on? 'Would you like me to make you a hot milk drink?' he asked.

She gave a choked bubble of laughter that sounded almost hysterical. 'Yeah, why not?' she said. 'Maybe put a shot of whisky in it for good measure. Two shots. That should knock me out.'

Emilio poured milk into a mug and placed it in the microwave set near the bar. He leant back against the counter as he studied her. 'I know from experience that running a business, even a successful one, is stressful,' he said. 'I've had plenty of sleepless nights myself.'

She curled her lip at him. 'I'm sure you've found plenty of women to distract you from your spreadsheets.'

'Not as many as you might think,' he said.

She gave him a cynical look. 'Well, just for the record, I'm not opening my legs like one of your cheap gold-digging whores.'

'You didn't seem to have any problem with it in the past,' he said. 'And at a cool two million, *cara*, you are certainly not cheap.'

Gisele raised a hand to slap him but he intercepted it, holding her slim wrist with the steel handcuffs of his fingers. 'Don't even think about it,' he warned. 'You might not like the consequences.'

She fought against his hold, clawing at him, but it was like a kitten trying to fight off a panther. He was too strong. He was too close. He was too everything.

'What consequences?' she asked. 'What are you going to do? Hit me right back? Is that what rough, tough Italian guys do?'

His expression tightened. 'I would never lay a finger on you and you damn well know it.'

She gave him a challenging glare. 'You've got five fingers on me right now.'

'And they're staying on you until you stop behaving like a wilful child.'

'I hate you,' she spat at him furiously.

'So you've said.'

'I mean it.'

'I believe you.'

'I want you to die and rot in hell.'

'I believe that too,' he said. 'But trading insults isn't going to make this go away.'

Gisele felt his thighs way too close to hers. She felt the warmth of his body, a radiating heat that her colder flesh craved. She felt his warm brandy-scented breath move like a teasing feather over her face. She felt her breasts go to hard aching peaks as the hard wall of his muscular chest loomed closer. Her lashes lowered as she looked at the line of his mouth. That mouth had kissed her so many times she had lost count. It could be hard and yet so soft, so demanding and yet so giving. 'I hate you,' she said again, but she wasn't sure if she was saying it for herself or for him.

She *needed* her anger.

She needed her rage and fury to keep herself in one piece. It was all she had. The only armour left that she could rely on. It had carried her through for so long.

Emilio cupped the side of her face with the broad span of his hand, his thumb moving over the hollow of her cheek, back and forth in a mesmerising rhythm that sent every thought flying out of her head. His eyes moved over her face, taking their time before they finally meshed with hers. 'Stop fighting me, Gisele,' he said. 'Don't give up on us before we've had a chance to set things right.'

'Some things can't be fixed,' she said. 'It's too late. Too much time has passed.'

'Do you really believe that?' he asked.

Gisele didn't know what to believe when he was holding her against him, his hard body fitting against her softer one as if no time had passed at all. She felt the hardened ridge of him, the surge of blood that lengthened him in the primal preparation to mate. It was so earthy and real. No amount of denying it could make it go away. Her body was responding to him in its own secret way. The silky moisture of her inner core was reminding her that she was no less immune to him than she had ever been. It didn't matter how much she hated him. It didn't matter how much she told him she wanted nothing more to do with him. Her body had its own needs and wants and they were overriding every other rational thought she tried to cling to.

'I believe you're only doing this because you're worried what the press and your precious business colleagues will think if you don't try to make amends,' she said, looking at him defiantly. 'It's all for show. The one-month reconciliation. You'll appear to do the right thing by me but it will all be for nothing because I won't come back to you for good. No amount of money will ever induce me to do that.'

He pulled her roughly up against him, his expression hard and bitter and thunderously angry. 'Then I'd better get my money's worth while I can, hadn't I?' And then his mouth crashed down on hers.

It was a blistering kiss, no hint of softness about it. Gisele felt its impact from the top of her prickling scalp to her toes curling into the carpet at her feet for purchase. His lips ground against hers with bruising force, making a dam inside her break its bounds. She kissed him back with all the fury that was inside her. She felt the demand of his tongue at the seam of her mouth and didn't hesitate in allowing him in.

She *wanted* him in.

She wanted to duel with him until they were both breathless with need. She wanted to taste him, to savour that essential maleness that had always sent ripples of delight through her body.

She wanted to hurt him. She wanted to remind him of what he had thrown away. She used her teeth, and not just little nippy bites either. She bit down on his lower lip and held on like a tigress with a prized piece of prey.

He bit her back, the alpha-male-taming-his-mate action sending a rapid blast of heat straight to her core. She tasted blood and wasn't sure if it was his or her own. She felt the rough graze of his stubbly jaw against her face as he changed position. His hands were clutching her head, his fingers buried deep in her hair, holding her captive to his sensual assault.

Gisele's hands moved up from lying flat against his chest to rediscovering the thick silkiness of his hair. He shifted against her urgently, his body so thick and full she felt her body quiver in reaction. Raw need clawed at her, an ache that was so tight and ravenous it burned inside her.

She wanted him.

She wanted him even though she hated him. She wanted the savage thrust of his possession to make her feel alive again. Oh, dear God, please make her feel *alive* again...

Emilio suddenly pulled away from her, his hands dropping from her as if she were a carrier of some deadly disease. He wiped at his mouth with the back of his hand, grimacing as he saw a smear of blood. 'Is that yours or mine?' he asked.

'Does it matter?' Gisele asked with an arch look.

'Actually it does,' he said, frowning darkly. 'I didn't intend to hurt you.'

She challenged him with her gaze as she touched a finger to where her bottom lip had borne the brunt of his kiss. 'Didn't you?'

He took a clean folded handkerchief out of his pocket and stepped back into her body space, lifting her chin as he gently held the cool cotton against her lip. His eyes were unfathomable coal-black pools as they held hers. 'It doesn't have to be this way between us, Gisele,' he said in a husky tone.

She took the handkerchief from him and moved away, turning her back on him. 'It's not going to work, you know,' she said. 'Nothing is going to change my mind. I will never forgive you.'

She heard the rustle of his clothes as he moved. Then she felt his hands come down on the tops of her shoulders and her whole body shivered in reaction. She closed her eyes, summoning her resolve. Where was it? What was happening to her that she wanted to turn around and melt into the warm protection of his broad chest? 'Don't…' she said, squeezing her eyes even tighter.

'Don't what?' he asked.

'You know what,' she said, suppressing a sigh of delight when his fingers began to massage the tightly knotted muscles of her neck and shoulders. If he was running true to form, any minute now he would slip the wrap from one of her shoulders and press his warm lips to her needy flesh. God help her if he did. She would have no power left in her to resist him.

'You want me, Gisele.' His still-aroused body brushed against hers from behind.

'You think.'

'I know.'

She turned and glared at him hotly. 'I want this month to be over so I can finally be free of you.'

His eyes roved her face, looking for what, she wasn't quite sure. She schooled her features into cool indifference, her version of it anyway. 'You should go to bed,' he said, brushing his thumb ever so gently against her bottom lip. 'It's a long flight tomorrow, even when travelling First Class.'

'What?' she said with a mocking look. 'No private jet any more?'

His expression remained inscrutable. 'Owning a private jet is no longer my measure of a successful person,' he said. 'I have other things I would rather spend my money on.'

'Such as?'

His hand dropped from her face as he stepped back from her. 'Good night,' he said. 'I'll see you in the morning.'

'It *is* morning,' she said, just to be pedantic and annoying, but it was a wasted effort on her part as he had already left the room.

CHAPTER FOUR

OF COURSE she didn't sleep. Not even the chemical cock-tail the doctor had prescribed to help dull the night-mares about Lily had any effect on her tonight. Gisele tossed and turned and watched as the clock went round, her mind racing with thoughts of Emilio and the month ahead and how on earth she was going to get through it.

In the end she gave up. She padded over to her suit-case and took out Lily's blanket and cradled it against her chest as if her tiny baby were still alive and breath-ing, wrapped inside it. Tears rolled down her cheeks un-checked. How many nights had she spent doing exactly this? When was this searing pain ever going to ease?

She must have dozed off for she suddenly heard the rap of Emilio's knuckles on her door. 'Time to get up, Gisele,' he said. 'It's 7:00 a.m.'

'I'm awake,' she called out as she struggled upright off the bed. She put Lily's blanket safely back in her suitcase before heading for the shower.

Emilio was pouring himself a cup of coffee when Gisele came in. She had a stoic look about her as if she were being led to the gallows and was determined not to beg for last-minute mercy. 'Sleep OK?' he asked.

'Out like a light.'

He doubted it. She had damson-coloured shadows under her eyes and her face was deathly pale. 'You should have something to eat,' he said, waving a hand towards the food he'd had delivered to the suite.

'I'm not hungry.'

He drew in a breath. 'You think by going on a hunger strike that it's going to help things?'

She shot him a glare. 'I'm not on a hunger strike. I'm just not hungry.'

'You're never hungry,' he snapped at her in annoyance. 'It's not normal. You need food. You'll fade away to nothing if you don't eat.'

'What would you care?' she asked. 'Your last girlfriend was much thinner than me. It *was* a swimwear model you were dating last month, wasn't it? Or have I got her mixed up with that London socialite with the big boobs?' She tapped a finger against the side of her mouth as if trying to prod her memory. 'What was her name again? Arabella? Amanda? Ariel?'

Emilio ground his teeth as he pulled out a chair for her. 'Sit.'

She gave him a castigating look. 'You know you could have saved yourself a heap of money by buying a dog to obey your commands.'

'I thought it would be much more fun training you,' he said through tight lips. 'Now, sit and eat.'

She sat with a toss of her head. 'At least I don't pee on the carpet,' she said.

'I wouldn't put it past you,' he muttered.

She picked up a rasher of bacon and dropped it on

her plate. 'So did you sleep?' she asked. 'You don't look like it. You look like hell.'

'Thank you.'

She stabbed the bacon with her fork. 'You're welcome.'

Emilio watched her as she nibbled at the bacon. Her small white teeth and those luscious lips of hers had kept him awake for what had been left of last night. He tore his gaze away and refilled his coffee cup. 'Do you want coffee or tea?' he asked.

'Tea,' she said and, rolling her eyes, added, 'Sorry for being so *un*-Italian.'

'You're not sorry at all,' he said, putting a steaming cup of tea in front of her. 'Do you want milk or sugar?'

She raised her brows at him. 'You don't remember how I take my tea?' she asked. 'Or have there been so many women since me you're getting us all a little mixed up?'

Emilio pressed his lips together. He wasn't proud of how many women there had been. It was just like her to twist the knife as much as she could. 'You take it black with one sugar,' he said.

She pressed her finger to the table and made a buzzing noise like that on a game show. 'Wrong answer.'

He frowned. 'Are you sure?'

She gave him a look. 'Yeah, I'm sure.'

'So when did you give up the sugar?' he asked.

'I did that when I was...' She stopped and dropped her gaze to her plate.

'When you were?' he prompted.

She pushed back from the table. 'I have to get my things together,' she said. 'I haven't packed.'

'You haven't unpacked,' he pointed out wryly.

'I have to do my...my hair,' she said, ruffling it with one of her hands. 'It's a mess.'

'It looked perfectly fine until you just did that,' he said.

'I have to do my make-up.'

'You're wearing make-up,' he said.

She bit her lip and then winced and put her fingers up to her mouth.

Emilio felt his gut clench. 'Does it hurt?' he asked.

Her eyes fell away from his. 'I've felt worse pain.'

A little silence passed.

'I'm sorry,' he said heavily.

'For what?' she asked, shooting him another cut glass look. 'Buying me back into your life or throwing me out of it in the first place?'

Emilio held her brittle gaze for a lengthy moment. 'I have already told you I'm not proud of how I handled things back then. This is my chance to make it up to you.' He let out a rough-edged sigh. 'It must have been terrible for you the night I asked you to leave.'

'It wasn't a highlight of my time in Italy, that's for sure,' she said, affecting a couldn't-care-less pose. 'But what doesn't kill you makes you stronger, right?'

Emilio swept his gaze over her thin frame. 'You don't look stronger, *cara*,' he said softly. 'You act it but you don't look it.'

She seemed to be actively avoiding his eyes. 'I'd really prefer it if you didn't call me that,' she said.

'I always called you that in the past.'

'This is not the past,' she said tightly. 'This is now. It's different now.'

'Not so different,' he said. 'We are together again.'

She flashed him a defiant glare. 'Only for a month.'

He picked up his coffee and took a sip before he responded. 'Maybe you'll like it so much you'll change your mind and stay.'

'And do what?' she asked. 'Hang off your arm and your every word like some besotted bimbo with no mind of her own? No, thanks. I've grown up. I want more for my life than to be a rich man's plaything.'

Emilio buttoned down his anger with an effort. 'You were going to be my wife, not my plaything,' he said.

Her eyes clashed with his. 'Why did you ask me to marry you, Emilio?' she asked. 'Why not one of the many other women you'd been involved with before me? Why was I so special?'

He put his coffee cup down with a little thwack. 'I think you already know the answer to that, Gisele.'

'It was because I was a virgin, wasn't it?' she asked. 'What a novelty in this day and age to have a woman no one else had ever had. I was a perfect candidate as your future wife. I was perfect until that scandal broke and then suddenly I wasn't worth anything to you. I was soiled. Used goods. Imperfect. And there's nothing you like less than imperfection, is there?'

Emilio pushed himself away from the counter, the set to his mouth grim. 'We need to leave in less than an hour,' he said. 'I hope I don't need to remind you that your behaviour towards me will be under intense scrutiny as soon as we leave the privacy of this hotel. I will not tolerate your insults or your childish attempts to pick a fight in front of any member of my staff, or the press, or indeed the public. If you want to have a showdown with me, then at least have the decency and poise to keep a lid on it until we are alone.'

Gisele looked at him in alarm. 'You don't expect me to act as if I'm still in love with you, do you?'

He gave her a look that would have sliced through steel. 'That's exactly what I expect,' he said. 'We're meant to be trying to resurrect our relationship.'

She felt her stomach shift uneasily. 'I can't do it,' she said. 'I can't pretend to feel something I no longer feel.'

'You will have to,' he said implacably. 'I'm not paying two million dollars for you to look daggers at me while the whole world looks on. If you can't meet the terms, then tell me now and I'll tear up the agreement. It's up to you.'

Gisele hesitated, caught between wanting to walk away and wanting to prove something to him and to herself. Could she do it? Could she act the role she had played for real with such embarrassing enthusiasm in the past? It was just a month. Four weeks of playing for the press. In private she could be herself. She could hate him a thousandfold and no one would be the wiser. 'All right,' she said, mentally crossing her fingers that she was doing the right thing. 'I'll do it.'

Thankfully, the Australian press had not been present when Gisele and Emilio left the hotel for their flight. But it was a completely different story when they landed in the Leonardo da Vinci Airport in Rome. As soon as they stepped through Customs the paparazzi swarmed like bees. Gisele felt under siege as it brought back horrible reminders of the time when the scandal had broken. The camera flashes made her flinch, and her heart was racing so much she felt as if she was going to faint.

She had pretended to sleep on the plane rather than try and make polite conversation with Emilio, but it was all catching up with her now. She felt tired and sick and way too much out of her depth to cope with the barrage of comments firing like machine gun bullets at her. She had always found the intrusion of the press rather daunting from the moment she became involved with Emilio. She had felt as if she was under scrutiny all the time. The speculation on what she wore, how she looked or whether she was smiling or frowning was something she had never got used to. Rumours about their relationship would appear from time to time, which Emilio had laughed off, but Gisele—although she had pretended otherwise—had been distressed by the lack of privacy.

Emilio spoke in Italian, asking the press to keep back to give Gisele some room. His arm came around her protectively, and if it hadn't been for their terse exchange before they left the hotel, Gisele would have been tempted to believe he truly cared about her welfare rather than his reputation.

'Signor Andreoni—' a journalist pushed through the cluster of cameras with a microphone '—does this mean you and Signorina Carter will be getting married as soon as possible?'

'We are enjoying some time together before we make any firm plans,' Emilio answered.

Gisele had learnt a bit of Italian while she had lived with Emilio but it wasn't enough to follow every rapidly spoken word, although she did hear the word *matri-*

monio—marriage. What exactly was he telling the press?

'Signorina Carter?' The same journalist turned the microphone in Gisele's direction but this time spoke in English. 'Is it good to be back with Signor Andreoni?'

Gisele stumbled over her reply. 'Um… I'm very happy…'

'It has been two years since your very public breakup,' the journalist continued. 'You must be feeling very relieved the truth has finally come out about who exactly it was in that sex tape.'

Gisele felt uncomfortable talking about her sister's private life. Sienna had seemed reluctant to go into any details other than to say the press had blown it up to be much more than it actually was. Gisele suspected that ignominious incident had been devastating for her twin, although Sienna pretended otherwise. 'I'm happy that I've found my sister,' she said. 'That's been the most important outcome of such a difficult time.'

'Is your twin sister planning on spending some time with you now that you are going to be living in Italy?' another journalist asked.

'I'm not planning on stay—'

Emilio cut Gisele off. 'We are both looking forward to spending time with Sienna Baker. Now, if you will excuse us, we have to get moving.'

'Signorina Carter, one more question…' Yet another journalist rushed after them.

'Basta,' Emilio said and then repeated it in English. 'That's enough.'

He spirited her away to the waiting car, physically blocking the swarm of press as she got in. 'Remember what I said earlier about what you do and say to me in public,' he said.

Gisele caught the driver's watchful eye in the rear-view mirror. A glass partition separated her and Emilio from the front of the car but it was hardly what one would call being in private. She forced herself to sit with a relaxed pose beside Emilio even though she wished she had the courage to thrust open the door and throw herself out of his life, both literally and figuratively.

She drew in a sharp little breath as she looked out at the scenery passing by. The Colosseum suddenly appeared and a tight ache settled in her chest. She could still remember the excitement of her first trip to Italy after she had met Emilio while she was doing a needlework course at the London School of Embroidery. They had met at an art exhibition she had been invited to by one of the girls she had met doing her course, whose boyfriend couldn't make it at the last minute. Gisele had been in two minds whether or not to attend but in the end had decided to go so that her new friend wouldn't have to go alone. Within minutes of walking into the small privately owned gallery she had met Emilio's gaze from across the room. She could still recall the way her heart had fluttered in her chest as he moved through the knot of people to get to her. He had been head and shoulders above all the other men, not just in stature, but also in looks and in his proud, almost aristocratic bearing. She had thought he must be Italian royalty at the very least, and why he should single her out was beyond her comprehension. But single her out he had, and within a week she had been swept off her feet and totally, blissfully in love.

'I have a new housekeeper,' Emilio said into the silence that had fallen. 'Her name is Marietta.'

'What happened to Concetta?' Gisele asked with a frown.

His mouth tightened briefly. 'I fired her the day after you left.'

'Why?' she asked. 'I thought you said she was the best housekeeper you'd ever had.'

'She was.'

'So why'd you fire her?'

'She overstepped the mark in telling me I was a fool for throwing you out,' he said. 'I fired her on the spot.'

'Way to go, Concetta,' Gisele said. She pushed her tongue against the inside of her bottom lip as she studied his brooding expression. 'You didn't think to ask her to come back to you along with me?'

His brows moved together over his eyes as he looked at her. 'She wouldn't come back,' he said.

Gisele gave him a saccharine-sweet smile. 'Maybe you should've offered her two million dollars.'

He didn't answer but she saw his jaw flex just before he turned and looked out of the window.

The driver pulled up in front of Emilio's villa in the exclusive area near the Villa Borghese parklands. Gisele felt another pang as Emilio helped her from the car. She had been totally blown away by the magnificent building two years ago and she felt exactly the same way now. Built on four levels with gorgeous formal gardens and a huge fountain set in the middle of the circular driveway, it looked every inch the private residence of a person who had very much made their way in the world.

Emilio gave the driver instructions about their lug-

gage before leading Gisele to the front door, which magically opened, revealing a neatly dressed Italian woman
in her fifties with a welcoming but deferential smile
on her face. '*Bentornati*, Signorina Carter,' she said.
'Welcome back. Congratulations on renewing your engagement.'

'*Grazie,*' Gisele said, taking the housekeeper's hand
and returning her smile with an effort. *Engagement?*
What engagement? Anger bubbled up inside her. What
on earth did Emilio think he was doing? She could
hardly have it out with him in front of the housekeeper.
She stood with a frozen smile on her face, furious with
him for putting her in such an invidious position.

Emilio spoke to Marietta in Italian before turning
to Gisele. 'Marietta will unpack your things while you
have a rest,' he said.

Gisele faltered as she thought of Lily's blanket inside her case. 'Um… Do you mind if I do it myself? I
haven't brought much with me anyway. I feel…um…
embarrassed. I need some new clothes. There hasn't
been much money for extras just lately…'

He studied her flushed features for a pulsing moment,
his eyes dark and unreadable. 'You have no need to be
embarrassed,' he said. 'I will see to it that you have all
the clothes you need.'

'I'd still like to unpack my own things,' she said. 'I've
got out of the habit of having people waiting on me.'

He held her look for another beat or two. 'As you
wish.'

Gisele let out a breath of relief as he turned and issued
Marietta another set of instructions. She didn't want anyone handling Lily's blanket. No one had touched it but

her. She didn't want to lose that last trace of her baby's scent...

Emilio turned back and took Gisele's hand and toyed with the knuckle of her ring finger as he held her gaze. 'We have a little job to do, *sì*?' he said. 'I have your engagement ring in the safe in my study.'

'So you managed to fish it out of the fountain, then?' she asked with an arch look.

'It took three plumbers, but yes,' he said. 'I finally managed to locate it.'

Gisele waited until they were alone in the study where his safe was before she let fly. 'How *could* you lead your housekeeper to believe that we're engaged? I haven't agreed to that! I've only agreed to come here for a month but not as your fiancée.'

Emilio's expression remained calm, as if he were dealing with a small, wilful child. 'Relax, *cara*,' he said. 'There is no need for such hysterics.'

'I am *not* hysterical!' Gisele shrieked with a stamp of her foot for good measure.

His brows snapped together. 'Keep your voice down.'

She clenched her hands into fists and spoke through tight lips. 'You've done this deliberately, haven't you? You're making it impossible for me to deny we have a formal relationship by making me wear your stupid ring.'

'*Cara*, you're tired and overwrought,' he said. 'You're not making sense. Of course you will have to wear my ring while you are here. People will not accept our reconciliation as the real thing if we don't appear to pick up where we left off.'

She glowered at him. 'You think by putting that ring on my finger it gives you automatic licence to sleep with me, don't you?'

'You will sleep with me, ring or no ring,' he said. 'We will be sharing my room. I will not have it any other way. I don't want the servants to suspect anything is amiss.'

Gisele's heart tripped in her chest like a pony's hoof in a pothole. 'I'd rather sleep on the floor than share a bed with you.'

'It seems to me you don't sleep anywhere,' he returned wryly. 'Your little closed-eye routine didn't fool me on the flight, *cara*. That's obviously why you're being so obstreperous now. You're acting like a little child who has been kept up way past her bedtime.'

She swung away from him in fury, flustered because he saw too damn much. She was worried because she didn't trust herself not to turn to him during the night. If her nightmares about Lily hadn't been enough to deal with, so many times over the past two years she had found herself reaching for him during that half-awake, half-asleep phase of fitful rest. Her need for him had not automatically switched off just because he had thrown her out of his life. If anything, it had smouldered under the surface, building in intensity as each lonely month had passed.

Gisele heard the sound of the safe being opened and drew in a breath for composure. This would be another emotional hurdle for her to negotiate. How different would this be from when he had slid that ring onto her finger after he had asked her to marry him? She didn't want to think about how eagerly and excitedly she had accepted his proposal. She had gushed in enthusiasm and he had looked down at her with the sort of indulgent amusement that made her cringe now. How gauche she had been, how foolishly romantic to think he had adored her even a fraction as much as she had adored him. He hadn't loved her at all. She had simply ticked all the boxes for him under the compartment in his life marked: Find Suitable Wife.

'Give me your hand,' Emilio commanded.

Gisele turned around like a statue on a plinth, her body tense from head to foot. 'I don't suppose you're going to do a rerun of your proposal?' she said.

His eyes glinted as he took her hand in his. 'I had thought of it but decided against it.'

'Why?' she asked. 'Because you were worried I'd say no?'

He slid the ring onto her finger, holding it there with the warmth of his finger and thumb, his eyes still meshed with hers. 'Ah, but *would* you say no?' he asked.

'Why don't you give it a shot and see?' she challenged him.

He gave a little chuckle that was spine-tinglingly deep. 'I'm sure if the price was right you would agree to marry me,' he said, bringing her hand up to his mouth and pressing his lips against her bent fingers.

Gisele felt a butterfly wing–like flutter pass over the floor of her belly. She disguised a swallow as she felt his lips move to the sensitive skin of the underside of her wrist. She wanted to close her eyes and lose herself in his magical touch. The sensation of his warm velvet lips made her skin shiver in reaction. 'Stop it,' she said, not really meaning it and pretty sure he knew it.

He slid his tongue over her leaping pulse, a sexy lick that sent a dart of pleasure straight to her core. She suppressed a tiny whimper, determined not to show him how much he affected her by his proximity, by his touch, by his astonishing ability to dismantle her defences. Her legs felt like dampened paper, barely strong enough to hold her upright. Her spine was loosening, vertebra by vertebra, until she felt sure she would melt into a pool at his feet. Where was her resolve? Where was her anger when she needed it? They were like cowardly soldiers retreating from the frontline of battle.

'You taste like summer,' Emilio said against her wrist. 'Like frangipani and honeysuckle.'

Gisele shivered as his teeth gave her a playful but gentle bite. Her breasts peaked with longing, her insides contracting with need. How was she going to resist him if he kept this up? It was torture to be so near him and not respond the way she wanted to. 'I need a shower...' she said.

'Have one with me.'

The images those words conjured up! She had to fight with everything within her to keep them from flooding her mind. But it was impossible to eradicate every single one. She felt the heat build inside her at the memory of his hard body driving into her as the water cascaded over them: the memory of his hot, clever mouth feasting on her intimately and the memory of her doing exactly the same to him. Just thinking about the earthy rawness of it made her cheeks grow warm. 'I don't think so,' she said, trying to pull away.

His eyes came back to hers as he held her firm. 'It

won't be long before you change your mind, *cara*. We both know that, don't we?'

She glared at him, spitting out the words one by one. 'Let. Me. Go.'

He pulled her up against him, pressing a brief hard kiss to her mouth before he released her. 'Go and have your rest,' he said. 'I'll see you at dinner.'

Gisele felt unsettled and disoriented when he stepped away from her. It was a feeling almost like being cast adrift. She felt strangely empty without his hands holding her against him. That too-brief kiss had made her feel hungry for more. She swept the tip of her tongue over the tingling surface of her lips, the tantalising taste of him making her insides clench with longing. She didn't realise she was still standing there in a zombie-like daze until she heard the soft click of the study door, signalling Emilio had left.

Walking back into Emilio's bedroom suite was something Gisele had been silently dreading for all the memories being there would stir up, but when she pushed open the door she was surprised to see everything had changed. The decor was completely different, even the bed ensemble and the light fittings and soft furnishings. She wondered if he had done it deliberately, somehow purging his room of her presence after he had sent her from his life.

The master suite now had a Venetian theme to it with the boldest of gold and black in the fabric of the curtains and bed linen. Crystal lamps encrusted with onyx and gold were stationed either side of the massive bed, and the priceless thick carpet on the floor continued the theme.

The en suite bathroom was fitted out in highly polished black marble with gold tap wear and golden-framed mirrors. There was a large shower with two showerheads and a deep marble-surrounded bath and a heated towel rack with several snowy-white towels with a black-and-gold trim neatly folded there.

It was decadent and rich and luxurious, the perfect setting for seduction, Gisele thought as she came back to the windows that led out onto a balcony that overlooked the gardens.

She opened the French windows and went out to breathe in the warm spring air, the clovelike scent of roses drifting towards her from below. The rear gardens were much the same as before, lots of clipped hedges and herbaceous borders and roses everywhere. A lavender pathway led to another fountain, larger than the one at the front. The sound of the water splashing had always had a soporific effect on her. She had spent many nights lying in Emilio's arms listening to that wonderfully relaxing sound as she drifted off to sleep, dreaming of their future together...

She stepped out of her reverie by leaving the balcony and closing the doors, turning the key as a reminder to herself that the past was no longer accessible.

She found another room farther down the hall. It was decorated in tones of milky coffee and white, with large windows overlooking the gardens.

Once she unpacked her things from her suitcase and stored them in the wardrobe, she found a drawer to put Lily's blanket and photos in and gently closed it.

The aching tiredness she felt was suddenly so over-whelming she was barely aware of kicking off her shoes before she curled up like a comma on the feather-soft bed and closed her eyes...

Emilio searched through several bedrooms before he found Gisele lying sound asleep on the bed in the room furthest from his. Her silver-blonde hair was spread out over the pillow, her slim body barely making an inden-tation on the mattress. She looked like an angel lying there, a sleeping angel with features so perfect and yet so pale she didn't seem quite real. How was he to get through the wall of her anger? He had to dismantle it brick by brick, getting her to slowly warm to him again.

Looking back now, he could see how truly devastated she had been when he had cast her from his life. At the time he had read her body language as a greedy little gold-digger whose plans to wed a rich man had been thwarted at the last minute, but now he could see her shattered expression for what it was: a young woman who had loved and loved deeply, who by a quirk of fate had suddenly found her life in ruins through no fault of her own.

Where had she gone?

Who had she turned to?

How must she have felt to have her life ripped out from under her without warning? He didn't like think-ing about it. She would have been feeling so shocked and frightened, so upset that she hadn't been able to get him to see reason. Even worse, anything could have hap-pened to her that night. In her state of high emotional distress she could have come to some sort of harm and he had done nothing to protect her. He had cast her out of his life as if she had been nothing more than some trash he no longer had any use for.

He had got it so horribly wrong.

Emilio watched the soft flutter of her lips as she gave an inaudible murmur and the way one of her hands seemed to be searching for something on the bed next to her. Her face suddenly contorted as if she was having a terrible nightmare. She started to thrash about, her cries soft but heart-wrenching. 'No…oh, no, please *no…*'

'Gisele, shh, it's all right,' Emilio said softly as he perched beside her and captured her flailing hands.

Her eyes sprang open and she jerked upright. She seemed momentarily disoriented but then her expression turned hostile. 'What are you doing here?' she asked, pulling her hands away from his.

'I hate to point out the obvious, but this is my villa and you are in one of my bedrooms,' Emilio said.

She brushed her hair out of her eyes with an angry movement of her hand as she gave him a resentful scowl. 'You shouldn't sneak up on people like that,' she said.

'I didn't sneak up on you,' he said. 'It looked like you were having a bad dream. You were crying out in your sleep so I came over to comfort you.'

She bit down on her lower lip, a soft flush rising in her cheeks as she averted her gaze from his.

Emilio turned her chin so she had to meet his eyes. 'Do you often have bad dreams, *cara*?' he asked.

A shadow passed over her blue eyes. 'Not often… sometimes…'

He caressed her cheek with the pad of his thumb.

'I wish I could wipe out the last two years,' he said. 'I wish I could just reset the clock. I wish I could take back every horrible word I threw at you.'

She didn't answer. She just kept looking at him with that grey-blue accusing gaze of hers.

'What did you do the night I sent you away?' Emilio asked.

'I found a hotel,' she said. 'The press gave me a hard time but eventually I managed to shake them off. I caught a flight back to Sydney the next day.'

'You never tried to contact me,' he said, still stroking her creamy cheek. 'Not even once.'

She gave him a brittle look. 'You forbade me to, remember?'

He studied her for a long moment before dropping his hand from her chin. 'Dinner is in half an hour,' he said as he rose from the bed. 'I'll see you downstairs.'

CHAPTER FIVE

AFTER Gisele had a shower she dressed in a slim-fitting sheathlike taupe-coloured dress and a pair of heels. She dried her hair and scooped it up into a knot at the back of her head and put on a bare minimum of make-up. She looked down at the engagement ring on her finger. It was too loose for her now. The huge diamond kept slipping round the wrong way out of sight. Was that some sort of omen? she wondered.

Emilio was in the *salone* when she came downstairs. He was sipping at an aperitif, looking out of the window to the gardens outside. He turned and looked at her, his gaze moving over her body like a warm caress. 'You look beautiful,' he said.

'Thank you.' Gisele fought for cool poise but a blush crept over her cheeks in spite of her best efforts.

'What would you like to drink?' he asked.

'Um…white wine if you have it.'

He poured her a glass of wine and brought it over to her. She saw his nostrils flare as if he was taking in the fragrance of her perfume. She saw too the way his eyes darkened as they caught and held hers. 'Do you feel a little more refreshed after your rest?' he asked.

'Yes,' she said, taking a generous sip to settle her nerves.

'Why didn't you put your things in my bedroom as I asked you to?' he said.

She gripped her wineglass a little tighter. 'You can't force me to occupy your bed. I need more time. It's a big step for me.'

'Didn't you like the new decor?' he asked.

'It looks like no expense has been spared to rid your bedroom of every trace of my previous occupation of it,' Gisele said with a touch of asperity.

His expression was unreadable as he raised his glass to his lips. 'I thought it was time for a change.'

'Out with the old, in with the new?' she said with a cynical look. 'Did all your subsequent girlfriends like it'?'

A brooding frown appeared between his eyebrows. 'If you don't like it then we can occupy another room,' he said. 'But you *will* share a bed with me, Gisele. I will not have any rumours circulating that this is not a proper relationship.'

'How soon did you replace me?' she asked.

A muscle worked in his jaw. 'Gisele, this is not going to help matters.'

'How many?' she asked, feeling a lump rise in her throat.

'I could ask you the same thing.'

'Go on,' she said. 'Ask me.'

The muscle in his jaw worked even harder. 'All right,' he said on an expelled breath. 'How many lovers have you had since me?'

Gisele wished now she hadn't provoked him. Could

she lie just to hurt him? Could she play payback with a host of imaginary lovers, not one of whom would have come close to being as perfect for her physically as him? What was the point? She suspected he would see through it anyway. Hadn't the way she'd responded to him so far given him enough proof that she hadn't moved on?

'There's been no one,' she said after a tight pause.

'Gisele...'

'Don't get me wrong.' She cut him off quickly. 'I've had plenty of opportunities. I just didn't want to rush into anything. You don't have to automatically assume I was waiting for you to take me back because I wasn't.'

He took his drink and moved over to the windows again, his back turned towards her. It was a moment or two before he spoke and, when he did, his voice was rough around the edges, as if it had been dragged up from a place deep inside him. 'Would you believe me if I told you I was thinking of making contact with you even before the press release came out about Sienna being the one in the tape?'

Gisele felt her heart give a little hit-and-miss beat. 'Why?'

He turned from the window and faced her with an inscrutable look. 'I'm not sure,' he said. 'I guess I wanted to see if you had fared any better than me.'

'What do you mean?'

'Anger and bitterness are pretty corrosive things to be carrying around,' he said. 'I think I got tired of being angry. For two years I was totally consumed with it. I could think of nothing else. I finally got to the point where I wanted to move on. I thought if I contacted you, perhaps met with you face to face to ask you why you'd betrayed me, it might've helped.'

'But I hadn't betrayed you.'

He let out a heavy sigh. 'No,' he said. 'You hadn't. And that's what I have to live with. I made a mistake. It's new territory for me. I'm not usually wrong about anything.'

Gisele looked at the wine in her glass and thought about what he had said about carrying around anger. Her anger had burned like acid inside her. It was still burning, eating away at her, keeping her awake at night. But she wasn't quite ready to relinquish it.

Marietta appeared at that point with the announcement that dinner was ready.

Gisele followed Emilio to the dining room where the long highly polished table had been beautifully set up for a romantic dinner for two. Flowers from the garden made a fragrant centrepiece along with the flickering candles in the candelabra that added to the tone of intimacy. So many times in the past she had sat here at this table and looked lovingly across the table at him. She had pictured their children one day joining them there, their little faces shining with good health and happiness and vigour. How far from her dreams and romantically infused imaginings had she travelled? There would be no happy family now. Not for her at least.

Emilio seated her before he took his own place. 'I've been thinking about your business,' he said. 'Do you outsource any of the needlework?'

'No,' she said. 'I do it all myself. I like working to commission. I think it gives the customer that sense of a personal touch.'

He reached across to pour her some wine. 'But you surely can't expect to keep up with demand if things were to take a sudden upswing?'

'I've managed to keep ahead so far.'

'Yes, but that will change as soon as things take off over here,' he said. 'How will you keep up then?'

She bit her lip. 'I've brought some work with me...'

'Gisele.' He sounded like a world-weary parent speaking to a naive child. 'You can't expect to run things as you have done in the past. You'll have to consider outsourcing. You have no choice. You can hand-pick your needlewomen. You'll still have total control over the standard of your product.'

She flashed him a defensive glare. 'I know what I'm doing. I'm good at what I do. I love my work.'

'The creative side of it is not the problem, *cara*,' he said. 'I've seen your needlework. It's exquisite. You are extremely talented. I'm not saying you aren't. I'm just saying you can't possibly do it all. You need to think about how to meet demands for more of your work, otherwise people will go elsewhere.'

Gisele pressed her lips together before answering. 'OK, I'll think about it.'

He gave a sigh and reached for her hand across the table. 'Look at me, *cara*,' he commanded gently.

She met his gaze with resentment burning in hers. 'I won't allow you to take over my life. I've been doing perfectly fine without you. My shop is the busiest one on that stretch of the street.'

'I know that,' he said. 'You've done amazingly well. I'm just trying to help you do better, to maximise your profits. At least if things don't work out between us you will have a stronger base to go home to.'

Marietta came in with their meal and Emilio deftly steered the conversation into less contentious areas. Gisele made an effort to do the delicious food justice but being in Emilio's presence made her feel nervous and excited at the same time. He could be such charming company when he put his mind to it. She felt the intoxicating lure of it each time he looked at her with that sexy slant of a smile. His eyes took on a dark mesmerising heat as they held hers, the sensual promise in them making every hair on her body stand up and take notice.

After Marietta had served coffee in the *salone* she announced she was leaving for home.

'She doesn't live here like Concetta did?' Gisele asked once the housekeeper had left.

'No,' Emilio said. 'She has a husband and a couple of daughters who still live at home. She likes to spend the nights with them.'

'So if she's not here at night then there should be no problem with me having my own room,' Gisele said.

His expression tightened. 'She is back first thing in the morning,' he said. 'What are you going to do? Run along the hall and jump in beside me just for show?'

She put her coffee cup down and rose to her feet agitatedly. The thought of jumping into bed with him for real was far too tempting. It was all she could think about. Her body burned with hot flames of need and there was nothing she could do to dampen them down. 'Lots of couples don't sleep together,' she said. 'My parents didn't share a bed for most of their marriage.'

He came over to where she was standing. 'That is not how this relationship is going to be run,' he said. He took her hands in his and held them gently but firmly. 'Why are you fighting what is inevitable? I know you were hurt by our break-up. I understand that you're still angry. We have this chance to reconnect but you seem intent on sabotaging every attempt on my part to put things right.'

'Some things can never be put right,' she said, looking down at their joined hands rather than meeting his gaze. Her belly quivered as his thumbs began stroking her fingers, his darker-toned skin against hers a spine-tingling reminder of how very masculine he was and how she couldn't help but respond to his primal call to all that was feminine in her. She could feel the flicker of desire between her thighs, a tiny rhythmic pulse that was like a faraway drumbeat deep inside her, each throbbing second bringing it closer and closer...

Emilio tipped up her chin, his eyes so dark she couldn't make out his pupils. 'Are you fighting me or yourself, *cara*?' he asked.

She sent the point of her tongue out over her lips, testing his hold but it remained firm. 'I hate you,' she said, but somehow the words didn't sound as feisty and determined as they had even a day ago.

'That doesn't mean that the sex between us won't still be good,' he said as his mouth blazed a hot trail over the sensitive skin near her left ear.

Gisele felt her senses go into a tailspin as his teeth gently tugged on her earlobe. It sent a delicious shiver down her spine as he moved back towards her mouth, slowly, tantalisingly, awakening each and every nerve beneath her skin, making her lips tingle in anticipation for the hot, urgent pressure of his. She gave a soft little whimper and turned her head just a fraction, just enough to make that final devastating contact.

His mouth sealed hers but it was nothing like the bruising kiss of the other day. This was a kiss that was sensually soft, exploratory and yet unmistakably commanding and arrantly sexual in its intent. She felt the stroke of his tongue at the seam of her lips and she opened to him, their breaths mingling, their tongues mating in an erotic ritual that sent lightning bolts of need straight to the heart of her femininity. One of his hands slipped to the nape of her neck, the warm cup of his palm causing the entire length of her spine to shudder in delicious response. His mouth changed position, his lips still moving gently against hers, but she still sensed an undercurrent of urgency, of his control still tightly leashed but straining for freedom.

His other hand pressed her in the small of her back, bringing her closer to the pulsing heat of his erection. She felt its thickness, the potent power of it stirring her body into a maelstrom of feeling. Her skin tightened, her heart fluttered, her legs trembled and still the kiss went on and on.

It was so wonderful to *feel* again. To feel alive and vibrant with sexual energy, to feel the way her body inflamed his by its closeness. His hand at her back pressed harder, a low groan emitting from his throat as she rubbed against him, her feminine mound aching to feel his possession. It was a deep ache inside her, a pulsing, throbbing ache that she could feel vibrating in his body as he ground himself against her, hungry for relief.

'I want you,' he growled like a wolf against her mouth, the primal deepness of his voice and the scrape of his teeth as he tugged at her lower lip making Gisele melt like honey under intense heat.

She didn't need to say she wanted him too. Her body was doing all it could to relay the message of how much she needed him to relieve her of this voracious need that was clawing at her insides. She pushed herself closer, her breasts jammed up against the hard wall of his chest, her mouth feeding greedily off his.

Emilio pulled down the zip of her dress, his hands moving over the naked skin of her back in tantalising strokes that made her legs feel as if they were going to go out from beneath her. He deftly unhooked her bra and it slid to the floor along with her dress, leaving her in nothing but her knickers and her heels. He brought his mouth to her achingly tight breast, sucking on her erect nipple before doing the same to the other. Gisele whimpered as her senses screamed in rapture. It was so good to feel him on her naked flesh, to feel the sexy rasp of his masculine jaw with its pepper of stubble on her soft skin.

She took her hands from around his neck and worked her way down his shirt, button by button, tasting the sexy saltiness of his skin with her tongue, teasing each of his flat male nipples with her teeth. He shrugged himself out of his shirt as she moved her hands down to the waistband of his trousers. She ran her hand over the proud jut of his body, her insides clenching with feverish anticipation as he moved against her hand with a guttural groan.

'I knew you would come back to me,' Emilio said in a gravel-rough tone as his lips hovered above her mouth. 'I knew you wouldn't be able to resist.'

The ice-cold water of common sense doused the flames of Gisele's desire at the hint of arrogant assurance in his tone. Did he really think she was *that* predictable? That he only had to beckon to her and she would come running back as if nothing had happened? 'Wait,' she said, dropping her hands from his body.

He frowned at her. 'Is everything all right?'

Gisele took a deep steadying breath and covered her naked breasts with her crossed arms. 'I can't do this,' she said. 'Not like this…not here…'

'Then we'll take it upstairs,' Emilio said.

She sent him a speaking glance. 'No.'

'No?'

'I'm sorry,' she said, bending down to retrieve her dress and her bra, her cheeks so hot they felt as if they had been scorched. She got dressed with as much dignity as she could, putting some order to her hair as she faced him once more. 'I'm sorry, Emilio. I know I should have called a halt earlier. I don't know what I was thinking. Maybe I wasn't thinking. I don't seem to do a lot of that when I'm around you.' She made a self-deprecating movement of her lips. 'I guess that's one thing that hasn't changed in two years.'

He gave her a wry smile as he brushed her cheek with the tip of his index finger. 'I like it when you're not thinking,' he said. 'I like it best when you're just feeling.'

Gisele chewed at her lip. 'It's been a long time for me,' she said softly.

He cupped her cheek with the warmth of his hand, his eyes dark and surprisingly tender as they meshed with hers. 'I know,' he said. 'That's why I want our first time back together to be special. I don't want to rush things just for the sake of it. I want to savour every moment with you.'

'You sound like you missed me,' she said a little wistfully.

His thumb brushed over her bottom lip like a teasing feather. 'Those first few days after you left I was unbearable to be around,' he said. 'The contract I was working on securing fell through. The man I was negotiating with was a very conservative family man. He gave the contract to the other architect who, unfortunately, was my biggest rival. I was so blind with rage I felt sure you must have had something to do with it. I thought you had been planted as a spy.' His mouth twisted. 'I became totally obsessed after that. I had to work hard to make up for the loss of that commission. The first real block of time I've had off since then was when I flew to Sydney to see you.'

Gisele thought of him working himself to the ground in an attempt to put her out of his mind. He had always been an intensely driven man. She had recognised that when she'd first met him. It had inspired her to think of how hard he had worked for his success. He had told her once it had been his dream since childhood to become an architect and he had determined nothing would get in his way. And it hadn't. He had become one of the world's leading and most innovative designers with a string of accolades to his name.

To suddenly find out he had been wrong about the accusations he had hurled at her must have come as a horrid shock to a man with his level of pride. The fact that he had put everything on hold to fly out to see her to make amends was certainly admirable, but she still suspected it was his pride and reputation that was at stake, not his heart.

His heart was for no one. Whatever had happened in his childhood had left scars that cut deep. That was another thing Gisele had suspected right from the start, but she had been determined to be the one to heal him. How deluded had she been to think that the strength of her love could unlock his fiercely guarded heart? He had trust issues that no amount of love would ever heal. She had been a casualty of that lack of trust, and she very much doubted that she was the first or even going to be the last.

'Have you spoken to Sienna about us?' he asked.

'I didn't go into a lot of detail,' Gisele said. 'I didn't want her to feel responsible for what happened between us. You have to remember that although we're identical twins we're virtual strangers. It will take some time to get to know each other properly.'

'Do you like her?' Emilio asked. 'Is she someone you could warm to?'

Gisele thought of her vibrant, vivacious twin, with her generous and impulsive nature. From what she had picked up so far, Sienna had got herself into plenty of scrapes because of her somewhat reckless take on life, but it was impossible not to like her. 'I think she's

lovely,' she said. 'She's smart and sassy and sophisticated. But I think the press misrepresent her. They paint
her as a hedonist, a wild child without morals. I don't
think she's anything like that. I think she's very sensitive but hides it behind the party girl façade.'

'I have a client to see in London towards the end of
the month,' Emilio said. 'I'd like it if you came with me.
You can introduce me to Sienna and perhaps spend some
time with her while I'm at work.'

'I'd like to see her,' Gisele said. 'But I don't want to
lie to her about our relationship. Putting on an act for
the press is one thing, lying to my sister is another.'

'Perhaps by then it won't be an act, *cara*,' he said,
brushing her lip again with his thumb.

Gisele felt the sensitive surface of her lips tingle from
the gentle caress. It was true what he had said: she was
fighting herself rather than him. Her unruly desires
were annihilating her resolve like a hurricane against a
house of cards. She had no hope of withstanding him,
not while her feelings for him were still so ambiguous.
She stepped back from him, giving him a brief on-off
smile. 'I think I'll go to bed,' she said. 'Good night.'

Emilio didn't answer but Gisele felt his scorching
gaze follow her as she left the room.

CHAPTER SIX

Gisele was pulling back the covers of her bed when she heard the bedroom door open and Emilio came in dressed in a bathrobe, his hair still damp from a recent shower. 'What do you think you're doing?' she gasped in shock.

'Coming to bed,' he said, slipping off the robe.

Gisele's eyes drank in the sight of him: that hard muscular chest, that gorgeous flat washboard abdomen and the arrantly masculine heart of him that was already partially aroused. Her heart gave a jerky kick inside her chest and her throat almost closed over. 'But I told you I—'

'And I told you how things were going to be,' he said before she could complete her sentence. 'We will share a bed for the month even if we don't make love. I will not force myself on you. You should know me better than that.'

She swallowed deeply, wondering if it was possible to share a villa of this size with Emilio without wanting to make love, let alone a bed. It was a big bed certainly, but not big enough for her to avoid those long, strong hair-roughened legs coming into contact with hers. 'That's not the point,' she said, running the tip of her tongue out over lips so dry they felt like ancient parchment.

'What *is* the point, Gisele?' he asked with a glittering look. 'You don't seem to know what you want. One minute you look at me as if you want to throw yourself back in my arms and never leave, and the next you look like you want to claw my eyes out. At some point you're going to have to make up your mind.'

Gisele had thought she had made up her mind but her body had chosen an entirely different path. It was calling out to him now in a secret sensual language he couldn't fail to misinterpret. But in her haste to disguise how much she wanted him she swung away from the bed and in doing so accidentally knocked the glass of water and her pills off the bedside table. The glass landed with a thump on the carpet and the little bottle of pills rolled across the floor and came to a stop right in front of Emilio's left foot.

She watched, dry mouthed, as he bent to pick them up. 'What are these for?' he asked, frowning as he read the label.

'Give them to me,' she said, trying to make a grab for them but he held the bottle just out of her reach.

He frowned as he read the label. 'Sleeping tablets?' he asked, looking at her again.

'So?' she said, throwing him a defensive look. 'Lots of people take them.'

'How long have you been taking them?' he asked.

Gisele folded her arms mutinously, her mouth in a flat line.

'Gisele?' He tipped up her chin, forcing her eyes to

meet his. 'How long have you been taking sleeping medication?'

She let out a shaky breath. 'A while…a few weeks… a couple of months maybe…'

'Sleeping tablets are meant to be a temporary thing,' Emilio said reprovingly. 'You shouldn't be on them any longer than a few weeks. They're highly addictive.'

Gisele rolled her eyes. 'You sound just like my doctor.'

He caught her just before she made to turn away from him. His eyes were dark and a concerned frown sliced deep into his forehead. '*Cara*, did *I* do this to you?' he asked hollowly.

Gisele thought of the weeks after his rejection when she had done nothing but sleep most days as well as the nights. She had slid into an abyss of depression that had made every little task an impossible feat. Having a shower hurt her skin. Brushing her hair felt like torture. Getting dressed in street clothes made her muscles ache. Walking to the front door had seemed like a marathon. Getting through each day felt like a lifetime. The warm, secure nest of her bed had been a reprieve from a life she didn't think she could live without him in it.

And then she had discovered she was pregnant. The news had pulled her out of her depression. She had started to look forward to life again with hope and a tentative happiness that had all too soon been torn away from her.

Was Emilio to blame that Lily had died?

For a while she had felt as if he was, but over time she had come to realise no one was to blame. It was just one of those things, or so the doctors had said—a genetic abnormality, a mistake of nature.

'No...' Gisele said in a voice so soft it was more of a whisper. 'No, it's not because of you.' It was the sound of Lily crying that haunted her sleepless nights. The only way to escape the torture of hearing that tiny mewling cry was to numb herself to sleep. Not that it always worked.

Emilio looked deeply into her eyes as if he wanted to see into the very heart of her. His eyes were pitch-black, still etched with concern as he cupped her face. 'Is it because of the business? Your father's death? Finding out about Sienna?'

Gisele put her hand on his to peel it off her face and stepped backwards, wrapping her arms about her body. Should she tell him about Lily? She could feel guilt nipping at the heels of her conscience. Didn't he have the right to know he had been a father, even for such a short time? She would have to tell him one day. What if he somehow found out by some other means? The thought was terrifying. Wouldn't it be better to hear it from her rather than someone else? But how could she drop that sort of bombshell into the conversation? Her chance to tell him had been right at the start. She couldn't talk about it now. Not like this, with no preparation. 'I...I've just been under a lot of stress,' she said. 'It's no one thing but everything, I guess.'

'You should wean yourself off them,' he said, still frowning. 'I don't like the thought of you drugging yourself to sleep. You never used to have any problem sleeping.'

She gave him a wry look before she could stop herself. 'As I recall, we didn't always do a lot of sleeping.'

The words seemed to hang in the air for a moment, the erotic images they conjured up gathering around like ghosts from the past.

Gisele saw the flare of heat in Emilio's eyes as he took in her scantily clad body. She had slipped off her wrap just before he had come in and her creamy satin nightgown left very little to the imagination. She felt the tight buds of her nipples pressing against the soft fabric and knew he could see them too. Her belly gave an excited flutter as his eyes skimmed her lower body, the heat in her core liquefying as if he had touched her there. His body responded to her as if she had stroked her fingers along his length. She saw him swell and rise, the sheer power and potency of him taking her breath away.

'No, we didn't, did we?' Emilio asked with a smouldering look as his eyes slowly came back to mesh with hers.

Gisele drew in a quick breath, her chest feeling prickly and tight. The heat from his body radiated out and touched her like a caress. Her skin felt tingly and supersensitive, as if all the nerves had repositioned themselves on the outside of her body. 'Don't do this, Emilio,' she said in a hoarse whisper.

'Don't do what, *cara*?' he asked as he shrank the gap between their bodies by taking half a step. 'This?' He touched his lips to the skin of her neck just below her ear, not a kiss, not a bite, but something sinfully and sexily in between.

She shivered as his tongue grazed her skin as he

moved down to the fragile scaffold of her collarbone. 'Or this?' he asked as his breath moved over her like a sultry summer breeze.

Gisele's lower body ached to move forwards to find his. It was like a magnetic field she had inadvertently stepped inside. It was pulling her inexorably towards him. She could sense him there, thick and hard, pulsing with the same longing that was making her heart race and her breathing become shallow and uneven. His feet touched hers, a sexy bump of toes that sent a shockwave of forbidden pleasure right through her body. She felt him then against her belly, the blunt head of him as scorching as a naked flame against her skin.

He worked his way back up towards her mouth, slowly, each brush of his lips setting her skin alight. 'This is what used to keep us both awake, remember?' he said just above her quivering mouth.

Gisele moistened her dry lips, her heart hammering as he slipped a hand beneath the curtain of her hair. The sensations shimmering down her spine made her dizzy with need. She remembered it all. It had never left her. How he made her feel. How he could set her aflame with just a look.

How much she still wanted him.

Time stood still for a heart-stopping pause.

She prepared herself for the press of his mouth; her eyelashes came down, her lips were softly parted, her breath had stilled...

But Emilio suddenly broke the spell by stepping backwards and moving to where he had dropped his bathrobe.

Gisele blinked a couple of times in bewilderment as

she watched him shrug himself into it and tie the cord around his waist, seemingly untouched by what had just transpired between them. How could he leave her like this? Was he doing it deliberately to prove how little he needed her? That she was just another woman he could have sex with if he could be bothered?

He was the *only* person she wanted to be intimate with. She couldn't imagine wanting anyone else the way she wanted him. Her body felt as if it *belonged* to him. It had belonged to him for more than two years.

'I'll give you the rest of the week to settle in,' he said. 'I'll make up some excuse for Marietta for why we're not sharing a room.'

'And after that?' she asked.

His eyes pulsated as they locked with hers. 'I think you know what happens after that,' he said in a gravel-rough, oh-so-sexy tone.

Gisele felt her belly do another crazy little tumble turn but she hid behind her increasingly fragile armour of pride and haughtiness. 'You think two million dollars is going to be enough to make me enjoy being back in your bed?' she asked.

His mouth curled up at the corners in a confident smile as he opened the door to leave. 'I'll make sure of it,' he said and, with a soft click of the lock falling in place, he was gone.

Gisele spent the night in a fitful state of tossing and turning. Emilio's promise had made her so edgy and agitated she hadn't had a hope of sleeping a wink in spite of her pills. Her body had been so uptight with longing she had felt like a tightly coiled spring. She hadn't been able to rid her mind of his aroused naked body so close to hers, *touching* hers. How dared he entice her like that with his mouth and hands, only to step back from her as if she was nothing to him? It made her so angry she had been so close to giving herself to him. It made her absolutely furious to think he knew how weak she still was. He was playing with her, toying with her like an angler with a fish on his line. He was biding his time before he reeled her right in.

She would show him.

She deliberately lingered in her room, taking an extra-long shower, dawdling over her hair and light make-up, determined to keep her distance for as long as she could, hoping he would have long ago eaten breakfast and headed off to work.

She walked down the stairs with an assured smile hovering about her mouth. She would show him how little she needed him. She would keep herself busy all day, sending him the clear message she wasn't waiting around for him to crook his finger and summon her back to his bed.

Marietta was on her way out to the terrace with a tray of fresh rolls and fruit. 'Signor Andreoni is waiting for you,' she said. 'You like tea, *si*?'

'Grazie,' Gisele said, forcing a smile. It looked as if she wasn't going to be able to escape Emilio's disturbing presence after all. It was almost eleven in the morning. He was not one to linger about the villa. He had never taken a day off in the past. He had even worked most weekends, leaving her for long periods on her own.

He was sipping a cup of coffee when Gisele stepped out onto the sun-drenched terrace. He looked fabulously rested, his skin glowing from good health and his eyes clear. He was dressed in black trousers and a white business shirt but it was rolled back over his tanned forearms in a casual manner, making him look even more arrestingly handsome.

He put down his cup and rose to his feet, pulling out a chair for her. '*Cara*, you look like you had a rough night,' he said. 'Your little pills not working, hmm?'

She gave him a gimlet glare as she plonked herself down on the chair. 'Why aren't you at work?' she asked.

'I took the day off to spend it with you,' he said. 'That's what a newly reconciled couple would do, is it not?'

'You shouldn't have bothered,' Gisele said crossly, flicking her napkin across her lap. 'I don't feel like being around you or anyone.'

'Too bad,' he said, picking up his coffee cup again. 'We will be expected to be seen out and about together.' He took a sip of his coffee, looked at the contents frowningly for a moment before looking at her again. 'I have a business function to attend this evening. I thought we could go shopping for you to find something suitable to wear.'

'I can go shopping by myself,' she said, shooting him a look across the table. 'I don't need you to carry my bags.'

Emilio placed his cup back down on its saucer with unnerving precision. 'Gisele,' he addressed her sternly, 'you are walking a very fine line. I am trying to be patient with you but there is only so much leeway I'm prepared to give.'

Gisele saw the steely determination in his dark eyes

and had to look away. 'What did you tell Marietta about me sleeping in the other room?' she asked to fill the heavy silence.

'I told her you have a snoring problem.'

Her eyes flew back to his. *'You what?'*

He gave a little shrug as he brought his cup towards his mouth. 'It's OK, *cara*,' he said. 'Lots of people snore.'

'I don't!' she said, bristling with outrage. 'Why didn't you tell her it was *you* with the problem?'

'Because I'm not the one with cold feet about sharing a bed, that's why,' he said smoothly.

Gisele scowled as she took a roll and tore it into little pieces. 'You could've thought of something a little less demeaning,' she said. 'Snoring sounds so…so unsexy.'

'Are you going to eat any of that roll or just play with it?' Emilio asked.

She pushed the plate with the decimated roll to one side. 'I'm not hungry.'

He challenged her with his narrowed coal-black gaze. 'Are you doing this deliberately to annoy me?' he asked. 'Because, if so, it's working.'

Gisele felt a little frisson race down her spine. She liked the sense of power it gave her to get under his skin. He was still in control but she could see the leash on it was straining. There was a muscle pulsing at the corner of his flattened mouth and his eyes had hardened to chips of black ice.

The air between them seemed to crackle like electricity along a wire.

'You are not leaving this table until you've had something to eat,' he ground out. 'Do you hear me?'

She glared back at him. 'If you want me to eat, then why don't you stop deliberately upsetting me?'

The sound of Marietta's footsteps sounding on the flagstones broke the tense moment.

Emilio sat back and visibly forced himself to relax and Gisele did the same. She sensed the housekeeper's intrigue and wondered how much she had overheard of their heated exchange. How well did Emilio know this new housekeeper? Concetta had been the soul of discretion. Was that why Emilio was so determined that Gisele should occupy his room? Journalists on the hunt for a story paid well for leaks and for photo opportunities. Marietta could exploit the situation if she sensed a lack of harmony between them, and clearly Emilio was fully aware of it.

'Here is your tea, *signorina*,' Marietta said as she placed a teapot beside Gisele, her gaze watchful.

'*Grazie*, Marietta,' Gisele said, trying to smile but not quite managing to pull it off.

'Is everything all right?' Marietta asked, hovering about the table.

'Everything is fine,' Emilio said firmly.

Once the housekeeper had left he raked a hand through his hair. 'I don't mean to upset you, Gisele,' he said. 'This is a difficult time for both of us. There are adjustments and compromises to be made. I want this to work. I really do.'

'Why?' she asked.

He frowned as if she was suddenly speaking a different language, one he couldn't understand. 'Because what we had was good,' he said. 'You can't deny that.'

'I do deny it,' Gisele said. 'What was good about me

having to sign a prenuptial agreement? Where was the trust that most good relationships are built on?'

'I've worked hard for my money,' he said. 'I have the right to protect my interests. If you were so unhappy about it, why didn't you say something at the time?'

Gisele looked away again, embarrassed that she had been so biddable back then. She had felt terribly hurt when he had told her about it but she had kept her feelings well hidden. She had signed the wretched agreement with a heavy heart, wondering if he would ever trust her, or anyone, enough to believe they weren't going to rip him off or betray him in some way.

'Gisele?'

She blew out a breath and set about pouring a cup of tea for herself. 'Can we just forget it?' she asked. 'It's not like we're getting married now. It's irrelevant.'

'It might not be so irrelevant if we do decide to make our reconciliation permanent,' he said.

Gisele's cup rattled against the saucer as she put it back down. 'Are you crazy?' she asked. 'There's no way I would ever agree to marry someone who didn't love me enough to trust me.'

'Love and trust are two different issues,' he said. 'They don't always come hand in hand.'

'Well, they come hand in hand to me,' she said, picking up her cup again and cradling it in her hands.

He studied her with an inscrutable look on his face for what seemed like an endless moment. 'You think I didn't care about you, *cara*?' he asked.

Gisele felt her heart contract. Like a lot of people, he cared about a lot of things but it didn't mean he couldn't imagine life without them. He had lived quite well without her for two whole years. 'Where was that care when you threw me out of your life without giving me the benefit of the doubt?' she asked.

His expression tightened. 'I can do no more than apologise,' he said. 'I was wrong and I have admitted it. What else do you want me to do?'

Love me, Gisele thought. 'Nothing,' she said, lowering her gaze from his. 'There's nothing you can do.'

He reached across the table and took her hand in his. 'Where's your engagement ring?' he asked.

Gisele met his gaze across their joined hands. 'I left it upstairs. It doesn't fit me properly any more. I'm frightened I'm going to lose it.'

He frowned as he stroked where her ring should have been. 'Then we'll have to get it readjusted so it does fit,' he said.

'Why did you keep it?' she asked after an infinitesimal pause.

He released her hand and leaned back in his chair, his face like stone. 'It's worth a lot of money.'

'I know, but you could have sold it,' she said. 'Why didn't you?'

He pushed back from the table and got to his feet. 'I have a call to make,' he said curtly. 'The driver will be here in ten minutes. Don't be late.'

Gisele let out a long breath as she watched him stride across the flagstones and back inside the villa. There were times when she wondered why she had given her heart to such a complex and unreachable man.

'Signor Andreoni asked me to tell you he will meet you for a late lunch,' the driver said when Gisele went out to the waiting car. 'He has some urgent business to see to. He gave me this to give you.' He handed her a credit card and a piece of paper with the details of a restaurant on it.

'Why couldn't he have told me himself?' she asked, feeling annoyed.

The driver shrugged. 'He is a very busy man. He never stops working.'

'I don't need you to drive me,' she said. 'I'm happy to walk.'

'Signor Andreoni insisted on me escorting you.'

'Have the morning off,' Gisele said, placing the credit card and note in her purse.

'But I will get fired if I don't—'

'No, you won't,' she said with determination. 'I'll deal with Signor Andreoni. Ciao.'

Emilio was already waiting at the restaurant when Gisele came in. She hadn't done much shopping, other than pick up a dress and shoes for that evening, but she hadn't used Emilio's card. She refused to be sent off like an overindulged child by a too-busy parent.

She weaved her way through the busy restaurant towards him, conscious of his dark brooding gaze focused solely on her. 'Hello, darling,' she said, offering her cheek for a perfunctory kiss for the sake of onlookers.

Emilio took her face in his hands and planted a hot, drugging kiss on her mouth. Gisele felt her senses spin like a top, round and round and round until she was barely able to stand up. She had to place her hands on his hard chest to steady herself. She stepped back when he released her, sure her face was as red as the single rose in the centre of the table.

'You don't look like you've had a very successful shopping spree,' he said as he seated her.

'I don't like spending other people's money,' she said, throwing him a look over her shoulder. 'If I want to buy clothes then I'll buy them for myself.'

'You seem very determined to disobey my instructions,' he said as he took his own seat opposite her.

'You seem to have trouble accepting that I will not be told what to do,' she tossed back.

He drew in a little breath. 'Careful, *cara*,' he said. 'We are in public now. Keep your claws sheathed until we are alone.'

Gisele had to fight not to glower at him. She picked up the menu and buried her nose in it. 'How did your urgent business go?' she asked.

'Fine.'

A stiff silence passed.

Gisele wondered if his urgent business had been female. A sick feeling opened up in her stomach like a canyon. She hated thinking of him with someone else. For two years she had tried *not* to think about it. Did he have a current mistress he was keeping as backup? Her chest tightened painfully at the thought. So many rich men led double lives. Was he one of them?

'I have something for you,' Emilio said.

Gisele put the menu down again. 'What is it?'

He handed her a jeweller's box, his expression as blank as a sheet of paper. 'I hope it fits.'

She opened the black velvet box and looked down at the staggeringly gorgeous diamond sitting there. It looked frightfully expensive and yet it was much simpler than the one he had given her previously. 'I don't understand...' She looked up at him again. 'I thought you were going to get the old one adjusted?'

'I thought you might like this one instead,' he said. 'But if you don't then you can choose your own. It doesn't matter either way to me.'

Gisele bit her lip as she took the ring out of the box and slid it on her finger. It was a perfect fit and suited her hand so much better than the old one. She had never really liked the previous one but she hadn't had the courage to say so. It had been too heavy and cumbersome for her hand, too flashy, and the claws had caught at the finer fabrics of some of her clothes. This one, with its delicate setting, looked as if it had been designed for her and for her alone. She brought her gaze back to Emilio's. 'It's beautiful,' she said. 'It's the most gorgeous ring I've ever seen.'

He gave a dismissive grunt and picked up his menu. 'What would you like to eat?' he asked.

Gisele looked at him as he flicked through the menu, as a cricket ball of bitterness and hate slowly loosened in her chest. 'Was *this* your urgent business this morning?' she asked, holding up her hand.

He put down the menu and looked at her with a brooding frown. 'Can we get on with the meal or are you still on a hunger strike?' he asked.

'Was it, Emilio?'

'I had several things to see to,' he said, shifting in his chair as if someone had put marbles beneath him. 'That was one of them.'

'It was very thoughtful of you,' she said softly.

'Think nothing of it,' he said, turning another page of the menu with a look of acute boredom on his face. 'It's just a prop, anyway. I didn't want people to talk about why you're not wearing an engagement ring.'

She chewed at her lip as she looked at the sparkling diamond, watching as the light caught at it from a thousand different angles. 'Looks like a pretty expensive prop,' she said.

He closed the menu with a little snap. 'It's just money.'

She met his gaze across the table. 'Do I get to keep it after I've…you know…got through this?' she asked.

'"Got through this"?' he said, with a rueful quirk of his mouth. 'You make it sound like something dreadful you have to endure, like torture or a prison sentence.'

Gisele pursed her lips as she examined the diamond again. 'I don't know…maybe there are some compensations to be had.'

'Well over two million at the last count,' he muttered.

She flicked her gaze back to his. 'So, do I get to keep it?'

'What will you do with it?' he asked with a curl of his lip. 'Sell it or toss it in the nearest fountain like you did the last time?'

Gisele held his mocking gaze for a beat before she picked up her menu. She still couldn't work out why he had taken the time and effort to choose her such an exquisite ring. Was she fooling herself he cared more than he was letting on? She wasn't used to thinking of him being hurt by their break-up because he had been the one to end their relationship. She had thought he had only orchestrated this temporary reunion for the sake of appearances.

But what if he really *did* want a fresh start? What if the new ring was his way of communicating that? Was it crazy of her to look for love where hate had resided for so long?

What if he had only bought the ring to lure her back into his bed? It was way too soon to be jumping to any conclusions over his motivations. She had to tread carefully or risk everything all over again. 'I think I'll keep it as a souvenir,' she said. 'A girl can never have too many diamonds, now, can she?'

His expression hardened all the way to his dark-as-night eyes. 'I'm surprised you didn't keep the old one,' he said. 'The sale of it could have set you up for a year or two at least.'

'I found it much more satisfying to throw it away,' she said. 'It seemed appropriate, given the circumstances.'

His mouth tightened even further as he held her look. 'You're never going to let it go, are you?'

'Is that why you bought the ring?' Gisele asked. 'You thought a little bauble would soften me up enough to occupy your bed once more? You'll have to try harder, Emilio. I'm not that easy for the taking.'

He elevated one dark brow as he ran his smouldering gaze over her indolently. 'That wasn't the message I was getting last night,' he said. 'You were hot for it as soon as I kissed you.'

Gisele felt the heat rise from her neck to pool in her cheeks. She pushed against the table and got to her feet, all of her movements stiff with outrage. 'Excuse me,' she said. 'I need to use the Ladies' room.'

'Don't even think about it,' Emilio said before she had even stalked two paces from the table.

She turned and looked at him haughtily. 'Excuse me?'

'I know how your mind works, Gisele,' he said. 'But running away is not going to help things.'

'I'm not running away,' she said, shooting him a livid glare. 'I'm simply removing myself from your hateful presence.'

His expression became as unmalleable as marble and his voice just as hard and unyielding when he spoke. 'If you walk out of this restaurant without me I will call every contact I have in Europe and tell them not to touch you with a barge pole. The knock-on effect will follow you all the way back to Australia. Can you imagine what the press will make of that?'

Gisele felt the scorch of his glitteringly determined gaze as it warred with hers. It made the backs of her knees tingle with a sensation like pieces of ice chugging through her veins.

Dared she call his bluff?

What if the press dug a little deeper into her private life? Somehow she had managed to keep Lily's birth and death out of the public arena. She couldn't bear having her grief splashed over the press for the world to see.

It was a king hit to her pride to resume her seat but she didn't see what other choice she had. She threw him a look of undiluted venom. 'Happy now?' she asked.

'You've turned into quite a little spitfire, haven't you, *cara*?' he said. 'Taming you is turning out to be quite diverting.'

'Would you like me to sit up and beg while you're at it?' she threw back.

'No,' he said, giving her another smouldering look.

'I'm much more interested in you rolling over and playing bed.'

Gisele felt the incendiary heat of his play on words at the very base of her spine. How could he reduce her to such a quivering wreck of need with just a look or a teasing comment? 'You might be in for a disappointment,' she said with deliberate coolness. 'What if I don't live up to your lofty expectations?'

He sat back and surveyed her features at his leisure, pausing for a moment on her mouth before his eyes came back to mesh with hers. 'I'm sure you haven't lost your touch,' he said. 'I still remember what you feel like wrapped around me.'

She gave him a cynical look to disguise the way her insides were coiling with red-hot lust. 'All cats are black in the dark.'

'I've met a few cats in my time,' he said. 'But none purr quite the way you do.'

'I might scratch and bite instead,' she said, crossing her legs to try and control the surge of longing that was rippling through her. 'Or I might just go through the motions to get it over with. Lots of women do.'

His lips curved upwards in a glinting half smile. 'Do you really think I wouldn't be able to tell if you were faking it?'

Gisele shifted her gaze from his, her face flooding with colour all over again. He had known her body so well. Every pulse point, every curve and indentation, every sensual hotspot had been his to tease and please. Her body had sung for hours afterwards. The memory of his touch was still on her skin. It was still *in* her body. She could feel it even now, the on-off pressure of aching need building deep inside her. She would have no hope of holding back her response even if she wanted to for the sake of her pride. Hadn't last night proven that? He had been the one to call a halt, not her. She had been incapable of it. Desire had consumed her common sense. It had always been that way with Emilio. She had no defences against the attraction she felt for him. She suspected he knew how fragile her armour was. How could she keep herself safe from further heartbreak? 'Can we please talk about something else?' she asked, darting a glance either side in case other diners were listening in.

'What are you embarrassed about, *cara*?' Emilio asked. 'That I know your body almost as well as I know my own?'

'You don't know it *now*,' Gisele insisted.

He leaned across and picked up her left hand, bringing it up to his lips as his eyes held hers in a mesmerising trance. 'Then perhaps it is time I reacquainted myself with it, hmm? The sooner the better, don't you think?'

Gisele's whole body shivered as his lips brushed the tips of her fingers. The diamond he had placed on her hand glittered as a reminder of the contract he had drawn up between them: two million dollars for a month of her time. 'Why didn't you do so last night?' she asked. 'You had the opportunity. Why didn't you take it while you had the chance?'

He stroked his thumb across the soft dish of her palm, sending powerful lightninglike sensations all the way up her arm. 'You weren't ready last night,' he said. 'It wouldn't have been fair to take advantage of you when you were tired and overwrought.'

'I might never be ready,' she said with a pert lift of her chin. 'What will you do then?'

His coal-black eyes caressed hers until she wondered if she was going to disappear in their bottomless depths and never come out. 'You'll be ready,' he said with bone-melting conviction. 'Your body is already there—it's just your mind that has to catch up. I'm prepared to wait until it does.'

Gisele pulled her tingling hand out of his. She buried her nose in the menu and chose a dish she had no real appetite for, just so she didn't have to meet Emilio's percipient gaze. It unnerved her how well he could read her. But, even more disturbing, it *touched* her that he hadn't exploited her last night. So many men would have taken advantage of her vulnerability but he hadn't. How was she supposed to hate him if he didn't do hateful things?

'You don't seem to be enjoying that,' Emilio said a little while after their meals had been served. 'Would you like me to order something else for you?'

She put down her fork, which she had been using to push the rich, creamy food around on her plate. 'I'm sorry,' she said. 'I guess I'm just not hungry.'

He looked at her for a long moment, his expression dark and serious. 'Does my presence upset you so much?' he asked.

Gisele made a rueful movement with her lips. 'It's not just you…it's the situation between us. It feels… I don't know… I'm not sure what you want.'

'I want you.'

She felt his statement brush along her spine like a caress. 'Apart from that, I mean.'

'You mean in the long term?'

She ran her tongue over her tinder-dry lips. 'I'm not sure we want the same things now.'

'Isn't it a little early to be worrying about that?' he asked. 'At this point we need to take each day as it comes. We have to try—surely you see that?'

Gisele nailed him with her gaze. 'How much of this is about restoring your good reputation with the public?'

His brows moved together over his eyes. 'Is that what you think this is?' he asked. 'Nothing but a publicity stunt?'

She let out a wobbly breath. 'I don't know... How can I know? You bought me a beautiful ring and yet you've never said anything about your feelings. Not before and not now.'

'What do you want me to say?' he asked. 'You hate me. You've said it several times. What would be the point in me saying what I feel? It's not going to change how you feel, is it?'

She took a breath and dived straight in. 'Did you *ever* love me?'

His expression turned to stone, muscle by muscle. 'I was prepared to marry you, wasn't I?'

Gisele looked at him in disdain. 'So I'm supposed to feel grateful that you selected me from a line-up of hundreds, if not thousands, of potential candidates?'

'Why are you bringing this up now?' he asked.

'I want to know what you felt for me back then,' she said. 'I want to know what foundation our relationship was built on.'

He scraped a hand through his hair. 'It was built on a mutual desire to build a life together. We wanted the same things—children, a solid family base and a secure home life. All the things most people want.'

'Most people want to be loved,' she said with a sigh. 'It's what most people want more than anything.'

'I realise that, Gisele,' he said. 'I would be lying if I said I didn't want it too. I've wanted it all my life but I've learned that it doesn't always happen just because you want it to. It also doesn't last, or at least not in my experience.'

Gisele could sense the conversation was over even before the waiter appeared to clear their plates. Emilio's expression had closed over like a page being turned in a book. She knew it would be pointless pushing him to reveal more of his childhood. She wondered how many people had come and gone in his life to leave him so cynical about love. Had people made promises and not kept them? Said words that had no actions to back them up? Children were so trusting and relied heavily on the adults around them for stability and security. Had *he* grown up feeling he had no one he could truly rely on, no one he could trust to have his best interests at heart?

'Luigi will drive you back to the villa,' Emilio said. 'I have some paperwork to do at my office.'

'So you didn't fire him?' Gisele asked with a sheepish look.

He put a hand to her elbow as he escorted her out of the restaurant. 'He's on notice,' he said.

'Oh, but you mustn't do that,' she said, a frown puckering her brow as she stopped to look up at him. 'He's probably got a family to feed. It was my fault. I wanted to avoid the press. I wanted to melt into the crowd rather than turn up in a flash car and draw attention to myself.'

He smoothed the tiny frown away from her forehead with his finger. 'I don't like it when my orders are disobeyed,' he said, 'especially by members of my staff.'

'Thank God I'm not on the payroll...' She flushed and sank her teeth into her bottom lip. 'Well, maybe I am, now that I come to think about it.'

Emilio brought her chin up. 'You are not a member of my staff.'

'What am I then?' she asked.

His eyes measured her gaze for a long moment. 'Try and rest this afternoon,' he said and brushed a light kiss on her lips. 'Tonight might be a late night.'

Gisele got in the waiting car, but when she turned from adjusting her seat belt Emilio had already gone.

CHAPTER SEVEN

EMILIO watched later that evening as Gisele came down the stairs towards him. She was wearing a simple but elegant fuchsia-pink cocktail dress with a matching chiffon wrap. She had skilfully styled her hair into a smoothly coiffed up-do that gave her a regal air. He had never seen her look more beautiful as she smiled at him, albeit briefly. Her smile was like sunshine breaking through the clouds on a bleak day. He had forgotten how wonderful it made him feel to see it. It was like a spill of warm fluid inside his chest, slowly spreading until all the places inside him were no longer echoing with emptiness.

It was a big step for him, taking her with him tonight. He had thought about going alone, like he usually did. Few people outside the charity knew how deeply he was involved and why. Over the past year or so he had felt the need to stop ignoring where he had come from and do something to help others escape the hell he had escaped. He had done it through sheer grit and determination but he had come to realise others didn't always have the confidence or willpower to do it.

Giving Gisele a glimpse of his former life would be uncomfortable for him but that was the price he had to pay for wanting to make a difference. It wasn't easy facing the dark shadows of his past. He always came away from these things feeling unsettled. He felt as if those ghostly shadows were reaching out of the darkness to drag him back to the gutter and leave him there, cold and shivering and alone.

Emilio took Gisele's hand as she stepped off the last stair and brought it up to his mouth, pressing his lips against the soft skin of her bent knuckles. 'You look stunning,' he said. 'Pink suits you.'

She gave him another fleeting smile. 'Thank you.'

He reached for the jewellery box he had left on the hall table. 'I have something for you to go with your ring.'

Her eyes looked at the box and then up at him with a little frown. 'You shouldn't be spending so much money,' she said.

'I have the right to spoil my fiancée, don't I?' he asked.

He opened the box and she touched a finger to the diamond-and-sapphire necklace glittering there. 'I'm not really your fiancée,' she said. 'It's just a game of pretend to the press.'

'We could make it real,' Emilio said.

Something flickered in her grey-blue gaze before she turned so he could put the necklace about her neck. 'You want the old Gisele back but she's gone, Emilio,' she said. 'You can't get her back, no matter how much money you spend trying.'

Emilio put his hands on her slim shoulders once he had fastened the necklace, breathing in the summery fragrance of her until he felt intoxicated. He felt her skin lift in a shiver beneath his fingers, just as it always used to do. He liked that he still had that effect on her. He liked the way her body instinctively reacted to him, in spite of what she said to the contrary. 'Is the money issue worrying you?' He turned her back to face him. 'The fact that I paid to have you back in my life?'

She gave him a pensive look. 'It's not about the money…not really…'

'What, then?' he asked.

Her eyes dropped from his to study his bow tie. 'You want everything to be as it was,' she said. 'But I'm not sure life comes with a reset button. You can't just pick up where you left off and expect things will be exactly the same as they were before. Things change. People change… *I've* changed.'

Emilio studied her for a moment with an uneasy feeling in his stomach. She said she had changed and she had. She didn't eat. She didn't sleep. She looked pale and frail. He had done that to her. *He* had been the one to change her. How could he change her back? He wanted it all to go away. A fresh start was what they both needed. It was no good looking back. He, of all people, knew that. It didn't change things, brooding about what could have or should have been. Moving forwards was the only way to heal the past. He was living proof of it. Perhaps tonight would help her to see that.

He tipped up her chin again. 'Let's just take it from here and see how it goes, shall we?' he said. 'No promises. Just time to explore what we have now, instead of what we had then, OK?'

She moved her lips in a semblance of a smile but

her eyes looked as if a cloud had passed through them. 'OK,' she said and slipped her hand in his as he led her out to the car.

When they arrived at the luxury hotel where the dinner was being held, Gisele realised the function wasn't actually anything to do with Emilio's architecture business but was rather a fundraising event for a homeless kids' charity he had set up over the past year. She found out through the course of the evening that he had developed a drop-in centre in the city where young people could get a meal and a shower and a bed. His charity also offered educational and vocational schemes to help kids get off and keep off the streets. Counselling services were provided as well as drug and alcohol rehabilitation for those in need.

Gisele spoke to several young people who had benefited from the charity personally. They told her stories of how they had come to be on the streets—desperately sad and heart-wrenching stories of neglect and abuse. It was an unsettling reminder of how little she knew of Emilio's background.

He had told her almost nothing about his past. Had she known him at all back then? Had *he* grown up like some of these young people? Why else had he set up such a charity? What had happened to him on those dark, dangerous streets? What sort of horrendous horrors had he witnessed or experienced? She wondered how he had survived it. How had he overcome such desperate odds to be the successful man he was today?

What had happened in the past year or so that he had decided to do something as big as this? She'd always suspected he deliberately shied away from his past, that he wanted to leave it well behind him. But putting himself out there in such a public way spoke of a deeply moving concern for others less fortunate than himself. It was such a change from the super-successful businessman persona he presented to the world. He was no longer using his wealth to show how far he'd come up in the world; rather he was reaching back down into his dark past to help others climb out of it.

One of the young volunteers, called Romeo, told her how Emilio did a lot of the hands-on work himself on the streets, speaking to kids to help them realise there were other options for them other than crime or prostitution or gang warfare.

'He's not afraid to get his hands dirty,' Romeo said. 'I was one of the first he helped get off the streets. He helped me see a better future for myself. He taught me that you mustn't let what happens to you define you. It's how you handle it that counts. You must be very proud to be his fiancée, *sì*?'

Gisele hoped her smile didn't look too unnatural. She was still feeling so incredibly shocked. The world Emilio came from couldn't be more different from hers. She couldn't imagine how hard it must have been for him to drag himself from such a rough start in life to achieve all that he had. So many obstacles must have stood in his way. How had he overcome them? 'Yes, I am,' she said, 'very proud.'

After a few more words of conversation, Romeo got called away to help with serving food.

Emilio came back over with a drink for her. 'I hope

Romeo wasn't telling tales out of school,' he said. 'He has a tendency to exaggerate.'

'Is this how you grew up?' Gisele asked, looking up at him with a shell-shocked expression. 'Like some of these kids? Why didn't you tell me?'

'Lots of people have it worse than I did,' he said with a dismissive shrug as he took a sip of his drink.

'Why didn't you tell me about your charity?' she asked. 'You've not said a word to me about any of this. In fact, this morning you said this was a business function.'

'Does it matter?' he asked.

'Of course it matters,' she said. 'I thought I'd be forced to speak to stuffy old businessmen and their wives, and instead I'm meeting young people whose lives you've saved from God only knows what.'

'Romeo would have made it without my help,' Emilio said. 'He just needed a leg-up.'

'Who helped you?' Gisele asked. 'Who was your leg-up person?'

His eyes became shuttered. 'Some people need more help than others,' he said.

'So you did it all on your own?' she asked.

He touched her on the elbow to position her to face a man who was approaching them with a camera. 'The official photographer is coming over for a photo for the newsletter,' he said. 'Put on your happy face.'

Gisele schooled her features back into happy fiancée mode as Emilio put his arm around her waist, drawing her into his hard warmth. She felt her skin react to his closeness, to his smell, to the sense of protection he offered. It was hard not to want to get closer, to start to imagine a future where she would always be by his side, helping him help others. He had mentioned they could make their 'engagement' real again, but how could she give him what he wanted most? The one thing he had always been clear on was that he wanted a family, but there was no way she could risk going down that path again.

The evening soon drew to a close. Emilio escorted her out to the waiting car, but he barely spoke on the way back to the villa. He spent most of the short journey staring straight ahead, his eyes blank, the different-coloured lights of the city passing over his features like a special-effects film, making his handsome face take on grimly distorted shadows and angles.

Although he had cleverly evaded answering her question about his background, Gisele wondered if he was thinking of the life he had left behind, the life of poverty and neglect and unspeakable cruelty that lurked on the underbelly of the eternal city. She thought of him as a young teenager out there, huddled under a bush or park bench, cold, hungry, thirsty, terrified, lost and alone. It made her heart ache to think no one had protected him, no one had taught him how to love.

'I think it's amazing what you've done,' she said into the silence.

He frowned and looked at her as if he hadn't realised anyone was sitting beside him. 'Sorry, did you say something?' he asked.

She gave him a soft smile and took one of his hands in hers. 'It must feel good to have made a difference,' she said. 'To think that you're responsible for so many young people getting a chance to live a decent life—

a life they would never have been able to have without your help. It must make you feel very satisfied.'

He rolled his thumb over the diamond on her finger before meshing his gaze with hers. 'In my experience money fixes just about everything,' he said. 'You just need enough of it.'

Gisele felt a little frisson scuttle down her spine at the glittering darkness of his eyes. 'I guess you have to decide which projects are going to be worth pursuing,' she said. 'You wouldn't want to be throwing good money after bad.'

His half smile had a hint of ruthlessness to it. 'I don't take on projects unless I'm sure I'll succeed with them,' he said.

'Success isn't always up to you, though, is it?' she said. 'Other people or circumstances can influence outcomes in spite of what you've planned.'

His bottomless brown eyes moved from hers to slowly gaze at her mouth. She felt her lips tingle and fizz, her heart stepping up its pace as he touched her bottom lip with the pad of his thumb. 'Overcoming obstacles is part of the challenge,' he said, returning his eyes to hers. 'The harder they are, the more satisfying they are when accomplished.'

Gisele felt another shimmery sensation move down her back as the car drew to a halt outside his villa. There was a premonitory weight to the air as he helped her from the car. His fingers as they curled around hers sent livewires of electricity along her arm. She followed him into the villa, all her senses on overdrive as he led her to the *salone*.

'Would you like a nightcap?' he asked.

Gisele sent her tongue out in a quick darting movement to moisten her paper-dry lips. 'Um…I think I might give it a miss,' she said. 'I think I'll go on up to bed.'

'As you wish,' he said, moving to the bar to pour himself a finger of whisky.

She hovered for a moment, not sure why, but unable to tear herself away. She watched as he lifted the glass to his lips, how they rested against the rim and then how his strong throat moved up and down as he swallowed the liquid.

He put the glass down and looked at her. 'Is something wrong?' he asked.

'No… I… It's just I wanted to say thank you for this evening,' she said. 'I had a good time. It was very… revealing.'

He picked up his glass again. 'Don't go out making me out to be a hero, *cara*,' he said grimly. 'I'm anything but. You, of all people, should know that.'

'I think you care much more than you let on,' she said.

He gave a grunt of something that might have passed for mocking laughter. 'Got me all figured out, have you, Gisele?' He took another swallow of his whisky, a generous one this time.

'I think you hide who you really are and what you really feel behind that I-couldn't-give-a-damn façade,' she said. 'I think that deep down you're afraid you're going to get let down so you do everything possible to protect yourself.'

He put the glass down with a crack that sounded like a gunshot. His eyes were blazing with a heat that threatened to consume her. She felt the lick of the flames as he raked her with his gaze, an incendiary heat that ran along her flesh like a river of fire. 'You should've gone to bed while you still had the chance,' he said, moving towards her.

Gisele stood her ground, determined not to be threatened by his devilish and roguish manner. 'You don't scare me, Emilio,' she said. 'You might scare the warlords and the pimps and the drug dealers of the backstreets of Rome, but you don't scare me.'

'Such brave words,' he said, taking a handful of her hair and pulling it free from its restraining clip, unleashing with it a flow of sensations that showered over her like the sparks from exploding fireworks.

Gisele sucked in a much-needed breath. He was so close. He was *too* close. She could feel *him* there: the heat, the hardness, the need that was as hungry as hers. It was pressing against her, calling her body into play. A call she could not resist, even if she wanted to. It was too primal, too overwhelming and way too rampant to be held back any longer.

He tugged her towards him with a roughness that thrilled her as much as it terrified her, pelvis against pelvis, need against need. She could not hide behind her smart comebacks now. Witty words were no defence for the onslaught of feeling that was rushing through her like a tumultuous tide. There was nothing between their bodies now but the desire that had always pulsed and throbbed between them. 'Such brave, foolish words,' he said and then his mouth came down on hers.

Gisele revelled in the fiery heat of his kiss. He took control from the start and refused to relinquish it. He thrust through the seam of her mouth with a bold stroke of his tongue and she whimpered in submission as she gave him total access. He explored her thoroughly, staking his claim, leaving her in no doubt of who was in charge. Teeth and tongues collided, hands groped and grabbed, clothes were unzipped, unbuttoned and at one stage even torn.

'If you don't want this then you'd better tell me now,' Emilio said as he all but slammed her up against the nearest wall.

'I want this,' she said against his mouth, her lips nibbling at his, her hands searching for him, aching to feel him. 'I want this. *I want you.*'

He groaned deeply as she finally found him, her fingers closing around his hot, hard heat, rediscovering the length of him, the strength and power of him. She felt him shudder as he fought for control. He was just as she remembered him: sleek and hard, an intriguing combination of satin and steel.

Somehow she was naked from the waist down; she couldn't remember how it had happened but it didn't matter. There was barely time for him to put on protection before he positioned her and drove into her with a force that sent her head back against the wall, a gasp exploding from her lips as she welcomed him all the way. He grunted with deep male satisfaction and her skin rose in a fine layer of goose bumps as she held him to her. He rocked against her savagely, deep pumping actions that made her body sing with delight, a rapturous melody that struck on chords that had been played in the distant past.

She didn't take long to reach the summit. She only

teetered there for a moment before she lifted off, her body convulsing around his, squeezing, contracting, milking him of his essence in those few blissful seconds where common sense and rational thought had no place, no foothold.

He followed close behind, a shudder going through him that ricocheted through her as she held on to him.

Long seconds passed.

'Sorry,' Emilio said against her neck, still breathing heavily. 'I probably rushed that a bit.'

'No,' she said, sliding her hands over his back and shoulders. 'You don't need to apologise.'

After a moment or two he eased back to look at her. 'You OK?'

Gisele wondered what he was really asking as she looked into the black unreadable pits of his eyes. 'I'm fine,' she said. 'It was...amazing...'

He pushed himself away from the wall, his expression rueful as he dealt with disposing of the condom. 'It wasn't supposed to happen this way,' he said, raking a hand through his hair in a distracted manner. 'I wanted it to be better than a rough grope against a wall. I wanted it to be memorable.'

Gisele stepped forwards and placed a gentle hand on the side of his face, loving the feel of his raspy skin under the softness of her palm. 'It *was* memorable,' she said. Being back in his arms was unforgettable. She knew she would have to live off the memories all over again, but at least she had this time with him.

He studied her for a moment before placing his hand over hers, holding it to his jaw. 'I want you in my bed,' he said. 'I want to wake up in the morning with you beside me.'

How could she say no to him when he made her feel things she'd thought she would never feel again? He might not love her but he wanted her.

He might *never* love her. Some people were just incapable of it and, from what she had picked up about his past, it certainly hinted that he might be one of them, too damaged to open himself to anyone else. It was a heart-wrenching thought but it was something she would have to accept. She could not stay with him permanently without the love she needed, but for now this felt right. She looped her arms around his neck and looked up into his dark eyes. 'Make love to me,' she said softly.

Emilio lifted her and carried her to his bedroom, laying her down as if she was the most precious cargo he had ever had in his possession.

'Emilio…' The soft sound of her voice was like a caress over his skin.

'I'm here, *cara*,' he said, threading his fingers through her hair. 'I'm here.'

'Did you miss me?' she said, looking into his eyes with her grey-blue ones. 'Did you miss doing this with me?'

He pressed a soft-as-air kiss to her mouth. 'I've missed everything about you.'

And he had, desperately. His life had seemed so pointless and empty without her in it. He had worked like a man obsessed over the past two years but none of it had given him any real sense of purpose. He had made money—lots of money; more than he had dreamed possible—but it hadn't filled the gaping hole she had left in his life. The charity helped a bit but it wasn't enough. He wanted more. He wanted her.

He kissed her again, a long drugging kiss that stirred up deeply buried longings that he could no longer ignore. He wanted to feel her convulse around him again in ecstasy, he wanted to feel her grasp hold of him as if he was her only lifeline—the only person on this earth who could make her feel complete.

He peeled back the spaghetti-thin straps of her dress to press a kiss to her bare shoulder. Her skin tasted of summer, an exotic tropical fragrance he had always and only associated with her. He worked his way around to her neck, lingering on the sensitive flesh there, delighting in the way she wriggled beneath him, her soft gasps of pleasure fuelling the raging fire of his need. It was a blistering furnace of want, hot flames leaping beneath his skin, making him aware of her in every cell of his body. She was his nemesis, the completion of him, the missing other half that he had been seeking for most of his life.

'I want you,' he said, pressing a hot kiss to the skin just shy of her earlobe. 'I want you so badly I can't think straight. It's all I can think about. How much I want you back in my arms.' He moved his mouth to the soft temptation of hers.

'I want you too,' she whispered back, her soft lips moving around to play with his in a cat and mouse game that set his senses on overload.

At least he had her desire for him to build on, Emilio thought. It was the one thing he could count on. She might say how much she hated him but her touch and the press of her lips against his told another story entirely.

He felt the sexy tug of her teeth, the way they pulled on his lower lip in a tantalising bite that made his spine tingle. He nipped her back gently, sucking on her lip and then stroking his tongue over the plump softness until she whimpered and did the same back. Their tongues met and mated in a moist duel of wanton need, each one seeking the other in sensual combat.

Emilio slipped the other strap of her dress off her shoulder and planted a kiss to the creamy softness of her skin. She tilted her head, her long hair falling back over his hand where it rested in the middle of her slender back. She made a soft noise of acquiescence, a murmur of want, of need, of red-hot desire, and his blood surged in response. No one made him feel more of a man than she did.

He uncovered her breasts and gently cupped one of them with his hand while his mouth continued to explore hers. She arched up into his palm, her erect nipple driving into the centre of his palm, her slender hips inciting his to press down to meet her feminine softness. He ached to fill her with his presence but this time he wanted to take things slowly, to savour each moment. He stroked his fingers against her folds, delighting in the scented moistness of her body that told him she was more than ready for him. But still he took his time, gently stretching her with a finger, feeling the tight clasp of her body around him.

'Please…' she begged breathlessly.

'Not yet,' he said against her mouth. 'You know how much better it is when we both wait.'

She writhed restlessly beneath him, pushing her body up to meet his, her mouth ravenous as it fed off his. He kissed her back with the same intensity while his fingers continued their gentle exploration. He felt her swell beneath his touch, the tight pearl of her need so delicate and yet full of such feminine power.

Her hands began to search for him and when they found him he groaned out loud in pleasure. Her soft fingers stroked along his length at first before she made a sheath with her hand and rubbed him up and down, slowly at first and then with increasing vigour. He felt all his senses roar for release and had to fight not to explode right there and then.

She wriggled some more, grasping the cradle of his hips with her hands, positioning herself beneath him. 'Now,' she said. 'I want you *now.*'

He quickly found another condom and applied it before he positioned himself above her with the bulk of his weight supported by his arms as he surged into her with a deep thrust that drew a gasping breath from her body and a guttural groan of pleasure from his. He felt her body wrap around him, the tight ripples of her flesh massaging him, torturing him, luring him into the deep swirling pool of blessed oblivion. He held himself back from it with an effort; no one challenged his ironclad control more than her. The physical act of sex always became something more with her. It was not just a joining of bodies; it reached him on a level he had not experienced with anyone else. It felt as if each time they made love she reached inside his battered soul with her soft fingers and soothed the torn and ragged edges until they didn't ache any more.

He felt it now, the way she stroked the muscles of his back with her gentle hands, long, smooth, gentle movements that made his flesh turn to gravel with goose bumps. He felt it in the soft but urgent press of her mouth against his, the way her lips were both gentle and insistent, her tongue searching and yet submissive to the driving command of his.

He moved within her, the slide of his flesh in hers slick and sexy, slow and then fast, her body rising to meet each downward movement of his, her legs wrapping around his hips as she urged him towards the edge of rapture.

He caressed her with his fingers to heighten her pleasure. He knew exactly what she needed to take that final plunge into paradise. She was hot and wet and swollen beneath his touch. He kept caressing her, softly and slowly, varying the pressure until he felt her finally give in to the pleasure her body craved. She threw her head back against the pillows and let out a high-pitched cry as her body convulsed around his. He felt every milking movement until he had no choice but to pour himself into her, his body finally collapsing with spent pleasure against hers when he was done.

She continued to stroke his back in the aftermath. He felt those softly padded fingertips move up and down his spine as he eventually got his breathing back under control.

'I'm assuming you're still on the Pill,' he said as he eased himself up on his elbows to look at her. 'Condoms are not always reliable, especially putting them on as haphazardly as I did earlier.'

Her eyes flickered before moving away from his to

concentrate on a point just below his chin. 'I'm sure it's not going to be a problem...'

'Are you currently using contraception?' he asked.

Her gaze met his briefly before skittering away again. 'I'm on a low-dose pill to regulate my cycle,' she said. 'It's been out of whack since...' Her teeth sank into her lip before she continued. 'Since we broke up...'

Emilio felt another dagger-sharp probe of guilt assail him. Gisele had done it tough since he had thrown her out of his life. So much had happened to her: the death of her father and the revelation of her twin sister, all the while juggling the demands of building up her business. No wonder she didn't sleep properly at night. She had said it wasn't his fault but how could it *not* be? Her life would have been completely different if he had stood by her.

He wanted to fix it all, to wipe out all the wrongs, but he sensed it wasn't going to be as simple as that. There was a streak of stubbornness in her that hadn't been there before. He understood how she would want to protect herself from being hurt again, but he wanted to break down her defences so she would come back to him, not because of her need for money, but because she valued him and the future they had planned together more than her pride.

He wanted her as the mother of his children. He couldn't imagine anyone else. He had never considered anyone else. He looked forward to becoming a father. He longed for a family to love and protect. He had dreamed of her swollen with his child. The images had mocked him over the past two years, but now it was something that was just within his grasp if only he could get her to put aside her pride and admit to her own yearnings. She was born to be a mother. She loved anything to do with babies. She just had to trust him enough to let go of the past so they could move forward.

Emilio played with the ends of her silky hair, running it through his fingers, watching as her features relaxed in enjoyment. 'You know how we talked about having a family one day?' he said.

She flinched as if he had slapped her. Then she pulled her hair out of his fingers and, using the flat of her hand against his chest, pushed him away from her. He watched in bemusement as she got off the bed and reached for a wrap, tying it roughly around her middle. 'Was it something I said?' he asked.

'I've changed my mind,' she said, spearing him with a glance. 'I don't want to have children.'

Emilio swung his legs over the bed and reached for his bathrobe, coming over to where she was standing with her arms folded tightly across her body. 'What are you talking about?' he asked. 'You adore children. You own and operate a baby wear shop, for God's sake. You spend hours doing exquisite embroidery and smocking on baby clothes. What do you mean, you've changed your mind?'

She gave him a defensive look. 'I mean exactly what I said. I've changed my mind,' she said. 'People do. I did.'

Emilio looked at her as if she had suddenly turned into someone else. Where was the young woman who spoke so excitedly of having a family? Two years ago she had talked to him about baby names, what sex their children might be, what they would be like, *who* they would look like. They had even talked about her coming off the Pill as soon as the honeymoon was over.

He was thirty-three years old now. He didn't want to leave it much longer before he became a father. He had hoped Gisele would settle back into his life and within a month or two everything would be back to normal. He had planned that once things had settled down between them they would marry and start a family. It was unthinkable to him that she wouldn't fall in with his plans. He hadn't factored in her refusal to give him the family he wanted so desperately. That would be admitting defeat.

Failure.

That word was like a ghost that stalked him. That word haunted him like no other. It was an invisible but all too real enemy from his childhood, the same one that had followed him out of back alley dumpsters in search of food and shelter. It had taunted him; it had tortured him with thoughts of not being good enough, not strong enough, not determined enough to get out of that hellhole. He had fought it off; he had wrestled it to the ground, determining he would never allow it back in his life.

He would not fail.

He would find a way to change Gisele's mind. Whatever it took, however long it took, surely she would change her mind. 'Has this been a recent decision or one you've thought about for a while?' he asked.

'What does it matter when I made the decision?' she said. 'I've made it and I'm not unmaking it.'

'Gisele, you know how much I want a family,' he said. 'You've known that from the start. It's one of the reasons I asked you to marry me. I saw a future with us as parents, building a family unit together.'

'Just because you've made bucket loads of money doesn't mean you can automatically have anything you want,' Gisele said. 'Life isn't like that.'

Emilio tunnelled a hand through his hair. 'Look, I know you got terribly hurt by our break-up. It came out of the blue and shook you badly. Having a child is a big commitment in any relationship, let alone one that caused you so much pain in the past. But we can make it work. We'd make great parents. You'll be a fabulous mother. I just know it. I've always known it.'

She gave him a glittering glare. 'I'm not going to be a breeding machine for you or for any man,' she said.

'For God's sake, Gisele,' he said, frowning heavily. 'When have I ever referred to you as such? I want you to be the mother of my children. That's an honour that I have never asked of any other woman.'

'You'll have to ask someone else to do it because I'm not going to,' she said, shooting him a look that would have felled a lesser man.

Emilio felt his jaw tighten with frustration. How could he make her see reason? Was a month going to be long enough to make her change her mind? Was she doing this just to get under his skin? If so, she couldn't have picked a better weapon. He hadn't told her anything about his past. He had told no one. The loneliness he had felt, not having a proper home and family, not belonging, being constantly hungry, cold and dirty. The shame of not even knowing who his father was. The shame of being an outcast because of the poverty that had been all he had ever known. 'Is this about money?' he asked, barely managing to control his anger. 'You want more money? You want a business deal instead of a proper relationship? Is that what you want?'

Her expression turned bitter. 'That's what we already have, isn't it?'

'That's not what we have and you damn well know it,' he said, frowning at her furiously. 'You made love with me, not because of the money we agreed on, but because you wanted me. It wouldn't have mattered what amount of money I gave you. I don't believe you would have sold yourself. You're not that sort of woman.'

She turned away, her arms still wrapped tightly around her body. 'I don't want to talk about this any more,' she said. 'I'm only here for a month. That's what we agreed on. I haven't signed up for anything else.'

Emilio let out a harsh breath. 'I want a future with you, Gisele, and I want a family. Don't make me choose between one and the other.'

He saw her back and shoulders stiffen. 'I can't give you what you want,' she said.

'Can't or won't?' he asked cynically. 'You want to punish me for how I hurt you. I get that, I really do. I understand that was part of the reason you agreed to come to Italy with me. You saw it as a chance to be as difficult and demanding as you could so I would let you go at the end of the month with no regrets.'

She swung back round to face him, her expression taut with anger. 'And why shouldn't I punish you?' she asked. 'You broke my heart, damn you. I *hate* you for that.'

Emilio put his hands on her shoulders. '*Cara*, if you

truly hated me you would never have shared that bed with me just now,' he said.

'It was just sex,' she said with a worldly toss of her head. 'It's been a while for me. I wanted relief and you provided it.'

'I don't believe it was just sex.'

'Women can do it too, you know,' she said. 'We can separate emotion from sex when we need to.'

'Is that so?' Emilio asked with a curl of his lip.

'Yes,' she said, chin up, eyes defiant.

His hands tightened on her shoulders as he pulled her closer. 'Then if that's the case, you won't mind having sex again just for the heck of it, will you?' And then he brought his mouth down heavily on hers.

Gisele had fully intended to block his kiss by keeping her lips firmly closed, but just one stroke of his tongue had her opening to him with flagrant need. She felt the sexy thrust of his tongue against hers, calling hers into a tango that sent shivers racing up and down her spine. Her body was pressed tightly against his aroused one, the hardened probe of his erection searing her belly with the erotic promise of his potent possession. She returned the heat and fire of his kiss with wanton disregard for her pride or principles. She wanted him with a hunger that was beyond her control. It raced through her veins with breakneck speed, lifting her skin in earthy delight as he tore open her wrap as if it were made of tissue paper. His hands cupped her breasts, his thumbs rubbing over her nipples until they were tight and aching all over again.

He eased the ache with the hot, moist cavern of his mouth, sucking on her until her back was arched in pleasure, her hands clutching his head for support as the fiery sensations tore through her.

Her hands got to work on his bathrobe, pulling it off him while her mouth went back in search of his. She grabbed at him greedily, delighting in the hard sheath of his flesh and the way it throbbed under the caress of her fingers.

He picked her up and carried her to the bed, dropping her in a sexy tangle of limbs, his weight coming down over her, his body spearing hers with a hard thrust that knocked the air right out of her lungs. She heard him give a primitive male grunt of pleasure as her body wrapped around him, a sound that made her shudder all over in delight. He set a furious pace but she was with him all the way. She clawed at the skin on his back, she grabbed his taut buttocks and drove him on with a feral urgency she had no idea she possessed.

It was wicked.

It was racy.

It was thrilling to have him so close to losing control.

She felt the tension in her body rise with every rough surge of his body within hers. She felt her orgasm approach like a speeding train. She couldn't have done anything to stop it if she had tried. It smashed into her, tossing her high in the air, rolling and rolling her in a whirlpool of heady, blissful sensation that surpassed anything she had felt before in his arms.

He came with a stabbing thrust and a shout of pleasure that made her skin shiver. She felt the pulsing of his body as he discharged his essence, anointing her, branding her as his.

He rolled off her and lay with his chest heaving, his

body totally spent and the scent of their coupling fragrant in the air.

Gisele wasn't sure what to say, so said nothing. She was still struggling to get her breathing under control. Her body was still tingling from the sensual assault of unrivalled ecstasy. She wanted to hate him, but how could she when he made her feel this way? He had dismantled every one of her defences with his hot, drugging kisses and his fiery possession. She squeezed her legs together and felt the stickiness of him. It was such a stomach-hollowing reminder of the passion that still flared between them. Would it ever go away? Would *she* be able to walk away once the month was up?

Emilio turned back to her, propping himself on one elbow as he toyed with the wayward strands of her hair. 'I want you to move into my room,' he said.

Gisele quickly hid a nervous swallow. She had wanted some space but he clearly wasn't going to be satisfied unless she was in his arms every night. The intimacy of it terrified her, not because she didn't want to sleep with him. She did. It was just that she knew she would fall in love with him all over again if he got too close.

'What, now?' she asked.

'Not right this minute,' he said, rolling her so she was lying on top of him. 'I have other plans for you just now.'

'Oh?' she said with a coolness she was nowhere near feeling. Her body had already betrayed her. It had welcomed him with slick moistness, gripping him so tightly she could feel the hot, hard length of him filling her completely. She couldn't just lie there without moving. She just *had* to feel the delicious sensation of being in control. She rode him all the way to heaven and back, finally collapsing over him when she had shattered into a million pieces. She felt him plunge himself deeper and deeper before he let go with a raw groan of ecstasy.

And then, without the need for anything other than the sheltering circle of his arms, she fell soundly asleep...

CHAPTER EIGHT

EMILIO lay awake for long hours, watching Gisele sleep. She was purring softly like a kitten beside him. She had curled up against him, one of her arms thrown across his chest in the way she had used to do. He stroked the silky flesh of her arm, thinking how much he had missed moments like this. She was the first woman he had wanted to spend the entire night with. He had never felt comfortable doing that with any other lover. The physical closeness of sex became something deeper with her. Her natural sensuality was something that had attracted him from the first moment he had met her.

He had loved that she had been a virgin. It was perhaps a little old-fashioned of him to have been so ridiculously pleased, but he admired her for not putting herself out there for just anyone. All the women he had slept with had been experienced. It had stopped him in his tracks to think Gisele had waited until she felt she had met the right man to give herself to.

He had been that right man.

She had waited until she was absolutely sure she was ready for that level of intimacy. He had enjoyed tutoring her. He had always thought there was something highly sacred about her giving herself to him. It wasn't just her body she had given him, but her trust.

It had been such a precious gift, one he had savoured and treasured…until the sex tape scandal had erupted and he had mistakenly believed her virginal status had all been a hoax, a deliberate ploy to gain his confidence in her—an act to put a ring on her finger and a steady income in her bank account. His extensive experience of gold-diggers and social climbers had made his judgement skewed. He had not for a moment considered Gisele had been innocent. That was the thing that still plagued him the most. He had not looked long and hard enough for another explanation. He had gone with the pack on calling her out as little more than a high-priced whore.

It pained him to think of the way he had let her down. Would she ever forgive him? Did the fact that she had let her guard down enough to be intimate with him again mean she was softening towards him? Or had she only done it to ease her conscience about taking the money he had promised her? Was the only thing tying her to him two million dollars? It was a disquieting thought and one he couldn't readily dismiss from his mind.

She moved against him, stretching one leg and then the other before her eyes slowly opened. 'Have I been sleeping?' she asked, struggling to an upright position, her blonde hair all tousled like a bird's nest around her shoulders.

Emilio smiled and brushed a strand of hair out of her eyes. 'Like a baby,' he said.

Something flickered in her eyes before she lowered them, her fingers plucking at the edge of the sheet covering her chest. Her face had taken on a stricken look. He even saw the colour leach out of her face.

Emilio propped himself up on one elbow. 'Are you OK?' he asked.

'Why wouldn't I be OK?' she said, affecting an indifferent tone.

He trailed a gentle finger down the slope of her linen-creased cheek. 'Did I hurt you?' he asked. 'Things got pretty intense there last night.'

She still didn't look at him but her cheeks filled with colour again. 'No, of course not.'

He tipped up her face with a finger beneath her chin. 'Still just sex?' he asked.

'Of course,' she said with a haughty look. 'What else could it be?'

His eyes continued to study her as he outlined the contours of her mouth with the tip of his index finger. 'Liar,' he said. 'It's never been just sex, has it, *cara*?'

She pushed against his chest and rolled away from him, reaching for a bathrobe and tying the ends around her waist, her lips pressed tightly together as if she didn't trust herself to answer. She gave him a final chilly look and stalked across the room.

'Where are you going?' he asked.

'I'm going to take a shower,' she said with a little flash of her gaze. 'Is that OK or should I have asked permission first?'

Emilio frowned at her. He was getting a little tired of her game-playing. One minute she was sobbing with pleasure in his arms and the next she acted as if she couldn't wait for the month to be over. He wanted their relationship to settle down, not be a constant battlefield.

He wanted the past put behind him. It wasn't his way to dwell on things. He had to move forwards. There was no other choice. 'Do what you like,' he said, throwing off the bedcovers as he rose from the bed. 'I'll see you downstairs.'

When Gisele came downstairs Marietta had set out the breakfast things and the morning papers out on the terrace. She sat down and poured herself a cup of tea, but just as she was lifting it to her mouth she saw there an English paper sticking out from beneath the Italian one. She pulled it out and looked at the headline below the main news item. The cup in her hand fell with a loud smashing clatter to the flagstones of the terrace. Her heart jerked, stopped and then started to stutter. Her breathing stalled for so long her head swam.

She heard the firm tread of Emilio's footsteps come out on the terrace. 'Gisele?' he said. 'Are you all right? Have you burnt yourself?'

She pressed the paper to her thumping chest, unable to get a single word out past the sudden constriction of her throat. Her heart was thudding sickeningly, a kick-blow beat that was as painful as it was erratic.

There were two photos. One was of Emilio and her at lunch yesterday. The shot showed her looking crossly at him. It wasn't very flattering to her at all, but that wasn't the worst of it.

The other photo...*oh, dear God...* How had it happened? How had the press sourced a photo of her at her baby's grave? Had someone followed her there the last time she had placed flowers on Lily's grave?

She tried to think through the haze of pain inside her

head. The cemetery had been a little busier than usual that day. Had someone recognised her and cashed in on the opportunity to sell the shot to the press? She knew there were websites where members of the public could sell phone pictures of celebrities: candid shots, catching people off guard with no make-up on or having an intimate argument with a partner—private moments made public for cash. Not that Gisele thought of herself as a celebrity in any shape or form, but re-establishing her connection to Emilio made her an instant target. Was this how life was going to be for the next month? Her still raw, agonising grief splashed over every paper for others to gawk at?

To have her private pain made so public was devastating. She couldn't bear it if her tragic loss was going to be cheap fodder for the press. Lily's short, precious life would be wrapped around someone's fish and chips or vegetable scraps—discounted as yesterday's news.

How on earth would she bear it?

Emilio's dark gaze went to hers. 'What on earth's the matter?' he asked.

She opened and closed her mouth, her lips too dry to make them move. She felt sick. She was *sure* she was going to be sick. Her insides were churning with such anguish and despair she felt as if she was going to drop in a faint. She vainly tried to keep the paper against her chest but her hands were shaking so much she could do nothing but watch in sinking heart-stopping dread as Emilio took it from her.

Time seemed to come to a standstill as he unfolded the newspaper. Even the sound of the paper crackling as he opened it was magnified a thousand million times.

And then she saw as his eyes went to what was printed there. Every word was carved on Gisele's brain like a cruel tattoo: *Andreoni Reconciliation Haunted by Tragic Death of Love Child.*

Gisele saw the flinch of Emilio's dark gaze, the camera shutter flick of shock, surprise and disbelief. Every muscle on his face seemed to freeze for an infinitesimal moment.

There was no movement.

No sound.

She couldn't even hear him breathing.

But then the column of his throat moved up and down, once, twice.

'What?' His one word was a rasping gasp, a choked, strangled sound that contained so much agony it resonated in her trembling body like a loud echo.

She could feel his tension. She could feel every tight band of muscle in his body. His face was ashen. He looked as if he had aged a decade right before her eyes.

She hadn't wanted him to find out like this. She'd wanted to work up to it, to make sure she had a more secure footing with him before she told him what she had gone through.

She slowly released the breath she hadn't even realised she had been holding. 'I was pregnant when I left you two years ago,' she said. 'I didn't find out until a couple of months after I got back to Sydney.'

His throat moved, rose and fell again as if he was trying to swallow something that didn't quite fit inside his oesophagus. 'Pregnant?' he said hollowly.

'Yes...'

The silence was so intense she heard him draw in a

breath. She even heard the sound of his hand against his skin as he dragged it downwards over his face, catching on his stubbly regrowth.

His eyes took on a haunted look. 'You had a baby?'

Her throat tightened over the word. 'Yes...'

He swallowed again. '*My* baby?'

For a moment all she could do was just stare at him as the hurt of his question smashed against her heart like a knockout punch. Then she took a breath and sent him a look that would have stripped wallpaper off a wall. '*How* can you ask that?' she said. '*How can you?*'

His expression contorted with remorse as his hand came back up to rub over his face. 'Sorry, I wasn't thinking,' he said. 'Of course it was mine. Forgive me.' He dropped his hand back by his side. He looked completely floored, dumbstruck, shattered. 'Was it a girl or a boy?'

'A girl,' Gisele said, squeezing back tears.

'What happened to her?' he asked in that same raspy croak.

She let out another painful breath. 'I found out at sixteen weeks there was a problem,' she said. 'I was offered a termination. But I wanted to give her a chance. There was a slim chance she might've made it. I wanted her to make it. I *wanted* it more than anything but she didn't live past a few hours. Six hours, twenty-five minutes and forty-three seconds, to be precise. Not much of a lifespan, is it?'

Emilio felt as if he had been hit with an anvil that had come out of nowhere. He had not seen it coming. Nothing could have prepared him. He stood there in a shell-shocked silence as his thoughts ran riot, each one pointing a finger of blame at him.

Gisele had been pregnant when he had cast her from his life. He had thrown her out on the streets while she had been carrying his child.

A child he would never meet.

A child he would never touch or hold in his arms.

A child he would never know.

What had stolen his child's life from him? What had gone so terribly wrong that she had been advised to terminate the pregnancy?

He thought of his tiny daughter suffering. Had she felt pain? Distress? His gut twisted with anguish. Why hadn't he been told?

'What was the problem?' he asked. 'What happened to her?'

'She had a genetic abnormality,' she said. 'Some of her organs hadn't developed properly. There was nothing they could do to fix it.'

His little daughter had never stood a chance. Would it have been different if he had been there? Could he have saved her? He would have shifted heaven and earth to do so.

Frustration and grief besieged him. He felt the weight of it like a straitjacket made of lead. His emotions—emotions he had never allowed space enough to breathe—were now gasping for air until his throat felt as if it had been scraped raw with rusty razor blades.

'What caused it?' he asked hoarsely.

She looked down at her hands. 'Who knows? The doctors said it was just one of those things but I've always wondered if it was something I did or didn't do...'

Emilio felt another smashing blow of guilt assail him. If it was anyone's fault, wasn't it his? The stress she had been under would have been enough to jeopardise the baby's development.

His baby.

'Why didn't you tell me you were pregnant?' he asked. 'I could have helped you. It might have made all the difference. Did you ever consider that? Why did you keep my own child's existence a secret from me? Surely I had the right to know?'

She gave him a hardened look. 'Have you forgotten your parting words to me?' she asked. 'You said you never wanted to see or hear from me again. I had no reason to suspect you didn't mean it.'

'Did you even try and contact me?' he asked. 'Did you even give me a chance to do the right thing by you and the baby?'

She glared at him, her grey-blue eyes flashing with accusation. 'And have you pressure me to get rid of her because there was something wrong with her?' she said.

Emilio opened and closed his mouth, trying to locate his voice. His chest felt as if someone had landed a heavy blow to it, knocking the air right out of his lungs. How could she think so lowly of him? Didn't she know anything about him? 'Did you really think I would've asked you to do that?' he finally said.

'I wasn't prepared to risk it,' she said. 'You strive for perfection in everything you do. I wasn't sure how you would handle the news of a baby that wasn't perfect in every way, especially since our relationship had ended so bitterly. I thought you'd be better off not knowing. I thought you wouldn't want to know.'

Emilio kept looking at her in bewildered dismay. Did she know him so little that she thought he would not want to give his child every possible chance at life? He would have done anything—*anything* and *everything* within his power. 'What sort of man do you think I am?' he asked. 'Do you really think I would've rejected my own flesh and blood?' *Like my mother did to me.* The words were like a flashback of horror. He blinked to make it go away. 'I would never have done that, Gisele. Never in a million years.'

She bit down on her lip and swung away, her arms going around her body protectively. 'I had enough trouble dealing with everyone else's opinions on what I should do,' she said. 'I didn't think I could cope with your input as well.'

Emilio swallowed against a king tide of regret. 'You should have told me,' he said. 'Damn it, Gisele, do you realise what this is like for me, finding out like this now, and via the press, for God's sake?'

She swung back to face him, her expression full of bitterness. 'So this is all about you, is it, Emilio? What about me? What about what I suffered? You have no right to tell me *how* you feel. As far as I'm concerned, you brought it on yourself.'

Emilio felt his spine tighten with anger. He had never felt so blindingly angry. He was angrier than when he had thought she had betrayed him two years ago. How could she be so cold and callous to deny him the knowledge of his own daughter? 'You did it deliberately, didn't you?' he said. 'You could have told me but you chose not to because you knew that would hurt me far more than anything else. It was your chance to punish me for not believing you. It was a perfect payback. And it worked, goddamn you. You couldn't have thought of a better revenge.'

She gave him a defiant look. 'You always think the worst of me. It's your automatic response, isn't it? Blame first, ask questions later.'

'Were you *ever* going to tell me?'

A flicker of guilt came and went in her gaze. 'I wasn't sure how to bring it up. It's not easy talking about it… about her…'

'You should've told me the day I came to see you at the shop,' he said. 'I came all that way to apologise. I did my best to make it up to you. You should've at least met me halfway.'

She threw him a withering look. 'Some apology that turned out to be,' she said. 'We both know I wouldn't be here now if it hadn't been for the money you offered.'

Emilio ground his teeth until his jaw ached. He felt blindsided by pain and a sense of loss that was unlike anything he had felt before. He was unaccustomed to being bombarded with such deep emotions. Emotions were something *other* people felt. He had cauterised his heart a long, long time ago. He wasn't supposed to feel like this. He'd always made sure he never did.

He had *never* felt so out of control.

How could he ever right the wrongs of the past? Gisele had lost their baby. She had suffered that loss all by herself. He hadn't been there for her. He hadn't protected her or provided for her. He could see now how a simple *sorry and let's try again* wasn't going to cut it. Nothing could make up for that loss. There was noth- ing he could do to bring their child back. A chasm of pain and bitterness divided him from Gisele now. Was there any bridge that could span that canyon of bitterness? Was there any amount of money or machinations on his part that could fix things? The powerlessness he felt was like being thrown back on the streets all over again. 'I'm sorry,' he said, but his voice sounded nothing like his own. It was hollow and empty, lifeless, soulless. *Dead.*

A long pain-ridden silence passed.

'I have some photos,' Gisele said quietly.

Emilio blinked himself back to the moment. 'Of the baby?'

'I brought them with me…' She lowered her gaze from his. 'I have her blanket too. She spent her short life wrapped in it. I would have buried her in it but I didn't want to part with it.'

A spasm of pain gripped Emilio's chest again. 'You have it *with* you?' he asked.

She gave him a defiant look. 'I suppose you'll think it's weird or sick or pathetic of me, but I've never felt ready to let that final link with her go.' Her eyes suddenly filled with tears. 'Do you know what it feels like when people ask you if you have kids? What am I supposed to say? I had one but I lost her?' She choked back a sob. 'I don't even know if I'm supposed to call myself a mother or not…'

Emilio reached for her and enfolded her in his arms, pulling her stiff little body close, resting his chin on the top of her head as he rocked her gently in his arms as she quietly sobbed. He couldn't speak for the roadblock of emotion in his chest. He thought of her holding on to her baby as long as she could. How had she endured such heartbreak? Who had supported her? How could

she have juggled the demands of running a small business with the tragedy of carrying a child that had never
been given a guarantee of making it? And how cruelly
ironic to have been surrounded by constant reminders
of what she had lost?

Baby wear.

His stomach plummeted as he thought of all those
tiny outfits, all those little vests and booties and bonnets
and christening gowns. Could she have chosen a harder
way to navigate her way through her loss? Seeing other
mothers day after day with their babies. Helping those
mothers choose outfits for their little ones. How on earth
had she done it? No wonder she hated him. No wonder
she had asked for more money. 'No, I don't think it's
weird or sick or pathetic,' he said.

She leaned back to look up at him with reddened eyes.
'You…you don't?'

He shook his head, feeling humbled by all she had
suffered. His anger seemed so pointless and inappropriate now. Hadn't she suffered enough without making
her feel guilty for not contacting him? Besides, there
was every chance he might have blocked her attempts
to speak to him. His stubbornness had helped him in
his business life but he had paid a high price for it in
his personal one. 'I think you're still grieving,' he said,
blotting a tear as it rolled down her cheek. 'You'll know
when it's time to finally say goodbye.'

Her bottom lip started to quiver again. 'My mother…
Hilary thinks I'm a basket case,' she said. 'She thinks
I'm morbid. But what would she know? She's never lost
a baby. She's never even *had* a baby.'

'That's not true,' Emilio said. 'She had you. Not in

a physical sense, but she was the one who stood by you and reared you. She might not have been the best mother in the world, but at least she didn't leave you on some cold, rat-infested doorstep in the middle of winter to fend for yourself when you were less than four years old.'

The silence reverberated with the horror of his words.

Emilio wished he hadn't blurted that out. This wasn't about what he had suffered. This was about her. About her loss. About her devastation. He had put his behind him a long time ago.

'Your mother left you on a *doorstep*?' she asked with wide incredulous eyes.

He stepped away from her. 'You think you're hard done by? I know it's been tough on you, finding out about a long-lost twin. I know it must have been devastating to find out your mother is not really your mother. But she's your mother in every sense that's important. You can't cut her from your life just because you don't share the same genetic make-up. It wasn't her fault. It sounds to me like she did the best she could, given the circumstances.'

She looked at him narrowly. 'Have you been talking to her?'

'No, but I can imagine what she feels like. She's been shut out of her child's life due to circumstances beyond her control. At least her child is still alive and breathing. I don't even know my child's name.'

'I called her Lily,' she said softly.

His throat rose and fell again.

Lily.

'Can I see the photos?' he asked.

She gave a nod. 'I'll go and get them.'

Emilio turned and bent to pick up the shattered remains of Gisele's cup. There was no way the fine china could ever be put together again, which was just like his heart felt right now…

Gisele took the photo album out of her drawer and cradled it against her chest for a moment. Emilio's statement about his childhood had shocked her to the core. She couldn't bear thinking about him as a little boy, cast aside, frightened, alone, vulnerable. How could his mother have done that to him? Who had taken care of him? Had anyone? Was that why he was so closed off and so determined to put the past behind him? He couldn't stomach thinking about his wretched childhood. It was something he wanted to forget. And yet he had set up the charity, throwing himself into the hands-on work with the strength of character she was only now coming to understand.

She put the album back down and took out the soft pink blanket she had so lovingly made for Lily, holding it up to her face for a moment, breathing in that sweet baby smell. She wondered what Emilio had been wrapped in, whether he had ever been loved and cherished even a fraction of the way she had loved and cherished Lily. It was too painful to think he might have never been welcomed, never loved or wanted. How could he have been if he had been left to fend for himself at less than four years old?

When Gisele came back Emilio was standing looking out over the gardens. He turned when she came in, even though she was sure she hadn't made a sound. His eyes went straight to the album she carried. She handed it to him silently, her throat closing over with emotion.

His large hands held the album as if it was the most precious item in the world. She watched as he stroked his fingers over it reverently where she had placed a photo of Lily on the cover inside a pink-and-white embroidered heart. It was a moment she knew she would never forget. He might not have been there for her pregnancy and Lily's birth and all too short life, but he was a father in every sense of the word, meeting his daughter for the very first time. His dark brown eyes melted, a sheen coming over them like the glisten of wet paint. His expression was one of wonder and deep, heart-squeezing emotion. She had never seen him with his guard down. She had never seen such softening of his features, with such raw humanity on show.

He turned the first page and there was the one taken straight after birth, with Lily's tiny body still vernix- and blood-streaked, her minuscule mouth open like a baby bird, but she hadn't had the strength to make much more than one mewling cry.

There was another one after the nurse had washed her. She was wrapped in the pink blanket, looking almost normal. When that photo had been taken Lily had had less than four hours of life left. So little time to say all she needed to say to her. She'd had to pack a lifetime of mothering into a few short hours...

'She looks like you,' Emilio said in a gravel-rough tone.

'I thought she looked like you,' Gisele said.

He met her gaze and her heart contracted when she

saw the glimmer of moisture shining in his eyes. She hadn't expected him to care about a baby he had never known about until now. She hadn't expected him to feel the way she felt when she looked at photos of Lily. She had assumed it was different for men. They didn't have the physical connection with their offspring that mothers did. But it looked as if he was grieving every bit as much as she was. She saw the agony etched on his face.

'She looks like both of us,' he said in a low, deep, pain-filled burr.

She bit the inside of her mouth to keep control of her emotions. 'Yes…'

'Can I…?' He cleared his throat and began again. 'Can I have these copied?'

She nodded. 'Of course.'

'How much did she weigh?' he asked after a long aching silence.

'Just under four pounds. She was like a doll. I could hold her in one hand. See in that picture?' Gisele pointed to the one where Lily's tiny frail body lay in her hand.

He touched the photo, his long finger making their baby look even tinier in comparison. 'She's beautiful,' he said. 'I wish…I wish I'd been able to hold her. To touch her. To smell her. Photos are so one-dimensional.'

Gisele handed him the blanket she had been clutching against her chest. She had never let anyone else touch it before now. 'I can still smell her on this,' she said. 'It's faint but when I close my eyes I can imagine I'm still holding her. I made it for her. She was wrapped in it as soon as she was born. It was the last thing she was wrapped in before she…' She swallowed before she could continue. 'Before I dressed her for the burial.'

He took the blanket and held it up to his face, closing his eyes as he breathed in the lingering trace of their baby's sweet, innocent smell. A mixture of talcum powder and newborn baby, a fragrance so precious Gisele wished she could stop it from ever fading.

She watched as a single tear rolled down Emilio's cheek. She felt for him then in a way she had not felt before. For so long her anger had shut down her feelings for him. How must he feel to have missed out on their baby's short but precious life? She felt dreadful for not telling him now. She had misjudged him, just as he had misjudged her. Would he ever forgive her?

After a long silence he handed the blanket back to her. 'Thank you.'

'Emilio…' Gisele met his tortured gaze. 'I'm sorry I didn't make the effort to tell you. I realise now how wrong that was of me. I should've at least tried.'

His mouth twisted ruefully. 'I probably would've cut you off before you could tell me. I was too proud, too stubborn. I made a bad situation a whole lot worse.' He pulled a hand down over his face again; it made a sound like sandpaper. 'I've handled all of this appallingly. From day one I've been so wrong, so unforgivably blind.'

'We've both made mistakes,' she said softly.

'I don't know how to fix this, any of this,' he said with a haggard look in his eyes. 'For the first time since I was a small child, I find myself totally defeated, powerless. I can't turn any of this around.' He sighed again, a deep serrated sigh that sounded painful as he exhaled. 'You were right, *cara*. Life doesn't come with a reset button.'

Gisele swallowed the lump of emotion clogging her throat. 'I'm so sorry...'

'For what?' he asked, frowning at her. 'What did you do? You're the innocent one in all of this. I was the one in the wrong. None of this would have happened if I'd trusted you.' He walked to the windows and looked out over the gardens, his back a stiff plank of self-recrimination.

'I've been thinking about what you said...' Gisele cradled Lily's blanket close to her chest. 'About if things had been the other way around?'

He turned to look at her, his expression so full of pain it was agonising to witness it. 'Don't try and make excuses for me, Gisele,' he said. 'You would've handled it differently. We both know that. This is my wrongdoing, not yours. I have to live with it. I got it wrong and apologising is not enough. But then, it was never going to be enough, was it? You always knew that.'

Gisele wasn't sure what to say, although she didn't think she could have spoken even if she had known. Her throat had closed over completely, her eyes were burning with more tears and her heart was compressed by the weight of sadness that she had carried for so long. Sharing it with Emilio hadn't halved it; rather it had *doubled* it. She felt his pain as well as her own. She had learned to manage her grief. She had no idea how to manage his. The misery of his childhood had been bad enough; now he had the loss of his child to deal with. It didn't seem fair, but then what in life was fair?

Emilio came over to stand in front of her again. 'I know it's a lot to ask you to stay on in Italy after this,' he said. 'But I will do my utmost to protect you from the media. I can handle the business meetings for you. I can meet with the executives on your behalf. You can stay here, within the privacy and protection of the villa. You don't have to go out in public at all.'

'I'm not sure hiding away is going to solve anything,' Gisele said. 'I'm not sure how the press got hold of that photo, but if they've got that one, they probably have more. I don't want to become a victim and I certainly don't want to be seen as one either.'

'So you're still happy to stay the full month?' he asked.

Gisele studied his expression for a microsecond. She thought about leaving. She thought about packing her bag and walking away, drawing a line under her relationship with him, never to look back. He was giving her permission to do so. Could she do it? But, more to the point, did she *want* to do it? He had, for the first time ever, revealed something about the horror of his childhood. How much more might he tell her if she stayed on the full time? Wouldn't it help her to understand him better? She *wanted* to understand. 'I'll stay on,' she said.

He put his hands on her shoulders, his fingers cupping her gently in an embrace that touched on something deep in her soul. He had touched her in a thousand different ways in the past, but somehow this was different. His charcoal-dark eyes held hers for a long mesmerising moment before he bent his head and briefly but tenderly brushed her mouth with his. 'Thank you,' he said. 'I will do everything in my power to make sure you don't regret it.'

CHAPTER NINE

OVER the next week the meetings Emilio had set up went off brilliantly. Gisele came out of each one with a renewed sense of purpose and vision for her work. It was all happening so fast but she was happy to be swept along with it, as it was just the distraction she needed.

In private, Emilio was tender but distant. She knew he was still coming to terms with the knowledge of being a father to a child he would never meet. She found it hard to reach out to him. Part of the reason was because she was frightened of talking about it in case he brought up the topic of having another child. It was the proverbial elephant in the room. It made her conversations with him stilted. She knew she sounded distant and removed but she couldn't do anything to stop it.

But, in spite of her assiduousness at avoiding the subject, there was a heart-stopping moment when she was confronted with how much Emilio had missed out on by not knowing about her pregnancy and how dearly he still wanted a family of his own. They had been visiting one of the main baby wear outlets in an exclusive department store. Gisele was showing the manager some of her samples and had not realised Emilio had moved to a selection of infant toys farther along. The store manager excused himself to speak to a staff member about something urgent and that was when Gisele's gaze went to where Emilio was standing. He had picked up a soft teddy bear dressed in a pink tutu, his expression so wistful she felt an ache that took her breath away. She bit her lip and turned away, relieved when the manager came back from dealing with his little crisis so she didn't have to deal with her own.

After the first day or two the press's interest in her relationship with Emilio had died down a little, but not enough to make her feel totally at ease. The sense of living under a microscope was petrifying at times. She wondered how big-name celebrities coped with it. And yet Emilio seemed to handle it all in his stride. But then he seemed to know what places the paparazzi frequented, cleverly managing to avoid them. He took Gisele to quiet, off the radar restaurants where the food was magnificent and the wines like nectar. As the days passed, she felt she was gradually getting to know the real Emilio, not the super-successful architect, but the *real* man. The man behind the mask he wore in public. He was making an effort to lower his guard with her, perhaps because he had sensed her closing off from him.

It came home to her in a powerful way when they were walking back from having dinner in one of the less trendy suburbs of Rome. They suddenly came across a young girl who was obviously stoned on some drug. She staggered up to Emilio, teetering on her shabby and scuffed high heels, her skin-tight skirt showing more than was decent of her scarily skinny thighs. She said something lewd in Italian and put a hand out to Emilio's chest. He covered the girl's scabby hand with his and pulled it off his chest, but he still held it within his. He spoke to her like a concerned father would do to a wayward daughter.

Gisele watched in amazement. Although she couldn't understand much of what he had said, she could tell that he hadn't berated the girl. He took her to one side, out of the way of passers-by, chatting to her for a minute or two before he made a call to his homeless kids' hot-line. Within a few minutes a van arrived and one of the youth workers came over and escorted the girl into the vehicle, presumably to take her somewhere safe.

Gisele came over to where Emilio was standing watching as the van drove down the street. She looped her arm through his and moved her body close to his. 'You seemed to know her,' she said.

He drew in a ragged breath and released it. 'Yes, her name is Daniela and she's been in and out of our detox programme three times,' he said. 'She wants to beat the cycle but she's got so much going against her—the wrong family, the wrong friends and the wrong beliefs about herself.' He turned and looked at her, his expression haunted. 'I'm terrified I'm going to find her dead in some back alley one day. The police will write her off as just another overdose.' He scraped a hand through his hair and continued. 'Do you know the thing that gets me the most? She could have been *anything* she wanted. She's bright and beautiful but look where she's ended up. How can I stop her from self-destructing? How many young women are out there just like her? Some of them have children. Do you realise that? Who is looking after them while their mothers are out working the streets?'

Gisele swallowed tightly. *He* had been one of those

little children. She knew it, even though he hadn't said anything further about his childhood. She had tried to get him to open up over the past week but he had seemed reluctant to reveal anything else. 'You're doing all you can, Emilio,' she said. 'You're doing more than anyone I know to try and help.'

'It's not enough.' He stalked a few paces away, his hand going back to his hair, making it stick up in disarray. 'Goddamn it, it's not enough.'

She went over to him and hugged him from behind. He was so rigid with frustration, but eventually he softened and turned to face her. His expression looked as if he had come to some sort of definitive decision—a decision he had taken a long time to make. 'I want to show you something,' he said.

'What?' she asked.

He took her hand and led her down a side street and then another and then another. It was a labyrinth of dark alleys and shadows, of scuttling rats and strewn and rotting rubbish. Gisele's skin crawled but she clung onto Emilio's strong hand, somehow feeling safe in a world that she had never visited before. A world she had not even known existed. She felt ashamed that she hadn't made herself more aware. How had she lived for twenty-five years and not have known that life for some people was a daily struggle for basic survival? It made her grievances over the lies she had been told about her origins pale in comparison.

Eventually they came to a back alley that had only one working streetlight. The insipid light it cast was just enough to show the disrepair of the buildings, the neglect that spoke of desperate people in desperate times.

Emilio led her to the front of a run-down building that was abandoned. No lights shone from inside. Graffiti-sprayed slats boarded the windows up. It looked like a soulless body, a shell of something it had once been but would never be again, no matter how much money was thrown at it.

'This is where my mother left me,' he said in a tone-less voice. 'I was a month or two off turning four. I re-member it as if it were yesterday.'

Gisele gripped his hand, her throat so tight with emo-tion she couldn't speak. She let the tears run down her face as she looked at the worn step. She imagined Emilio as a little child, not even of school age. What had he felt to be left here? To watch in bewilderment as his mother walked away, never to return?

'She was a teenager, barely out of childhood herself,' Emilio said into the silence. 'She probably didn't know who my father was. I've heard since there were four or five possible candidates.'

'Oh, Emilio…'

'She told me she would be back.' His hand suddenly gripped Gisele's so tightly she felt her bones protest but she wouldn't have indicated that for all the money in the world. She stood there silently, watching as the memo-ries flashed through his haunted gaze.

'She *promised* me she would be back,' he said. 'I be-lieved her. I waited for her. I waited for her for hours. Maybe it was days. I can't remember now. I just remem-ber the cold. It was so cold.' He gave an involuntary shudder. 'It crept into my bones. Do you know, there are some times when I can still feel it?'

Gisele put her arms around him and held him close,

trying to reach inside him to the little abandoned, bewildered child he had once been. 'Oh, Emilio,' she said, her voice breaking over a sob. 'I can't bear that you went through that. I can't bear to think of you so alone and so helpless.'

His arms were like steel bands as they wrapped around her. He crushed her to him, his head buried against her neck. She breathed in the essence of him, the pain and the wretchedness, drawing into her being the lost, lonely soul he had hidden from everyone for so long.

After a long moment he set her from him. 'I don't want other kids to go through what I did,' he said. 'I don't want them to spend their lives wondering where their mother went to that night and why she didn't come back—to not know if she's alive or dead. I don't want them to wonder if every man of a certain age they pass on the street is the father they never met.'

'You're such an amazing person, Emilio,' Gisele said, putting a gentle hand to his face. 'I don't think I've ever met a more amazing person.'

'I've never shown anyone this place,' he said gruffly. 'Not even the shelter workers know this is where I came from.'

'Thank you for showing me,' she said. 'It makes me admire you all the more.'

He gave her a twisted look and linked his hand with hers. 'Let's get out of here,' he said. 'This place gives me the creeps.'

Emilio closed the door of the villa when they got home and turned off the exterior lights. 'You go on up to bed, *cara*,' he said. 'I'm going to call the shelter to make sure Daniela is settling in OK.'

'I'll wait for you,' Gisele said.

He brushed the underside of her chin with his finger. 'Wait for me upstairs,' he said. 'I promise I won't be long.'

He watched as she made her way up the stairs; every now and again she turned back to look at him over her shoulder. Her grey-blue eyes were full of the longing he could feel pumping through his own veins.

Telling her about his childhood had felt good. It had felt cathartic. It made him feel as if that part of his life was truly behind him. Gisele had not been repulsed by his wretched background but rather had embraced him with the sort of acceptance he had been hungering for all of his life.

After he made his call he went upstairs and opened the door of the master suite. Gisele had showered and was now wearing his bathrobe. It was way too big for her, almost covering her from neck to ankles, but even so he could tell she was naked beneath it. 'You're wearing my bathrobe,' he said.

'Yes,' she said with a coy smile. 'What are you going to do about it?'

He pushed the door behind him closed. 'I'm going to take it off you.'

Her eyes teased his. 'What if I put up a fight?'

A glint of amusement lit his gaze as he came towards her. 'Then it will be twice the fun.'

She gave a little squeal when he scooped her up in his arms, carrying her caveman style to the bed, where he gently dropped her. He stood back and dispensed with his clothes, watching as her pupils flared as each layer hit the floor. He came back to her and tugged the ties of the bathrobe free, watching as it fell away from her body. He feasted his eyes on her beautiful breasts, the cherry-red nipples already tightly budded. He bent his mouth to each one in turn, tasting her, suckling on her, delighting in her unrestrained response. 'Some fight you're putting up,' he said teasingly.

'Maybe I can't resist you,' she said, toying with the hair on his chest with her soft fingertips. Her hands moved lower, tantalising him with her touch. He sucked in a breath as she closed her fingers around him. How could one woman's touch work such intense magic on him? He wanted her so badly it was like a raging fever in the surging river of his blood. He pressed her back down and came over her with his weight supported by his elbows. 'Am I too heavy for you?' he asked.

'No,' she said, pulling his head down so she could press her mouth to his.

Her tongue danced with his, darting away and then coming back for more. Her lips were impossibly soft, like velvet against his.

He stroked his hands down her body, delighting in the silk of her skin before going to the heart of her womanhood. She was so warm and wet and he was so hard and aching he couldn't resist sinking into her. She gave a little gasp and he immediately stilled. 'Sorry, did I hurt you?' he asked.

'No, it's just you're so big and I'm still a little out of practice...' Her cheeks took on a rosy hue that he found so incredibly endearing.

He went to pull out but she stalled him with her hands on his buttocks. 'No, stay,' she said softly. 'I want you.'

He took it slowly, conscious of her tender muscles accommodating him. She felt so wonderful, so silky and yet so tight. She lifted her hips for each downwards thrust, urging him on, her hands caressing his back and shoulders, her mouth like fire on his. He caressed her breasts, taking his time over each one, his tongue rolling over her nipples, stroking along the highly sensitive undersides where he knew her nerves danced triple time. She writhed with pleasure as he continued his sensual feast on her body, his teeth and tongue working in tandem to bring about maximum excitement for her. She became more and more restless as her need grew, her body rising to meet his as he sank deeper into her. He felt the tension grow in her, the way her thighs gripped him around the waist, her body open to him in wanton abandon as she sought the ultimate in human release.

'Now…' she gasped brokenly against the hot damp skin of his neck. 'Oh, please *now*…'

He played her with his fingers, his touch light but sure. He knew exactly what she needed to go over the edge. He had taught her himself how to relax into the whirlpool, to let it carry her into oblivion. She had been hesitant in the past; she had been almost frightened of the overpowering sensations clamouring in her body, but he had gently coaxed her into embracing what her body craved. Now as he felt every contraction of her body as she orgasmed, the pulses of her flesh triggered his own cataclysmic release. He fell forwards, pumping through those precious few seconds of bliss as her body welcomed him home.

He lay in the quiet aftermath, still with her in the circle of his arms, her silver-blonde hair splayed out on his chest. He heard the rhythmic sound of her breathing, the way on each soft breath out it blew across his chest like a feather dancing ahead of a teasing breeze.

He closed his eyes, sighing deeply as he breathed in the fragrance of her hair and skin, the taste of her, vanilla-sweet on his tongue.

It was the closest he had ever felt that he had finally found somewhere to call home.

CHAPTER TEN

WHEN Gisele woke the next morning she was disappointed to find Emilio wasn't beside her. But as she lay there covered in fine Egyptian cotton, in that richly furnished suite, she thought about why he worked so hard and so tirelessly, why he drove himself day after day after day. Visiting the bleak desolation of that back alley and finding out the true horror of his childhood had finally made her understand why Emilio was so driven and determined. In the past she hadn't fully comprehended his ruthless ambition, but now she saw it for what it was. All the long hours he worked, his single-minded focus on projects that kept him awake at night were not to make him become yet another mega-rich self-indulgent man, but rather a passionate quest to make the world a better place for others less fortunate than him. He wanted to be successful so he could help others escape the life he had once led.

After her shower Gisele went downstairs in search of Emilio but Marietta informed her he was taking a call in the study. 'I have served breakfast in the breakfast room this morning,' the housekeeper added. 'It looks like it is going to rain.'

'*Grazie*, Marietta,' Gisele said and went through to the delightfully appointed east-facing room to wait for him.

With an unnerving sense of déjà vu, she moved to where the newspapers had been laid out on a sideboard close to the table. The Italian paper had a large photograph of Emilio and her coming out of the baby wear department. She remembered the moment so clearly. She had been carrying some of her samples and Emilio had put his arm around her protectively as they came out on the busy street. Someone had been taking a photo with their phone but Gisele had thought they were taking it of a friend standing at the front of the store.

Her heart started to gallop as she picked up the English paper, where the caption was emblazoned there above the very same photo: *A New Baby for Award-winning Architect and his Australian Bride-to-be?*

Gisele went hot and then icily cold. Panic streaked through her. Her heart tripped. Her breath caught. Her hands and fingers tingled as if she was losing her blood pressure.

The elephant wasn't just in the room.

It had escaped. It was everywhere, stalking her. Crowding her, pressuring her to do something she could not do.

'I'm sorry about that,' Emilio said as he came in. 'I was just making sure Daniela had booked into rehab... *Cara?* What's happened?'

Gisele thrust the paper at him. 'I can't do this,' she said. 'I can't live like this. *I can't do this.*'

Emilio glanced at the paper briefly before putting it to one side. 'It's just a bit of speculation,' he said. 'You know the games the journalists play.'

'*Speculation?*' She glared at him. 'Is that what you call it? I call it pressure.'

'*Cara*, no one's pressuring you to do anything.'

'Aren't they?' she asked, starting to pace the floor in agitation. 'What about you and all your talk about having a family? It's what you want. You told me.'

'I do want a family but we'll take things slowly until you get used to the idea of—'

'Stop it!' Gisele put her hands over her ears. 'Don't say it. Don't tell me I'll get used to the idea of having another baby. I don't want to hear it.'

'Gisele, you're overreacting,' he said.

'Don't tell me I'm overreacting!' She felt close to hysteria. She had been in that scary place before and didn't want to go back. She struggled to get her emotions under control. 'I saw you looking at that teddy bear.'

He frowned at her. 'What teddy bear?'

'The pink one with the tutu,' she said, her heart racing so wildly she could feel it knocking against her rib cage. 'In the shop we visited the other day. You picked it up and looked at it. I could *see* it, Emilio. I could see how much you want another baby.'

'*Cara,*' he said soothingly. 'Can we talk about this some other time? You're upset just now. I can understand that. It was a horrible shock to you to see that article. You'll feel different in a few days' time.'

'I *won't* feel different,' she said. 'I'll never feel different. You have to accept that.'

A muscle worked in his jaw. 'Gisele, I'd rather not discuss this with you in this state of mind.'

'I'm not in a state of mind!' she all but screamed at him. 'I can't do it, Emilio. I'm *not* doing it. I'm not going to be speculated on and pressured and cajoled into a relationship I'm not sure I can handle any more.' She stopped pacing, snatched in a scalding breath and added impetuously, 'I want to go home.'

He stood very still, barely a muscle moving, except for that tiny one in his jaw. His eyes gave nothing away; they were onyx-black, fathomless. 'You are free to leave any time you want, Gisele,' he said. 'I am not holding you here by force.'

Gisele swept her tongue over her lips. Her heart gave an extra beat—a sickening thud that reverberated throughout her body like a church bell struck too hard. 'What did you say?'

'If you want to leave, then leave,' he said. 'I'll get Marietta to pack your things while I book you a flight.'

'But...but what about the rest of the month?' she asked. 'What about the money?'

'You've earned every cent,' he said with a slight curl of his lip. 'You owe me nothing.'

Gisele wondered if she'd heard him correctly. Was he really sending her away without a single word of protest? Had all they had shared in the past couple of weeks been reduced to a business deal that had now ended?

What about what they had shared last night?

What about what *he* had shared?

He had let her into the private hell of his childhood. Didn't that mean he cared about her? But how could he truly care about her if he was happy to let her leave? 'But I don't understand...'

'I'll have my legal people contact you with the details of the handover,' he said in his cold and detached businesslike manner that was so at odds with her seesawing emotions. 'You'll own the building and the business outright. You will be able to employ more assistants as things expand. I have engaged a web-designer to help you set up a better online presence. People will be able to order and buy from you online once it's set up.'

Gisele couldn't think beyond the fact he wanted her to go. If he wanted her to stay then why wasn't he saying it? Was it because deep down he wasn't able to forgive her for not telling him about their baby? Had last night brought that home to him afresh? The fact that he had never got the chance to meet his child in the flesh, just like he hadn't met his father? Or was it that he didn't want her in his life any more because he didn't want to be reminded of the pain they had both suffered? Was that it?

No, there was more to it than that, she realised with a sickening jolt.

He didn't love her.

He had never loved her. He was *never* going to love her.

'What about the press?' she asked, clutching at whatever straws she could. 'Won't they make a fuss about... about everything ending like this?'

He gave a careless shrug. 'I'll release a statement saying things didn't work out between us,' he said. 'Don't worry about it. I'll make sure they leave you alone. I'll get Luigi to take you to the airport.'

'So...' She moistened her lips again, trying her best to appear as casual as he was being about it all. 'So, I guess this is goodbye.' Oh, how it hurt to say the word! *Please let this not be goodbye,* she thought. *Don't send me away. Not again. Not like this.*

The shutter was still down over his face, every muscle locked down now. 'Yes,' he said. 'This is goodbye.'

She gave a little nod of assent. What else could she do? She had told him she wanted to go. He had virtually *commanded* her to leave. He had his driver waiting on call. Her bags would be packed within minutes. What was she waiting for? She hadn't wanted to come in the first place. She was only here under sufferance.

Why, then, when she left him standing there, did it feel as if her world had shattered into a thousand pieces all over again?

Three weeks later...

Gisele was hanging some new stock in her shop when Hilary, her mother, came in. Hilary had only been to her shop a couple of times, barely staying long enough to look around. It was the first time Gisele had seen her mother since she had come back from Italy. She had spoken once or twice on the phone to her but the conversation had felt stilted and awkward.

'The shop looks lovely,' Hilary said.

'Thank you.'

There was a little silence.

'You look very thin, Gisele,' Hilary said. 'Are you sure this new expansion's not too much to handle? It's a lot to take on.'

'I can handle it,' Gisele said, hanging another baby jacket on the rack.

Hilary let out a little sigh as she picked up a jacket with a row of baby rabbits stitched around the bottom.

'I know you're still upset and angry,' she said. 'I don't blame you. What your father did was wrong.'

Gisele turned and looked at her. 'What you both did was wrong. You told just as many lies as he did. You *lived* a lie.'

Hilary's eyes suddenly filled with tears as she held the baby jacket against her chest. 'I know, and every day of it I was terrified the truth would come out,' she said. 'I wanted you to know the truth right from when you were little but your father wouldn't hear of it. I didn't trust Nell Baker. I lived in dread that she would turn up and insist on having you back. I guess that's why I was always so distant and stiff with you. I was never sure if I was going to have you snatched out of my arms.'

Gisele had never seen her mother shed tears before. Not a single one. Hilary had always been so stiff upper lip about everything, so stoic, so in control, so emotionally detached. 'I never felt like you really loved me,' Gisele said. 'I never felt like I was good enough for you.'

'Oh, my darling,' Hilary said. 'I loved you so much. I loved all of my babies.'

Gisele frowned. 'Babies? What babies?'

Hilary fondled the tiny jacket in her hands. 'I had four miscarriages in the first couple of years of our marriage. I felt such a failure. Each time my hopes would soar and then it would all be over. I tried so hard not to get attached but I loved each one so very much.'

'Why didn't you tell me?' Gisele gasped. 'Why didn't you tell me when I lost Lily?'

Hilary's lower lip trembled. 'I lost my babies when they were just a few weeks along. You lost a full-term baby. How could I tell you I understood a fraction of what you were going through? I felt ashamed of not being able to be a proper mother. At least you were a mother, even if it was only for a few hours.'

'You *are* a proper mother,' Gisele said, with tears rolling down her face. 'You're the only mother I've got and I love you.'

Hilary's arms gathered her close. 'I love you too, my precious daughter. I love you too.'

Emilio pushed the computer mouse away in frustration and got stiffly to his feet. He stared sightlessly out of his office window. Almost a month had passed since Gisele had left and he still couldn't focus on work or indeed anything. He couldn't remember the last time he had slept more than a couple of hours. He had forgotten the last time he had eaten a full meal. He moved through each day like an automaton.

His life felt empty.

He felt empty.

Even the weather had joined him in his misery. The promising start to spring had been replaced with a ca-pricious sun that had stayed behind brooding clouds for days and days. The drizzle of intermittent rain was a poignant reminder of the aching sadness he felt deep in his soul.

He hadn't cried since he was six years old, when a particularly unfeeling foster carer had told him his mother was never going to come back. He had thought his tear ducts would have dried up from lack of use. But no, they were working all right. He only had to look at the photos of his little daughter for the tears to fall.

He had wanted to do the right thing by Gisele. Seeing

how distressed she was about the thought of having another child with him had made freeing her his only option. It had been the right and most honourable thing to do. But it hurt so damn much! Was this wrenching pain *never* going to go away?

He had received an email from her with a polite thank you for the help with the expansion of her business. He had stared at the typed words, looking for a clue between the lines, but there had been nothing. But then what else had he expected? If she had loved him, she wouldn't have wanted to leave him. But she had gone as soon as she had been given the chance.

His secretary, Carla, came in with his afternoon coffee. He didn't even bother turning from the window. She brought it in every afternoon, even though he never touched it. It would sit on the desk, forming a skin over the top as it went cold. 'Leave it on the desk,' he said tonelessly.

'There's a parcel for you,' Carla said. 'It came by registered mail. It's marked private.'

Emilio turned and looked at the package she had placed on his desk next to the cup of coffee. 'Who's it from?' he asked.

'It's from Signorina Carter,' she said. 'Do you want me to open it?'

Emilio felt a fist tighten over his heart. 'No,' he said, raking an unsteady hand through the thickness of his hair. 'That will be all, Carla. You can have the rest of the day off.'

'But what about the Venturi Project?' she asked, frowning at him. 'Don't you have a deadline on that?'

Emilio gave a negligent shrug. 'It'll get done when

it gets done. If they're not happy with that, tell them to get someone else.'

Carla's finely groomed brows rose. *'Sì, signor,'* she said and left with a soft click of the door.

Emilio traced a finger over Gisele's neat handwriting where she had printed his name on the package. It was probably the jewellery he had given her. He'd been expecting her to send it back. He was surprised she hadn't left it behind the day she had left. He could imagine she wouldn't want any physical reminders of their relationship.

The package was securely wrapped with packing tape. He worked at it methodically. He could have used the silver blade of his letter opener but this time he preferred to do it by hand. He wanted to touch where her hands had touched. It was ridiculously sentimental of him, but that just about summed him up these days. He peeled back the tape and opened the cardboard box where a tissue-wrapped parcel lay nestled safely in a bed of Styrofoam cushioning.

His hands shook uncontrollably as he peeled away the tissue wrap to find the pink hand-embroidered blanket his tiny daughter had spent her short life wrapped in. Emotion burned like fire at the back of his throat as he cradled it gently in his hands. He felt as if he were holding his own heart.

There was a single sheet of paper in the box, neatly folded over. He took it out and opened it to read:

You said I would know when I'm finally ready to say goodbye. You were right. Gisele.

Emilio felt a juggernaut of emotion assail him. He hadn't been there at the beginning of their daughter's short life or at the end, but he was to be with her for ever more. Gisele had given him that privilege. How much had it cost her to do so? She had sent him her heart.

A lightning bolt of realisation hit him.

She had sent him her heart.

Mio Dio, what had he done? He had sent her away when all he had ever wanted was to have her close. Why hadn't he told her how he felt? Would it have hurt to have at least said the words? Even if she had still left, it would have been better for him to tell her he loved her. She deserved to know she was the only woman he had ever loved, *could* ever love.

He had been a coward. A pathetic coward, not man enough to own his need for her. Too frightened to feel like that little abandoned boy he had once been, he had kept his feelings locked away. He hadn't even admitted them to himself, let alone to her.

How could he have been so stupid?

So stubborn?

So blind?

He pressed the intercom on his desk. 'Carla? Are you still there?' he asked.

'*Sì, signor,*' his secretary said. 'I was just tidying my desk.'

'Get me a flight to Sydney,' he said. 'I don't care how much it costs. You can even hire a private jet. Buy one if you have to.'

'Urgent business again, Signor Andreoni?' Carla asked.

'No,' he said. 'This is personal.' *This is my life. This is my love. This is my everything.*

Emilio saw the 'Closed' sign on Gisele's shop as the taxi drew up outside. His heart slipped like a Bentley on black ice. But then he realised it was only seven-thirty in the morning. In his haste to get here he'd forgotten the time difference. He kicked himself for not having phoned first. But he had wanted to see her face to face. He *ached* to see her face to face.

He directed the driver to Gisele's home address and waited with a thudding pulse for the journey to be over. He mentally rehearsed his speech. He had been awake for the entire flight, thinking about what he would say, but in the end he knew he really only had three words to say to her: *I love you.*

The taxi turned the corner into her street and Emilio's stomach nosedived when he saw the 'Sold' sign on her flat.

He stumbled out of the taxi, issuing a brusque order over his shoulder for the driver to wait.

There was no answer when he pressed the doorbell. He peered through gaps in the drawn blinds but there was no sign of her being inside.

'Can I help you?' an older female voice asked.

Emilio swung around to see an elderly lady with a walking frame standing by the letterboxes. 'I'm looking for Gisele Carter,' he said. 'Do you know where she is?'

'She left a little while ago,' the old lady said.

Panic gripped Emilio by the throat. 'Left?'

'Yes, she's taking a holiday before she moves to her new home,' she said. 'She's meeting her mother and her sister in Queensland. A tropical island, I think she said. I can't remember the name of it now.'

Emilio mentally groaned. How many tropical islands were there in Queensland? *Hundreds*. How on earth was he going to track her down? 'When did she leave?' he asked.

'You just missed her,' the old lady said. 'She only left half an hour or so ago.'

'Do you know what airline she was booked on?' Emilio asked as he walked quickly backwards to the waiting taxi. 'It's really important. I need to see her. I'm going to tell her I love her. I'm going to ask her to marry me.'

The old lady smiled as she told him the carrier's name. 'I think I remember now the island,' she said. 'Hamilton Island—yes, that's the one.'

Emilio rushed to the gate lounge after he had cleared Security but it was empty. The illuminated board said the flight was closed.

He was too late.

He scraped a hand through his hair and stumbled to the window overlooking the tarmac. The plane was backing out, preparing its journey down the runway, its lights along the wings flashing in preparation.

A choked-up feeling seized his chest. He couldn't breathe. He planted his hands on the glass in front of him for support.

He was too late.

He rested his head on the window. He *knew* this feeling. It was the same feeling he had on that step. He remembered all too well the feeling of being abandoned, of having no one to turn to, of not knowing what was going to happen next. The uncertainty, the bleakness, the loneliness, the aching emptiness...

'Emilio?'

The skin on the back of his neck prickled. He was imagining it, just like he had imagined his mother's voice, reaching out to him in the dark while he had been sitting on that cold stone step for all of those long, lonely, terrifying hours.

He slowly turned and saw Gisele standing in front of him. She looked pale, wraithlike, just like a ghost. Was his mind playing tricks on him? It must be. He blinked a couple of times but she didn't disappear. 'You sold your flat.' *What an inane thing to say*, he chided himself.

'Yes,' she said. 'I felt it was time to move on.'

He shifted his weight from foot to foot. 'I thought you were on that flight.' *Even more banal.* Why couldn't he just say what he wanted to say?

'My flight isn't for another forty minutes,' she said. 'I'm going to Heron Island. Mum and I are meeting Sienna there. Mum thought it might be a good chance for us all to get to know each other. It leaves from the other gate down there.' She pointed farther down the concourse.

'Oh... I thought you were going to Hamilton Island,' he said. 'Your neighbour said... The board said the flight was closed... I saw it leaving.' He stopped because he was rambling like a tongue-tied lovesick fool.

Gisele rolled her lips together, looking just like a shy, uncertain schoolgirl. 'I was coming back from the rest-room and saw you standing here,' she said. 'I thought I must be imagining things. Why are you here?'

'I wanted to see you,' Emilio said. 'I wanted to thank you for...for giving me our daughter's blanket.'

A shadow passed over her face before she lowered her gaze. 'She was made in Italy,' she said in a tiny whisper-soft voice. 'I thought it was appropriate that a part of her rested there too.'

Emilio felt his emotions rise like a flash flood within him. He had no control over it. His chest ached with the pressure. It was building to a crescendo. He felt every tidemark. They were etched indelibly on his soul. He brushed away the tears that were falling with the back of his hand. 'What if you still need to hold her sometimes?' he asked.

Her bottom lip quivered uncontrollably. 'It's your turn to hold her.'

'She needs both of us to hold her,' he said, gulping back a ragged sob. 'No one can take your place. No one can *ever* take your place. She loves you. *I* love you. I've always loved you. Please come home, *cara*. Come back to me. Come back to us.'

She paused for an infinitesimal moment before she stumbled towards him, a flurry of arms and emotions that he welcomed with every cell of his being. He had never felt so close to another human being. Her arms wrapped around his waist, but he felt them around his heart. *'Il mio prezioso,'* he said. 'My precious one. I thought I had lost you for ever.'

Gisele clutched at him, terrified he would suddenly vaporise, that she would open her eyes and find this was all a dream. Had he really said those wonderful, amazing words? She looked up at him with tears streaming from her eyes. 'Do you really love me?' she asked. 'You're not just saying it?'

He grabbed her hand and pressed it against his thudding heart. 'I love you, *tesore mio*,' he said. 'My life is meaningless without you. I can't imagine how I will cope if you don't say you will marry me. You will, won't you? Marry me, I mean?'

She smiled at him with immeasurable joy. 'Of course I will marry you,' she said. 'I can't think of anything I want more. I love you.'

He crushed her to him again, holding her tightly, as if he never wanted to let her go. 'You are everything to me, *cara*,' he said. 'I am ashamed of how long it has taken me to realise how much you mean to me. How can you ever forgive me for taking so long to come to my senses? How can you ever forgive me for how I misjudged you, which started this crazy affair in the first place?'

'Don't torture yourself any more,' she said. 'We were both victims of circumstances beyond our control.'

Emilio held her from him so he could look into her eyes. 'I was such a fool. I can't believe I got it so wrong. If only I had stopped and thought about who you were as a person, your values, the strength of character you had demonstrated so many times. I ignored all of that. And then, to add insult to injury, I practically forced you back in my life. I wanted to wipe the slate clean but you taught me that it's not always possible. The hurts and blows and mistakes of life are things you sometimes have to carry with you. You can't erase all of them. Those are the very things that make us who we are.'

Gisele stroked his lean cheek with her hand. 'I love who you are,' she said. 'I love everything about you.'

He rested his forehead on hers. '*Cara*, I want you to know that if you can't bear the thought of having another baby, then that is fine. God knows I've got enough on my hands with all the street kids I'm taking in. Daniela has brought in some of her friends. Having you will be enough. More than enough.'

Gisele blinked back fresh tears. 'For all this time I could never imagine going through a pregnancy again,' she said. 'I couldn't bear the thought of going through that terrible loss again. But this time you'll be by my side. I think I could handle just about anything with you standing beside me.'

He cupped her face in his hands, his gaze soft and tender as it held hers. 'And that's exactly where I plan to be for the rest of our lives,' he said. 'By your side, loving you, protecting you and worshipping you with my body and my soul.'

Gisele closed her eyes as his lips sealed hers in a kiss of promise and hope and healing. She wrapped her arms around his waist, leaning into his strength, delighting in the feeling of being loved and cherished.

It was like finally coming home.

Sienna Baker was sitting by the pool on Heron Island, sipping a Manhattan when she got the text message from Gisele. She picked up her phone and, propping her sunglasses on her forehead, squinted against the bright sunlight as she read the words: *Sienna, sorry, slight change of plan. Mum's on her way but I'm off to Italy to prepare for my wedding. PS Will you be my bridesmaid? Gisele X*

* * * * *

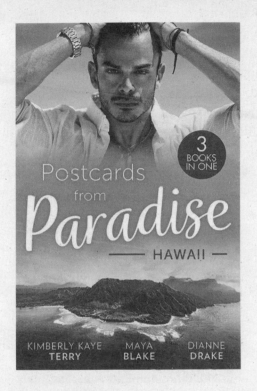

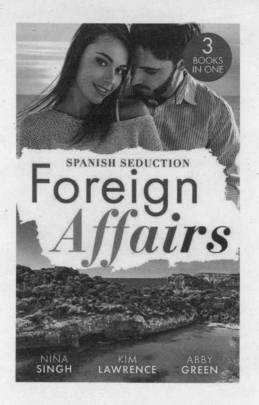

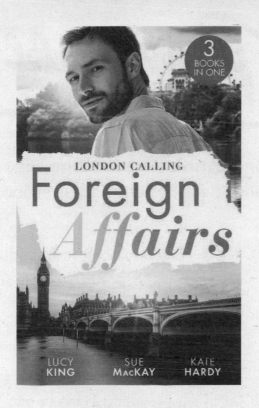

LET'S TALK

Romance

For exclusive extracts, competitions
and special offers, find us online:

- facebook.com/millsandboon
- @MillsandBoon
- @MillsandBoonUK
- @MillsandBoonUK

Get in touch on 01413 063 232

For all the latest titles coming soon, visit
millsandboon.co.uk/nextmonth